EMBARK

Book 1

Jon "Justice" LoGiudice

JON JUSTICE

ISBN-13: 9781730787126

www.MyNerdWorld.net

Join the mailing list
TalkShowNerd@gmail.com

EMBARK

For Melinda,
whose love of books encourages our sons, Logan and Kyle, to read
and inspired me to write this story.

Chapter 1

Arizona

Taft decided to get working on his Traverse Craft (T-Craft) earlier than usual as the sun slowly began to rise over the barren mountains in the distance. He was hoping to be farther along with the upgrades he started the week prior, especially after his futile attempts at bragging to his friends, which were nothing more than not so subtle comments trying to impress Kaytha. He knew she probably saw right through him, but he didn't care and deep inside was hoping she did. Taft had known Kaytha for a few years now, and while they had become fast friends and primarily the "leaders" of their self-proclaimed squadron of pilots, they weren't nearly as close as Taft would like. He was convinced she felt as he did, but that she was way too stubborn to admit it and refused to let any man, boy, or whatever else potentially get in the way of her becoming a better pilot.

Kaytha would visit Taft almost every day unless she messaged him ahead of time to let him know she was busy.

The time she arrived varied, sometimes before sunrise, other times she didn't show up until the sun was setting, and anytime in-between.

But even if she came too late to take advantage of the daylight, she always insisted on making flights in darkness with the thinking it would help in the cold vastness of space. For Taft, whenever she would touch down on the tarmac, it felt like Christmas morning: a feeling of excitement, anticipation, and potential for more, maybe the start of something he always desired.

Taft rolled his nearly ten-year-old T-Craft from its designated hangar and worked on it just outside the bay doors. He didn't much like working behind the steel walls of the T-Crafts' housing, but he mostly wanted to be able to hear the sound of Kaytha's thrusters as she neared his location. Taft could determine the cruising flight time of Kaytha's newer, yet continuously evolving T-Craft, just by listening. He knew the sound of her ship so well that he could tell exactly when she would arrive from the moment he heard the pitch of the thrusters as she passed downtown Camelback.

It was just past 9:00 am, and Taft was sitting in the cockpit with the canopy up, making some much-needed adjustments to the joystick. The foot pedal directional controls had been entirely out of sync with the joystick controls ever since his last mock dogfight with Kaytha. She'd won, again. Although this time it was legit and he hadn't backed off. Taft noticed the wind dying down and at that moment he heard the sound of Kaytha's thrusters faint in the distance. It was clear she wasn't cruising; the wailing harmonies from her T-Craft motors grew louder by the second.

Usually, Kaytha would travel over the mountains to the south, flip on the lift manifolds, and come down for a normal landing.

On rare occasions she would come flying over the ridge at top speed, buzzing the flight line as though seemingly angry that Taft wasn't already in the air ready for her arrival. Taft immediately knew that this was one of those moments and, in clothes barely worthy of wearing while in flight, he quickly reached for his helmet sitting just outside the cockpit. He could hear Kaytha was almost to his location as he flipped the toggle switch, lowering and locking the canopy, helmet already strapped, visor down. By the time Taft's T-Craft was fully engaged through its takeoff cycles, the sound of Kaytha's DeCorp thrusters were almost deafening in his head, and she wasn't even in sight yet.

Taft didn't bother to use the lift manifolds to get the craft clear of the ground, deciding instead to punch the power to the thrusters and take off from a dead stop on the tarmac. His decade-old T-Craft, which used to be his father's—at least the frame and a quarter of the panels still were of his dad's old ship—rumbled to life.

Most T-Craft thrusters when powered up glowed a brilliant, almost neon yellow, and Taft's was no different as he mashed forward the throttle controls. The feet of his landing pads scraped the concrete for just a few feet before the ship lifted from the ground.

Taft's Traverse-Craft bolted toward the sky. Knowing that Kaytha would be in his airspace at any moment, Taft gained a few hundred feet and turned his T-craft in the direction she would be entering his valley.

The scream of three DeCorp MXF multidirectional propulsion thrust engines at full power drowned out all sound. Taft was scanning the skies out of his cockpit window, when suddenly a brilliant blur of white, gold, and gunmetal gray, reflected by the sun, went flashing right past his canopy, causing him to put his T-Craft through three barrel rolls as the shock of adrenaline went

6

coursing through his veins. Once he righted his ship and figured out which way was up, he immediately saw Kaytha's contrail and made a sharp turn to follow it. Before Taft knew it, she had already come up from behind him and was flying just off to his right. Taft, looking out his cockpit canopy, saw the exact moment that Kaytha lifted up her full face helmet visor. It was the first time he'd seen her face that day. Even from a distance and behind the canopies of both their ships, Taft still instantly locked on to her piercing, green eyes.

Standard flight helmets were pressurized for space travel and could be connected to both flight suit and on board oxygen while in flight. The visors, when closed, would seal air tight and could be tinted, or smoked, with the swipe of a finger on a flight control screen.

"You know you really should pay more attention if you're going to fly like that," said Kaytha through their ship to ship comms.

Taft clamored for a witty comeback, looking over again to see her putting her visor back down.

"I assume you're fueled and fed?" continued Kaytha.

"You know it," replied Taft. This was not a total lie; he hadn't eaten anything yet that day, but his T-Craft was fully fueled, and he had some provisions stowed away on board would such a day like today occur.

Kaytha tended to be temperamental, and he'd had too many circumstances where he was unprepared. Kaytha was known for changing her mind instantly on whatever "adventure" she wanted to go on. Their fellow flying friends always pegged her as being bitchy because of this, but Taft knew that it was really her insecurity that made her react that way. Taft was about to comm from his helmet mic and ask Kaytha which direction they were heading, but she'd already turned her newly painted T-Craft east and started her descent toward the terrain. Kaytha repainted her ship and made modifications about as often as she changed her hair color. If it weren't for Taft being able to unmistakably recognize the sound of her engines, he'd never be certain who was approaching the airfield.

He dropped down in the sky just off her right rear thrusters, speculating on what color her hair would be this time under her helmet, thinking, *It's been black with a tint of blue for the past few weeks. Before that, red, brunette!? It's been almost a year since she's been brunette.*

Kaytha and Taft were heading west now following low and close to the terrain, picking up speed.

Kaytha then keyed her comms again, "Let's be sure to keep the chatter to a minimum, for now. Keep up and stick close."

"I assume we are doing this for a reason, Kay?"

"Absolutely. I have something to show you."

Chapter 2

Caserta, Italy

For a reason, thought Sint Argum as he walked the grand halls of the Royal Palace of Caserta. Looking at the centuries-old craft work, he wryly smiled to himself that after all this time even a place as wondrous as this could succumb to modern day society and technology. *For a reason, it had to be this way,* Sint's thoughts continued, now that the Palace was home to the United Earth Galaxy Coalition. To the public, this was where the worlds' superpowers would meet to discuss the most critical issues facing humanity. In reality, it was where DeCorp and EnerCon, the only real superpowers, debated the future and how they would one day populate the stars. Sint worked for Development Corporation (DeCorp) which had, over a few decades, become the largest employer on the planet, with factories in every civilized country and in the United States almost every state. DeCorp provided the best static lift and propulsion technology on the planet.

Energy Contributions (EnerCon) was the second largest to DeCorp but not by much. EnerCon provided the fuel cells needed to power the tech that DeCorp produced.

Once they were one company, but in the early days of DeCorp's success, they decided to split into two entities to better maximize their efforts roughly ten years ago, and maximize they did, for a reason.

The UEGC was in the process of debating the issue of just how humanity would populate the stars. Sint was in Italy to represent DeCorp. The latest session was on break, and Sint took this time to wander the great halls before returning back into the Galactic Coalition Chambers. All the major countries that made up UEGC had placed large stone plaques with raised letters that spelled out their spiritual beliefs and how they'd arrived at them.

Some carried messages from the Quran, another with inspiring words from the Buddhist, Tripitaka, etc. Sint stopped in front of the plaque representing the United States. It read: _For a Reason_

Americans, with our proud history and grand traditions that span generations, hold on to the cherished belief that regardless of situations, decisions, and outcomes, it all happens according to a design and for a purpose, regardless of your religion. America continues to be the land of the free and home of the brave.

The plaques were each set side by side one another in the large circular gazebo with a raised tile roof held up by stone pillars. The courtyard was open apart from the one side which connected to the main hall. It was along that wall that the various nations were represented.

Sint Argum admired the accomplishments of those who made up the UEGC. He too had goals, grand aspirations of his own. For a reason. Those three words carried significant meaning for Sint, just like millions of others in the United States.

Above each plaque, a holographic display would appear when visitors passed their hand over a scanner prompt.

After choosing the appropriate language, the projected video footage would provide images, along with narration further detailing the meaning behind each nation's core beliefs.

Sint passed his hand over the panel located on the wall. Flashes of key moments in American history appeared above the plaque as the female narrator, voiced by an American actress of world-renowned fame, began to narrate over the footage.

"Over several decades, organized religion in the United States changed drastically. Generations shifted away from traditional churches, leaving the pews empty. Churches became increasingly unable to keep up with operating expenditures. Due to a lack of donations, a huge shift occurred in how religions spread their messages.

Several different denominations within Christianity along with the nation's most prominent religions decided to pool their collective core values and beliefs into one unifying message. Not unlike the non-denominational teachings of the past, this began revival and further melding of ideologies that spread across the country. It became popular to simply have a belief in a higher power even if that specific higher power differed from person to person. Explicit teachings detailed in various religions were specifically taught at home. Traditional churches now focused on general principles that applied to everyone. While many fundamentalists across the variances of religions absolutely did not agree with what they believed was a watered-down version of their beliefs, the majority of people understood that times had changed and more people were accepting a belief in something. A higher power."

An associate of Sint Argum, Akens Ember, arrived to notify Sint that it was almost time for him to rejoin the council as the session was about to begin again. Sint continued to watch the program, raising his hand. Ember understood not to disrupt him at that moment. He continued to watch and listen along with Sint as the program continued.

"...Americans still respect all forms of religion and non-religious beliefs, such as atheism. One fundamental principle guides all of the new church teachings. 'For a reason' is now a widely accepted belief that everything happens for a specific reason and purpose. Under this belief, regardless of what was at the center of your religion and what you called your higher power, the overwhelming majority of Americans now hold dear the idea that regardless of situation, decisions, or outcomes, everything happens according to a design and for a purpose, even if we do not immediately understand what that reason is. This phrase is now used by many Americans in everyday life and brings the nation a sense of belonging and unity. 'For a reason,' the United States of America is the Land of the Free and the Home of the Brave."

The familiar refrains of the National Anthem faded as the holographic projection ended.

"Quite the renaissance of religion, wouldn't you say, sir?" asked Akens.

"Very much so, Ember. But it's not without its dark, unexpected consequences."

Akens' face turned solemn. "It is unfortunate that something which provides so many so much hope could be used to justify the evils that men do." What Argum was referring to and Ember agreed with was the absence of having guidelines from which to pull from that 'for a Reason' provided. Many people who believed in a higher power beyond their own reasoning decided 'for a reason' also justified their bad behavior.

For some it was a pure, blind ambition that they would use to rationalize stepping on whomever they needed to achieve their goal. Believing that it was with purpose, 'for a reason'. For others in a life of crime, that even without a belief system in place they would be pursuing, they now falsely used this rationale to actually convince themselves they were doing no wrong. In a sense, nothing had changed; people throughout the ages would make excuses for their bad choices and behavior. The difference now was they were living in a time when, while many people had found a positive purpose and therefore were less self-centered, others were motivated to do harm and now had a belief system to justify it. After decades upon decades of religious division, America had once again found, as best as it could, the common ground under 'everything happens for a reason.'

"It's as if those silly ancient bumper stickers touting 'COEXIST' with symbols for letters that automobile drivers would slap on their bumpers finally came true. Fascinating," said Sint as he turned his attention away from the Wall of Nations.

The roar of Transport-T-Crafts could be heard thundering overhead.

This drew Sint's attention as the last officials of both DeCorp and EnerCon arrived. Sint watched them land on the platform, floating off the lake connected by a ramp leading to the Coalition chambers.

The lake lit up in every shade of yellow, red, and orange imaginable in the fading light of day as the sun set.

"Commander Argum, the DeCorp dignitaries have arrived. It's time to rejoin the meeting, sir."

"So it is."

Chapter 3

Old Pueblo, Arizona

Kaytha was obsessed with flying. When she wasn't in the air, she would immerse herself in books, streaming documentaries about the history of air travel (long before DeCorp made it possible for everyone), films, technical manuals—anything she could get her hands on to learn more. One particularly special morning, it was still dark outside, and the sun wouldn't be rising for another forty-five minutes. Kaytha boarded her newly custom painted T-Craft. She lived by herself in the home she grew up in Old Pueblo, a small suburb just outside Camelback, the current capital of the state. Kaytha was headed north to see her friend Taft. She was excited to share some news she'd recently received. Kaytha often listened to BlasterCasts on her T-Craft's internal audio system.

Blaster was the app that everyone used for all audio related content.

News, entertainment, sports, music, podcasts and more could all be found on Blaster. People could post live streaming or recorded audio snippets, commentary, etc., on any subject they wished. Regardless of what you wanted to listen to, it could be searched for and found on Blaster.

Kaytha stored hundreds of recordings on a wide range of topics from movies, current events, and a host of BlasterCasts covering all manner of flight, both Earth-bound and interstellar.

Kaytha strapped into her vehicle, but before lifting off she chose a specific BlasterCast she'd been listening to recently. The host, well-known talk personality Jerrod Doyle, focused this particular show on the history of Traverse Craft, how they came to be and the global impact of accessible flight. With a flip of the large red toggle switch on her cockpit dash, her ship rumbled to life. As Kaytha rose into the sky from her home's landing pad, she swiped play, starting the show titled "How T's Changed the World". Focused on her ship's flight controls, Kaytha listened to the host's speaking into her helmet speakers, picking up where he'd last left off:

"After the split with EnerCon, DeCorp research and development experienced a major breakthrough, creating the single lift system able to carry several tons off the ground with little effect on the areas surrounding where the manifolds were attached. By combining several of these "lift manifolds," massive space vehicles could leave Earth's gravity.

With smaller vehicles and just one or two lift manifolds, combined with powerful quasi-jet propulsion pods and nuclear fusion drives, DeCorp and EnerCon put manned air and space flight within everyone's grasp. DeCorp provided the opportunity for almost anyone with means to purchase, build, or retrofit vehicles. People could not only fly with ease inside Earth's gravity, but also outer space. EnerCon's fuel cells and recharge capabilities made global flight as easy and as accessible as it used to be to travel state to state by car.

Atmospheric travel only required rudimentary pilot training. A T-Craft flying license was now as simple as getting a driver's license. Spaceflight was considered easier in the weightlessness of outer space, but substantially more dangerous and required special permits, though they were often ignored.

One didn't leave the breathable air of Earth unless they flew a ship that could withstand the cold vacuum of space and carried the proper gear. When once you owned a car for daily travels, now, in the late 21st century, you owned a T-Craft, fully customizable and affordable. Many restrictions were placed on flying, with most authorized recreational space flight reserved for just outside the stratosphere. Countries maintained orbital stations to monitor activity over their airspace and outer space. Former Earth car culture had gone away and was replaced by T-Craft culture with every shape, size, color, and speed capability one used to see at vintage car shows. T-Crafts made it as fast and efficient as an eight-hour road trip by car to fly to the Moon, and that was cruising speed.

Those thermal nuclear engines and more advanced quasi-jet propulsion pods I was talking about earlier? It's because of them and the secondary market creators that space flight in our solar system had changed forever. Combined with EnerCon's AI assisted power plants, ships could travel throughout outer space at tremendous speeds. With interstellar "Speed Jumps," a single vehicle or a combination of vehicles could visit parts of the solar system and one day beyond, in a fraction of the time it used to take."

Kaytha continued to listen to the show as she continued her trip north, passing near Arizona's DeCorp factory just outside Camelback which used to be known as Phoenix (although most locals still called it Phoenix).

17

Years ago the cities and towns in southern Arizona merged together after the downtown regions fell into poverty. The trend happened nationwide. With the outlying areas of the larger metropolitan regions thriving, they would all eventually redistrict the areas and become a larger whole, combined with elected leadership better suited for each district's needs. The politics never really changed, but the players and the game did for the better.

Kaytha was nearing the end of her morning journey. Switching off the BlasterCast, she tuned in her embedded OS flight audio feeds to local air traffic control. After confirmation of clear skies, she continued listening to host Jerrod Doyle.

The talk was focused on how rapidly flight culture grabbed the imagination of the world.

"Quickly, all across the globe people took to the skies and, over just a few years, cars began to disappear from sight. The roads remained, but few people bothered to use them. The car manufacturers, along with their factories, were purchased by DeCorp and EnerCon, converted to R&D centers and T-Craft factories. Bodies, frames, power plants, onboard computers systems, analog control parts, and fuel cells, were now all being made by what had become the two biggest companies on the planet.

To keep some standard for travel, whether it was to the store for groceries, or out of state for business or pleasure, an Air Way system was developed by EnerCon. This "skyway" would appear on every vehicle cockpit heads-up display, utilizing outboard camera monitors and the roadways that destinations still occupied. Advance holographic "HUDS".

Beams of projected yellow tubes would guide pilots to their destinations, with bright blue lines indicating exit paths to specific destinations. Columns of brilliant red where flight paths would potentially cross paths let fliers know of oncoming air traffic. The OS AI was so advanced, "HUDS" would update on a second by second basis in order for the pilot to reach their destination.

While local police departments still did their jobs maintaining the peace, if someone were to fly out from the directed paths before them, law enforcement in their own patrol craft seldom attempted to stop anyone unless they posed an immediate danger. The colored "HUDS" projected skyways usually ended at the edges of the major populated areas, replaced by larger dual yellow beamed visual pathways over more rural areas connecting to other states and their cities. These were almost exclusively used by leisure travelers who felt more comfortable being guided like the roads below that generations before used to travel. High above the turbulent air, where airliners formerly conducted their business, were now filled with smaller scale personal T-Crafts along with DeCorp and Enercon large occupancy transport crafts."

"All the technical specs of both DeCorp and EnerCon creations were proprietary and kept as trade secrets. As I've discussed in the past, many of their secrets got out from employee turnover, despite confidentiality agreements. Most of those who leaked info never got caught. That's the problem with providing the public with easy ways to travel—they can get away and never be seen again, on or off the planet. Because of the rapid expansion of travel, some of DeCorp's factories began to consolidate in order to better serve the demands of the public.

Almost no layoffs occurred, but many people had to relocate, and most of those were the parents working, leaving their young adult children behind."

It was at this point Kaytha turned off the recording, thinking about her dad. Kaytha's parents had joined DeCorp right out of high school, like the parents of so many of other twenty-somethings living in the cities and their suburbs. Twelve years ago, Kaytha's dad Wilicio left to join the growing exploration endeavors of NASA.

It was then that both her parents moved back east. Wilicio's actual role in the organization had remained a mystery to Kaytha. She assumed her parents lived on the Gulf Coast of Texas, but since his location was kept secret, by association, her mother was too.

Kaytha wasn't far from her destination now. She skipped ahead a few minutes in the recording, past the talk of families as the host continued.

"Using both DeCorp and EnerCon resources channelled through governments of various countries, decades' worth of effort resulted in an energized NASA.

Now combined with the space programs of allies like China and Japan, space travel occurred often. With so many unmanned missions to set up and drop off supplies for future colonies on reachable and potentially habitable planets, large-scale excursions from Earth became routine. Currently, with the UEGC locked in a power struggle, no one was supposed to leave the planet until the debates ended. Mars and Europa had supplies and resources set up. Mars was equipped by DeCorp for potentially hundreds of thousands to live on the red planet. Most of what was actually happening on the planets wasn't public knowledge. Although there were many rumors that some of the Chinese and Japanese run missions out of NASA had pushed further into space, setting up atmospheric processors well beyond the known, traveled solar system. But as I've said before, that was just the stuff of rumors as far as most people were concerned.

They also weren't the only rumors, especially among those in the highest levels of both DeCorp and EnerCon. Next week on Doyle-Cast I'll be continuing the commentary on the history of DeCorp. Until then, thanks for downloading and listening to Mr Know It All."

With the episode over, Kaytha couldn't help but keep thinking about her parents. Kaytha was never really close with her mother; she always had much more in common with her dad. A year ago Kaytha's mom had comm'd her to let her know that her father had passed away. The way that her mom worded her father's death was such that Kaytha got the impression that her mom hadn't seen him in a while. Kaytha was told it was due to natural causes, but Kaytha never bought that excuse. Wilicio was only in his late sixties and always in excellent health. The position Wilicio held in NASA and because of the their privacy policies, kept her mother from getting access to the body. Kaytha and her mom attended a small funeral in her dad's home state of California. NASA and EnerCon paid to have her father's body put to rest at the cemetery just outside the city of Redlands, California (the city where Wilicio was born and raised). Kaytha and her mother were not allowed to view the body as per the agreement he'd signed with both organizations. The loss of her father was devastating for Kaytha and impacted her personal relationships. At the time of the funeral, she and her mother had vowed to communicate more and rebuild their relationship.

Kaytha's mother Tellsea even claimed she would move back to Arizona, but it never happened, and they slipped even further away from each other. Kaytha's one-on-one time with her dad was gone when he left for NASA, but she always knew she could comm him whenever she wanted, or at least when he was available and allowed to. Now he was gone forever. It had taken the better part of the year for Kaytha to let go. Her friendship with Taft helped take her mind off her father, and she hoped that one day she could emotionally return the favor.

She was almost to the Valley and the flying field she was headed for. She knew Taft would be waiting for her, and she couldn't wait to surprise him.

Chapter 4

Taft lived alone just north of Camelback, Arizona, although a few days of the week one or two of his flying-mates shacked up at his place, mostly because of its proximity and short flight time to the abandoned airfield they flew out of. Taft's parents were quite a bit older than most of his friends' moms and dads. Taft had just turned twenty-seven, and his mom and dad were already retired. They lived in their home only a few miles from Taft's apartment.

The airfield they used was in a fairly remote area, due to the abundance of different options for pilots to store and fly their craft. No one had much use for most airstrips since T-Craft garages had replaced car garages decades ago. No one knew what the name of the field used to be, although Taft would call it Kay's Place, but never out loud. The self-proclaimed squadron of friends was made up of Taft and Kaytha along with Ven, Oshly, and Jebet. Ven, the oldest of the bunch, had served in the air-force. His experience provided a unique offensive perspective on their hobby.

Ven was also incredibly protective of the whole group and would be the first one to get in the face of anyone that took issue with his friends. Oshly was a handyman and the digital guru of the group. Oshly had an incredibly quick wit that he used to hide the fact that he wasn't very comfortable in his own skin. Jebet was by far the best mechanic out of the bunch. She could fly and fix anything they had in the hangar.

The friends had come together over the past few years. Taft and Oshly had grown up together, while Oshly knew Ven through flight school.

At the time, Ven had been dating Jebet, but that relationship lasted as long as flight school since that's all either of them had in common at the time. Kaytha was friends with Jebet from school and a couple of years ago had invited Kaytha to join her at "Kay's Place," although at the time Taft just called it the airfield in his head. Before Kaytha joined their group, the four of them were flying together for a year, doing mock dogfights, pylon races, heading north for weekends in the mountains, avoiding air patrols and registration fees that were supposed to go along with traveling with T-craft in and out of national parks. Something always seemed missing, however. Regardless of how long Taft had known Oshly and how well he got along with Ven and Jebet, Taft never felt quite at ease with himself.

The day Taft first met Kaytha, it was late in the summer season when the chill in the morning air reminded everyone that fall was just a few weeks away.

Taft was waiting for the others to arrive for another day of whatever would happen. No one really ever set plans for what they would all do together. During the week they all held various day jobs focused around flying in some way. Saturday mornings the four of them would gather at the airfield, have breakfast, work on their ships, and then decide what the day would bring. On this morning, however, Taft heard something different.

Taft could easily recognize the sound of multiple T-Craft approaching. Ven, Oshly, and Jebet rarely flew in alone, and normally on Fridays either Ven or Oshly stayed overnight at Taft's, leaving the other to travel with Jebet. Seeing how no one had stayed at Taft's the night before, he fully expected to hear all their ships together.

This morning, however, he only heard one T-Craft, and it sounded nothing like anything he'd heard his friends flying before.

Taft was in the hangar trying to mount a new set of DeCorp thrusters he'd purchased and was in the process of locking down the primary engine cooling tubes when the wailing of a T-craft echoed inside the steel hangar walls. He was a little concerned. It was incredibly rare for anyone to come flying into his relatively small valley unannounced.

If someone did, it usually was either a mistake or they were looking for trouble. Taft's concern grew since his T-craft would need at least another hour before it would be flight worthy.

Grabbing a nearby crowbar that served no purpose apart from being something to trip over in his hangar, he cautiously stepped out on the flight line. Even if it was one of his friends, something still wasn't right; none of them ever approached at the speed this ship was apparently flying.

The sun hung brightly in the morning sky, forcing Taft to raise his left arm over his face to shade his view, and as he did a T-Craft came flying up and over the nearby ridge. Entering deeper in the valley and beginning to slow, the ship pitched at a steep angle and flew toward where Taft stood. He raised his right arm, crowbar in hand as if he was a threat to this intruder. This was no ordinary T-Craft. The vehicle's metal skin was covered in shimmering red. The ship itself looked like one of the newer DeCorp models, but heavily modified. Taft's concern shifted to curiosity. Still holding the crowbar raised in his hand, he analyzed the oddly aggressive looking T-Craft. Its canopy was situated to the front of the craft which was preferable by only the most skilled of pilots.

Having the pilot sitting so far forward offered the best view but also made the operator the most vulnerable. The bars that housed the canopy glass were a gunmetal gray and the glass itself had a smokey tint, keeping Taft from getting a solid look at the pilot.

The undercarriage had gun and missile mounts that showed signs of use, yet no actual artillery was attached. The right of the ship had a large DeCorp multi-directional interstellar thruster that could not only power the craft but also had reverse capabilities that a skilled pilot could use as a massive forward blaster weapon.

The barrel-shaped thruster was painted the same color as the canopy bars. The left side had a smaller but still incredibly powerful DeCorp Ultra-Focused dual thruster package giving the ship needed directional variation. The body of the craft was powder coated in metal flake, candy apple red. This T-Craft was one of the most impressive T-Crafts Taft had ever seen. The sight was something aggressive, scary, and beautiful.

The ship's gray landing gear deployed as the pilot glided down to earth with ease under the power of its lift manifolds. T-Crafts gave off an array of beautiful colors from their power sources. From the yellow, red, and orange glow of the engines in flight, to a slight hint of magenta that radiated from under the ship as the manifolds did their work.

The pilot landed about several yards from where Taft stood. As the canopy of the cockpit opened, he could see the pilot removing their helmet and placing it on the T-Craft's joystick. The female's hair was pitch black and cropped short, all of which in Taft's mind just added to the mystery of the entire situation.

Her face, he thought, looked like an old-school fighter jet: fast, lethal and gorgeous, but with a classic feel of nostalgia.

She wasn't the type that would turn heads, but she was the type that would stop Taft dead in his tracks. She began to push herself up out of the cockpit with both arms, but paused briefly. "Hey Sandy, I come in peace. You can put the stick down."

Taft hadn't had his wavy brown hair cut in several months, which was the only conclusion he could come to as to why she called him Sandy. Already taken aback by her unconventional good looks, not to mention the exotic look of her T-Craft and apparent skill, Taft nervously muttered, "Oh yeah…sure…no problem." He tossed the crowbar off to the side.

The pilot stepped out of her ship, wearing a worn but well kept gray flight suit, tailored to fit her slender frame and average height. Taft stood about 6'2" and struck a lean shadow. He didn't work out but kept busy enough to stay in good shape.

The pilot flipped the small external switch on the side of her T-Craft which closed the canopy, and walked over toward him. "Taft, right? Sorry for the unannounced entrance. I'm Kaytha. I guess Jebet didn't tell you I was coming?" She removed one of her flight gloves as she reached out to shake his hand.

Taft immediately noticed her nail polish matched the red on her ship. "Oh, yeah, she's mentioned you a few times I think. Nice to meet you."

Kaytha responded quickly back, "Yeah, I doubt that... Jebet doesn't like to share a lot, but either way nice to meet you too."

Taft immediately knew that he probably shouldn't try impressing this girl as she carried a level of confidence that he already found intimidating.

Several hours passed before the others arrived, and in that time Kaytha had helped Taft finish mounting his new thrusters to his ship and get it prepared for flight for once the rest of the group joined them. Most of their talk was about flying, but Taft did everything he could to sneak in questions trying to get to know Kaytha better without being too obvious of his intention. It had been some time since he had feelings for someone, mostly because he spent almost all his time flying with Oshly, Ven, and Jebet, never really being anywhere he could meet new people.

Kaytha wasn't all that different from Taft in as much as she didn't have a dating history worth discussing either. In Kaytha's case, however, it was her ambition to work R&D at DeCorp that kept any potential boyfriends at bay as she spent almost all her time either flying or working on her T-Craft.

The most coveted jobs in the United States and for most of the globe were in the Research and Development centers at DeCorp, and only the most skilled pilots were able to fill the highly sought-after positions. But Kaytha too felt something missing and filled the void by devoting all her time to her goals. Regardless of how hard she worked, it never soothed her, which just drove her to work harder. Meeting Taft for the first time was the rare occasion when she let her guard down.

Kaytha didn't even realize how much time had passed working in the hangar or how much information she had actually given up to this "stranger." It wasn't until the others arrived that Kaytha started to realize the hours that had passed.

Taft was so focused on every word coming from Kaytha that he didn't even hear the three T-Crafts land next to Kaytha's. The moment Jebet walked inside the hangar, Kaytha's demeanor totally changed.

Over the sounds of the T-Crafts winding down, Jebet yelled out, "Hey Kay…how long you been waiting for me?"

Kaytha responded, "Not long at all!"

Taft was puzzled at her response considering they had been working on his ship and talking for over three hours.

He wasn't sure what to make of it at first, but a passing glance back from Kaytha as she greeted Oshly and Ven was an indication from her to him that she was fully aware of her white lie and was trusting him to not make a big deal about it. Taft wasn't immediately sure how to take that, but indeed at that moment, he kept his mouth shut. His gut instinct told him this was the first, but indeed not the last time he would be trusted to not divulge the entire truth, and would be shown many times over that he was absolutely right.

Taft didn't know exactly what just happened in those first few hours he spent alone with Kaytha; he was only sure that something had happened, and for the moment he was glad that it did.

Chapter 5

Southern California, current day

A few hours passed by in Taft's mysterious trip with his friend. The trip took longer than Kaytha wanted; she had them flying close to the terrain, hugging the contours of the mountains between the two states. Staying low helped in avoiding any detection. So far it had worked. They still had some flying time left in the trip so Kaytha pulled up another Doyle-Cast to listen to. She'd listened to them dozens of times before. Once again the show picked up where the host left off.

"During the split between DeCorp and EnerCon, they still held on to many of each other's available resources. Both companies were not all that different from one another apart from their focuses on technology and also philosophy. Especially when it came to exploring the galaxy, a debate that mirrored and was perpetuated by the conflict among the leaders in the UEGC. Each organization held different views on how the universe would be populated.

DeCorp firmly believed that massive oversight should be employed when it came to who lay claim to any part of the galaxy and its planets. EnerCon felt it was best to look to the past and the pioneers of America's west, a first come first claim situation, that would be in the best interest of all who traveled among the stars. While it was never official record why the companies parted ways, most believed this was the reason.

At this point in time, EnerCon's way of thinking was winning the debate. Most of the space exploration being pursued was under the idea that if you dropped off supplies, set up atmospheric processors on what was formerly uninhabitable planets, you were claiming the right to those regions if not the worlds themselves. DeCorp knew that it was losing ground and its leadership desperately wanted the United Earth Galaxy Coalition to put forward an agreement to divide up the known regions fairly among all nations with the ability to colonize. As time passed, the more that seemed unlikely and heads at DeCorp were beginning to strategize other ways to gain control of the most valuable resources the stars had to offer.

"Both companies kept most of their supplies in colossal space vehicles, which were, in simplest terms, large space going warehouses. Each vessel was loaded with everything a new society would need to survive from scratch. Before the two entities split, the choice was made that the most logical thing to do was to make all but the manufacturing portions of operations mobile. With both on Earth and space flight now the standard mode of travel, it made sense to store everything in large building sized vehicles.

This not only solved any potential issues of relocation on Earth but also with the desire to begin taking Earth's interests and expanding them to the stars, it was an efficient and effective way to prepare for the future. I've heard behind closed doors, when the world leaders would gather in Italy, that even before the companies split, the final choice to make everything mobile came down to safety and survival.

The leadership knew that if there were ever any kind of global disaster, they would be prepared to get their assets off-planet as soon as possible.

Most never imagined such an extinction level event could ever occur, even I don't believe that anything that significant is possible.

Because of the massive production efforts, especially the enormous facilities DeCorp needed to fill the demand for flying vehicles and thusly for EnerCon to create the power plants for them, a disaster at any one of each of the hundreds of locations would be a massive catastrophe. But it was the unpredictable scenarios that had these experts most concerned. The current technology always provides a level of safety and safeguards that made any chance of such an event occurring almost nonexistent. Regardless, everyone close to the companies knows it's not just trillions of dollars at stake—DeCorp and EnerCon hold the future of the human race in their possession."

Kaytha shook her head, as if she was shedding the negativity of the doomsday talk coming from the show host from her head. Shutting off the audio, Kaytha glanced at the HUD display on her cockpit canopy.

They were almost to their destination. Finally, she broke radio silence, keying her comms, "Yo, Taft, Taft...?"

Taft didn't hear her at first as he had been listening to one of his many playlists on board his T-Craft audio system. Most of them were themed, and he had more than a few "Kay" playlists.

Kaytha made a quick barrel roll over Taft's ship which immediately grabbed his attention.

"Hey, you lost in there?" asked Kaytha over her comms.

"Just in the music," Taft replied.

Taft turned down the volume on his Blaster App, currently playing *Depeche Mode, "In Sympathy,"* a band none of his friends were huge fans of despite the fact that they fell into the current trend of nostalgic music. The song still played quietly in the background while Taft looked over at Kaytha flying off his left.

Kaytha sounded almost giddy as she spoke, "We're getting close. Keep low, we're pretty much out of range from any local scanners, but there's no need to be risky."

Kaytha had flown Taft into the southern part of California, high up into the mountains a few miles from a town called Big Bear Lake.

While most of California had grown into large sprawling metropolises, this sleepy town—apart from technological advances in flight, building construction and communications—never developed in size from its inception in the early part of the 20th century.

Taft, finally tired of waiting for Kaytha to explain what they were doing there, decided to speak up, "So Kay, it's been a fun ride and all, but could you tell me what in the world we're doing out here? There's plenty of places to visit just like this in Arizona."

"Sorry, I figured you were getting a little restless. Your flight formation and steadiness was getting kinda sloppy," replied Kaytha.

It was little comments like that which gave Taft a feeling of satisfaction knowing she was paying closer attention to him then she led on.

"Slow up. Where we're headed is just up and over that upcoming ridge line," said Kaytha.

As they skimmed the pine trees up and over the next peak, they arrived at the top of a small valley nestled high up the mountain. Taft slowed down, following Kaytha's lead as she pitched his T-Craft sideways, flying in a clockwise pattern over the pristine natural landscape.

After completing a few circles of the valley, Kaytha scanned the area for any other signs of human life. Satisfied they were alone, she revealed the purpose of their journey.

"Taft, switch on your manifolds. Let's hold for a few minutes just over the lake."

Their T-Crafts floated to a stop about two hundred feet off the surface of the water. T-Crafts didn't give off much of any wake from their lift manifolds. Any real disruptions would come from the engines. Plus they were high enough above the water that it barely made a ripple on the lake's glass smooth surface.

Kaytha flipped up her visor. "Alright, so about four days ago I received a delayed communication. It was from my dad. I don't know who sent it or how, but it came from his personal communication code, and it was cryptic. It started off typical, saying how he was doing, hoping I was doing well, small talk but no insight or details about what he had been up to. Then he started talking about this camping trip the two of us took when I was ten years old when he flew us up to this lake.

"I remember it specifically because it was one of the only times he took me anywhere without my mother.

"We arrived in the morning, set up camp, and spent the day exploring the area and fishing on the lake. The next morning, we packed up his T-Craft and flew home.

It was one of my favorite times with him as a kid, but I never expressed that to him, and he's never brought it up since."

"Are you sure he wasn't just sharing a nice memory, Kay?" Taft spoke with more than just a little hint of skepticism.

"My dad's not one to ever really get emotional let alone nostalgic," Kaytha answered, adding, "It was the last part of the message that convinced me he was trying to tell me something. At the end of the message, my dad said that he wondered if the spot was the same, saying he would like to visit this place and if I ever had the chance I should come back here."

Taft adjusted the settings on his T-craft. Floating idly for as long as they were, some of the systems of the ship didn't like being static and had a tendency to heat up. Looking over at Kaytha, apparently realizing the same thing, she began flipping switches, resetting some of her ship's gauges. Kaytha then flipped her visor back down.

Taft did too, keying his mic, "Alright, so you're convinced your dad wanted you to come back here. Any idea why?"

EMBARK

"That's why I brought you along. You're going to help me find out."

EMBARK

"That's why I brought you along. You're going to help me find out."

Chapter 6

Sint Argum's home was a DeCorp funded base of operation south of Atlanta. Sint returned from the UEGC meeting in Italy for less than twenty-four hours when it was time for him to travel on work related matters once again, taking off just before dawn in his specialized DeCorp T-Craft. Most upper class preferred their vehicles to have some level of sophistication with the exposed mechanics covered with sleek, lightweight materials. This reduced the appearance of the T-Craft to various shiny surfaced, characterless shapes, looking more like pieces of art than transportation vehicles. This was a look consistent throughout DeCorp's specific hardware. The Massive Mobile Warehouses (MMW) for example, looked just like that of warehouses when not prepared for flight. A dark blue hue adorned Sint's T-Craft, the latest luxury model available. The ship was virtually seamless and completely streamlined. Even the large DeCorp custom fusion drive thrusters attached to the rear side panels were shrouded behind the smooth metal that covered the entire vehicle. One would have to be staring directly at the rear of the ship to see even a hint of its mechanics.

Sint only flew in this particular ship for appearances. He preferred the raw customizable look of the normal T-Craft that one would find dotting the skies over communities. But he was used to doing things against his own norm for the sake of appearances.

Sint, at just 35 years old, was the defacto head of DeCorp. He didn't have the command title, but those at the top never got involved in the day to day operations of the company.

Local leadership at each DeCorp location carried out the requirements of central command, and those orders usually came directly from Sint. These days things had become so routine that Sint found himself with little to do other than to make sure everything was running as it should. This granted him time to pursue other endeavors within DeCorp that went largely unnoticed. The world was a relatively calm place. Sure, there were always pockets in Europe that had their turmoil and groups staunchly opposed to both DeCorp and EnerCon, but the little protesting that did occur rarely made the global news. The UEGC had been debating the issue of populating the galaxy for years. Neither side wanted to give way, and both were seeing the advantages of continued debate over actually reaching a resolution. This stalemate created a situation that only perpetuated the idea of a rumored cloaking device having either been already built or currently in development, with everyone claiming the other had access or potential access to it.

The concern over the existence of such a "device" was so great that most entities with the right resources had started developing their own weapons divisions in relative secret from one another.

This line of thinking led to the inevitable conclusion that war for the stars could one day be a reality. In truth, everyone knew war was not in anyone's best interests. For all these reasons, the existence of a functional cloaking device was of great concern for leaders of both companies. If anyone had the ability and power needed to mask a vehicle the size of an MMW from detection, they could potentially create multiple devices.

While the UEGC considered the best way to debate issues of how they would populate the galaxy, the one who possessed such a device could begin to set up resources in secret anywhere in the known galaxy. In theory, by the time the UEGC actually ended any debate, that entity would already have control of the stars long before anyone else had a chance.

Sint had become so bored with the regular operations of DeCorp that he had quietly turned almost all his focus to weapons development. While this shift in his own personal agenda had helped maintain his interest in daily operations, Sint knew that eventually this would become tedious as well. What good was a strike force, military vehicles, and weapons if you never got to use them?

Sint's T-Craft was cruising on autopilot as he flew toward the DeCorp fields located in the Midwest portion of the United States. They were called "fields" because hundreds of MMW now occupied what were essentially miles upon miles of concrete parking lots. When passing above DeCorp property at high altitude, over flyover country, it didn't look all that different than they did decades ago.

Before where you would see miles of patchwork square crop fields, they'd been replaced by massive square MMWs. Sint was reviewing the most up to date info he could get on the weapons development taking place at various DeCorp facilities. In truth, DeCorp already had a vast array of weapons. But with the advances in technology moving as fast as they were, the R&D centers were constantly hard at work making more powerful and easier to utilize means of destruction.

All of the loaded MMWs had not just the means of survival for hundreds per ship, but also held large weapons caches: guns, cannons, ammo, military grade fuel, and recharge units. These provisions were largely seen as nothing more than accepted weaponry for law enforcement purposes. Most importantly, they carried weapons that could easily retrofit any T-Craft or even an MMW into a fighter or interstellar battle station. Most of the standard MMW weapons load were already preassigned or attached to the handful of stock vehicles on the MMW. The genius behind what DeCorp had created was the ease at which you could change and customize any vehicle.

This didn't just apply to style, luxury, and power, but also to weaponizing. Everything from the largest MMW, down to the smallest weapon, was seemingly interchangeable and customizable.

The combined effort of DeCorp hardware with EnerCon energy and ammo made it all possible. If you ever played with LEGO then you too could easily change, customize, build up, or take apart anything from a T-Craft to a handgun. Virtually nothing the companies made wasn't interchangeable with something it wasn't supposed to be placed with. Driver's education in schools was replaced with rudimentary flight training and most of the standards needed to work with DeCorp and EnerCon equipment was included with that education. All of DeCorp's larger vehicles had anti-gravity systems that at the time were not available to the public. The anti-gravity systems had been developed back when DeCorp and EnerCon were still a single company. The breakthrough happened when the lift manifolds were created and used much of the same technology, but scaled down in size.

The lift manifolds simplified the technology, making it cost efficient and therefore accessible for the masses.

EnerCon had their own versions of MMWs but many lacked the same amount of supply stock that DeCorp had amassed. EnerCon did have their own military; however, it was almost all focused on defense and therefore not nearly as robust as DeCorp. Most of the top leaders inside EnerCon never felt the need to bolster defenses.

Who would they have to be fighting? After all, no one was at war, currently. The biggest difference between DeCorp's MMWs versus EnerCon's was what DeCorp called Massive Mobile Station-Adaptation or MMSA. DeCorp had designed every single MMW with the ability to attach to each other once they reached outer space. Any number of MMWs could be attached together in formation to create one massive space station.

All crews could then move freely throughout the entire creation once the MMSAs had all attached to one another. Twenty or more MMSAs once combined turned into a giant orb-shape, with the thrusters of the outer MMWs working in tandem. Each MMW would be assigned a number with "One" being the flight command ship that would send out its commands to all the others. DeCorp knew that an MMSA was a threat deterrent unmatched by EnerCon or anyone else who could, however unlikely, pose a threat.

Sint's T-Craft began its final approach to the DeCorp's MMW fields. He took the ship off autopilot to fly it himself as he preformed his usual aerial tour of the main facility and the two dozen MMWs closest to the communications buildings.

These particular MMWs were of great importance to Sint, and he always took extra steps to ensure that everyone involved from construction all the way up to the flight crews was the best trained, most loyal, and brightest that DeCorp had hired. These MMWs were stocked in the same way as all the others except for one thing.

They all carried an armory of vehicles, weapons, and ammunition greater than the standard supply normally stocked for security measures only. Each of these MMWs could not only ensure vital supplies for hundreds, but the extra military grade hardware also meant they could be used as defensive and offensive kinetic action. Unlike the standard stock on the normal MMWs, these Sint-approved vehicles had extras of everything, meaning that the other standard travel vehicles could also be turned into military fighting T-Craft along with the already weaponized security vehicles on board. It was a top of the line, elite army in every flying box.

From the outside, these MMWs looked normal, but they were far from it. Among only those with direct knowledge of their capability, they were referred to as MMD or Massive Mobile Defense. They were always prepared for flight, with the needed crews staying in the mobile housing facilities close enough to the flight line that they could be on site and ready for taking off in an hour's time.

Most all employees lived on the work base, with rotating crews keeping staffing at a maximum. The DeCorp facilities, and to a slightly lesser extent EnerCon's too, were cities unto themselves.

The growth and rapid expansion of the companies was largely responsible for so many parents leaving their young adult children to live in the suburbs while moms and dads worked and lived at the factories.

Sint exited his T-Craft, swiping his hand over an illuminated green oval on the outside of the ship. The ship OS bio-scanned his palm and automatically closed the canopy. Sint stopped for just a minute to stare at his handiwork. His MMDs, boxy behemoths of state of the art technology, sat side by side, row upon row on the tarmac.

One of the MMDs was departing for a routine test flight. Sint decided to watch as the space vehicle began its transformation. Folding out from the front of the MMD structure was a massive multi-level flight and command center that closely resembled the head of a beetle with large crystal clear viewport windows. The bottom of the MMD lifted up from the ground with the assistance of six huge formally hidden landing legs. With the vessel no longer sitting flush against the concrete, the MMD's rows upon rows of slightly magenta glowing lift manifolds were exposed. All four lower corners of the MMD opened up, the doors giving way then sliding back out of sight into the sides of the MMD. From out of the open hatches came sets of hydraulic arms attached to the giant cylindrical DeCorp directional thrusters. The metal telescoping tubes stretched until the engines locked in place. The entire process only took an impressive few minutes, with everything working in tandem.

With clearance given, the huge MMD slowly began to rise, its powerful thrusters erupting, lifting it from the surface almost as if in slow motion. Because of their massive size, even the maximum amount of lift manifolds wasn't quite enough to get it off the ground.

The directional thrusters assisted the MMD as it elevated straight up into the air. After about three hundred feet, with momentum achieved, the manifolds were enough to keep the MMD aloft, and the directional thrusters began their real task of putting the vehicle into motion. Once an MMW or MMD was moving into the atmosphere, fighting Earth's gravity, they were almost impossible to stop as they headed straight for the stratosphere. Once in space, the ships were more nimble and maneuverable, able to reach tremendous speeds toward their destination.

Sint continued to watch until the MMD flew high enough into the blue sky that it was no longer visible. Walking now toward the communications building, Sint thought, *One day I'll see my creations in action, real action.*

Chapter 7

Mountains, Southern California

Kaytha and Taft circled the valley for roughly twenty minutes, flying in varying patterns, seeing if they could spot anything at all unusual.

"A few more minutes, Taft, and we can set down on the beach. I just want to be sure that we don't miss anything from above first before we go traipsing off on foot."

"Any idea on where you want to start? It's a lot of ground to cover, especially since we don't have any clue what to look for," Taft replied.

"The spot we camped that one time is about one hundred yards into the trees. I figured we could start there."

Just then Taft changed his direction suddenly, turning his T-Craft back out over the water.

"Did you spot something?" Kaytha asked.

"No, but I am noticing something. Come around alongside of me, let me know if you see it too."

Kaytha and Taft had been flying the entire time over the forest, trees, and ridge line with their ships angled looking down on the Earth below.

Having flown back to where they first started, Kaytha flipped up her visor and keyed her comms, "So what are we looking at?"

"I noticed this earlier but didn't think anything of it at first. Look at the tree line dead ahead. See that grouping, about six trees wide and well into the forest? The tree line is lower than the entire valley," said Taft as he floated in the sky, parallel to Kaytha.

"There looks to be almost a dent in the tops of the tree line." Kaytha was impressed at Taft's observations, but wasn't about to show it. "And look just beyond those trees. You can clearly see snapped tree trunks."

Taft, well aware of this as it's what reminded him of what he'd seen when they arrived, didn't bother to tell Kaytha.

"Something knocked down those trees and whatever it was cut a pretty big path into the forest. Look at how far back it goes," said Kaytha as they continued to examine the area from out their cockpit canopies.

"The forest is really thick. We both flew past that location several times already. I think we're going to have to go on foot," continued Kaytha.

Both of them immediately started flying for the beach, setting down their ships on loose dirt soil between the water and the forest.

Taft hopped out first, leaving his helmet in the cockpit. With Kaytha continuing to normalize the settings in her T-Craft, Taft walked to the back of his ship to a small supply hatch and grabbed a protein bar. "Before we head out, you hungry? I've got some breakfast bars."

Kaytha, now standing on the beach, replied, "Yeah you got blueberry?"

"Yep." Taft always kept enough flavors so Kaytha would have a choice.

Taft turned his head to look at Kaytha for what would be the first real time that day. When his eyes fell upon her, he stopped cold for a moment trying not to let his emotions show. Kaytha had unzipped the top of her flight suit, allowing it to fall around her waist, exposing her gray t-shirt, but that wasn't what totally caught his attention. He was right; her hair was brunette and longer than he remembered seeing it. Trying to keep his cool, Taft muttered, "Did you do something with your hair again?"

"I washed it?" Kaytha said somewhat sarcastically.

She wasn't entirely sure whether she appreciated that Taft noticed such things or whether she was annoyed at his lack of honesty about his noticing such things. Kaytha harbored no illusions that Taft cared for her, and while she believed it was probably healthier to have it out in the open, she wasn't entirely sure how she would actually react if it were.

Kaytha had feelings for Taft too; she always did, finding him attractive from the moment they met, and there was no one else she would rather spend time with, even Jebet. But Kaytha also knew that getting into a relationship with Taft now just wasn't ideal. She was so focused on her flight training and the future, she knew that a romance with Taft would slow everything down and ultimately strain whatever relationship they had. She just accepted that this was the place where they would be. She would keep them as friends.

Taft would do what he could to show her how much he loved her without ever saying he loved her and she would ignore those moments or make subtle comments to keep him guessing and his emotions at bay. It was why she would get annoyed that he noticed when she changed her style and expressed it by acting aloof. Deep down Kaytha wasn't really annoyed at him—she was really annoyed at herself. She knew she was at least half responsible putting him in that situation.

Taft tossed her the protein bar while he opened another storage hatch. This one contained some sidearms. "Do you know anything about the wildlife?"

Kaytha understood what Taft was driving at. "I'd grab your energy blaster. I've got extra charge clips if you need them."

Standard guns using conventional bullets were still in use, and so were next generation small arm laser blasters, but those were mostly used for either sport or military snipers. They were "cool" but not very efficient and oddly inaccurate.

Energy blasters, rifles, and when outfitted on T-Craft cannons, were the most popular weapons of choice. All energy based weapons were similar to shotguns, with a more considerable blast radius to damage your target.

These weapons could be adjusted on the fly from merely sending a shock wave, all the way to a destructive burst of energy that could disintegrate targets in its crosshairs. A standard sidearm energy blaster could fire off at least 12 rounds. The only downside was that if you had your weapon settings at their deadliest, the final rounds you shot might not pack as big a punch.

You had to be smart and thoughtful about the use of any energy based weapon. Much like all the significant innovations created between DeCorp and EnerCon, one usually had a slight advantage over another.

In this case, EnerCon energy weapons were far more popular and technologically advanced than DeCorp. DeCorp made up for this in volume, amassing exponentially more energy weapons, even though EnerCon made them. DeCorp always felt it best to be prepared. EnerCon directly supplied the need.

Kaytha pulled her flight suit back up over her shoulders and zipped up as they began to walk into the forest, both with blasters in hand. Now that they understood what they were potentially looking for, they could see something had moved through the trees with enough force to tear up decades worth of dense growth.

"It looks like the tops of the trees behind us were cut off."

"Whatever came crashing down did so at a pretty level angle, but had to be going fast for it not to come instantly crashing to the ground," said Taft, looking back over his shoulder.

As they walked further, the crash area was becoming more and more defined.

"I don't think this happened all that long ago. Look at the clearing ahead. I didn't spot it flying overhead. The tops of these trees created a canopy cover for whatever came plowing through here," said Kaytha.

They walked up and over a small rise in the terrain giving way to a large clearing and the cause of the devastation.

The soil, turned up and shoved away from where they stood, with a small berm made of dirt filled with sticks and pine needles, outlined like a pathway toward the object.

Kaytha immediately said out loud what they were both thinking, "That's a T-Craft or at least what's left of one."

They both spotted what looked to be a piece of DeCorp thruster that had broken off on impact wedged between two trees.

"That's a long-range transport thruster. Not much maneuverability but sturdy and you only need two. You find them almost exclusively on..."

"Drones," said Kaytha, interrupting Taft.

She walked to the front of the T-Craft wreckage.

There was no cockpit window which they both immediately knew meant there was no pilot.

51

"I'm shocked the cockpit section stayed intact. The rest of this ship got shredded," said Kaytha.

"Yeah, but that's mostly the other thruster and the lift manifolds. It looks like the rear storage and avionics section broke clean off the rear of this thing. But where is it?" said Taft.

"It's over there!" exclaimed Kaytha, pointing to about fifty yards from where the front of the ship had stopped. "It must have snapped, got blown forward on impact."

"There has to be something in the cargo hold adding enough weight for it to get tossed that far. These ships just don't break apart like that and when they do it's usually the entire T-Craft that gets decimated," replied Taft.

They both walked cautiously over to what remained of the rear of the ship. "Looks like it tumbled a few times," said Taft.

The rear was sticking up in the air while the section that had ripped away from the rest of the ship was stuck face down in the dirt.

"The fastest way to see what's in this thing is going to be pulling it outta the ground. It's way too banged up to try and open the hatches," said Kaytha.

Taft didn't entirely agree, but also didn't feel like arguing as he grabbed on to a corner of the rear of the destroyed ship. "Hey, grab the other side and let's see if we can uproot it."

It didn't take nearly as much strength as they both thought it would, and the rear of the ship came quickly crashing to the ground, knocking them both back with the weight of each of them carrying them to the dirt. Taft looked at Kaytha and they both started laughing.

"That was your idea, dude," said Kaytha chuckling.

"Maybe it was empty after all...?"

Kaytha sat on the ground staring straight ahead at where the rear of the broken ship had been. Once the chunk of ship hit the ground, it had rolled away, exposing the hole they wanted to examine.

Kaytha nodded to Taft. "Or maybe whatever it is just fell out?" Taft then noticed it too.

Then Kaytha saw something. "Taft, what the hell is that?"

"I've got no clue..." he replied.

Getting back to their feet, they wiped off the dirt that had gathered on their jumpsuits—neither was in a rush to investigate whatever it was the crashed T-Craft drone had been carrying. It wasn't that they were scared; it was more confusion.

They both knew, even without speaking to each other, that someone had to put this thing into the ship and sent it on its way so it couldn't be that dangerous. But still, neither could gather by just looking at it even a shape. They were staring at something and nothing at the same time.

"I'm not getting any radiation readings. How about you?" said

Kaytha, checking the small digital gauge on her flight suit located on her left jacket pocket.

All flight suits were equipped with radiation and toxicity monitors built in. Anything dangerous, the monitor would pick it up.

"Mine shows nothing harmful, apart from some of the fluids left over from the crash," said Taft.

They both started cautiously walking toward the mystery cargo. As they got closer, they could see a sense of shape, smaller than an old style beer keg and slightly more cylindrical, yet still shapeless. There was an almost glistening energy wake rippling off from the "device," distorting everything around it. Even the ground it was resting on had all but disappeared, giving it an appearance as if floating. The closer Taft and Kaytha got, the more it appeared as if you could see right through it.

"Are you sure your monitor is all in the green, Taft?"

"Yup. I read nothing harmful coming from it."

They stood about two feet away on either side of the device and stared at it, not sure what they should do.

"I think it's safe to say that this is what my dad was hoping I would find, but why was it here, who crashed the ship, and why has no one come looking for it?" said Kaytha.

Taft bent down and reached out to touch it.

Once his hand seemed to be at the edge of whatever was emanating from the device, he moved a little closer when suddenly...

"Taft!" Kaytha exclaimed as she watched as his hand disappeared from sight.

Taft was just as startled. He leaped back, yanking his hand away as fast and far as he could.

"What the hell? Is your hand okay?!" Kaytha asked.

"Yeah, it's fine. I didn't feel anything at all."

The slow realization washed over Kaytha and Taft as they started to understand what they had found.

"It can't be. No one ever thought it was actually real and I don't know what else it could be. But it would explain why your dad was eager for you to find it," said Taft.

"Right? And it would also explain why no one saw it in flight or go down."

"Even if they did, they wouldn't have known what they were looking at and the wreckage wouldn't have been exposed until impact," Kaytha replied.

"There is only one way to find out. You go to that side, I'll take this end," said Taft.

They both positioned themselves on what they were sure was either end of the device.

Taft instructed, "Okay, let's slowly reach down and see if we can find a place to grab on. Keep an ear and eye on your monitor too."

As they bent at the knees and reached down to try and pick up the device, both their arms disappeared in the wake of light waves rippling from in front of them.

"Okay, Taft this is fricken freaky."

"Are you feeling anything yet?"

"Yep, I got something. Feels like there is a ridge on the base of this end I can grab onto. Its circumference is bigger than I thought," replied Kaytha.

The closer they moved, the more of their bodies disappeared, almost as if underwater.

"There seems to be a grip on this end. Okay, I got it," said Taft.

"I'm good," replied Kaytha.

"On three. One, two...three!" said Taft, as they both raised the device off the ground and in doing so, whatever "it" was almost entirely vanished, as did their bodies, apart from their shoulders up.

They looked at each other and for the second time that day started laughing, this time at how ridiculous it was that they were essentially floating heads.

"It's not that heavy. I think I might be able to grab it on my own," said Taft, feeling along the cylinder. "Yeah, there are handles along it. Think I got it."

Kaytha was still holding onto it as Taft got a firm grip with both hands.

"It's a little cumbersome but the weight isn't bad. Go ahead and let go."

As Kaytha released her hands, Taft positioned the device closer to his body and prepared to walk it back to the beach. Most of his body was still transparent with only his neck and head showing.

"Let's get this back to the ships. We can't be the only ones that know about it," said Kaytha as they started toward the lake with Kaytha leading.

"Honestly, Taft, do you think it really is…?"

As Kaytha turned around to look at Taft, he had vanished entirely. As if on instinct, Kaytha began to walk swiftly in Taft's direction. Before she could yell his name, her body slammed into his.

"KAYTHA, LOOK OUT!"

Taft dropped the device and instantly reappeared, looking up at Kaytha who had landed on top of him. The "device" had rolled off to the side. They could see it again as it sat on the ground, radiating light waves as it did when they found it.

Kaytha was laying directly on top of Taft. "The moment you started walking, you were completely invisible. I didn't even see any distortion."

Kaytha's leg had landed in an unpleasant spot on Taft, yet he didn't for a second want to let on he was in pain, having only dreamed about being this close to her. They stared at each other for a moment. Taft, growing equally nervous and in pain, just stared at Kaytha as she began to speak.

"Taft?"

"Yeah…" replied Taft, looking pathetically dreamy eyed at Kaytha.

"I think my dad made a cloaking device."

Chapter 8

DeCorp, South Dakota

The sun was hanging low on the horizon, bathing dozens of MMWs in a wash of orange and lavender. Sint had landed his luxury T-Craft alongside the communications and control facilities tower. Several of the men currently in charge of the watch were waiting for their boss. This wasn't a military operation, so for those that had previously served in the armed forces, they were no longer military officers. They were all employees. Nevertheless, no one had any illusions that in this sector of DeCorp, these MMDs were the closest thing to a military operation you could get.

Sint was taller than average—almost six and a half feet—not very fit, and considered by most to be awkward, yet his appearance was no indicator of how absolutely vital he was to DeCorp. He was aware of this and used it to his advantage when meeting new people. He put on a no-nonsense, almost arrogant, front as if passive-aggressively relaying that while he might look gangly, he was not to be messed with.

"Welcome, Commander. We trust you had a pleasant flight," said Akens Ember.

"I did, Ember, for a reason," replied Sint in a formal yet forceful manner.

Since DeCorp was not a military operation, there were no military titles given to the leadership. Sint Argum was the only exception. It was rumored that early on in the development of Sint's fleet of MMDs, a new recruit who served in the US Navy had unwittingly called Sint "Commander," and no one had ever bothered—or dared —to correct him. Sint never corrected anyone either and actually enjoyed being in charge, using "commander" as his title, even if it was just a phony one.

As Sint entered the control facility, he asked, "Ember, is everything on schedule and what's the current state of readiness for my SF?"

"Sir, your Special Fleet is at Level One, on schedule, as you requested, with a twenty minute crew load and lift time available, if needed."

Sint's SF wasn't exactly common knowledge among all of DeCorp's employees. Sure, most of the leadership was aware of Sint's program, and a few had been briefed on its special cargo, but not much thought was given to the project or the expenses needed to make it happen. This was a welcomed opportunity for Sint to have as few eyes as possible on his plans, and DeCorp had never been in any budget crisis.

"Good. Any updates I should be briefed on? I heard that there may have been technical problems at the far West Quadrant of the facility," Sint asked in a tone that suggested that he already knew the answer to the question.

With unease in his voice, Ember replied, "Yes, that is correct. To the West, right on the border with Wyoming, there was a spike in the primary cooling conductor of the MMW fueling station in Quadrant Five. The reactor scrambled when the anomaly occurred, with no apparent damage to the reactor or the MMW that was being fueled at the time."

"Why wasn't I notified? I'm to be made aware of any issues that occur," asked Sint.

"The event happened just within the past few hours and was over in seconds," Ember said as he regained his composure. "I knew you were arriving soon and felt it better to explain in person."

"Fine, but follow my orders as I command them and do not deviate, or you will find yourself working in the northern fields loading seafood and two-by-fours on the humanitarian MMWs."

"Absolutely, sir!" Ember could not help but stand at attention, as if he was a soldier in front of his superior officer.

"Do we know the cause of the power spike? Are you concerned it might be indicative of a larger issue?"

"We do not have a primary cause. Although I suspect it was due to the systems cycling after the latest rounds of refueling and restocking from the newly returned MarsCorp supply run. I do not anticipate it to be a systemic problem."

"Investigate the incident until you have exhausted all possibilities and then report your findings *immediately* to me!" Sint then turned around and walked out of the control room.

"Yes, sir," Ember replied in a raised voice of respect, even though Sint had not waited for confirmation. As he watched the control room door slide shut, the sound of an alert warning began to echo from the far side of the room.

Ember yelled across the room, "Hindley! Is the control board sounding that alarm?"

"Yes, sir. I just got a power fluctuation alert on a refuel station to the West, but it doesn't say what the cause was," Hindley replied.

A wave of concern immediately washed over Ember. "What quadrant in the West?"

"That would be Five, sir!"

CHAPTER 9

Mountains, Southern California

Having stumbled into each other walking with the device, resulting in Kaytha inadvertently kneeing Taft's groin, whatever moment might have happened with her, no matter how painful physically or emotionally, had passed as she climbed up and off Taft. He was disappointed but also realized that if anything was going to happen, it probably wouldn't have been the best memory. Besides, there were bigger things to consider, much bigger.

Kaytha's thoughts immediately turned to the BlasterCast she had been listening to. "Jerrod Doyle talked about a cloaking device in one of his episodes."

"There was talk of cloaking devices in development or already created by either DeCorp or EnerCon, but no one had ever actually seen one," explained Kaytha.

"I imagine such a device could allow anyone to leave Earth undetected, and in the wrong hands lead to corruption or worse be used as a military weapon," said Taft.

Kaytha continued, "That's the same thing Doyle said. He talked about a free market of space sort of existing. How many believed in a first come first serve exploration of the stars. Something like that."

"I like this Doyle guy," replied Taft.

"I do too. Unfortunately, he passed away unexpectedly two years ago. But I've kept all his shows."

"Do you remember anything else, Kay?"

"He said leaders of DeCorp had been calling for regulation in preparation for the potential creation of a cloaking device."

"Until now," offered Taft.

"If that's what this is," said Kaytha, still sounding slightly skeptical. "Doyle said one more thing on that show. Everyone did agree that a cloaking device could destroy the dreams of future exploration of the stars without conflict, and in the wrong hands could grant power to the most dangerous of self-interests."

Taft rose to his feet, moving to pick up the device again. "Right before you knocked into me, I was about to tell you that I can see the whole thing once I am moving.

Motion seems to be part of the activation process. For the few feet I took, I got a good look at it. Here, see for yourself."

Kaytha just stared at Taft, the look that Taft absolutely hated. It said nothing and said everything, mostly that Kaytha, at that moment, was annoyed.

"How am I supposed to grab it from you if I can't see anything to grab?" Kaytha groaned.

For a brief moment, Taft thought about messing with her, walking around behind where she stood, but clearly, much like the moment he found Kaytha on top of him, this too was not the time or place.

"Heh, sorry...here." Taft set the device down.

Kaytha reached down, feeling beyond the bending, waving, and twisting of the light radiating from the device while it sat on the ground.

Once Kaytha got it up off the ground, Taft watched her body disappear. "Let's get moving. I'll follow you." With Taft in the lead, they started back toward the beach.

"You're right, you can see it. As a matter of fact, you can't even tell you're transparent," said Kaytha.

"There has to be an on-off switch, right?" asked Taft.

"Hold up real quick." Kaytha lifted the device up further to examine it.

It couldn't have weighed more than forty-five pounds. It was indeed cylindrical, with both ends slightly smaller than the center. It had a few seal points that might be ways to access its internal components, but there didn't appear to be any digital displays, gauges, or switches.

"Nope, wait, here we go." Kaytha was now holding it almost up over her head. Taft had let go and she was now holding it on her own.

Standing stationary with the device, the distortions appeared again. Taft could no longer see Kaytha's upper body. The only part of her that was visible was from her knees down to her flight boots. Taft chuckled to himself when he realized that she had customized her boot color to match her T-Craft.

"Looks like there's an input port for networking here on the bottom of this thing. I bet it will hook directly up to the ship's systems," said Kaytha.

She disappeared again as they both started walking along their path. "Let's be sure we both shut off all OverAir networks on everything. We don't know what signals this thing could send. We wouldn't want it telling anyone we found it," said Taft.

Kaytha agreed, "Yeah, as a precaution, sure, but I don't think whoever built this put in a tracking system. If they did, it could probably be tracked to whoever made it in the first place. I imagine they wouldn't want the attention. Besides, no one came here looking for it."

"Not yet, at least," Taft said, with more than just a hint of concern in his voice.

They both could see the beach through the dense trees standing in front of them. "I'm really having a hard time understanding what happened here." Kaytha sounded much more confused then she ever had in the past.

"My dad obviously knew this was here, and he wanted me to find it. He rarely if ever talked about work, but I know he paid attention to the UEGC. He was always watching the news and keeping tabs on issues."

"This is no small deal," Taft said, matching Kaytha's concern. "We don't even know what this is capable of at this point."

As they reached the beach, Taft turned around and didn't see Kaytha. Walking backward, he watched as her feet created footprints from nowhere. He could tell where she stood, however.

The effect the stealth wave had on the ground was apparent, creating similar light wave patterns of distortion in the same way the device did as it lay on the ground.

Kaytha set the device down and walked toward Taft. Taft was taken aback as Kaytha suddenly appeared, forming out of thin air. The event was in itself a thing of magic and made even more intense given his attraction to her.

"Don't look so stunned. I've been here the entire time," Kaytha said with a wry laugh.

Taft knew it was one of those times where he had been busted letting his feelings show, and his face turned red because of it. Kaytha noticed, but kept it hidden, secret. Now wasn't the time.

Taft headed over to his T-Craft and opened the canopy. "I'm shutting down the OverAir network." Taft's body leaned into his ship, shutting down any send and receive systems.

Kaytha had already turned off her system when they landed. She'd sensed it was best to be overly cautious. "I've had mine down since we arrived. Figured since we were together it was safe to do so."

"So now what? I'm not so sure sticking around is a good idea, but I'm not so sure how to go about taking this with us either," said Taft, still standing near his ship.

Kaytha opened up the utility panel on the side of her T-Craft and reached for a hardline connection cable. "I'd try to sync up with OverAir, but better to keep it old school for now."

Kaytha hopped into her cockpit and powered up the electronics. "Go ahead and plug it in."

Taft was now back standing beside Kaytha's T-Craft, kneeling down next to the "device" and watching his hands then arms disappear again into the distortion emanating from it. "I have a hard time believing this is healthy. I know nothing is reading on our flight gauges, but it's not all that reassuring."

Taft couldn't tell where to plug in the hardline so he decided to lie down on the sand so he could get his face into the stealth waves and see the input.

Kaytha leaned her head out of the cockpit, turning to the right to see what was taking so long, only to witness a headless Taft lying on the beach. "That's a good look for you, dude."

"Whats that?" asked Taft.

"Nothing," said Kaytha with a smile.

Just then, Kaytha's T-Craft digital display lit up. "It's connecting," she said under her breath. "Okay, let's see what we got..." The display showed a readout of all available options for the device. "Whoever built this knew what they were doing. There is a ton of data and options here."

"You're not kidding," said Taft, startling Kaytha for a moment. She'd not realized that he was now standing right outside her ship.

"See if you can find a way to power it down. We can spend time analyzing once we get it home," said Taft.

"Okay, I think I got it. Go take a look and see if anything changes." Kaytha found the power down option in the systems menu.

Taft walked back to the rear of Kaytha's ship to the device, and just as he did, the dark gray cylinder appeared on the sand. She'd successfully turned off its cloaking ability.

Kaytha climbed out of her ship. "Let's load it up in the ammo storage compartment and get it back home."

Ammo storage on their T-Crafts was constructed with a unique double-walled, Titan-steel lining to keep the contents hidden from scanners.

"Kaytha, I think we oughta talk about what we should do with this thing."

"We will, Taft, but right now we gotta get out of the area. Oshly and Jebet can spend time analyzing while we work out what this all means. We'll stay off comms, stick closer than the trip out, and speed up our pace. We'll be louder, but the less time we are in transit with this thing the better."

The sun was starting to set as Kaytha and Taft lifted off the beach. Taft flanked just right and behind from Kaytha, flying as close as he could while staying out of her thruster's jet wash.

Kaytha was doing her best to remain focused on the terrain and trying to assist Taft to stay in formation, while keeping her eye on the rearview monitor displays. Her mind was racing with thoughts of her father. *Why would he send me to find the device? Why did he have the device? Did he create it?* Doing so was throwing her focus off. She chose a random Doyle-Cast to listen to. This one included some tech talk.

"From the start, DeCorp and EnerCon made almost everything not only interchangeable but also computer tech compatible. All T-Craft had a main digital touch screen on the cockpit dash. Most often these were referred to as HIREZ, which served as displays for video and information. This onboard computer could give information, make calculations, adjustments, and take over as the autopilot if needed. As decades before when digital screens had a monopoly on everything— entertainment, schooling, reading military—an unexpected problem occurred. So much of the technology was created with durability that could last decades; unfortunately, that didn't include the screens created.

"Most people didn't care for viewing anything on holograms apart from military and construction use. It was functional for some means of communication but had a lot of limitations. HIREZ Screens were dominant, but also breakable, scratched easy, and just not built to withstand the decade's worth of using the technology they were created for. DeCorp and EnerCon both decided to incorporate a lot of

analog style controls in all their creations to supplement the HIREZ touch screens.

"Behind the control panel, the switches were simple relays to the digital onboard systems. It was an old school, new school technology that was widely accepted, especially in the youth flight culture. Along with most standard living space control functions, the all-digital sleek, clean technology in flight vehicles was used almost exclusively by the wealthy, upper class, and elites of society, not because of expense but merely as a way to show off or show status."

The show wasn't helping; Kaytha still couldn't pay attention. She decided maybe some music would help get her mind on something else and help focus her flying. T-Craft could be linked between each other, enabling autopilot, operation OS status checks, and even the entertainment systems. Kaytha didn't know what she was in the mood for so she tapped into Taft's playlist. Taft had turned his music system on the moment they left the lake. Kaytha and Taft roared through the skies at top speed, skimming over the mountains and desert terrain heading back to Arizona. Taft was tuned into a random mix of old Depeche Mode songs. While they listened to the same track, they weren't aware that each of them was thinking of the other. Of what had happened on the beach. It wasn't thoughts about the cloaking device as the song "I Am You" played in their flight helmets' speakers.

Chapter 10

Kays Field, Arizona

Ven was reaching so far into his T-Craft propulsion port that the only part of his bulky arms showing was his defined biceps. He was trying to reposition the locking mechanism to ensure the thrusters would connect correctly.

"You know, Ven, if your arms get any bigger you'll have to hire Jebet as your mechanic," said Oshly, feeling vastly inferior to Ven's physique, with sarcasm his only weapon.

"He'll have to grease up his arms to make them fit before that happens," yelled Jebet from under her stock T-Craft.

She'd been installing new lift manifolds. If there was one person in the group whose ship was always operating at 100%, it was Jebet.

"Why would I hire Jebet when you can just crawl inside for me?" Ven fired back at Oshly.

Oshly didn't mind. He was fully aware that it was all in good fun and knew if he was going to dish out the salty talk, he better be prepared for it to get dumped back on top of him.

The sound of loud guitars and keyboards, featuring an obviously young male lead singer belting out nonsensical lyrics of rebellion, bounced off the walls of the hangar.

"What on God's green Earth are we listening to?" said Ven, now annoyed. The music wasn't helping.

"It's Sad Milkshake Weekend. What? You're not feeling it?" answered Jebet.

"Oh, I'm feeling it. In my stomach," Ven replied.

"I like it," injected Oshly.

Looking up and over the top of his T-Craft, Ven stared in Oshly's direction. "You would."

Every generation had its new music. Just as every generation had its musical trends of the past revived. For the past few years the popular nostalgic music trend was the era between the late 1990s and early 2000s. Referred to as "Grand-Age Rock" due to it being the popular music of the grand and some great-grand parents of current twenty-somethings. This would include the five friends.

"Can you put on something we can all agree upon?" asked Ven.

"Like what?" asked Jebet.

"I don't know. Thirty-Seconds to Mars, M83, Pale Waves? Anything familiar would be better than this right now," Ven replied, his head shoved inside a rear thruster.

"Ugh. Maybe Waves. How about Chvrches? Either way, I'll put

Blaster on shuffle after this song," replied Jebet.

The sun had just set, but the three of them hadn't noticed since they had been in the hangar all day. It wasn't all that surprising for Taft and Kaytha to be gone, but the length of time and lack of communication didn't happen often.

Ven, Oshly, and Jebet decided to work on their ships once they arrived at Kay's Field and the others weren't there, figuring by the time they returned everyone would be ready for some group flights.

While Ven was giving his combat T-Craft a good overhaul, Oshly had been sitting in the cockpit of his "tricked out" T-Craft, reworking the settings of his ship's controls on its operating system. If T-Craft shows in the same vein as old 20th-century car shows had existed, Oshly's would be the one competing and would probably win. He always had the latest performance upgrades and new gadget gimmicks that he swore made a difference in the ship's flight ability, but everyone else just thought was a waste of time and money. Oshly's T-craft looked more like an early 21st century street rod than an aggressive fighter.

The rear of the ship was unique from most T-Crafts, sporting a single EnerCon Extended Duration Thruster which gave him unmatched straight flight speed. Everyone else always felt this was completely useless since you couldn't turn at those speeds and he never traveled far enough from home to maximize its potential, but he didn't care. The lower rear left and right of Oshly's ship were equipped with DeCorp Maneuver enhanced thrusters.

Smaller in size and power than your average thruster package, these engines made up for it by giving the craft extra turn speed with aid from the T-Craft's direction flaps. The nose and cockpit of his ship was also a custom job; he'd chosen to sport a look that echoed the front of a 2017 Corvette ZR-1, albeit with a larger window for the cockpit canopy for maximized viewing.

Most T-Crafts took on the characteristics of the era automobiles pre dating 2050. They were the last of the varying designed automobiles, after which most manufacturers went with standard base designs because of the rise of autonomous vehicles. The trend of driverless cars never entirely took hold with the public; the roads were cluttered with all the standard cars, driverless copycat automobiles, and newer vehicles that had drivers. When the T-Crafts were introduced, a big part of their rampant popularity, beyond the ability for virtually every former driver to fly, was the individuality of each vehicle. Decades upon decades of car culture had gone away but now returned for new generations with flight culture.

DeCorp/EnerCon made a choice early on to look to the past for its future designs. None of the automakers of the past existed any longer and their models, even ones that never went into production, had become public domain. When DeCorp/EnerCon introduced the custom designed packages, airplane styled options were made available but proved unpopular with the general public, save for the military custom options. UEGC and various countries' military all had standard looks for their vehicles, while the public could choose from an array of old fighter and bomber designs.

The base color of Oshly's machine was flat dark gray, but he spared no expense in being able to customize its appearance with a series of color changing panel accessories that started at the nose and ran along the side of his craft. He could choose any color in the spectrum at any time. This was probably the thing that everyone, especially Jebet, mocked him for the most, even though the rest of them also made appearance mods to their ships, especially Kaytha. Kaytha always felt painting one's T-Craft was more worthy of an effort than opening up the modification program and picking a color on the fly. Oshly couldn't care less. He loved his ship, and it showed. Jebet was no-nonsense about her ship. She preferred the latest stock T-Craft available. The most recent DeCorp T-Craft model didn't share any automobile characteristics apart from total size of the vehicle. The front of Jebet's ship featured a large half egg-shaped beam reinforced cockpit and canopy. For power, Jebet equipped her T-Craft with a multi-direction quad thruster package attached to the rear quarter panels.

She always kept her ship fully stocked with spare parts in the travel-ready cargo hold at the very back. Unlike most of the friends who would choose custom paint jobs, Jebet kept the factory gunmetal gray with dark blue accents look. Jebet did have her family crest, a red circle with a yellow sideways V pointing forward painted on the ship's side panel. Ven's T-Craft was a decommissioned military model. It was equipped with all the typical missile, ammo, and gun racks. His choice for ship design included a large metal framed cockpit canopy that echoed the look of an old military, forward full view circular quarter dome bomber nose, and two enormous DeCorp Max Output Thrusters attached to the rear.

It was the T-Craft version of an NFL lineman: large, bulky, imposing, and not to be messed with.

Covered in grease and metal parts, Jebet continued to work on her ship. "Hey, either of you know what time it is?"

Oshly's eyes were still glued on his systems monitor when he answered, "It's past eight. Sun just set."

Casually adding to the discussion, Ven asked, "Anyone bothered to try and comm with Kaytha and Taft?"

"Are we sure they are even together?" asked Oshly.

"Are they ever not together?" said Jebet, then, under her breath so Oshly and Ven couldn't hear, "Not as together as Taft would like."

"I sent out a few inquiries to both their codes but got nothing back," said Oshly, still making inputs to his T-Craft.

Ven sounded confused, "You mean they never replied?"

"No, I never even got a message received. It was as if their comms weren't even on," clarified Oshly.

The roar of two T-Crafts echoed through the air. The lights from the ships cut through the darkness outside and lit up the hangar bay, forcing the three of them to shield their eyes. Jebet rolled out from under her T-craft. "Jeez, Kaytha, turn off the high beams."

Kaytha decided to fly her ship into the bay, just beyond the hangar doors. Taft set his T-Craft down in his usual spot just outside. Taft was exhausted from the day, not only the events that had unfolded, but emotionally too from his interactions with Kaytha and his mind racing with thoughts of her the entire flight back.

He was slow getting out of his ship as he powered down his T-

Craft, ran a brief system's check, and made sure that everything was secure. In the time it took him to shut everything down, Kaytha had already started telling about details of all that happened that day. Taft always considered himself to be the leader of his small group of friends and if you asked Kaytha, Oshly, Jebet, and Ven, they would probably say he was too. Taft placed his helmet on the seat in his cockpit and flipped the external canopy switch.

As the canopy closed, he turned to look at his friends, who were amazed at Kaytha's story, asking all the questions that he also had. Taft was still beside his T-Craft and took a moment to himself while he watched the conversation. Oshly removed the device from Kaytha's ship, only to have Ven come over and help carry it to the primary workstation. Kaytha followed them as they continued to let their curiosity take over.

Jebet noticed Taft, his arms folded as he leaned against the nose of his T-Craft, and walked out to him. "Long day there, hey Taft?"

Letting out a sigh, Taft replied, "Yup long day." His eyes were fixed on Kaytha deep inside the hangar bay.

"Seems you and Kay got yourselves into something special this time. How you holding up?"

"I'm alright, Jebet. Just need to get some rest, start fresh in the morning." Looking down at his feet and thinking out loud, Taft continued, "Crazy day...crazy day." He looked back up to notice that Kaytha wasn't in his line of sight anymore. His eyes got wide as he looked confused.

"T, jeez, man, you must be exhausted. You usually don't seem SO vulnerable. You got it bad," said Jebet.

"Huh?"

Jebet knew Taft was fully aware of what she was referring to. "Kaytha just went to get out of her flight suit and get cleaned up."

"Oh, no, that wasn't..." stuttered Taft in his reply.

"Don't worry about it, Taft. I know you're tired," said Jebet, adding, "Look, I think we all should call it a night, stay here in the hangar quarters, and like you said, start over in the morning."

"Good idea, Jebet. See if the others want to."

"They are already planning on it. It was Kaytha's idea anyhow. She's exhausted too," Jebet replied as she started to walk away.

Taft was about to follow when Jebet turned around. "Oh, and Taft, she must be tired. She's already mentioned she was probably going to bunk with you in your quarters." Jebet clumsily winked.

Taft, trying desperately to not crack a smile, was about to make a smart ass remark when Jebet added, "Now don't go getting all weird, just play it cool...if that's possible."

Chapter 11

DeCorp facility, South Dakota

Akens Ember shut off the alarms as quickly as he could. West refueling station Five had its fair share of issues, and he assumed that even if this was an actual emergency, there was probably little he would be able to do to keep his job, especially after just telling Argum that everything was fine.

Ember's barking was getting louder with each line of questioning. "Hindley, I need updates. Is this getting worse?!"

Before the alarms began going off, Hindley was about to head out to his T-Craft and make the short flight to the mobile housing units he currently lived in. The sun had set, and he was already there an hour later than his shift required. "I don't yet know, sir," he replied.

Wendell Hindley had been a refueling tech for DeCorp for close to a decade. With opportunities to advance beyond the low-level position after two years, he had made a choice to stay at his current job post.

Because of this, he was one of the best techs at DeCorp. Wendell was also assigned to the West Quadrant MMW refueling stations because of his expertise.

The DeCorp facility was built in the west portion of South Dakota, but still at a safe distance from Wyoming and Yellowstone National Park. There was always an issue with the dangers of an industrial catastrophe.

Disaster at any DeCorp facility was a huge risk to anyone within a thirty-mile radius. Safety measures and decades without incident stripped away the public's fears. But the problem with West Quadrant was its proximity to Yellowstone Park. Experts had long dismissed the possibility of the volcanic region actually erupting. Many believed that if it was going to happen, it should have happened long ago. The concern with locating DeCorp so close by was the depth at which their underground facilities reached. If the fuel transfer pathways branching off the dozens of MMW refueling stations ever ruptured, it was theorized by experts and most enviro-alarmists that it could cause enough underground chaos and disruption to Yellowstone's volatile volcanic activity. The fear was a man-made eruption, an extinction level event of Yellowstone's volcano, could occur. Because of DeCorp's extremely entrenched relationship with the US government, any legit concerns were quickly put to rest as long as DeCorp could provide enough safety reassurances, which they always did and the government still accepted.

Akens Ember could see all the primary alerts on Hindley's control screen, and it was clear that the problem was much more than a heating issue.

"Status, Hindley, status!"

"Sir, Five started overheating again. No cause…the emergency cooling system activated, but so far it has no effect. Six and Seven are also showing overheating. I don't know what's causing this, sir," said a frantic Hindely.

"Can you get it stabilized?" Ember asked.

"The cooling seems to be at least stabilizing on Six and Seven for the moment," replied Hindley.

Just then, seated directly across the bank of monitors, another technician spoke up. "Eight!…Eight and Nine…it's almost half the West Quadrant, sir, overheating."

Ember's heart sank, not only because the gravity of the situation started to sink in, but also because he knew he had to tell Sint Argum as soon as possible. Not prepared to fully accept that the situation was spiraling gravely out of control, he continued to work the problem.

"Hindley, you're the senior tech. Give me your best assessment of the situation."

"Sir, my only conclusion is that…wait… Hey, Digby?! Are we getting any reports? Surface reports in West Quadrant?"

Gregor Digby was in charge of monitoring the Fields with a team of fifteen, eyes always fixed on dozens of HIREZ monitors.

"No, sir. We see personnel running to and from the MMWs and lots of commotion inside the West's command center, but no visual anomalies," Digby shouted back.

"Thanks, Digs…" Hindely replied. He continued, "My apologies, sir. But I think it's a deep core fire inside the primary refueling exchange lines."

"Fire! You think?!" shot back Ember, not satisfied with the uncertainty Hindley was giving him.

"Sir, the backup systems, shut down, cooling, redundancies—it should all keep a fire from happening. We shouldn't be having these heating issues. We don't keep fire monitors down there. It was always deemed pointless."

Ember was lost in confusion, frustration, and concern. "How are there no fire alarms!?"

"Sir, you're looking at the fire alarms. This is it. I'm the fire alarm and that's my conclusion. It's the ONLY explanation," said Hindley.

"What do we do?" Ember asked.

Hindley took much pride in providing the solutions to problems that arose under his watch, but only muttered, "I don't know sir…"

Chapter 12

Kay's Field, Arizona

While the others cleaned up, put away tools, and powered down various machinery, Taft closed the hangar bay door and walked over to the facility central computer system. As he did every night after a day of work or play, he double checked to make sure there was no equipment left on that didn't need to be on, set all the security systems in their monitoring mode, and prepared to call it a night.

Munching on an apple he'd taken from provisions stowed on board his T-Craft, Taft surveyed the room. He watched Ven turn off the final light display near his ship and walk over to the door that led to the rear of the hangar bay and the small visitor housing complex where he and Oshly both had rooms with overnight gear stored away. Jebet and Kaytha would ordinarily bunk in a multilevel five bedroom former military dorm located adjacent to the landing strip. Jebet had enough of her personal stuff there that one would think it was her home. Because of how furnished the house was, Kaytha had hardly anything of her own there, but she also rarely ever spent the night and usually chose to fly back to her home. Taft would spend the night in what used to be the office and living space of whoever was in lead command of the flying field when it was in use. It occupied a small amount of square footage relative to the massive vehicle hangar. Placed in the far back corner of the building, the area was primarily an enormous office with a full bathroom and shower attached to it.

The front was entirely glass, but with the press of the command from the room's systems display pad, the clear glass could change its tint and even effectively be blacked out for privacy.

Since Taft had been using Kay's field longer than the rest his friends, it was pretty much a home away from home. He had a refrigeration system stocked with food for himself and his friends, a small mobile cooking area, and positioned in the center of the room were two large sofas situated in front of an 80-inch HIREZ display. The system was filled with every possible form of entertainment immediately streamable. At least twice a month after a day of flying, one of them would start a movie, and it wouldn't take long before all of them were sitting around together watching. The sleeping area in the rear of the room was probably the least accommodating. You couldn't really call it a bed since it could be converted into a couch. Taft usually just slept on it without ever taking the few seconds to make the whole thing flat like a bed. He had clean sheets and pillows, but it was far from fancy. Taft never needed more than that to get a night's sleep.

Taft watched as all his friends left the hangar for the night and headed to their rooms, but he still hadn't seen Kaytha. He shut down the hangar system display and started walking to his office living space. He felt mildly disappointed that what Jebet had said apparently wasn't happening as he assumed Kaytha must have gone to Jebet's housing to get cleaned up and had decided to stay there. Shutting the door, Taft pressed the function on the display screen to smoke out the room's windowed walls.

Taft liked to keep his room chilly and as he walked toward the refrigeration unit, he realized the room was really humid even with the AC running.

Surprisingly, he heard the bathroom door open and then watched Kaytha walk out. She was drying her hair and wearing a pair of his own gray sweatpants and a tank top that was way too small for him, but fit perfectly for her.

"Has everyone closed down for the night?" Kaytha asked while she continued to dry the ends of her long currently brunette hair.

"Yeah. I didn't realize you cleaned up in here. I just locked up, but I am more than happy to walk you over to Jebet's place."

"I'm gonna stay here for the night, if that's alright by you?"

Taft did his best to not show any of the emotions that began to build at the thought of Kaytha staying with him. It helped that he was also exhausted.

"Sure...make yourself at home. I'm just going to go get cleaned up."

Taft grabbed his sleepwear from his dresser. This called for quick decision making as Taft carefully chose the right lounging pants, plain black with a white stripe down the side. *Comfortable yet still stylish,* Taft thought. The t-shirt was the more difficult of the two. *Do I go with a simple solid color? Maybe a logo'd name brand? Or do*

I go with a printed shirt? Maybe movie or band themed?

Taft opted for an older printed t-shirt from a T-Craft rally they'd all attended shortly after he'd met Kaytha. Frustrated slightly at the time he'd wasted, Taft headed for the shower room. As he did, Kaytha made her way over to the entertainment sofa and sat down.

As Taft cleaned up, thoughts of the day raced through his head. *What would happen tomorrow? What about the device? Why would Kaytha's dad deliberately crash it only to have Kaytha find it? Did anyone else know of its existence? Was Kaytha already asleep? I wonder if she is thinking about what happened at the lake? I'm starving...*

Taft got dressed, then made his way into the living area fully expecting to see Kaytha either watching TV or asleep on the sofa. The room's lights were dimmed, but he didn't see either. Taft suspected she might have been lying down and couldn't see from behind the sofa. As he carefully moved further into the room to confirm his suspicions, looking over the back of the sofa, she wasn't there. Taft, confused, looked around the room. D*id she decide to leave for Jebet's? Did I shower too long? Did she steal the device and go?* He chuckled at the thought when his eyes caught a glimpse of his bed off in the other corner of the room. Kaytha was resting on it. She had gone ahead and adjusted the sleeper from its usual couch position and put fresh sheets on. Taft continued to stand in question, wondering if he should just go sleep on the entertainment sofa or if it was safe and appropriate to climb in bed with her? Walking over, Kaytha came better into view from the darkness of the evening. She was sleeping only on one side of the mattress pad, leaving room enough for Taft, and she had turned open the sheets.

It was at this point when Taft realized even if he somehow was misinterpreting the situation, he had the excuse of being exhausted and most likely she was too worn out to care. Reluctantly, Taft keyed the light controls on the wall control display and slowly climbed into bed.

The lights grew dimmer over a few seconds as he pulled the sheets over himself and turned to his side facing Kaytha. Kaytha rustled a bit, feeling the weight of Taft lying next to her.

As Taft was about to doze off, Kaytha backed slowly against him and muttered softly, "I'm kinda cold."

Taft, trying to be gentlemanly and respectful, didn't say a word. Leaning in cautiously, he closed the gap between the two of them. Taft kept his arms close to his body. It was awkward, but he was too tired to care. Before either of them totally fell asleep to close the day, Kaytha reached back and pulled Taft's arm over her, connecting her hand with his. At this moment, Taft finally felt a sense of calm and relief. He leaned his head forward and rested it for only a moment on the still slightly damp hair of Kaytha. She let out a subtle sigh. Taft knew it was attached to a smile and they both fell asleep.

****

DeCorp Facility, South Dakota

The overnight staff contained the fire at West Quadrant DeCorp for several hours, communicating to Ember and Hindley of their progress. While the fire hadn't spread, where it was burning was heating to a breaking point.

All the construction of DeCorp facilities were built to withstand almost any fire, but everything had a breaking point, and with morning about to dawn, they were all going to discover just what the breaking point was. Alarms suddenly began to echo throughout every corner of the facility at West Q.

Meanwhile, at the control center of the Massive Mobile Defense landing field, Digby was standing up, looking over at a monitor located across the room. Ember and Hindley took notice when Digby, straight-faced, looked right past them, slowly, nervously, yet calmly sitting back in his chair and turning his attention to the view screen. They froze, knowing it could only mean one thing. Someone had entered the room.

Before Ember had a chance to turn around, the stern ,steel tinged voice of Sint Argum spoke up, "Akens, I seem to recall you mentioning that all was fine what appeared to be only minutes ago?"

Ember turned, standing at attention, all the more ridiculous considering the chaos in the form of flashing red and yellow lights, with alarms of every pitch sounding around them. "Commander, things were fine, sir, but it appears..."

"I know what the situation is, Akens, at least as much as you do." Sint had more than the usual disgust in his voice as he stared down Ember while walking past him and proceeding to look over Hindley's shoulder.

Sint spoke in a manner that said he really didn't need to be asking questions but was going to anyway. "How sure are you that we have a fire, tech? You're supposed to be the expert here, are you not?" said Sint, directing his question at Hindley.

Trying his best to sound confident and failing miserably, Hindley replied, "Sir, I don't see any other explanation. And it looks as if the rest of West Quadrant is starting to react in the same way as Five. I fear…"

Sint, with annoyance in his voice, demanded a swift response, "Fear what, TECHNICIAN!?"

"Sir, I fear that it's not going to be just West Quadrant. The entire facility is tied together via the underground networks. This is the worst case scenario."

Underground warning systems triggered in quadrants Six, Seven, Eight, and now Nine all but confirmed an unstoppable chain reaction. The scenario that had played out when the fire that started twenty-four hours before was about to repeat itself. The crisis would continue not only in the South Dakota facility, but it was highly likely that other North American DeCorp facilities would suffer the same fate. Over decades, DeCorp had created a deep vast underground pipeline that tied every facility in every state together. The pipeline network was equipped with fail-safes, but much like the Titanic centuries before, weakness would always occur regardless of how unsinkable you believed your efforts were. The fires were spreading, attempts would be made to contain them, but they would not be extinguished and breaking points would be pushed.

It's not that no one ever thought that the worst case couldn't happen; it was that no one believed it would.

The big unknown was if one of the facilities suffered a massive explosion, what impact would that have on the nationwide system? The safeguards, beyond fire control, were always believed to keep such a catastrophic event from ever happening, but if the past twenty-four hours had proven anything, with DeCorp facing a raging fire burning out of control, nothing could be assumed. The unthinkable was no longer.

Trying to keep up with all the incoming data, sitting behind his bank of HIREZ screens, Digby yelled out, "Sir! We're getting reports of fire coming up from Five!"

Ember shot back, "We know Five's on fire?"

"No, sir. It's breaching the surface. It's no longer underground!"

Ember, trying to keep his ever-growing fears to himself, looked around at the room thinking,...*how much worse could this possibly get?*

Chapter 13

Typically, when all of the friends spent the evening at Kay's Field, they would have all beat the sunrise, but not on this day. Ven and Oshly stayed up many hours into the night having more than a few beers and discussing the device Kaytha and Taft brought back with them. Late into the evening, they stumbled upon an idea they were eager to share with everyone else. Jebet had awoken with the sunrise as she usually did when staying in the base house; however, upon realizing that indeed Kaytha had not joined her, she decided it was best to not head to the hangar until she saw some other signs of life.

Taft slept later than he ever did and was still in a daze when he realized that yes indeed Kaytha was lying by his side. In the middle of the night, Taft had rolled onto his back, and with that, Kaytha had curled up next to him as if she was *cuddling with a giant, beloved teddy bear.* At least, in Taft's mind that's what he was imagining.

Taft expected that Kaytha might immediately withdraw from any signs of affection as she usually did, but as she woke up, she stayed right where she was. "Good morning. You still look as tired as I feel," said Kaytha, with the slightest of smirks on her face.

"Yeah, I slept great but still need to wake up."

Taft didn't want to move; he wanted to stay in this moment as long as he could, feeling like they were a couple.

Kaytha shared similar thoughts, a little surprised to wake up and still find her arms wrapped around Taft, but it felt familiar like they were a couple, a couple that had been together for a long time. But they weren't together, at least not in any permanent sense. Sharing a bed and the comfort of a friend still kept their relationship at arm's length, even if their bodies weren't. Taft was too insecure to ruin the moment by assuming that this was a tremendous step in their friendship-relationship-whatever it was or was going to be. Meanwhile, Kaytha, who always knew she had feelings for Taft and was finding herself more and more enamored with him, also knew that while this was a great moment, it still wasn't the moment. They were in the middle of something potentially huge, and turning their relationship into a boyfriend-girlfriend situation was not a good idea.

Taft knew if it was meant to be, it would be, and after last night he was closer than ever to the reality they could be together, but trusted her to be the one to allow it to happen. In the meantime, here they were, enjoying one another, trying not to make things complicated, but doing just that—making things complicated.

Kaytha pushed off Taft to start making her way out of bed. As she did, she leaned down and quietly said, "Well, good morning, Sandy." She lightly kissed his forehead.

"I'm gonna make some coffee," said Kaytha, walking into the kitchen area.

93

Making coffee was really just pouring coffee.

The automation system knew the number of people in the room, who they were based on the bio-scans that permeated from the building's central knowledge system.

It knew what to brew, how much to brew, and what time to brew the coffee based off all available data of the closest occupants and the combination of their sleeping habits. Albeit the analyzation had to do some guesswork, not ever having had Kaytha spend the night. The coffee machine had two pots of coffee, each with a digital projection of the person's name for which it was brewed. Kaytha poured both cups and took them back over to the bed. Taft sat up with his Digi-Info-Pad, checking out the details of the day, while Kaytha sat down beside him looking over his shoulder as he scanned the weather and headlines.

"Hey, check the news out of Southern California, the Big Bear area?" asked Kaytha, pointing to the screen.

"I was thinking the same thing. I'll look over the police sky patrol overnights, see if anyone reported us in the area." Taft kept scanning through screens and took suggestions from Kaytha until she said abruptly, "Can you set that down for a second?"

"Sure, what's up?" asked a more than curious Taft.

"Things are probably going to get hectic once we get going today and I need to tell you…well, tell you and ask you something."

This was wholly out of character for Kaytha. Taft quickly realized that this was going to be directly about the two of them. Her tone said there was something different about it.

"Of course. What's up?"

Kaytha began to explain something that she had held onto and never shared with anyone. Her explanation didn't get very far when Taft realized he knew what she was talking about and in detail. He too had not shared a part of his life either with anyone. They both spent a good hour in a discussion, having a few more cups of coffee and realizing they were much closer in many ways than either of them expected. The conversation was the turning point; they both knew the path laid out before them. Taft and Kaytha agreed that they would keep this conversation to themselves. Taft knew, as did Kaytha, that once this adventure they were about to embark on was finished, there would be a new one to start. With and without words, they confided in each other. They may not have vocally solidified their relationship as being exclusive, but they both knew they were tied together in a way few people would ever understand.

Kaytha freshened up in the bathroom and Taft did the same in the kitchen area. Taft took notice that Kaytha was still wearing his shirt she'd slept in the night before. Ordinarily, he would attempt to not think anything of it, but now he felt more confident than ever how Kaytha honestly felt about him. Wearing his shirt may have been nothing more than a convenience for Kaytha, but it was more for Taft.

Jebet got tired of waiting and had already joined Ven and Oshly at the hangar. The silence from the three of them was more than a little obvious and awkward as Kaytha and Taft walked through the hangar bay door, which Oshly had opened when he and Ven arrived about an hour prior. There was nothing anyone could say to help remove the assumptions that everyone was thinking about one another.

Even if Kaytha were to exclaim that nothing happened between her and Taft, it wasn't like Jebet, Oshly, or Ven was going to believe her. Although Jebet did find it curious that they arrived together, and there didn't seem to be even a hint of discomfort between Kaytha and Taft.

They all huddled around Oshly, who was sitting at his system's terminal with three large HIREZ screens in front of him, plugged into the device.

Ven was the first one to speak up, "Oshly's been going over specs and looks like this thing is capable of more than we think."

"More than just providing stealth capabilities?" Kaytha asked.

Oshly was giddy at this point as he continued to explain, "No that's pretty much all it does, but it's the stealth abilities that are so impressive. My understanding, just going over the preliminary details of STL-5..."

Taft interrupted, "STL-5?"

"Yeah, that's the code name on all the settings. It has the stealth capabilities beyond anything I would have expected for such a relatively small machine," Oshly replied.

"What about power consumption?" asked Taft.

"Not as much as it should. It doesn't have to do all the work. It does…well, not technically. The initial cloaking waves that emanate from STL are enough to cloak a person, which would explain why you disappeared when you were carrying it as you guys described," explained Oshly.

Ven took over the tutorial. "Before you guys got here, we turned it on, and it did exactly like you described. Sitting still, its cloaking waves affected about a three or four foot radius, but once you pick it up, the cloaking waves begin to spread, providing a larger cloaking area," Ven added.

Oshly picked back up where Ven left off. "Motion seems to be the key. It works while moving. This thing is constantly scanning the surrounding area, even while turned off.

I noticed it had a series of scanning reports it kept while it's shut down. I've been unable to determine what it's reading, however."

With concern in her voice, Kaytha asked, "Was the scanning area large enough to be detected by anyone off-site?"

"That was my first concern too," Oshly continued, "but based on the readings, it's only scanning a radius of about two hundred to three hundred yards."

Jebet had been biting her tongue but grew impatient, "Get to the good stuff, Oshly."

"Again, if I understand everything correctly, the reason it can stealth larger areas is that once it's attached to a ship, the ship itself, along with its motion, enhances the STL's capability. The cloaking waves are harmless and radiate off of what it's attached to."

"While any other vehicle in its wake not only gets cloaked as well. It too will radiate cloaking waves just as strong as the lead vehicle," said Oshly.

Ven hardly ever showed excitement but he too was borderline giddy as he laid out one possibility. "In theory, with this thing attached to any one of our T-Craft, we would be able to fly in a fairly close formation of about one hundred yards from each other and achieve full stealth capabilities."

Jebet, always the first one to bring things back down to Earth, said, "I agree with Ven, but there's only one problem, recharging."

Oshly explained the issue in further detail. "This has one of the longest lasting fuel cells, plus an extra shock-charged energy block of its size I have ever seen. It's not limitless and the charge it needs is not your run of the mill down the road kind of charge either."

"The only place I know that has the ability to charge it apart from DeCorp or EnerCon would be…"

"Let me guess…NASA?" said Kaytha.

"Yup. Well, there are some secondary options, but those would require a hookup that would connect to a network feed, and I think we all agree that's a bad idea. If what you said was true, your father obviously didn't want anyone—including his boss to have this thing," said Oshly.

"How much charge does it have now?" asked Taft.

"Oh, it's almost fully fueled currently. The energy block needs a recharge, but that's just backup. I imagine it could provide a decent amount of stealth for a few days of constant running, but after that, it's dead as a doornail."

"Any ideas on where to refuel or recharge it if we needed to and not raise any attention?" asked Kaytha.

"Glad you asked," Ven said.

"Remember that thing we always talked about doing? Well, maybe now we have a reason?" said Oshly.

"You're not thinking…" said Taft.

"Yes, we are," said Ven.

With that, Jebet's face grew wide with a smile, showing off her pearly white teeth, a sight seldom seen. Kaytha and Taft both grew concerned knowing the words that were poised to escape Oshly's and Ven's mouths. "Moon run!"

Chapter 14

Experts inside Yellowstone Park regularly sent out information to the public on the seismic activity below the surface. DeCorp always kept an eye on the incoming news streams as part of standard protocol. It wasn't that unusual to see swarms of earthquakes. This time, however, as the reports started pouring in from the park, scientists and the DeCorp staff in the control room tasked with assessments of the information knew that this was not a coincidence. The frequency of the earthquake swarms was matching up directly with the escalation of the situation at DeCorp. A perfect storm of extinction level proportions was occurring. Almost everyone who was privy to all the available data was still harboring the belief that the worst couldn't happen: a Yellowstone eruption along with state by state devastation to DeCorp facilities. The few people who had no qualms with what was happening were those who always prepared and, in some ways, no matter how twisted yet rational in their minds, had hoped this would happen.

Sint stood back up and turned to Akens Ember who was stunned at Sint's words. "Akens, give the command. This station only for the MMDs to prepare for launch."

With a tremble in his voice, Ember replied, "Which ships, sir?"

"All of them, Ember. I want the entire MMD fleet to prepare for departure. Who is currently in command?"

"That would be Tober Rosel, sir."

"Tell Rosel to commence with Operation Hot Springs, final destination MarsCorp. Is that clear, Ember?"

"Yes, sir, right away."

Everyone in the room was thinking the same thing. With the order given for all of the defenses to depart the planet, what were they supposed to do while the situation continued to spiral out of control? Akens Ember sat at his control center command post in the room. The elevated space, raised a few feet above the rest of the room, allowed Ember to keep a watchful eye over the entire internal operations. His attached computer terminal consisted of five HIREZ monitors which gave him all the data needed to run the show.

Sint continued to look over the alarms and analyze the data coming in from the overheating region of Quadrant Five.

On Ember's screens, he witnessed the reports that mirrored the chaos breaking out at the farthest western reaches of the facility. The disturbances at Yellowstone Park increased alongside the increasingly dire situation at DeCorp. Every monitor displayed flashing alert codes, while the external cams on Quadrant Five showed in high definition detail the DeCorp workers trying to put out the fires coming up from the fueling shed. Following orders,

Ember pulled up the communications screen on his central computer.

He would have called the MMD watch commander, Tober Rosel, directly, but the alarms were echoing too loudly in the room.

Message: T. Rosel On orders of Sint Argum you are to begin Operation Hot Springs, MarsCorp Destination. Lift off readiness level one upon acknowledgment of this message. A. Ember.

In a matter of seconds, Rosel's reply appeared on Ember's screen.

Orders Received, please provide authorization Argum code to execute. T. Rosel.

Ember knew his response was about to set into motion events that would change the course of everything. He shook his head as he typed his response.

Message: T.Rosel Authorization Execute Order K12375. A. Ember.

Ember waited for what felt like minutes but was only fractions of a second.

Message: A. Ember received and verified. Stand by for MMD flight departure readiness status. T. Rosel.

Lifting his head up from the screen, Akens Ember was startled to find that Sint was standing at his side by his desk.

"Is this the internal broadcast mic?" asked Sint.

"Yes, sir..."

Sint picked up the desk microphone and pressed the on switch located on its stem. This automatically turned off all the alarms so the broadcast could be heard.

"DeCorp employees, continue to work the situation as best you can. Contain where possible but also begin preparation for secondary disaster protocol. The MMDs will be launching in the next half hour. To those in charge of such things, internally and quietly tell all leads in flight control across the entire facility to prepare all MMWs for departure to MarsCorp."

Turning off the mic, the alarms resumed as Sint leaned over Akens while he sat in his chair.

"Ember, on the private channels send a message to all DeCorp personnel status five and above. Inform them that Operation Hot Springs has begun. Additionally, tell them to begin preparations at every facility for departure to MarsCorp. Make sure the Science and Genetics MMW is prepared to leave with my MMDs."

Akens Ember knew what this meant. It was what everyone in the room was beginning to realize: that the worst thing imaginable was now unavoidable. On the far right side of the room hung a massive HIREZ view screen. Usually set to one of the global news outlets, the employees preferred to keep to the US news coverage. In this case, the breaking news alert would be local. No one could hear the reporter, but they all could read the headline.

Reports coming in—earthquake swarms in Yellowstone Park.

For everyone watching, their fears were realized and the public was about to find out too.

Sint Argum knew he had more than enough time to get all necessary assets off the planet, but he also knew that getting the MMDs off planet before the worst happened was priority one.

The DeCorp defense program was recognized but not to the extent at which Sint had built up the resources, and only those who were in direct contact with him were aware. Secrecy wasn't a concern.

The top men like Ember knew better than to betray him and the others; the others were loyal. Sint also knew that those who weren't loyal were going to be dealing with what was about to happen.

Sint left the command center, it having turned into a chaotic mess in the wake of the fire that now continued to grow in the West Quadrant. Only fifteen minutes had passed since he had given the command to get his precious MMDs off the ground and off Earth.

Sint wanted to watch the spectacle of his MMDs leaving the planet. As he walked outside, the sound of the internal alarms disappeared behind the automatic steel doors. They were replaced by the thunder of DeCorp thrusters coming online, dozens of engines now exposed from their hidden compartments inside the massive flying warehouses. There were the sounds of a deep low hum as engines fired up, the buzzing of extensive hydraulic systems going to work as the MMDs came to life. All of the ambient noise was music to Sint Argum's ears.

Sint watched one by one as the bulky insect-like landing gear struts, ordinarily unexposed while parked, lifted each of the more than twenty MMDs off the ground, the glow of the rows of lift manifolds underneath lighting up the concrete in blues and purples beneath the vessels. The large flight command bridge of each armed transport folded out as the doors opened on the top and sides of the MMDs.

Weapons arrays with their missile launchers, huge cannons pointed forward, and a handful of rapid-fire interstellar blasters all pushing out almost as if their only job was to threaten an enemy. Sint realized that he should've given orders to keep the MMDs weapons systems hidden. The command he gave required them all to be at full defense preparedness. It was too late now and more than likely irrelevant given the disaster that was about to befall mankind. Those that had never seen one of Sint's MMDs wouldn't even know exactly what they were looking at after their military transformation had taken place.

Twenty minutes had now passed and as if he was the conductor orchestrating a fleet of unstoppable armed might, the MMDs slowly began to rise from the ground. The shaking, the rumbling, and screeching as the first MMDs to lift off started gaining speed and altitude was more glorious than Sint ever imagined. If things continued at this pace, in a matter of days the Sun could be blocked from the ash of an event many prayed would never happen. But at this moment, the Sun was blocked by Sint's achievement as the Massive Mobile Defense crafts flew up and away for the first time, casting a giant shadow where Sint was standing. At all of DeCorp's facilities in a matter of hours, this sight would be repeated as hundreds of standard supply MMWs prepared to depart the planet. The operation was designed to get as many people who were working for DeCorp evacuated as soon as safely possible.

The global disaster would take months to impact the population, save for those in the western states of America, but the idea was to get everyone out of harm's way. While the Yellowstone eruption would be terrible enough, West Quadrant's fire, once it reached the primary fuel manufacturing section, would create a disaster of almost equal magnitude and immediate devastation. The panic from the public alone was enough of a concern to warrant an evacuation of this size.

EnerCon, with their own versions of MMWs, had much of the same protocols as DeCorp. Once off-planet, most of the high ranking company members knew that the division between EnerCon and DeCorp would be taking on an entirely new dynamic. Survival would be a brand new game, and it would be waged in the vastness of space and the unknown. Many inside both corporations believed that the human race would find cooperation to be the key to longevity after Earth, but as Sint watched his military power disappear into the heavens, it was clear where the fight would eventually begin.

Governments across the globe would crumble overnight. DeCorp, and to a lesser extent EnerCon, were the only powers that had any plans at all of a future beyond planet Earth. Sint Argum knew the planet's military superpowers were so focused on geopolitical issues that they would not be prepared to keep their chains of command intact. Once the evacuations started, outer space would immediately become the wild west.

Fear of the unknown would drive most everyone to that which provided them with safety and security.

Sint had spent years preparing for this.

He would take control of the leftover interstellar military hardware, and he would give the protection that the fearful would be seeking. *Those foolish enough to align with EnerCon will regret their choice,* he thought. Those trained for combat could join the ranks of DeCorp and continue their service under the command of Sint Argum.

Sint's wrist comm sounded, alerting him that he was receiving a message. "Yes, Ember, what is it?"

"Sir, your fleet has left the atmosphere and has begun to make its calculations for the journey to MarsCorp," said Ember, his voice shaking.

"And what of the rest of DeCorp's population?"

"All locations reporting that the evac operations, including most of the staffing, should be departing as requested."

"Good, Ember. Keep me posted with updates. I am going to fly to West Quadrant and do an aerial assessment of the situation."

Chapter 15

Kay's Field, Arizona

Once the words "Moon run" were spoken, the friends launched into a debate on every pro and con each of them could muster. Sometimes solo pilots would attempt to sneak out past the Orbital-Observation-Stations (O-Stations) to make "Moon runs." Usually you could fly there and back with some fuel to spare before recharging, but that's only if you didn't bring extra fuel cells or didn't have time to charge on the Moon's shock-charging stations. Attempts by multiple pilots to make a group run past the O-Stations typically failed, as it was much easier to track, identify, and shut down evading craft in a group than one ship.

Back in the Apollo mission years, it took days to reach the Earth's Moon. However, flight time now had been cut to a few hours using the T-Craft propulsion systems, since the ships were lighter, the thrusters more powerful, and the fuel exponentially more efficient.

The Moon's population used to be made entirely of workers who would make monthly rotations at what was primarily a galactic rest stop with temporary crew living space and an extensive entertainment with hotel hub. Currently, the facility sat unoccupied with the UEGC halting all authorizations while the coalition was still debating how to populate the solar system.

Taft, Kaytha, Ven, Jebet, and Oshly were completely oblivious to any news coming out of Yellowstone or anywhere else for that matter.

It would most likely take days for the news to spread about the totality of what was happening, unless (or until) Yellowstone erupted or a DeCorp factory did. None of them read much in the way of social networks to hear the rumors. The only way any of them were going to find out what was happening was if they watched the news on the HIREZ screen in Taft's entertainment room, but with the STL-5 taking up their attention and the "should we or shouldn't we" discussion of heading to the Moon, no one was going to have downtime to watch TV.

Not surprisingly, Kaytha seemed to be the most ardent against making the trip. "There is no way we would risk a Moon run if it wasn't for this *thing* we brought home, and we still don't totally know its capability, let alone its reliability!" Kaytha argued.

Taft enjoyed the satisfaction of hearing Kaytha refer to them as "we."

Once Taft got his head out of the clouds, he was also leaning toward a no vote. Siding with Kaytha more than he wanted to for understandable reasons, he added, "I'm with Kaytha on this. It's really a matter of trusting that this device is going to keep us from being detected."

"Then let's test it here and now," said Ven.

Oshly said, "Look, this has more than enough in its power core to test and fly there and back. Not to mention if there is anywhere that has the ability to charge this thing without being noticed, it's the Moon's shock-charging stations."

Kaytha finally relented. "Fine. We'll test within atmosphere flights. If and only if we all agree that it works, we'll discuss heading to the Moon."

Taft leaned in so only Kaytha could hear him. "Just think of all the stories you won't be able to tell."

Kaytha got the joke but was dead serious when she told Taft, "We need to find out why my father wanted me to have this. He knew me well enough to understand that I am not just going to stick it in a storage locker. I get that on-planet testing and real interstellar use is the only way to really figure out what it's capable of."

Ven, Jebet, and Oshly wasted no time before getting to work on preflight preparations for their ships. Kaytha went back to Taft's hangar space to get her flight suit on. While she did, Taft took to the facility computer terminal, switching on all of the Kay's Field security measures, local, long-range ground and air scanning protocols. If ever there were a time to be overly careful, it was now.

Roughly an hour had passed, and everyone was about finished prepping their vehicles for what usually would have been a routine day of flying. Everyone, that is, except for Oshly.

Oshly made quick work of retrofitting the STL-5 with magnet connections for attachment to Ven's T-Craft. Oshly would also be staying behind to monitor the test visually and the computer scanning of the skies above the flying field. Ven piloted the largest of the friends' T-Crafts; logic dictated that Ven would be best positioned as the lead ship with the device. The others were to follow behind the stealth wake, what Oshly had decided to call the process of what the device did.

Oshly finished positioning the STL-5 under the nose of Ven's T-Craft. "Fits like a glove. Well, kinda fits like a glove, but it's not going anywhere."

Ven bent over to look under his ship. "Shouldn't cause any drag in atmosphere, it's seated deeper in the lift socket than I expected. Now what?"

"If it's working like it did when we found it, it should show up on your system's display," said Kaytha, as Ven opened up the front canopy and climbed in.

"Got it, STL-5 operations," Ven called out.

Kaytha said with a warning in her voice, "Everyone keep to comms for this flight. Keep all networks off. We need to know if this is being picked up on any of the scanning Oshly does, and we don't know what this thing sends out and who might be listening."

With a snap of the slightest digital twang, everyone took a short step back, startled by witnessing Ven's T-Craft disappear in front of their eyes, replaced seemingly by an energy wave that distorted everything surrounding the ship. The T-Craft was nowhere to be seen.

"That doesn't look very invisible guys," said Jebet, both annoyed and dismayed.

"Wait until he gets moving. Ven what do you see?!" asked Taft.

"You don't need to yell. I'm two feet away from you."

"Sorry, what do you see?"

"Looks kinda like it does after a late Friday night and too many shots," quipped Ven.

Taft responded to Jebet, "Once in motion, the visual displacement should go away. At least it did when I was walking with it when we found it."

"From what I can gather, motion seems to be the trick, and once objects enter into its stealth wake, the process should replicate itself with each added mass, in theory, " explained Oshly. "Before we all take part in this grand experiment, Ven, why don't you go for a quick flight and let's see what happens?" suggested Oshly with more than a hint of reservation in his voice.

Ven strapped into his T-craft, flipped the switch to close the canopy, then put on his helmet.

He normally wouldn't for a quick flight around the complex, but for the sake of the unknown it made him more comfortable.

Oshly was already wearing his headphone comms, listening to Ven key his mic. "If I disappear and never come back, I'm making a point to hold you responsible."

Ven's T-Craft, under power from the lift manifolds, began its rise off the floor of the hangar. The landing gear slowly retracted as he throttled forward. From the moment his ship began to move, the energy waves emanating all around the vehicle began to dissipate.

Ven noticed immediately as his view started to clear from behind the circular metal reinforced viewport of his custom

World War Two-era bomber styled T-Craft. For everyone watching, it was all the more exciting as they witnessed nothing; the energy waves that were causing the visible distortion where Ven's ship had been all vanished and were replaced with nothing but the sound of his thrusters. Ven slowly piloted his ship out of the hangar. Taft followed the sound coming off the T-Craft, and yet was looking at nothing but the open runways and clear blue sky of the valley where Kay's Field rested.

Once clear of the hangar doors, Ven pitched up and powered off into the sky. "Hey, Osh, how do I look?"

"Lost apparently. We don't see anything at all," Oshly replied turning back to walk toward his computer terminal.

"Are scanners picking up anything?" asked Kaytha as she followed Oshly.

She leaned over his shoulder as he sat down at the chair behind his desk.

"Nah, Kay, I got nothing. Well, I don't see Ven at all. Ven, copy. What's your flight path currently?" asked Oshly.

"I'm circling the perimeter of the buildings about a thousand feet off the deck. Here, I'll drop a few hundred and park over the hangar," replied Ven.

As soon as Ven went into hover mode, everyone could hear the low hum of the lift manifolds echoing inside of the steel walls from above the hangar, then a faint blip on the radar screen appeared, so slight that viewing it one would think it was a giant bird.

Taft realized what was happening. "Oshly, you were right. The motion is the key."

Taft grabbed the control stick and rotated the camera to the external hangar security monitors. Taft focused it on the location of the tiny blip on the screen while Ven's ship floated above the hangar.

Kaytha was looking at the camera monitor. "Look, the visual disruption the device made on the ground while not in motion is gone, even though Ven is still stationary in the sky."

"Maybe it needs time to warm up?" said Oshly, who continued to speculate. "In theory, heat radiating from the engines or even the ship's vibration might be just enough to fully activate its stealth ability?"

"Ven, continue your flight and keep within the boundaries of Kay's field," said Taft.

The moment Taft turned off the mic, Ven disappeared. The sounds of his T-Craft engines hung in the air as he took off. Taft's calling the field Kay also was heard by Kaytha. Truth be told, she'd heard him say it before; they all had.

Taft wasn't very good at keeping that a secret and had grown so accustomed to calling it Kay's Field in his head that, when he said it out loud, he rarely noticed.

Oshly continued his monitoring of the test. "As soon as he was moving again, the scanner blip disappeared too. The only thing I'm picking up now are two large objects to the North. It's probably the Otto Brothers out on a flight."

The Otto brothers were two twenty-something siblings who'd been left behind like so many others their age when their parents moved to go work for DeCorp or EnerCon. None of the friends much liked them. They were known to sneak around the field and were even accused of stealing some equipment that had been left out after a weekend of recreation. Unfortunately, none of them were ever able to prove it. Every once in a while they would come into the valley, buzz the hangar in some beat-up-unworthy-for-space-abomination and then cowardly fly off before anyone could get after them. Several weeks had passed since anyone had noticed them. That was until they showed up on Oshly's scanner.

"Well, what do you say? Convinced and ready for some flying?" asked Taft excitedly.

"Oshly, remember to keep off the network and stay on comms with all of us. Once we're up, make sure the scanners pick up our signals. So we know they are functioning properly. Then monitor visually outside as we conduct our maneuvers," Kaytha said, sounding more and more like the leader everyone knew she was.

"Jeb, you in?...Jebet?" said Taft.

From the comm speaker sitting at Oshly's terminal, Jebet spoke, "I've been waiting for you guys."

Just as Jebet finished her words, the roar of her T-Craft shook the walls of the hangar. Already strapped into her ship, completely unnoticed by everyone, she flew straight out and up from the hangar bay.

The combination of turbulent air and lift manifold power rushed off the rear of her T-Craft, blowing off all the loose papers, rags, specks of dust, and dirt. It almost made Taft and Kaytha lose their footing.

Jebet keyed the mic again. "Ha, sorry about that, guys. VEN?! Where are you!?"

Chapter 16

The news reports were exclusively covering the seismic activity happening within Yellowstone Park. Those who studied the Park's active volcanic activity were becoming increasingly convinced that the park was headed for the catastrophe they'd been dreading for years. News reports were less concerned, providing updates with caution so as not to start a panic. Inside the state, government warnings went out to all officials, spreading to neighboring states that evacuations were to begin within days if the activity of the Park continued at its current rate. No mainstream media outlet was ready to broadcast the potential of what a volcanic eruption would mean, but the news was beginning to spread on secondary social networking outlets like Blaster.

The states surrounding Wyoming would be destroyed in a matter of ten minutes and the west would be cut off from the rest of the country. Ash would fall on all of the United States, blocking out the sun.

With DeCorp and EnerCon providing the means for most of the population to get off the planet, the majority of the company families already had priority placement on departing transport vehicles. With the global economy tied almost exclusively to DeCorp and EnerCon, a disaster of this magnitude would plunge the planet into global chaos, and that would be before the environmental catastrophe made it uninhabitable. The bottom line for everyone that currently knew what was about to happen and what the rest of the Earth was about to find out was when Yellowstone's volcano erupted, everyone would have to escape to the stars.

EnerCon kept a watchful eye on DeCorp and all their facilities. Orbital substations monitored all activity; EnerCon did the same. When the MMDs left DeCorp's western facility, EnerCon took notice. Both companies had virtually unlimited travel access from the United Earth Galaxy Coalition, at least by those who granted final authority and typically didn't raise attention to interstellar liftoffs. As a part of Operation Hot Springs, the UEGC was also made aware of the incident unraveling in the West Quadrant and the underground fuel catastrophe bringing Yellowstone to the brink of eruption. The information alone was enough for the highest in the chain of command of the UEGC to ignore the military power DeCorp exposed when they left Earth. Those top officials also knew that the UEGC too would face extinction in the wake of the planet's pending devastation. Many inside members didn't raise attention to the UEGC guidelines. Those guidelines required any organization to divulge its large-scale military assets.

Those with knowledge of what DeCorp was doing within the UEGC hoped to find a new place to serve, if not just survive, inside of DeCorp.

EnerCon had its own suspicions of what DeCorp was doing, but it wasn't until EnerCon's O-Station above the western United States watched as the large fleet of MMDs passed by that they had any idea how militarized DeCorp had become. EnerCon kept themselves within the guidelines of UEGC's rules. They had some military hardware and resources to expand, but it was nothing compared to how comprehensive DeCorp's build-up of armament and employee troop training had become.

EnerCon's own chain of command, not including its population of employees, scientists, engineers, and almost all of NASA, was beginning to realize that DeCorp had prepared for something far more significant than just survival were this day to arrive.

There was no perceived or immediate threat if mankind were to leave its home. No extraterrestrial intelligence had ever been discovered apart from radio wave signals that Earth had been listening to for decades that never amounted to anything coherent. It was always assumed that life in space, and the possibility of finding a home on one of our closest planets before venturing further into the cosmos, was going to be challenging enough, even with modern technology.

EnerCon now knew what they had only fearfully speculated, that somewhere inside DeCorp there was a desire to conquer the stars in the event of a planetary catastrophe. As EnerCon watched DeCorp's ships fly out into space, they also watched the news reports and images from the O-Station of the growing fire and imminent destruction of the West Quadrant of DeCorp. Within minutes of receiving all the data, messages were being sent across the country to all EnerCon authorities to prepare for evacuation. For EnerCon, evacuation meant getting as many people in their own transports, T-Crafts, and MMW's off the planet and out of harm's way. Apart from that, there were no further plans

****

Houston, Texas

One man sat alone inside his office at NASA. He had the highest level security clearance of all EnerCon, although he didn't have a title worthy of how people perceived him.

From the moment the western states' O-Station picked up the signal of a DeCorp MMD launch, he was watching. Even before that happened, he was alerted to an underground explosion at West Quadrant. Almost as soon as Sint Argum knew that what was happening was irreversible, so did this NASA officer. He immediately began the process of compiling the needed contacts and codes to send out the evacuation orders when his worst fears were realized. As he watched the MMDs, he needed no more confirmation.

It would take a significant number of hours, and maybe even a few days, for EnerCon to get their assets off the planet. DeCorp was going to have a massive head start on everyone looking to save themselves and others. The inevitable Yellowstone eruption, the blast radius and ash cloud to follow, public panic, global economic collapse, and everything not anticipated was more than enough to get as many people to safety as quickly as possible. He knew that the apparent threat DeCorp posed would mean EnerCon and anyone else who decided to defend themselves, were DeCorp to attempt any acts of aggression, would be outmatched.

While the current safety and security of everyone he knew under EnerCon were of utmost priority, there was one person he couldn't stop thinking about. He knew Kaytha had plenty of means to get off the planet but wasn't certain she had enough time to do so. What he also didn't know was whether or not she received the delayed message. The message he knew he shouldn't have sent. The message that if anyone inside NASA found out he'd sent, he would probably be prosecuted for accessing. Most importantly, it wasn't the only message; there were hundreds of others, filled with valuable info and data.

He was an honest man and knew that those messages were intended only for Kaytha. He sent the one because it was the only one he felt safe sending and knew that if she were to get any of them, it should be that one. But now he wouldn't know how to reach her. Now he didn't know if he would survive to find her.

He stashed away the data in the encrypted security box at his workstation. That box would be going with him and one day, *for a reason* he thought, with its contents, he would find his way to Kaytha.

****

DeCorp, South Dakota

Sint Argum, in his luxury T-Craft, lifted off from the airfield where his fleet of MMDs had just left, beginning the journey of fulfilling their purpose. All he had to do now to find his way to West Quadrant was to fly straight to the massive cloud of smoke covering the horizon. This portion of the DeCorp facility was now burning out of control.

Sint already knew from what he'd witnessed on the monitors of the command center and in keeping up with the private communication channels of DeCorp that there was no saving any of it. For a reason, he had given the command to initiate Operation Hot Springs. It was why he had sent the MMDs off into deep space. It was also why once all his orders were being carried out, he would have to make his own plans to get off the planet and assume command of his DeCorp military.

Sint was secretly pleased all this was happening, and it explained why he needed to witness with his own eyes the events that would set everything in motion and chart a new path for not only the future of humanity, but more importantly his future. The fact that he didn't cause the accident himself gave him all the rationale he needed. Sint was now motivated to use any means necessary to gain control of the equipment and infrastructures that had already been laid out on the various planets for future endeavors, especially MarsCorp. Sint knew that DeCorp's chain of command would be in complete disarray. He knew that his army of loyal DeCorp employees, soldiers, and mercenaries he'd handpicked throughout the years would remain in his command. Would any of the upper management attempt to maintain their control once off-planet, it wouldn't matter. Sint would be in charge. Sint always anticipated DeCorp to be the only essential global player, and he resented when the board allowed EnerCon to break from the company. Sint believed DeCorp should have done the equivalent of an old-school corporate takeover. Inside his head he would scream over the lack of vision from DeCorp board members during the UEGC council meetings in Italy. Sint was keenly aware not to show his anger and frustration when faced with opposition from upper management. That was the moment when he formed a plan to build an arsenal of his own design and have DeCorp pay for it. For almost a decade, Sint played by the rules, kept out of trouble, and made DeCorp billions of dollars. And in return, he quietly prepared for this very moment, which he never dreamed would be so easy.

Sint always figured that one day he would have to forcibly take over both DeCorp and EnerCon, but that thought was always more fantasy than reality.

He knew it would take extraordinary circumstances for him to pull off such a coup, but he prepared for it none-the-less.

Manually taking control over his T-Craft, Sint circled from a safe distance over West Quadrant, watching the explosions and fires that destroyed hangars, control towers, along with the businesses and housing of the company. He knew all his hard work was coming to fruition in the form of massive devastation.

Sint keyed in Ember's call number to his comm controls. After a few short bright tones, his ship's speakers gave a slight static crackle, "This is Ember, Sir! Have you reached West Q?"

"I have, Ember. Continue forward with all orders. It's as bad as we expected."

"Yes, Sir. Should I continue to maintain control here?"

"Stay on command. Keep watch on the Yellowstone seismic feeds. We should have fair warning before it blows. You'll want to prepare everyone to evacuate east or grab a ride on any departing interstellar MMWs. Message forward to Atlanta and tell them to prepare for my arrival and my ships for interstellar departure per the Hot Springs orders."

"I will, Sir. Local authorities are requesting any data and

information about our current plans. They have been asking for it, sir."

"Maintain privacy, no outside communications. All relevant information will be kept for DeCorp personnel only. Any info from us will only scare them and the public into an even greater panic. It's in our best interest, Ember, to get off the planet before the public erupts into chaos."

"I understand. Safe travels back to Atlanta, Sir!"

"I'm already heading east. Sint out."

Chapter 17

Kay's Field, Arizona

Once Jebet was airborne, it was quickly apparent to Ven that he needed to shut down the STL-5 for fear that Jebet, along with Kaytha and Taft once they were in the skies, might mistakenly fly right into him.

Jebet spoke over her comms, "Ven, shut off the device and let me fall in behind you."

"You got it, J." Ven put the STL-5 setting on inactive and in an instant appeared circling the sky over the hangar.

Kaytha and Taft were seated in their T-Crafts when Kaytha got an idea. Kaytha opened up all comms to the group. "Let's get organized. We know that the stealth stream, wake or whatever, is supposed to duplicate the process when other objects are nearby, right, Oshly?"

"That's right, Kay, and once everyone is in motion, you all should be fully cloaked," answered Oshly from his computer terminal in the hangar.

"So, what we need to find out is the distance we can be from the lead ship carrying the device but remain cloaked," Kaytha suggested as she powered up her T-Craft and began to hover out of the Hangar Bay.

Taft's ship was already on the field. He had been sitting idle waiting on Kaytha.

"Ven, Jebet, let's start on runway 12 at ground level," said Taft.

Oshly, feeling slightly left out of the planning, keyed his comm. "Taft's right. Ven, take the lead position on the runway. Everyone else park behind him, and we'll start from there."

Kaytha was already floating off the concrete that led from the hangar bay to the runways, drifting slowly about twenty-five feet from the ground. She throttled up slightly, pitching the nose of her T-Craft forward, and started toward Jebet and Ven, who had already landed out on Runway 12. Taft switched to active on his lift manifolds, rising from the ground with more efficiency and grace than the last time he took off when Kaytha arrived a little more than 48 hours earlier. Catching up with Kaytha, he followed her the few hundred yards to their friends. Jebet had landed just off of the rear and to the right of Ven's T-Craft. Kaytha landed to the right of Jebet, while Taft landed behind both of them, centered between the two.

The group formed a diamond shape, similar to the formation flying they'd done hundreds of times before.

They all sat quietly for a moment when Kaytha decided to get the ball rolling. On all comms, she said, "Oshly, you spotting us?"

Oshly had walked away from his hangar bay terminal to see if he could spot his friends in the sky. While they lined up on the airstrip, Oshly ran back inside and grabbed his only pair of Bionoc-Enhancers glorified-sunglasses that magnified the view of the person wearing them.

They were not all that different from the standard binoculars, but the technology of the day had shrunk all the needed components into standard sunglasses, with adjustable range on the earpiece, and the view out the lens was as if you were standing a hundred yards or closer.

"I got eyes, Kay."

"Ven, on my word turn the device back on. Oshly, when he does, give us a visual of how much energy wave distortion we collectively make. Everyone, once we have the range at a standstill, Ven will take off as the lead. We'll follow behind and try to keep our same distance," said Kaytha as she continued, "Once we are in flight, let's keep standard D formation. Oshly, you make us aware of what you see or more specifically what you don't see?

Okay, it's going to be crucial that we don't talk over one another and fly true. If anyone drops out of the stealth wake, fly clear from what path you're on and comm Ven to shut off the device."

Taft chimed in, "Can't have anyone flying into nothing while being something."

Jebet offered her thoughts, "You're right, Kaytha. This is going to be trickier than I thought. Once any one of us is out of the stealth stream, it's going to be near impossible to fly back in without breaking cover."

Oshly attempted to put the growing concerns to rest, "If the system's parameters are correct, once Ven is at speed and, provided the STL-5 is expanding with each of your ships, you should all have a large flight path to work in."

Ven sounded more tired than excited and a little annoyed. "Guys, if we're all going to crash into each other and die, can we at least get on with it?"

Kaytha agreed, if not in so many words as Ven. "Okay, if no one objects, Ven, turn it on."

Watching from just outside the hangar, Oshly's eyes grew wide from behind his tech-enhanced glasses at the sight of all his friends disappearing. All that he could see were the energy waves that now replaced where they had been parked on the runway.

From Oshly's view it was like he was looking through a fingerprint smudge on his lens.

The deep hum of the four T-Crafts grew louder as Ven started rising and moved forward off the concrete of the runway.

Once Ven's ship was in motion, the stealth waves behind him began to disappear. As if on cue, Jebet and Kaytha increased the power to their lift manifolds, pulling back on their control sticks and throttling forward slowly to follow Ven. Once all three of his friends were off the ground, Taft was about to do the same but hesitated for just a moment. Ven, Jebet, and Kaytha were now totally invisible as they continued to lift up off the tarmac. Oshly keyed his comm, "Taft, I still see the energy wave around you and it's beginning to diminish. Everyone else is gone from view."

Taft noticed this too, and that caused him to wait. He wanted to see what distance he could be from the others before the stealth wake would no longer reach him. Taft started his takeoff cycle right as the visible tail sections of Kaytha's and Jebet's T-Crafts were about to disappear from his sight, and he timed it almost perfect.

"I know, Oshly. Everything is fine. Just doing my thing," said Taft, as he gave power to his T-Craft thrusters and lurched forward. At first, the only thing he could see before him was open sky as he flew toward the rears of Kaytha's and Jebet's ships. Then they appeared right in from of him.

"All visuals lost, guys. You're cloaked completely. I'll monitor and keep on comms if you need me, but so far nothing on the scanners or in the skies shows you are here."

Ven replied, "Roger that."

Taft relayed his observations, "I waited to lift off, and after about 200 to 250 yards I was out of the stealth wake."

Kaytha, taking the lead on how everyone should proceed, said, "Ven, let's get about one thousand feet and circle the perimeter of the valley. Taft, drop back again and see if your range stays the same while we're at cruising speed."

Taft used his onboard scanner, having his T-Craft systems zero in on Kaytha's ship only. Taking a position directly behind her, he slowly dropped back and watched the distance on the monitor grow. "Visual, 180 yards, 200, 220…visual lost at 230…throttling up to 220. I see you again, Kaytha."

"Good work, Taft. Jebet, I'm going to fly left. Taft, stay in my path. Jebet, you line up behind Ven."

Oshly continued to monitor the group. "I picked you up there for a moment, Taft, on the scanner and caught a brief visual until you disappeared again. Kaytha, I think you're on to it; the 230 yards should be the max distance for everyone, which would greatly expand your flight path as long as one of you is within that range of Ven."

The years of flying together paid off as the group continued to show off their skills in the sky.

"Ven, go ahead and free fly. Let us do our work behind you."

"You got it, Kay."

Ven picked up speed and began his own dance among the clouds as the friends followed behind him. Apart from a few brief moments when one of them would drift too far and lose the cover of the STL-5, they were able to stay in range of one another, even while Ven simulated as if he was being tracked down by a DeCorp fighter.

From the ground, Oshly offered up his words of encouragement. "You guys are doing a fantastic job figuring this out, so much so I'm bored."

Forty-five minutes into the flight Taft realized something.

"Everyone form up again. Diamond formation cruising speed."

"What's up, Taft?" Ven asked.

"I think we're going at this wrong," Taft replied.

The friends got quickly into formation. "Alright, Taft, now what?" asked Kaytha in a direct comm to Taft.

Taft didn't directly respond to Kaytha, opting for all comms in reply to everyone.

  "I'm going to leapfrog to the lead position. Ven, you take position behind me. Kay, Jeb…"

"Ahhh I see what you're doing," said Jebet.

"Good, because I'm still confused," replied Ven.

"Ven, use your system's tracking and lock onto me. Call off the distance and visual." Taft didn't so much leapfrog as he did dive under the other T-Craft.

He throttled up his engines, passing Kaytha, Jebet, and Ven and throwing his ship into spiral, taking up position 200 yards out from Ven.

"Show off," said Kaytha sarcastically under her breath on a direct comm with Taft. This put a grin on Taft's face.

"You're 210 out front Taft," keyed Ven.

Taft was keeping an eye on his rear view external cam monitor positioned next to his system's display in his cockpit, calling out the distance as he read it. "220...225..." said Taft, watching the energy wave distortion.

"230, Taft," said Ven. Just as Taft had guessed would happen, Ven disappeared from his view.

"You're at 240 now, Taft, and gaining," called out Ven.

"Taft, did you lose visual?" asked Kaytha.

"Yup, you guys are off my sight and scanners. Backing it down. Ven, stay behind me," Taft replied.

"235...228," said Ven continuing to count off the distance.

Taft eyed his monitor as all three ships appeared again. Oshly had moved back to his workstation and listened in to what Taft had revealed. On all comms, Oshly gave his analysis. "230 yard bubble is what we are working with. Each ship is capable of extending the stealth range, as long as they are in the sweet spot of the stealth bubble."

Taft was still leading the group as they banked their ships in the sky to stay in range of the airfield valley.

The other three followed in silence for about a minute, then Kaytha spoke up on all comms. "I think we learned all we needed to know. Let's bring it in."

Ven keyed his mic. "Going to full visibility. Turning off STL."

All four ships appeared on Oshly's scanner. " I see you guys. Bring them in. I want to show you something."

Chapter 18

Sint's luxury T-Craft was set to auto-pilot as he headed back to Atlanta Command and Control, which was also his home base. Sint was asleep when a communication chime roused him awake. Gelina, his internal female voiced vehicle operating system, spoke from the cockpit speakers, "Incoming message, Mr. Argum, from Akens Ember. Do you accept?"

"Yes, Gelina, patch him in."

"Commander, Sir, we have an update on the situation."

"Go ahead, Akens. What's our status?"

"Sir, Hindley was able, for the time being, to keep the fire from spreading further beyond our South Dakota facility. So far the pipeline network is shut down and blocked. However, Quadrant 5, as you saw, is being destroyed at ground level, while Quadrants Six through Ten all have fires that, despite our best efforts, will reach the surface as well."

"How long do we have, Akens?"

"That's the problem, Sir. Our calculations show that cutting off the pipeline network, for now, is going to escalate the destruction of the entire South Dakota facility within 24 hours. We could slow that by opening the pipeline back up and allowing the fire to spread. The working theory is that we could delay the eruption of Yellowstone Park, but at the expense of speeding up the destruction of the DeCorp facilities statewide. It's your call, Commander."

"Evacuations per Operation Hot Springs are still ongoing, is that correct, Akens?"

"They are, Sir, but it's taking much longer than anyone expected to begin interstellar flights."

"Open the pipelines back up, Akens. That will buy us some time. Be sure the evacuations continue as ordered."

"Yes, Sir, I will report back with an update."

Sint knew he bought himself maybe twenty-four hours before the mainstream news outlets informed the public that this was more than just an issue for Yellowstone Park and the surrounding states.

As Sint continued his flight back to Atlanta, his mind raced as he considered the next steps needed during and after Operations Hot Springs to ensure success. With his T-Craft on autopilot, Sint called up the latest reports from MarsCorp.

DeCorp's colonization of Mars was done with the approval from the UEGC. The permission was granted under the condition that they wouldn't lay claim to the planet and allow for EnerCon to also install infrastructure there. EnerCon sent a handful of automated MMWs to a portion of the red planet for future exploration and expansion, but never made it a priority and the supplies sat on the surface untouched. DeCorp, on the other hand, at the urging of Sint, not only continued to send supplies, but they also launched interstellar drone crafts designed for one task: to carry the automated atmosphere processors.

The launches went unnoticed by the public and the O-Stations over the United States picked up the ships, but not a thought was given as to the cargo they were carrying.

Once the vehicles entered the Mars orbit, the drone crafts deployed separate box-shaped ships.

As the machines, each one ten stories tall, entered the atmosphere with thrusters similar to those you'd find on MMWs, they expanded from the sides of the cube, slowing the rate of fall for each of them.

As the ships traveled closer to the surface, the lift manifolds took over, bringing them safely to the ground. Each machine landed in the exact position they were programmed for around the DeCorp facility on the surface.

After they were in place, in an orchestrated fashion, they began to transform from their square shape into something more akin to a piece of postmodern art. Massive airflow exhausts pushed into the sky, with a single curling spire in the center that stood just over fifty feet tall. Several feet thick, each processor had five metal spikes that pushed deep into the red planet's surface. From a distance, the atmosphere processors looked like a combination of a hardened steel flower and church pipe organ with a sinister, twisted spike in the center.

Once the transformation was complete, the processors went to work, sucking in the toxic air and pumping out breathable atmosphere. The difference in air density had thickness to it, creating a natural bubble of breathable oxygen. A dome would form around the DeCorp facility, stretching for miles from the center in every direction and all the way to the edge of space. The manufactured air pocket created a variance between the native atmosphere and the life-sustaining CO_2, giving the false dome an almost bubble-like prismatic appearance.

When a craft flew into and out of what most referred to as the "atmodome," it was like passing your hand through rising steam; the visible vapors would swirl around and then reform their shape. Atmodomes, visible from space, appeared on any moon or planet with atmosphere processors. Depending on a planet's native atmosphere, the atmodomes took on a variety of variations, including color and density.

The atmodome on Mars, given the planet's already vibrant color, had a dream-like appearance. Passing through the dome took on a magical quality. Strong martian winds would often push through the atmodome. While the winds would eventually lose strength, storms would often wreck havoc on the processors' ability to trap the breathable air. Residents on Mars were often forced inside until the atmodome could reform after the storms cleared. Following the launches of the atmosphere processors, further missions were carried out. MMWs with crews and all the supplies needed to create the required infrastructure traveled to Mars to help in construction. Massive housing, and more importantly for Sint Argum, a military installation inside the city-sized engineering portion of DeCorp's facility were both in place, running like any metropolis on Earth. The processors would come to serve as landmarks—gateways that surrounded the miles and miles of what ended up becoming DeCorp's MarsCorp facility.

Sint already had a foothold on Mars. Both EnerCon and DeCorp had much broader public goals in mind: future travel to Earth's closest inhabitable planets—Wolf 1061C or Proxima B.

Current technology, fusion reactor drives, and quasi-propulsion made travel a goal within reach, although no ship had made the journey. Mars was always going to be the future hub for such a journey. Sint's plan to own Mars was a bold move, but one he knew would pay off in light of what was now happening on Earth.

Chapter 19

Kay's Field, Arizona

After their test flight of the STL-5, Ven, Kaytha, Taft, and Jebet landed just outside the hangar bay doors. It didn't take long before they all exited their T-Crafts and made their way to Oshly. The five friends now gathered around three HIREZ monitors attached to the hangar's OS communications system.

"Tell us what we don't know, Osh," said Kaytha.

"I patched into Ven's systems to get the reading off the STL. By the way, Ven, your music library is horrible. I didn't realize you liked that girly dance stuff," said Oshly.

"I'm gonna girly dance all up and down your back if you question my musical tastes again," Ven fired back.

Jebet wanted in on the teasing. "I always pegged you more as a show tunes kinda guy, Ven."

Ven just glared back, knowing full well it was futile to get into a sarcastic sparring match with Jebet.

"Knock it off, guys. Oshly?" said Ven, trying to get things back on track.

"Right, so it doesn't look like the strength of the stealth coverage is lost at all on secondary masses, if you're in the stealth bubble or wake. I haven't decided which I prefer. Anyhow, your ability to stealth a range of 230 yards every direction is the same, and that's the bubble of anyone, not just the primary device carrier, but…"

"Yeah, I knew that was coming," said Taft.

"Yes, can't gain without losing something—and that's power. When you're not in the primary device carrier or lead ship, and you're cloaking, it draws significantly more power from the STL-5. The good news is the power cell holds a long range, more than enough for say, a Moon run there and back, provided you were all staying in the primary stealth bubble. The moment you extend stealth to anyone outside the primary bubble, you can see the increase in power drain. It spiked every time one of you extended the range and normalized when you didn't," said Oshly.

"I'm worried about having to stay in any of the stealth bubbles. We can't rely on scanner distance monitors. If we're cruising, sure, but it's risky if we're still talking about doing a Moon run. Certainly takes the fun out of it if we're going to be worried the whole time," cautioned Jebet.

"Glad you mentioned that, Jeb. I have already thought of that. While you guys were testing, I put together STL-5 stealth maintaining protocols and already uploaded it to all your T-Crafts' operating systems."

"This is the part where Ol' Osh here explains why we should all sit back in awe of his resourcefulness," said Ven, with a roll his eyes.

"Thanks, big guy. And, well, you should," Oshly sarcastically fired back.

"OSH, PLEASE GET TO IT!" Kaytha had just about had enough of the tomfoolery.

"Fine," chuckled Oshly. "You all have a stealth guidance system now, a visual cue when flying in the cover of the STL at the top of your display screen. This is the color bar." Oshly pointed to the duplicate of his ship's monitor. "Green you're good. Yellow means you're flying outside the primary stealth wake but still cloaked. Red means you're not concealed at all. It's a sliding scale too, so a quick scan of the bar should tell you how much room you have relative to what you're doing."

"Alright, I'm kinda in awe, Oshly. Good work," said Kaytha.

"What's with the purple and orange ones?" asked Ven, pointing to colored dot indicators located right next to the stealth visual bar.

"Oh yeah, those are the stealth emission and proximity indication lights. Purple means you're not cloaking anyone else outside the primary stealth bubble; the orange one lets you know that a mass is in range of your bubble. Good to know if you're saving STL-5 power."

"Why Purple?" grimaced Ven.

"Because I like purple," said Oshly, acting as if this should come as no surprise to anyone.

"And he gives me grief over girly dance music," muttered Ven under his breath.

"Just because we're asking, and the orange?" asked Jebet

"I was running out of colors," Oshly said, with a smile.

"Alright, Oshly, anything else?" asked Taft.

"There is one more thing. It's a given, but remember if we are flying in a wide formation, especially in space, you all know it's harder to maintain consistency in the distance out there.

If any other ship, or anything at all for that matter, comes within 230 yards of your ship, they will be in the wake and will see you. Hopefully the guidance system will help. It's also got an autopilot function set for stealth either in the primary or secondary bubble. That'll be useful for the Moon flight," said Oshly.

Kaytha had been thinking of something else entirely. Asking Oshly, "If all of this is true, given enough power for the STL-5 to maintain a stealth wake, you could, in theory, hide a fleet couldn't you?"

"You would need a lot of power to keep it up and running. My thought was if someone made a bigger one or made more of them this size," replied Oshly.

Taft understood the gravity of what they were all saying. "Maybe we know the reason why we were the ones meant to find it."

While Oshly continued to pour over the data gathered from the test flights, Kaytha motioned for Taft to follow her away from the others. Ven and Jebet were mindfully listening to what Oshly had to say.

After walking away and out of earshot of everyone, Kaytha expressed her concern to Taft. "What are we supposed to do. Just use it for fun? Obviously, my dad wanted me to find it. If not, someone else did. Who knows how that message got to me after so much time, but it did. Are we just supposed to act like my father left me some "toy" to play with?"

"I don't know either, Kay, but we have it now. And as for me, I'm just trying to learn what it's capable of," said Taft.

"But don't you think it's a little dangerous to just go flying off into space?!" argued an increasingly frustrated Kaytha.

"Okay, let's think about this. Who would we give it to? DeCorp? I don't trust their leadership, and they are tied into the UEGC more so than EnerCon. We could contact someone in EnerCon, but it's not like they are any authority, and I certainly don't want to hand it over to the government."

"You're right about that. And besides, NASA would have made the feds aware of it. My dad wouldn't have gone out of his way, like it appears he did, to have me find it."

"Exactly, Kay. If someone were looking for it, they would have found it, especially if they were tracking it. It wasn't exactly buried on that mountain. I'm shocked no one just came across it by accident. I hate to bring it up, but your dad has been gone now over a year, so it's been there at least that long we assume, right?"

Kaytha's face soured at the reminder of her dad and then quickly changed to confusion. "Wait a second...HEY OSHLY?!" Kaytha shouted.

"YO!"

"HOW COULD THAT THING STILL BE RUNNING WHEN WE FOUND IT!?"

Taft once again hid his smile as Kaytha referred to them as a "we." It was always the little things to him.

"WE FIGURE IT HAD TO BE THERE AT LEAST A YEAR?" Kaytha continued.

"GOOD QUESTION. I SUPPOSE IF IT WAS JUST SITTING THERE IT PROBABLY WASN'T EXTENDING MUCH POWER WHILE IDLE. I'LL THINK ABOUT IT."

Jebet and Ven turned their attention back to Oshly as he got back to data collecting, mumbling under his breath, "That is odd... maybe it didn't power up until they moved it?"

Ven noticed his babbling. "What was that, OSH?"

"Nothing, just thinking out loud."

Kaytha was only somewhat satisfied with Oshly's answer, but with so many other more significant questions to ask, she accepted it, and turned back to Taft.

"Kay, if you want to turn it into the authorities or EnerCon, I'll have your back, but I think your dad wanted you to have it. And since we do, let's make good use of it."

"I dunno, Taft," Kaytha replied.

"It's a few hours of flight to get there if we make good time and don't cruise. Once we get past the O-Stations, there's nothing between us and the surface... Come on, it'll be fun."

"Fun?" Kaytha was now annoyed but starting to remember how much she always wanted to try a Moon run.

Just then Oshly shouted over, "GUYS YOU NEED TO COME BACK OVER HERE."

Everyone gathered back around Oshly's monitors.

"So, we burned way more power than I thought. What I mean is, between how long it had been sitting before you guys found it and your flight today, it's down on power," Oshly explained.

"So, no Moon run?" Ven seemed most disappointed.

"Well, that's the thing. We can make it there without a recharge. But we'll need to uncloak once we were clear of the Earth scanners. With it shut down, there should be enough power for the return trip. But I don't think that's going to be needed."

Jebet chimed in, "The Moon's shock charging stations, we can power it back up there."

Taft was the one to ask, and Kaytha already knew the answer, "Why don't we just charge it here...well, not here, but take it into Camelback?"

"Because once we're connected with the rechargers on Earth, the technical data would be sent through the networks. If someone were looking for it, that would be the first place they would monitor," Ven explained, reminding everyone how they ended up having this entire debate in the first place.

"So it looks like we don't have much of a choice?"

Kaytha was getting weary from all the debating and decided to put an end to it. "Okay, gang, if everyone is on board here's what we'll do. Let's all get a good night's sleep. Once we're done gathering the gear we need here and at home, we'll plan on meeting back here and start our run at dawn. Once we're a few hours out, provided we slip past the O-Station, being mindful of our power consumption and out of precaution, we'll uncloak. Even if someone picks us up, we'll see them before they see us. If we can't charge on the surface, then—Oshly—you need to be sure we have enough juice to get home. If we do get a full charge, we'll fly back, and then we can decide what we do next."

"I might be able to grab a shock charger from the Moon command post. Then I could, in theory, attach it to the power bands here and keep it off the network," said Oshly.

Ven had other concerns in mind. "I also suggest that we stock our ships with extra ammunition. I'm not planning on going to war, but if we get caught we're in trouble anyhow, and we might as well be prepared just in case we run into any roamers." Ven with his military background knew that the talk of modern day space pirates was more than a rumor.

Roamers were wayward rejects who decided to live a life of crime and globe trotting to evade authorities. They'd been known to fly out to remote parts of the planet and evade the O-Stations before heading out into space. Some UEGC supply runs had been attacked; Ven was right to be concerned.

Kaytha agreed, "Good idea, just grab what you need, no need to weigh ourselves down. Besides, if the O-Stations don't see us neither should anyone else."

The friends started to gather their things and load them into their T-Crafts. Taft knew that Kaytha would need to head home, but he was hoping maybe she would do a quick turn around and stay again with him. But he also didn't want to press the issue. "So, I'll see you in the morning then," said Taft.

Kaytha closed up the back of her ship. She knew what he was thinking. "Yeah, I have to lock down everything, and I have lots to grab. I might even switch Ts. I'll keep on comms though if anything comes up. You staying here?" she asked, stopping at the edge of her cockpit before climbing in.

"Everything I need is already here. No need to make an extra trip, ya know?" Taft replied.

Kaytha glanced back at the hangar to be sure no one was looking and then threw her arms around him.

Resting her head on his shoulder and holding him tight, she quietly said, "I'm trusting you that this is the right thing to do, but also know I wouldn't be doing it if I wasn't doing it with you."

"Same here," Taft replied, knowing she would let go but not

wanting her to.

As Kaytha pulled away, she kissed him gently on the cheek. Before climbing into her ship, Kaytha flipped the canopy switch for it to close. Timing her positioning in the cockpit seat with the locking of the window, Kaytha knew her T-Craft's functions that well. Putting on her helmet, she gave Taft one last smile before she flipped the visor shut. Taft waved slightly as her T-Craft roared to life and began to rise from the ground.

"Hey, TAFT?" Oshly was walking out of the hangar as Kaytha began to turn her ship to the south.

Taft tried to watch Kaytha fly off, but, not wanting to be completely rude, he gave Oshly half his attention as he listened to her depart and started walking back toward the hangar bay doors.

"I was checking out the socials, and there is a lot of news coming out of Wyoming—earthquake swarms, strange stuff."

Distracted, Taft replied while turning his head back around, "Huh? It's that time of the year, I guess. Seems like they get a rash of those and everyone always freaks out and nothing happens."

Oshly looked relieved. "I suppose you're right. Still pretty weird. Looks like a record."

"Yeah, uh, that is weird." Taft was still watching Kaytha as she flew over the ridgeline.

Before she left the valley's view, she did a single barrel roll. Taft chuckled. *Kaytha figured he was watching,* and she was right.

Chapter 20

In the skies over Georgia

The sun was setting as Sint reached the Atlanta DeCorp facility. His "home" was situated just outside the main MMW field. On his approach, a flurry of activity signaled that preparations were underway for evacuation. Sint wasn't much concerned with the departure of DeCorp's fleet of MMWs and other T-Crafts. His specialized MMDs were on their way to MarsCorp, and, most importantly, they were no longer sitting around; they were actively engaged.

As a part of Operation Hot Springs, a few MMDs would be positioned in various locations on the direct interstellar route to Mars. Those in DeCorp's chain of command who were aware of the MMDs believed this was to ensure that all of the DeCorp assets would have safe passage, but Sint had his other reasons as well, most of the classified kind for only those whose job it was to command the military armed vehicles. Obviously, survival of the people along with the infrastructure and supplies were crucial for a post-Earth future, but Sint's desire to rule that future was of equal importance.

Because of this, the MMDs were built in part to one day let EnerCon know that while they would be allowed to have a future in the stars, it wouldn't be one that they would have a complete say in.

Sint landed just outside his own hangar, a massive structure almost big enough to house an MMW on its own. The large automatic doors were wide open as Sint stood outside mentally assessing the preparations for his own private fleet of vehicles.

Sint commissioned his own specially trained military pilots that flew four prototype T-Craft fighters with full armor plating, each outfitted with two massive DeCorp commissioned long-range multidirectional thrusters. In flight, the T-Craft main engines glowed with a shining hot blue hue, both a beautiful and threatening display of color and power. The front of the ships all had limited view titanium steel barred red tinted canopy viewports. The specialized fighters took on a bulky military look compared to most conventional T-Crafts. The limited view provided the needed combat protection due to the reinforced cockpit canopies and more than made up for it with the T-Craft onboard computer guidance system. Each ship carried plenty of firepower between its short range plasma blasters hidden on the top, to the undercarriage missile launchers located on the lift manifolds, down to the large and ominous double rail gun mounts protruding from the front of each ship. Combined, it was more than enough to take out several MMWs on their own.

Taking up the bulk of the hangar space was Sint's command ship, an SMTC named the "Oberkorn."

It was large enough to cargo Sint's personal T-Craft, but still agile for deadly combat. If the military T-Crafts or MTC were an elite soldier unit, then this was its leader. Sint took the MTC design and made everything four times bigger and faster. The Oberkron still maintained a single pilot cockpit but had room for three others to handle the various duties generally associated with a ship this size.

Director Vivsou, the man in charge of all flight operations for Sint, was standing just under the Oberkorn.

At about six feet tall, and in his late 40s, Vivsou wore an ensemble that could only be described as part business casual, and part military.

He had a body builder's physique and looked like he could be a mercenary. Regardless of what he was wearing, his presence was enough to be imposing and relatively threatening, which was why Sint hired him.

"I've been reading various reports of the disaster in the midwest at West Quadrant. I'm to assume this is the reason for Operation Hot Springs, sir?" the Director asked since he would be Sint's second in command in the case of the operation going active. That would mean Vivsou's wife of fifteen years and two children—a boy and a girl, both in their early teens—would be in jeopardy as well.

"That is correct, Vivsou.

I'll provide you full details once our travels are underway. I trust your family is already in preparations?"

"They are, sir. Already moved on board one of the executive MMW transports," Vivsou replied.

"Good. I prefer not to have any distractions during the operation. I'm sure you will see them in good time. Until then, are we on schedule?" asked Sint.

"We are. All craft are charged, fueled, armed, and pre-flight ready. Departure team HS is still gathering your personal effects and should have all preparations finished in the next few hours. Will you be loading your personal craft, sir, on the Oberkorn?"

"No, Director. I believe I'll fly alone until we are off-planet and then dock once we're out of the atmosphere. Might as well make the most of this departure. Until then, I'm going to go home one last time. I'll see you in the morning. Carry on."

Vivsou nodded and proceeded to walk up the boarding ramp. From the outside, Sint's home looked like a typical operations building situated just behind the hangar. Walking through the massive structure and out a single unmarked back door that led to a connected path, Sint made his way to a plain white door.

Once inside, he walked down the featureless hallway to a decorative door, designed to look like crafted wood, although it was made of steel, with a large Victorian oval shaped glass.

The decorative center was made of explosion proof poly glass. Just to the right of the door was a handprint entry pad. Sint placed his hand on the pad and heard the familiar female voice of his personal operating system Gelina, "Welcome home, sir."

The door opened automatically into a room with a huge vaulted ceiling that looked like a turn of the century ski lodge lobby. On the left side of the great room sat a desk made of oak that had all of

Sint's favorite alcohols in various glass dispensers. Pouring himself a single glass of his most prized rum, he examined the bottle from which he poured. Sint decided one drink would not be nearly enough for his remaining hours in his home, so he brought the bottle with him as he sat in his favorite chair, placing the rum on the handcrafted end table beside him. Sint considered how he would miss this place, but he also knew it would be a long forgotten memory soon enough.

****

DeCorp, South Dakota

West Quadrant was a smoldering ruin, virtually unrecognizable in the flame and smoke.

All personnel had evacuated from the area, gathering mostly to the east of the enormous DeCorp facility. Underground, the situation was growing worse. With the fire spreading, the pipeline containment systems to the other DeCorp locations were doing their job but not well enough.

It was only a matter of time before every DeCorp facility would suffer the same fate as West Q's.

The most pending concern was how long would it take the disaster to spread. Would facilities simply burn to the ground or would the worst case be realized with the explosive destruction of any of the main manufacturing facilities? Another concern was if the fire would break through the closed-off pipeline to the EnerCon factories. There weren't as many EnerCon sites as DeCorp, but the factories Enercon did have used to be tied together when the companies were still one entity. None of this really mattered as much as the environmental damage from a Yellowstone eruption along with DeCorp's disaster, which was enough to warrant evacuation. However, if the EnerCon factories were affected, it would drastically speed up the catastrophe.

In Yellowstone, the quakes continued to swarm. The geologists had all but come to a consensus that the park was going to erupt.

Many had already left while others still couldn't believe what was actually happening and felt they would have plenty of warning from the seismic monitors to fly away to a safe distance. Reports were being sent from the Park to authorities, but data still wasn't enough for local officials to force a mandatory evacuation.

Akens Ember gathered all he could from his living quarters and transferred everything to the Officers MMW (O-MMW). Wendel Hindley and Gerger Digby moved their operations to the onboard systems while they awaited departure.

Upon arrival to the O-MMW, Akens was greeted by the ship's pilot. "How close are we to departure readiness?" The pilot's name tag read Dyn.

"The ship is fully prepared to leave on your command. Should I put forward the order to commence?" Dyn asked.

"Not yet, Dyn. I wish to not only get situated in my living quarters, but I believe we will wait for daybreak and depart along with the rest of the evacuating fleet. Safety in numbers, wouldn't you agree?"

Dyn didn't agree. He along with almost the entire crew knew about the pending calamity and were eager to get off the planet, but he also understood that he had no final say in the manner.

"Yes, Sir. The safety of you and everyone on board is priority one," Dyn replied.

"Outstanding, pilot. Inform the crew of our intention and that everyone not currently on duty should rest now for the journey ahead. I'll be heading in now to my cabin. I am to remain undisturbed unless absolutely needed," said Ember.

Dyn nodded as Akens walked away.

Once he was out of view, Dyn turned to the crew standing with him and visually confirmed with a glaring eye roll the frustration and concern they were all feeling. In the meantime, Digby and Hindley kept watch on both the DeCorp and the seismic reports coming out of Yellowstone. Digby's attention had moved off most of the monitoring of the facility they still occupied. The concern of volcanic eruption was the more pressing concern of the two problems at the moment.

"Hindley, this latest batch of data and analysis is getting worse and worse," said Digby.

"Is this news that changes anything we are doing right now or just news that makes me wish I had more drinks that I already don't have, but wish I did?"

"Of the two, it's the latter. Even then I am not quite sure exactly what it is you just said?" replied Digby, comically, in spite of everything going on.

"I just want to be drunk. How drunk do I want to be based off what you read?"

"Ahhh…passed out?"

"Greeeeeat," said Hindley, in the most sarcastic tone he could muster.

Digby decided to offer specifics.

"Look, there is no broad view on when Yellowstone is going to erupt, but my concern is that the consensus is growing about as rapidly as the analysts are leaving. So in a sense, I am getting fewer opinions on the matter while the ones I have heard are starting to say that the eruption is happening on the sooner rather than later side."

"Well, Digs, that actually gives me comfort."

"Huh? Why?"

"Well, if any of them are staying at this point they can't be that worried. So why don't you just let me know when no one is providing updates inside the Park then I'll either start getting 'panicky' or, better yet, too drunk to care."

"None of that made me feel in the least bit better. At least we are on the ship to get outta here," said Digby, optimistically.

"If Yellowstone blows and we're still sitting on the tarmac, I'm not sure they can get this giant box in the air fast enough to avoid the blast," said Hindley, knowing it wasn't what Digby wanted to hear.

"On that note, why don't we split up and get some sleep? Dyn just sent out a flight update. We lift off at dawn. That should give each of us a few hours of shut-eye."

"You first, Digs. I'm having too much fun sitting here watching the fire burn and pondering the end of the world."

Digby was done trying to make light of everything, "See you in a few hours then, and hey, Hindley, if the Park does blow, just let me sleep."

"Will do."

Chapter 21

Kay's Field, Arizona

After hours of rest, Taft woke up just before dawn broke as the sun light brightened the room. While getting himself ready for the day, it almost seemed routine as he went through his morning rituals. Today would be far from routine. He hadn't heard from Kaytha since she left the night prior. This wasn't a huge surprise or out of the ordinary. But still, Taft was hoping maybe she would break from tradition and message him before she started to make her way back to the flying field. Taft knew these desires and assumptions were all his own doing and took comfort knowing that he was currently in a closer relationship with her than he had ever been before, even if it wasn't the "boyfriend-girlfriend" label he wished he could put on. The thoughts running through his head were occupying his attention so much so that he never bothered actually getting the cup of coffee he intended to get. Taft blamed his scattered thoughts of the future and flights of fancy on not having drunk the coffee yet.

He finally started to focus, reminding himself that if everything went according to plan, he would be standing on the surface of the Moon in a matter of hours.

The windows of Taft's room were set to private, though he was still able to see movement going on inside the hangar. Taft walked over to his control systems desk and sat down, with his coffee finally in hand.

Looking over the HIREZ security monitors, he saw that Oshly was sitting at his workstation with the STL-5. He'd removed it from Ven's ship after yesterday's test and placed on the workbench next to him.

Oshly looked frustrated, so Taft keyed his comms to Oshly's desk speaker. Oshly jumped as it crackled to life. "Good morning, Osh. What's going on?"

Oshly wasn't expecting the comm and wasn't prepared to answer Taft's question. Nervously he replied with an annoyed tone of continued frustration, "Hey, Taft. Yeah, nothing, I'm fine. Just going over some more of yesterday's readings and my computer was freezing up."

Taft bought Oshly's explanation well enough, even if he didn't believe it. Taft's instincts were right, Oshly was frustrated, and for a good reason: the STL-5 was offline and not only offline, it wouldn't wake up.

"Alright, I'll be out in about twenty. Coffee is fresh if you want to come grab a cup," said Taft before turning off his comms.

The hangar began to rumble. Taft recognized it, as only Ven's T-Craft and his piloting style made the walls shake like that. With Ven's arrival, Oshly's attention turned to outside the hangar doors. He needed to talk with him and quickly.

Taft took a few minutes to look over some of the streaming sites, taking quick notice of the news reports coming out of Yellowstone and some various unconfirmed reporting of a fire at the South Dakota DeCorp facility. Taft didn't bother to look past the headlines.

His attention was on the day ahead, and Kaytha wasn't going to allow much more head space for reading the news or concern over what headlines he might have seen. Getting up from his desk, he went to the shower room to get cleaned up, geared up, and further prepared for the day.

Ven exited his ship, decked out in his favorite flight suit. This one he only wore for the most important of missions. It was dark blue, white, and gray trimmed, with pockets and tech connections hanging from every available space on his arms and thighs of flight pants, equal-parts functional, necessary, and awesome, at least in Ven's mind. Oshly had only seen Ven wearing this flight suit on two other occasions.

Although as he walked into the hangar and out of the morning sun with his backpack slung over his shoulder, Oshly chuckled to himself noticing Ven's strut was always a little more pronounced when he did wear it.

"How long you been here, Osh?"

"A little over an hour now, but we've got a problem…let's not tell the others until I figure it out," said Oshly, his tone both sarcastic and severe, knowing that Ven had the loudest mouth of the three of them. Although Ven would say Oshly's lips were much looser than his.

Not taking Oshly all too seriously, Ven replied, "What did you do now, try and upload the hangar's entertainment data?"

"No, that would have been simple, but I couldn't do that if I wanted because it's not working."

"What do you mean it ain't working?"

"Just that. It was still booted up to my mainframe when I powered everything down last night but when I got here, nothing."

"I'm not even going to bother offering any suggestions." Ven was legitimately concerned, mostly because he knew that this was the only shot he had at the Moon run, setting aside the broader implications of what the device meant.

It wasn't that he was irrational to its significance, but because of his military background, he was confident that if someone wanted to find it, they would have located the device long before Kaytha and Taft did.

"The weird thing is that it's technically still on. I mean it's running cycles.

I can hear it working, and my own computer scans show it's radiating the same signal it always had whether it was fully functioning or in power down mode," continued Oshly.

"You think someone from the outside hacked in and disabled it?" asked Ven, not really aware of whether or not that was possible.

"No, OverAir is disconnected. I have the global network setup on a totally different system. Even if someone had remotely shut it off, my own system would have picked up an invading signal."

"So, now what?"

"I'm going to keep going into the connected mainframe. I must be missing something. Until then, let's hope the others take their time preparing because right now we aren't going anywhere," Oshly said. Eyes wide, staring at the HIREZ screen he shook his head in exasperation.

The noise from Jebet's thrusters echoed off the valley walls. Stock T-Craft gave off a distinct low hum compared to non-standard EnerCon or high-end DeCorp propulsion. Jebet preferred to keep her ship "pure," as she called it. She made a few modifications, but nothing extreme. She felt the manufacturer must know best. Jebet set down next to Ven's ship. She too was dressed in her favorite flight gear.

Gunmetal gray and black with and bright orange accents, it expressed more designer wear then fighter pilot, but it had all the needed bells and whistles of any modern non-leisure flight outfit. Exiting her ship, Jebet was greeted by Ven before she had a chance to walk to Oshly's workstation.

"You got here late?" called out Ven, with the fakest of smirks on his face.

"Since when do you care, Lump?" That was Jebet's nickname for Ven ever since the day she walked in on him working out shirtless and said he looked like a gigantic lump. It was the closest thing to a compliment she was ever going to give him, even when they dated.

Jebet looked past Ven who was now standing in front of her. "How you doing, Oshly?"

"I'm good!" replied Oshly, not looking up from his screen. He acted like he was busy even though he really was at a loss as he poured over the computer settings.

"Jeb, Oshly wants some coffee. Why don't you come with," said Ven, motioning with his eyes and bald head for Jebet to join him.

Jebet shook her head. Knowing something was up, she decided to go along. "Ok, dude," she said with a smile. "Let's get some coffee." They started to walk toward the kitchen area of Taft's living space.

Taft zipped up the only flight suit he owned. He had a few before but had worn them out. This one was a standard, no-frill dark green with black accents. He liked it ok enough.

Seeing people approaching, he finger swiped the wall control pad taking the windows off privacy. The smoke effect cleared and he could see Jebet and Ven making their way over. His desk comm crackled. "Taft, it's Kay. You there?"

Taft turned around with a smile appearing on his face. "Room system, open-air mic to desk communication."

"Open air on, Taft," the OS system replied.

"Hey, Kaytha. You on your way?"

"Yeah, I'm about 15 miles south. I'm going to make a valley perimeter sweep before I park it. Figured it won't be long before we leave and I want to do a long range visual, see if anyone is out on flights this morning." Kaytha sounded upbeat.

"Everyone's here. I haven't been to the workshop yet. See you soon."

Kaytha disconnected right as Jebet and Ven walked in to get coffee.

Kaytha swung west about five miles before she entered the valley, climbing to about five thousand feet.

It was a beautiful morning, and she could see for days in the morning light. After making a full circle, she noticed what she figured were the Otto brothers out on flight maneuvers. They were trouble, but as of late they kept to themselves. Now flying north of the valley, Kaytha decided to join Taft and the others. Turning south then pointing her T-Craft straight up into the sky and into a stall, the nose pitched over, sending the ship into a steep dive. Throttling up, then straightening her ship out, Kaytha wanted to have some fun before the adventure began.

Taft was keeping small talk with Jebet and Ven, exchanging looks with Jebet as Ven kept blabbering on about what he saw coming from the news feeds. It was out of character for Ven to care about the news. He did back in his military days when it mattered, but not since. Assuming the same thing, Taft and Jebet just figured it was nerves that had him chatting away, but the truth was Ven was stalling.

Taft's attention was diverted from Ven's talk of rumored exploding volcanos as he heard three, no four, wait...did he hear five thrusters on full? Combined with a low altitude scream, he didn't recognize the ship's growl at all, but he did recognize the maneuver. *Kaytha, coming in from the north,* he thought.

A massive roar shook the roof of the entire hangar bay. Taft looked out the windows to see the dust cloud kicked up from the sudden blast of thrusters as Kaytha came floating down just outside the hangar bay doors.

Kaytha never flew in anything that wasn't personally and extensively modified. Taft liked to believe that even in another T-Craft he could still tell if Kaytha was piloting it. Today she was flying a beast of a ship. Even Ven's eyes got wide seeing the modified and armed to the teeth dark gunmetal gray and flat black T-Craft. Her custom painted ship was accented along some of its contours with a candy apple red metal flake paint job. It looked similar to the older ship she flew when she first met Taft, although this one was a little less attention drawing. It was outfitted with four EnerCon Vector multi-directional thruster blasters on both sides to the rear of the ship. Kaytha's ship also carried two additional high velocity energy pulse weapons situated to the rear on the top of the ship. Placed to the center on the T-Craft roof was a conventional rapid fire dual cannon turret. Under both thruster packages sat a missile rack carrying six military grade EnerCon heat seekers with internal-external reloading capabilities for another dozen projectiles.

The sleek, high-visibility titanium bar-reinforced canopy gave the T-Craft a menacing look that was compounded by two laser-emitting gun barrels, alongside the rapid-fire micro bullet and high-velocity explosive tip missile combo gun clusters. Ven looked like he was practically in tears at the sight, while standing next to him, Jebet sipped her coffee simply admiring the sight of Kaytha's ship. Taft, meanwhile, stood there admiring Kaytha as Oshly walked into the room, getting his coffee unnoticed. Oshly grabbed a baby carrot from the breakfast tray on the kitchen counter and threw it, hitting Ven in the back and getting Ven's attention.

While Taft and Jebet continued to be distracted by Kaytha's arrival, Ven quietly walked over to Oshly.

"All good," said Oshly quietly.

"It's working? How did you fix it?" replied Ven.

"I was running another system check, and it came back on about ten minutes ago. I ran it through the reboot cycle with a clean mainframe search for any anomalies and nothing. Must have been a glitch."

Just as Taft and Jebet were about to turn their attention over to Ven and Oshly's side conversation, as if on cue, Kaytha came walking into Taft's living space. "Hey, everyone...who wants to go to the Moon?"

Chapter 22

Akens Ember entered the command control deck of the massive MMW and gave the final order. "Dyn, prepare for departure. First destination: O-Station One."

"Excellent, sir."

Wendal Hindley and Gregor Digby secured a few hours sleep before nervousness, commotion, and duty called them back to their jobs. Most of the South Dakota DeCorp facility was on fire, and any efforts to gain control had been lost. Everyone on board knew that it was time to leave and most felt they should have gone long ago. Back on the control deck, Dyn was running a systems check when he realized that the ship wasn't as prepared as he'd originally thought.

Dyn turned to Akens Ember. "Sir, it's going to be at least another hour. The primary hydraulic cooling lines have not been charged, and the connections to the fueling station are just now being attached. As soon as we are at regulation, we can depart."

"Speed up the process any way you can and tell all staff to stay at departure readiness.

As soon as those lines are filled, get us out of here!"

"Yes, sir," replied Dyn.

****

Director Vivsou handed control of the Atlanta base of operations to his second in command to have the ships prepared and was able to also catch a few hours sleep. The second in command was well trained and given specific orders, including moving to immediate evacuation departure status if the situation in Yellowstone or any of the other DeCorp facilities worsened, which was precisely what happened overnight. Sint had given advance clearance to his hangar command staff, and they were receiving incoming transmissions not just from the global DeCorp system feeds but also the data coming out of Yellowstone.

The updated info that had been coming in every half hour, now had slowed to nearly nothing. Even the most die-hard geologists had evacuated and the underground monitors had all been destroyed from the heat radiating off the volcanic activity. Steam was rising from every pool in the Park and visibility in the area had been reduced to almost zero. The experts were in agreement that unless a miracle were to occur, the situation had reached the point of no return—the eruption of Yellowstone Park was imminent.

The truth, however, was far worse. The pending eruption was now impossible to stop and it was DeCorp that had caused it. The pipelines that ran from each facility—specifically the lines that fed from West Quadrant to the west—were built dangerously close the seismic activity that existed for centuries under Yellowstone. Whether it was the Earth that ignited the spark that lit the DeCorp pipeline causing the original fire at West Q or the fire at West Q that caused the unstoppable chain reaction, the two were now undeniably connected. The firestorm from West Q had moved on past the Park to the west and was about to reach the DeCorp West Portland facility.

Between West Quadrant, South Dakota and West Portland, the fire had completely destroyed the pipelines as it spread. Under the earth's crust, the smoldering fire was heating by the second. In Yellowstone Park, the combination of man-made fuel and the history of the Earth was bringing everything to the brink. Across the country, the same situation was going to play out. The disaster from West Q was spreading like wildfire and would destroy every facility DeCorp had spent decades building. It was the beginning of the end.

****

Director Vivsou woke in his quarters aboard Sint's SMTC the Oberkorn to find that the vehicle along with the accompanying MTC fighters were all outside the hangar and ready for departure.

Vivsou keyed his room comm to his second in command. "Seand, this is Director Vivsou. Why are we in departure readiness? Over."

"Sir, the situation at both Yellowstone and DeCorp commands has deteriorated. I expedited Operation Hot Springs' orders and was about to wake you. It is my assessment that we depart immediately, and we're prepared to do so."

"Very well, Seand, good work. I'll wake the commander, finalize departure, and warm up the fleet."

****

Sint woke up on his own, bringing to life his room via the touch screen next to his bed, surprised that he had slept through the night. Sint's home had been cleared of any items that he'd wished to take with him, all a part of Operation Hot Springs protocol. Sint maintained a higher opinion of himself than he should have. He commanded the respect of those around him mostly because of his accomplishments in his many years of DeCorp management. His core group of supporters and underlings respected his vision more than anything. Many of them stayed with DeCorp after the EnerCon split, anticipating that one day there would be a struggle for power and Sint was the only one with the foresight and resources to prepare for that day. For those under his command, with the full knowledge of what was currently happening, they were proud to have made the choice to stay behind Sint.

In an attempt to gain a specific level of respect, Sint tried to use fashion as a means to influence people's opinion of him. Often this attempt at style as an influence was projected in an almost ridiculous way. To that end, the outfit that Sint had specified to wear for Operation Hot Springs reflected precisely that: a simple, black military style ensemble, adorned with reflective silver accents along the pant legs and the edge of the long sleeved heavy duty button shirt. The utility pocket flaps on the pants and chest were bright yet deep, purple as was the color of his shirt. What really set the outfit apart was the black waist-length cape he wore with it. The liner of the cape was half silver and the other half purple to match the rest of the ensemble. On a fashion runway showing the latest military-style dance wear, it might have been appropriate, but for a commander of essentially an army, let alone, in reality, a high ranking manager of a corporation, it was more than over the top, especially given Sint's long-legged lanky and borderline out of shape appearance.

Most of the men and women in his command took his choice of appearance as one of confidence—who else would wear such extravagant clothes? For others closer to the "commander," they believed it was more about insecurity, even if they did fear him.

As Sint latched his cape, Director Vivsou's voice crackled over his room comm. "Good morning, I took the liberty to look at your room's system settings to see that you were awake.

I need to inform you that the plans had been moved up, and we need to depart as soon as you are prepared."

Sint scanned the flight line HIREZ monitors in his room to see his private fleet on the tarmac. After gathering what was left of what he would take with him, he strapped on his waist gun, utility belt, and bandolier. Vivsou continued to provide Sint the necessary details and updated information about the new departure status. "Continue preparations. We can leave as soon as I arrive. Make sure all personnel are in place. Oh, one more thing, Director. Change of plans, load up my personal Craft into the Oberkorn. I'll be taking command in the lead ship."

Chapter 23

Kay's Field, Arizona

Taft was the last one to be boarding his T-Craft. He had been going over the final security measures of the airfield. It was quite some time since he'd felt the need to lock everything down. With the hangar secure, he made his way toward his ride, a walk and sight he always enjoyed.

Taft's T-Craft was special: it was his sanctuary.

Not just because it had been his father's, nor that it was particularly unique in its capabilities, but there was just something about it that made him feel at ease from the moment he climbed into its cockpit. DeCorp and EnerCon technology were made with such precision and care that being a decade old didn't mean there was any loss in quality, especially with the available upgrades.

Taft's ship was dull blue, almost gray, but when the light hit it just right, you could see the subtle shimmering flakes of blue tint on the metal paneling. His cockpit carried a poly glass view canopy with a titanium frame and large main window to maximize his view. Taft preferred a totally clear field of vision. This particular model had a customizable on-the-fly tint option that allowed him to black the window out but wouldn't disrupt his view. He'd recently upgraded the thruster package to have two large Enercom multidirectional, booster-assisted engines placed symmetrically on both sides to the rear of the ship.

Taft liked to fly out to a nearby old military practice bombing range and blow stuff up when he had time plus enough missiles, gun rounds, and bombs. His hobby meant that he usually left all the needed artillery mounts on the vehicle. He loaded up every available spot with missiles, cluster bombs, energy cells filled to the maximum for the plasma blasters, and all the ammunition he could carry. He preferred a clean looking T-Craft so most of the launch racks folded into the belly of the ship, but as for the gun mounts—that was different. He spent the better part of last year reconfiguring the nose of his ride.

Tucked underneath the front of the vehicle was a rotating gun mount that housed two long-range rapid-fire cannons, target-specific machine guns, and a pair of high-velocity plasma blasters. The dual heat-seeking propulsion-assisted seeker missile mount hid beneath the skin of the ship under the main thrusters.

It was so impressive that Taft had a hunch that even Kaytha, though she had never outwardly admitted it, was jealous.

With Ven's military grade T-Craft, Oshly's flying roadster, Jebet's reliable stock ship, Kaytha's armed-to-the-teeth costume craft, and Taft's ready-for-his-own-war vehicle, the friends unknowingly formed a team fit for any fight and equipped for survival. Taft put on his helmet as he walked toward his ship. He'd parked on the tarmac next to Kaytha and behind Ven, who would again be flying lead just as he did during the training exercise. With his helmet now fastened, Taft connected the power cable to his system's relay located on the hip of his flight suit, then climbed in and heard Kaytha's voice on comms to him only.

"We locked down?"

Taft, settling into his seat and strapping down, answered, "Yeah, we should be good. Been a while since I put the field on total lockdown." Taft wanted to say something to all of them; this was a big moment for everyone, but he opted to instead solidify it with Kaytha. Taft's visor was down already as his canopy closed and then magnetically sealed.

Looking to his left, Taft saw Kaytha sitting in her cockpit, her visor up, and she was staring right at him.

"Glad I'm doing this with you, Taft. Be safe," she said, flipping her visor down as her canopy tinted over black.

Taft replied, "You too." She did what he had hoped, and it meant everything to him.

Ven's voice interrupted Taft's thoughts. "I've been waiting a long time to make this trip. You guys ready to get moving?" It was a comforting ritual that Ven would be the first to speak and lead the group out when they all flew together, as was the roll call that came after.

"O-one on the ready."

"J-two on the ready."

"K-three on the ready."

"T-four on the ready."

Ven was last to sound off, using the same phrase he always did, but this time it took on a more literal meaning. "V-five on the ready. Let's disappear." And just like that, they did as Ven switched on the STL-5 and began his liftoff exactly as he had done hundreds of times before. Ven and Oshly had conceived the flight plan and had it programmed to the shared portion of their personal networks.

Kaytha reminded the group of what needed to happen. "Okay, everyone, we're going to stick to manual flight mode. Stay within Oshly's stealth guidelines and off the global network to keep us from being tracked."

Oshly wondered out loud if that was necessary. "No one even knows who we are so why would anyone be looking?"

Taft was quick to agree with Kaytha. "Better for all of us to be overly cautious."

The flight plan didn't take them on a direct route up into space; everyone agreed it was better to cross the country until they got farther east and then north of the southern states. That was the least traveled space route in the country with the fewest O-Stations in low orbit. The commercial flights were a thing of the past, but any cross-country flights that did occur still occupied the same sub-stratosphere flight paths as the airlines did, so it was still the smoothest route regardless of the technological advances. These flight paths were heavily traveled now, and it wasn't uncommon to find rows of T-Crafts or transports flying in opposite directions. With no need for air traffic control, these were the new highways. The group decided to maintain a lower altitude and stay stealth rather than potentially getting separated in the crowded yet smoother skies above.

An hour into the trip and Ven was already complaining. "Whose idea was it to fly at this altitude? I think my teeth are going to rattle outta my head."

Jebet was quick with a quip. "Probably be an improvement. We could change your name to gums."

"Seriously, guys. I know this sucks but just hang in there. It should smooth out soon," said Kaytha, her own voice shaky, the sounds of clanking metal echoing over the comms. "Besides, we're getting used to staying in formation and think how smooth it's going to be when we leave the atmosphere."

Taft keyed his private comm to Kaytha. "Hey, Kay, I'm with you on the flight plan, but the altitude is knocking the hell out of us, and it's not helping that we're all loaded with so much extra gear."

"I've got the same concerns, but it's a risk regardless. If the ships can handle this then we know we're in great shape. I'd rather find out now if we have an issue before we're interstellar."

Taft switched back to all comms and said, "Just hang in there, everyone. The crafts are sound and we'll get through this."

EMBARK

Chapter 24

DeCorp Facility Base of Operations, Georgia

Sint Argum settled into his commander's chair aboard the Oberkorn. This wasn't the pilot's seat, but moving the console on a swivel to his right, he could take over the flight controls if he wanted.

Director Vivsou had the honor of leading Sint's evacuation plans under Operation Hot Springs. Truth be told, the commander's chair was a more suitable position at which to pilot Sint's ship, but no one ever wanted to argue that point. Sint normally would want to be the pilot on such a momentous occasion, but he needed to monitor the increase in destructive activity of Yellowstone Park and the DeCorp facilities. From the latest reports, it was clear they couldn't leave soon enough.

"West Q. official requesting Commander Argum. Akens reporting," echoed from Sint's chair speakers.

Sint keyed his comm from terminal in front of him. "We're lifting off, Akens. Report."

"We've evacuated South Dakota DeCorp Facility. We are an hour

177

behind schedule. Systems fueling delayed our departure; however, most staff are clear. Senior leadership has been aloft for five minutes and is heading to High Command O-Station per orders, sir."

Operation Hot Springs protocols had all of DeCorp senior managers and their families board the DeCorp Craft Shuttles immediately to an O-Station. They would be reunited with family later after the evacuation was complete.

"Set the quickest path, Ember. You know what protocol demands and time is running out."

"Absolutely, sir. I'm setting the course now. I'll keep you posted. Ember clear."

As Akens pressed the orange square button turning off his comm, the alarms of the MMW began to ring out. The MMW jerked to one side and started to shake, dropping in altitude. The vessel had yet to gain the needed momentum from the thrusters, still relying on the lift manifolds to remain aloft. A massive explosion rocked the giant spacecraft off balance.

"Full power thrusters! Straighten us out!" Akens yelled at the pilot as the MMW began a violent tumble in the sky.

The vast storage compartment was causing further complications as supplies broke loose and shifted the weight of the MMW.

The thrusters were at max power as three different command center personnel working in tandem tried to right the ship. Ember and the entire crew felt the shock wave of the blast before they heard anything. The explosion of the central South Dakota DeCorp Facility was beyond anything anyone expected. Miles upon miles of civilization was leveled in the wake of the explosion that stretched thousands of feet into the sky. Every craft flying across the area was impacted. Depending on the altitude, most were either immediately destroyed or rendered un-flyable, crashing down to Earth, right into the expanding devastation below.

Ember's MMW fell a few thousand feet before finally coming to an awkward stationary position in the sky. Several of the lift manifolds had been destroyed, but, thankfully, the four enormous interstellar thrusters were all operational and holding the ship in place. Ember took a moment to assess the situation, when an alert message flashed onto his main HIREZ screen.

SD DeCorp destroyed. Yellowstone eruption imminent.

Ember immediately comm'd back to Sint Argum.

"Yes, Ember?"

"Sir, the situation has worsened. South Dakota facility has been completely destroyed. Volcanic eruption will occur at any moment. I would extrapolate that all the facilities are now in immediate jeopardy.

We're currently in a holding position at 5,000 feet after the initial blast," said Ember, desperate not to show fear in his tone.

"Ember, continue your departure. Get clear of the atmosphere and proceed with operations. Message Tober Rosel and inform him of the current situation. Report back once you're on your interstellar path."

"I will, Commander."

Sint leaned forward in his chair to speak with Vivsou. "Get us airborne, Director."

From his pilot's seat, Vivsou opened the vehicular communications channels. "All ships on my mark, depart on my lead."

With his right hand on the throttle control to power up the engines, Vivsou guided the Oberkorn from its parking spot on the tarmac with his left hand on the control stick. The vehicles rose from Earth with military precision. The powerful DeCorp advanced ships quickly gained speed and altitude as Sint Argum took one final look at his former home from one of the half-dozen viewport HIREZ monitors.

"Approaching 1,000 feet, sir. All ships in the green," voiced Vivsou.

"Execute house cleaning procedures, stage one," replied Sint.

Vivsou comm'd the four support fighters. "Dow, go with S-One House Cleaning."

"Copy that," replied the pilot, Uray Dow, as he immediately broke out of formation and started a deep dive back toward the hangar.

The MTC came down from beneath the cloud layer screaming at top speed. Dow flipped on his weapons display. He was given no instructions on how Stage One would accurately be executed, only that the entire facility must be destroyed. Rather than going with guided munitions, the skilled pilot opted for a close-range attack on the facility's power and fuel production plant. In doing so, it should destroy everything attached, and if it didn't, he could always make another pass.

Slowing his speed as the target buildings came clearly into view, Dow selected the two thruster blasters for his primary weapon's trigger. The pilot continued to slow his approach as he lined up his shot on the cockpit canopy overhead display. Squeezing the trigger while at the exact moment shoving the throttle forward, this provided for a short burst of power. Dow pulled back on the control stick, and, in unison, two bright, glowing red blasts shot from the front of the MTC thrusters as the fighter pitched up and thundered away from the explosion. The plasma blast instantly destroyed the building in a blinding display of structural carnage. The MTC was clear of the blast radius as Dow turned his ship around to watch the results of his orders.

The power and fuel building was still in the process of exploding when a series of smaller explosions began around the entire property.

Uray Dow keyed his comm to Director Vivsou. "Stage One complete, sir." As he turned off his comm, another considerable explosion occurred, reassurance of a job well done; the entire facility was destroyed.

"Stay in attack readiness, make your way back to the convoy, and await further instruction," commanded Director Vivsou, as the small military fleet was about to enter space.

Vivsou put their ship on autopilot and turned to Sint. "Sir, before we proceed with Stage Two, I need to inform you that not all officials have left the O-Station. There was a delay and…"

Frustrated, Sint cut him off and, in a terse tone, replied, "That is not our concern. Our *concern* is making sure that any data on that station doesn't fall into the wrong hands."

During the Stage One operation, Sint alerted Akens Ember on his ship to remote link and transfer all data on the orbital station OS computers.

This particular O-Station carried terabytes of DeCorp files that could prove useful were someone to get their hands on it.

Sint was already patched into the outbound O-MMW. "Has the file transfer been completed?"

"Yes, sir," replied Ember.

Vivsou heard the exchange between Argum and Ember and anticipated what Argum's next command would be. "Vivsou, have our pilot lay waste to it!" ordered Sint.

"Very well, sir," said Vivsou, although he didn't agree. There were still dozens of employees and high ranking officials on board the O-Station, behind schedule from the initial departure after Operation Hot Springs was implemented. Director Vivsou was all too aware that following through with the murder of these individuals also meant securing the safety of his own family, yet not following orders and going with his instinct to save those lives on the O-Station would probably cost him his own life. Sint Argum used fear to command most of his officials, and now he had more power than ever.

The fighter arrived back with the convoy just as Vivsou gave him his next instructions. "Uray Dow, proceed with the house cleaning Stage Two."

"Copy that," replied Dow.

The pilot punched in the required information to reach the O-Station and turned away once again from the convoy.

The "House Cleaning protocol" was a part of Operation Hot Springs that only those within Sint's inner circle were aware of.

The plan was to destroy any entity that might still carry DeCorp data, especially data that could be traced back to Sint Argum. The protocol was created without the approval of the higher chains of command. How far the protocol went was solely in Sint's hands.

Chapter 25

In the skies over Georgia

Oshly was about to start complaining again when Ven announced, "We've reached our window, everyone. Prepare for atmospheric departure." The words were technically meaningless; very little needed to be done to the ships as they flew into outer space. Ven was merely attempting to change the mood now that this rough part of their journey was ending.

"Everyone, keep flying in tight formation and stay in the green on the STL proximity monitor. We've got one O-Station we need to clear," comm'd Taft.

The group was climbing at a steep and rapid rate, with their thrusters now doing all the work. The ships' lift manifolds went on automatic shut down once the vehicles reached altitude.

"Do we have to fly that close to that station?" asked Jebet on comms.

Taft answered, "It's a choice between passing close to one monitoring station or flying a different route with the potential of being picked up by multiple stations."

"We're almost out of the atmos, everyone shut down on comms. Radio silence until Ven gives the all clear. If we're going to be undetected, that means total silence—engines too, when Ven gives the command."

Once they were clear of the Earth's gravity, the ships could shut down everything apart from the computer systems and maintain their speed with the momentum they gained.

Ven called out orders on comms to the other ships. "Okay everyone, get ready to throttle up, full speed, maintain formation, and complete power plant shut down on my command, and in three, two, one...throttle up!"

Everyone knew each other's vehicle capabilities and could match the speed as Ven, Kaytha, Jebet, Oshly, and Taft all powered up thrusters to their max potential, throwing them back into their seats while they all fought to stay in stealth formation to avoid detection.

After calculating that they had more than enough speed, Ven comm'd, "And in three, two, one, shutdown with radio silence."

The roar suddenly silenced as they shot away from Earth and toward the Moon.

The O-Station was getting closer in view out the windows of their ships. The lights from the orbiting station made it easily identifiable against the star-studded blackness of space. This O-Station was about one quarter the size of a standard MMW, a big box floating in space, with outer vehicle docking spaces and a communications dish attached to the bottom pointed toward Earth.

Several DeCorp transport shuttles were still attached to the outside, and three others had just cleared the station's port.

The departing shuttles, known as T-Buses, were showing up on everyone's tracking system as they continued to get closer to the station. Taft went over his HIREZ data screens, and so far no one was picking them up—their attempt to avoid detection was going as planned.

With only seconds left before passing the O-Station, Taft felt confident that success for this portion of the journey was going to be achieved. Just then his scanners picked up on a fast approaching ship flying up from the surface of the planet.

Ven noticed it too and steered slightly away from their present course knowing the rest would follow. He wanted to see if that ship was heading toward them or toward the O-Station. A moment of panic quickly subsided when the approaching vehicle stayed its course toward the floating facility.

****

Uray Dow was closing in fast on the O-Station. "Dow to the Director, ready to commence orders, do I have clearance?" he comm'd to Dir Vivsou.

Before Vivsou could respond, Sint did it for him. "Fire when ready," he said with more than a hint of glee in his voice which also showed on his face.

****

As the five friends were about to pass the station, Ven realized the oncoming ship was no ordinary T-Craft; it was military grade and before he could even start to conceive why it was there, the onboard monitors immediately picked up on the heat signatures that erupted from the MTC.

****

Not wanting to get as close as his last command, Uray Dow squeezed the trigger that launched two programed DeCorp explosive warhead-tipped missiles from the gun mounts attached to the side thrusters. Once the projectiles were clear, the pilot slammed his control stick sideways, violently turning his ship back toward Earth.

****

With the missiles launched, Ven's military training immediately kicked in. He knew exactly what was about to happen and that they were all flying way too close to where the missiles were about to meet their mark.

"Break radio silence, power up all thrusters, prepare for evasive act...." But before he could finish, the first missile hit one of the evacuating T-Buses pulling away from the station. The shuttle blew apart, scattering fragments in every direction as the missile ripped right through it. The warhead didn't detonate until it hit the side of the O-Station and as it did, the second missile made direct contact. The entire station exploded in a massive ball of debris and blinding red, yellow, and white light.

The blast was enough to send all five friends hurtling out away from the shock wave and each other. None of them had enough time to power on their ships' thrusters. Jebet and Taft were both knocked unconscious as their T-Crafts were sent spinning out of control and away from one another, chunks of debris from the O-Station and the departing ships flying past them.

****

Dow was changing course to meet up with Sint Argum's military fleet which had already reached outer space hundreds of miles away and at a safe distance from the destruction. Looking at his data screen, he picked up on the five floating T-Craft located in the middle of the chaos he had created. At first glance, Dow figured it to be just remnants of O-Station, although they were so large he was considering turning around to make sure there was nothing that could be retrieved.

Dow opened up his comm once again. "Director Vivsou, operation successful; however, there appear to be large remnants of the station remaining. Would you like me to mop up?"

Giving pause for Sint to answer the pilot's question, Vivsou turned to Sint.

"You're the Director of this operation. I'll hold you responsible for any failure. However, it is your call Director," said Sint.

Vivsou was about to give the pilot clearance to destroy what was left when the pilot noticed something odd on his ship scanner.

"Director, the objects now appear to be moving," said Dow on his comms.

Sint heard the pilot and leaned up in his seat. "What was that, pilot?"

****

Ven comm'd on all channels. "Maintain radio silence. Power up and get behind me. Follow my lead and get back on course."

Ven, Kaytha, and Oshly fired up their engines immediately. Taft woke up halfway through Ven's comm but understood what needed to happen. Following suit, he throttled up his thrusters to get back in line. In no time the four of them were flying up behind Ven, but the STL-5 wasn't operating, and Ven had yet to realize this as he course-corrected back toward the Moon.

"Ven! Is the STL off? I can see you!" comm'd Oshly.

Without turning communications back on, Ven looked over the STL data screen. Oshly was right—the STL had gone dark; only the proximity scanner seemed to be operational. Ven didn't want to start an open discussion on what to do next as he continued to normalize his ship's systems and point his craft in the proper direction.

Taft pulled back into formation. It took Kaytha and Oshly a few moments to catch up. The blast had tossed them farther away from the others. They hurried to close the distance between their T-Crafts and Ven in the lead ship. In a moment with the series of notification whooshes and bleeps, the STL came back online.

****

"Director, the remnants appear to be T-Craft of some kind, but..."

"But WHAT, pilot?!" bellowed Sint.

"They are disappearing off my scope. It showed five objects, four began to change direction, the largest flying away from the debris site, three started their approach to the larger ship. But now they're gone."

Uray Dow could now see the debris field in view. He watched as a T-Craft flew up to another disabled ship. "I see two custom T-

Crafts, sir. One appears to be disabled; the other just arrived at its location," said Dow back to the Oberkorn.

****

Oshly had only been in the stealth wake for a few moments before he noticed Jebet was stalled. Maintaining radio silence, he turned his ship around as fast as he could and flew to Jebet's still drifting ship.

Oshly angled just right so he could look in to see Jebet through the cockpit window. She was still unconscious in her pilot's seat. After quickly scanning her ship to check her vitals, he saw the MTC heading his direction on the data screen. Oshly switched on his roof panel magnets, flipped his T-Craft over to connect her roof to his, and throttled up to head back on course. Kaytha had been monitoring Oshly and, knowing he would not be able to find them, she switched on her ship's detachable homing beacon.

The MTC was now tracking in on Oshly, who was closing in on Kaytha's signal, which was also being received by the MTC pilot.

****

Uray Dow comm'd to the Oberkorn, "Director, I am almost to the evader. He's following a homing beacon ahead of him, but I don't detect the object."

Sint's worst fears were now becoming a reality. *Someone did it and these people have it,* he thought.

Dow on comms continued to keep Vivsou and Sint updated. "Sir, I am seconds away, but I'm no longer able to pick up the homing beacon."

190

Oshly was flying as fast as he could toward his friends, keeping an eye on his stealth monitor as it began to pick up the STL-5 signal. Kaytha, knowing Oshly was in range, shut off her homing beacon.

Ven went active on all comms and spoke in almost a whisper. "As soon as Oshly is in the stealth wake, full throttle ninety degrees up and off course."

Oshly's program, the one he built, finally registered green on his monitor as all five ships were hidden again. Jebet's T-Craft was still being towed by Oshly's as they all rocketed up and away from the fast-approaching fighter.

****

"Uray Dow, have you caught them?" asked Vivsou.

Not knowing exactly how to respond, Dow comm'd back. "They are no longer on visual or monitor. They up and disappeared right in front of me. My ship got knocked off course for a second, it felt like a blast of some kind and…"

"WHAT, PILOT?! I NEED ALL AVAILABLE DATA!" fired back Sint.

"Sir, for a moment I could have sworn I saw all five vehicles in front of me before my ship was knocked out of control."

"Uray Dow, head back to the fleet and dock on the Oberkorn, We'll debrief and pull the data from your onboard systems once you have arrived."

****

As soon as Ven was convinced the MTC was heading away from them, he changed his flight path back toward the Moon. Jebet woke up and was immediately confused by the position her T-Craft was in relative to the rest of her friends.

Looking up only to see a smiling Oshly looking down at her through his cockpit canopy only a few feet away, she deduced what had happened.

She thought to herself, *Oh, hell no, he's not towing me the rest of the way.*

Jebet motioned at Oshly to disconnect from her ship. Oshly, trying to be funny, acted like he didn't understand, but as Jebet fired up her thrusters and gave them a loud rev, he knew she wasn't having it. Once he turned off his roof magnets, Jebet boosted the power to her engines, maintained speed, and rolled away from Oshly, directly back into formation with the others. Ven wanted to get more distance from Earth before he opened communications, as they continued on toward the Moon. It was probably for the best, since none of them had quite yet come to grips with the dozens of lives that were just taken and why anyone would have committed such a heinous act.

****

Yellowstone Park, Wyoming

Only those who refused to believe the historic Park's ancient volcano would ever erupt or those who wanted to see it happen, knowing it would cost them their lives, remained.

Oblivious to what had happened at South Dakota DeCorp, having no way to communicate with the outside world inside the park boundaries, they were witness to the largest volcanic explosion the planet would ever know. As if the gates of Hell themselves had opened up, plumes of molten lava went rocketing hundreds of feet into the sky from the hole several miles wide that had broken open the Earth's crust. The shock wave radiating out from the first blast laid waste to a hundred miles in every direction...and this was just the beginning.

****

Outside Earth's orbit

Sint Argum sat silently as his small but powerful fleet powered on away from Earth. He was waiting for the MTC pilot Dow to return, his mind filled with frustration. The knowledge that someone created a stealth device, the one thing more powerful than anything he had.

Dr. Vivsou received the communication as he looked out back at the Earth; the Yellowstone eruption was so big they could see it from the cockpit window. Sint turned his chair to view the devastation himself, then under his breath, but loud enough for all to hear he spoke, "Good."

Chapter 26

The friends continued on course for the rendezvous with the Moon, maintaining radio silence longer than they needed. At least an hour had passed since the events just outside Earth's orbit and each of them, for the time being, was satisfied to soak in what they witnessed while trying to go undetected. Kaytha's mind raced thinking that DeCorp might be aware that they were in possession of the very thing that her father was trying to hide. *So could the vile scum who ordered and carried out the attack on the O-Station,* she thought. Being that it was a DeCorp fighter, Kaytha presumed they attacked their own O-Station, murdering over dozens of people.

She wasn't the only one with this thought either. "Kaytha? Kaytha, you read me?" Her comm quietly crackled to life as Taft broke silence to talk one on one with her.

"I read you, Taft. How are you holding up?" replied Kaytha.

"I was about to ask you the same thing. That pilot was coming back for us, flying right behind us, close enough to be in the wake, even for just seconds. If anyone suspects...?"

"I'm thinking the same thing, Taft. Again I have to assume my father didn't want it to fall into the wrong hands. If someone from

DeCorp suspects we have the STL—hell, even if they just assume we have that kind of tech—they are going to come after us. But why destroy the station? That makes no sense."

"Kaytha, have you looked or listened to any of the network feeds?"

"Bringing them up now." Kaytha's concern was growing by the second.

With the streaming feeds open on Taft's and Kaytha's ships, the network channel back to Earth was giving off notifications to everyone's HIREZ data screens. Ven immediately opened the ship-wide comms. Barely audible gasps and Jebet's quiet cry of, "Oh, my God," could be heard as the news gave details about Yellowstone Park's volcanic eruption's destruction. On their data screens a news ticker provided up to the minute reporting of the disaster.

...Yellowstone Park's explosion stretches hundreds of miles, the estimated mounting death toll in over one million lives... new reports of the extensive damage from the DeCorp South Dakota facility before the eruption...the fires continue to rage at the DeCorp locations in the neighboring states...

"Did any of you see the Atlanta report mixed in there? Sounds like a deliberate attack on that DeCorp airfield.

Could be the same O-Station fighter we came across," said Ven.

Jebet asked, "But why would they attack their own facility?"

"Could be they were trying to cover their tracks," replied Ven. "One of the reports has predictions that all the DeCorp factories are doomed—the underground pipelines starting from the west are on fire, and it's spreading. Half the western US facilities are already on fire or exploding." Ven began to monitor the air traffic feeds. "Guys, I'm looking at the Earth traffic flight data. Thousands are exiting the planet. Dozens of DeCorp's MMWs are leaving the atmosphere, and it looks like EnerCon is starting to follow their lead on a large scale."

"I see it too, Ven. I can't believe it. It's almost a planet-wide evacuation," said Taft.

"Could it be that bad already?" asked Kaytha, growing more concerned that someone else might suspect they might have a cloaking device.

"The Yellowstone eruption was bigger than anyone could have imagined. Reports are saying it won't be the only one. It'll be a global catastrophe," said Ven.

All five friends seemed relatively calm, given the gravity of the situation, that was until Jebet cried out, "What about our friends, our family? We have to turn around! We can't just leave them all there!"

"I agree with Jebet. We have to go back, but we're going to lose our stealth capability on the return trip if we do." Oshly wasn't about to be the one to make such decisions.

"Our families are out of range of the blast area and anyone working for DeCorp weren't in South Dakota. I know we're all worried about our loved ones, but is there anyone in your family that doesn't have the ability to evacuate?" asked Taft.

The others all confirmed that the people closest to them could leave Earth and agreed that right now it was too risky to try to reach out on the networks, potentially exposing their location.

Kaytha spoke up next. "We have to keep the STL operational. My father wanted me to find it, and I'm pretty sure he wanted to keep it out of the hands of someone like those people who just destroyed that O-Station. Ven, is it possible to safely send a brief, coded message to all our families telling them that we're safe and we'll contact them when we can?"

"That's doable, but I obviously can't guarantee it's going to reach any of them."

"Works for me," said Taft and everyone quickly agreed.

Ven's military and leadership training kicked in. "We're only about ninety minutes out from MoonStation. I just did a scan. We're in range and it appears there's no one around.

It'll take a few hours at least if someone decided to come here. We should have more than enough time to stop, rest, refuel, and charge the STL while we figure out what to do. Everyone agree? Sound off."

"T four agree."

"K three agree."

"J two agree."

"O one agree."

"Okay, now let's all rest up as best we can during the final leg. I'll have the systems monitor the Earth feeds for updates and make sure we have a full data collection source to look at when we arrive. Keep the comms closed for now unless we have an emergency, for a reason."

When the ship-wide comms turned off, Kaytha comm'd one-on-one with Taft. "Taft, I'm scared."

"I got you, Kay." Taft couldn't remember a time he heard her actually frightened. "We have each other, and I'm sure our families will be fine. We'll figure it out, for a reason, Kaytha, for a reason."

****

Space, beyond Earth's Orbit

Sint Argum was now in his private quarters on the Oberkorn. The room amounted to nothing more than bed space, a few compact communication monitors, comm equipment sitting on a desk, and two chairs. He leaned forward in his chair turned backward, arms crossed over the backrest facing the pilot, Uray Dow. It was Dow who lost sight of the evaders of the O-Station blast after they disappeared before his eyes. Over and over Sint made Dow recount what had happened and over and over the fighter pilot repeated the same version.

"I had them on the scanner, I had them in visual sight, and they just vanished from my view."

"Are you sure they didn't fly off under power and out of your sight?"

"No, sir, there was no way they just flew off. There was quite of bit of debris around us, and, when they disappeared, there was a clear path that whoever it was had cut through. I tried following it, but within seconds, I was out of the debris field. I had no way to track them. They were no longer on my scanner...they were just gone."

Sint had a growing concern that Dow knew too much, but he was also one of his most skilled pilots and, according to his records, one of the most loyal to DeCorp.

"Have you told anyone else, apart from those involved with the mission, about what you saw?"

"No, Commander. Everything I've said has either been on comms to command here that you heard and our discussions, sir."

"Good, we shall keep it that way. I'm going to have you reassigned, Dow. Do not worry, you'll still be working for me, but I have new orders I'll be including you in. Do not discuss with anyone the details of your last mission. You're free to go about your business until I call for you."

"Thank you, sir," Dow said, breathing a sigh of relief before he exited Sint's quarters.

Sint moved his chair back to his room's comm desk and opened the direct, private messaging channel.

Urgent action Message from S. Argum to T. Rosel, contact via private comm, Sint Quarters SMTC Oberkron Immediately.

A few minutes passed when the room's systems, after scanning the bio readings in the area, informed Sint he'd received a return message. "Sint Argum, T.Rosel requesting private communique," said the A.I. voice of Gelina.

"Go live," replied Sint.

"Rosel, what is your current status?"

"My MMD is in position per Operation Hot Springs. We've been monitoring the region. Quiet so far, but awaiting your instructions."

"Gather two of your best attack pilots. I have a mission I want you to take part in. Put whoever you trust most to take over command on your leave. One of my fighter pilots will round out your team. We have a group of ships that have gone rogue. We believe they're heading to the MoonStation. I need you and your team in route immediately to track them down."

"Yes, sir. I'll have my drone attack units on standby to keep the MMD under guard while I'm away."

"Make sure all the fighters are equipped for confrontation. Inform Director Vivsou once you're in route. He will send along the mission details and put you in contact with my pilot."

"Understood, sir," replied Tober.

"One more thing, Rosel. I've already privately sent over details for operation *Put a Bow on It*—be ready for execution."

Chapter 27

Still maintaining a tight formation to remain cloaked, the five friends approached MoonStation. Atmosphere processors covered a tiny portion of the Moon, giving breathable surface air around most of the infrastructure. The buildings were all large enough that few ever ventured outside apart from routine maintenance. The entire complex took on a brutal industrial look, most of which was made up MMWs now permanently a part of the Moon. The entire facility was dotted with communication towers and retrofitted with reinforced viewport windows on the now permanent buildings. With landing pads located on the dozen or so structures, it resembled a military installation more than an interplanetary gas station. Only the entertainment wing of the station showed any kind of culture or style with brightly contoured buildings, lined with overhead neon holographic projections that displayed a variety of visitor attractions, themed clubs, sports bars, and movie theaters. However, the Moon had been left unoccupied ever since the UEGC clamped down on Earth departures. The workers, a combination at the time of EnerCon and DeCorp employees, were sent home six months ago.

The facility was still fully functioning with a power plant buried deep beneath the surface which could supply electricity to the station for decades. Unauthorized visitors had landed on the Moon since the worker crews left, the few who actually made it off Earth on a "Moon run," some subsequently captured by Earth's interstellar police upon return. Those who were authorized to visit were supply runs to other parts of the solar system of either EnerCon or DeCorp, stopping off to refuel, rest, or recharge. No one really knew who or what was watching. Those who did visit were respectful not to trash the place. The stock of supplies, provisions, and gear were meant to last a few years even if there were a steady flow of visitors.

Ven opened all comms as they made their final approach. "Let's do a quick sweep of the complex before we land. We'll park behind the entertainment district after we're done. Stay in range to keep cloaked when we land."

"Better to keep us out in the open if we need a fast lift off," said a smiling Jebet over the comm.

Oshly said, "Probably the last place they'd look. Plus, the refueling and charging lines run right past that area and the supply buildings are in walking distance."

As they finished their flight around the area, Ven began his descent to a large landing pad behind the huge entertainment arena, normally a spot for supply drop-offs.

It didn't take long before Kaytha saw the real reason why Ven had picked this spot. "Hey, Ven, is that the main transportation hangar?"

It was one the most significant buildings situated adjacent to the arena, unmarked, but undoubtedly important. The building had a series of military-grade sensor arrays, plus more than a few visibly closed hatches which anyone with knowledge of armed safety defenses knew meant there were probably weapon turrets ready to deploy if needed.

"Yeah, it's the private hangar for the important people. The civilian spaceport is on the other side where we first flew in," Ven said in his stern military voice. "I did a quick scan of the interior and picked up a ship inside. If it's what I think it is, you're all in for a surprise."

After their long journey, the friends landed in the same positions as when they left Kay's Field. The STL-5 was still doing what it was created to do—anyone scanning the surface would not pick up their T-Crafts on the scopes, but they would see lifeforms. The rainbow of neon colored lights cast a glow on the spot where their ships were parked. The holographic dance of light acted like a welcome sign akin to celebrities at a movie premiere.

Exhausted, tired, and hungry, the group took in their surroundings, stretching their arms and legs, while still attempting to make sense of the situation they were in.

"The door to that hangar bay is huge. What's it hiding, Ven?" asked Taft, staring at the hangar.

Most of MoonStation was left open. There was little reason to keep everything locked tight with so many security monitors scattered throughout the complex. Ven had already made his way to the building's control pad. This particular building did have an extra layer of security. Ven still held rank in the Earth defense military even though he wasn't currently serving. With that came both DeCorp and EnerCon access as both required federal security at many of their installations. Ven keyed in the universal military code needed to open the massive steel doors. Kaytha, Taft, Oshly, and Jebet stood in awe as the doors rumbled and began to separate. The hangar bay lights were off, but as the gap in the door grew wider, the overhead lights, starting from the back, flickered to life. High-intensity spotlights began to illuminate what Ven had picked up on his scope when they flew in.

Jebet asked what everyone else was wondering. "Is that what I think it is?"

Ven was the first one to walk inside the hangar to get a closer look and the rest followed his lead. Even Ven felt like a small child standing next to this magnificent feat of flight engineering.

In a handful of seconds, their suspicions were confirmed by the proof in the little bold, black, italic letters painted just underneath the ship's enormous control deck window: ANNIVERSARY.

Chapter 28

Space, The SMTC Oberkorn

Tober Rosel and two highly trained, lethal T-Craft fighter pilots had Sint Argum's fleet in sight. Now out in deep space, Earth a tiny dot behind them, they'd completed the several hours it took from where Rosel's military team was stationed, flying at top speed, to join with Argum's fighter pilot. The pilot was docked at the top of the Oberkron and was going over the detachment procedures to join with Rosel's squadron.

"DeCorp craft, I see you departing. This is Rosel. Acknowledge," comm'd Rosel.

"I read, Rosel. This is Uray Dow."

"Detach and fall in behind the group. We are not stopping."

Uray had already been given the orders since he'd helped to work out the details of what was relayed to Tober Rosel.

With his T-Craft MTC clear of the Oberkorn, he could see the three ships approaching fast. Turning his T-Craft into their projected flight path, he sped away from Argum's fleet. As he picked up speed, the others grew closer in his rear view HIREZ monitor, and within seconds Rosel and his fighters blasted past him. Pushing the throttle lever forward, Uray fed more power to the thrusters to catch up. Quickly matching in speed, he followed to the rear behind the other heavily armed DeCorp attackers. Dow mounted his T-Craft with as much weaponry and ammunition as it could handle—and it was a good thing he did. Looking over the other ships as they continued to pick up speed, having slowed to regroup, he had never seen such a display of destructive might loaded onto fast attack MTCs like these before.

Tober Rosel, Uray Dow, Sint Argum, and Director Vivsou were the only ones with the knowledge of what they were specifically looking for: the device.

The pilots that Rosel chose only knew this was a hunt and would be informed of what to disable, take over, or destroy when it was time to act. Rosel was given all the details because Sint trusted him fully to not betray him. Uray Dow was a question that still had to be answered—would he stay loyal to Argum? It was a risk for Sint. In the mission details given to Rosel, instructions to capture the device was priority one. Priority two was destroy it if the possibility of obtaining it was deemed impossible. Priority three was eliminate *anyone* who knew of the device but was *not* loyal to Argum.

Unfortunately, all the mission team members were expendable if they compromised the mission's priorities in any way.

Rosel direct comm'd Uray Dow. "Just to remind you, from here on out you will be referred to as Number Four. The others are Number Three and Number Two. I am Number One, or for the sake of argument, you can call me out as Leader, understood Number

Four?"

"Understood, Leader," replied Dow.

Rosel switched to all comms. "We have our orders. Number Four had direct contact with our targets, so he will help advise when contact is made. Maintain max flight speed for long distance travel and power consumption. At this cruising speed, we should be arriving at Moon Station in eight hours."

****

Moon Station

The Anniversary was a ship of myth and legend in the T-Craft community.

"Sorry, Oshly, but that ship makes your ride look like a T-Taxi," said Jebet.

Oshly didn't argue. "It's gorgeous alright. I'd always heard that a small flying group out of Texas had created a freighter sized T-Craft.

We'd tell stories, huddled around bonfires at night after an air show, drinking," Oshly continued, raising his arms in the air and shaking his palms with mock enthusiasm. "The ship with unmatched speed and maneuverability, ooooh."

Ven spoke as he walked around, examining the hull of the ship. "The story goes one of the creators had a father who worked for EnerCon before the split and creation of DeCorp. His dad was one of the lead engineers. He designed the original T-Craft."

"I've heard this story too. He had a small runway and a really big hangar bay on his property, right?" added Taft.

"Wait, hold the phone! Was this the same guy who was sick with some rare degenerative disease and worked from home, building ships?" asked Kaytha.

"Yep, same guy," replied Ven.

Taft continued, "I'd heard of the Anniversary, but I never put the two together. The story I knew was of a guy who worked for the company and built all types of experimental stuff from home, and that kept him close to his nurse's aide and medical equipment."

"All the same guy. We're looking at his life's work," said Ven.

Jebet, doing her best deep-voiced sarcastic impersonation of Ven, said, "I always thought it was just made up.

I know people always talk about the 'infamous' Anniversary, three times the size of a T-Craft, covered in lift manifolds, and faster than any ship of any size."

"If you're quite done, Jeb, I'll tell you the rest of the story."

Jebet rolled her eyes and crossed her arms, staring at Ven.

"So, *as I was saying,* before passing away, he was working on a secret project for EnerCon. I actually went to his home once on assignment, and the setup was impressive."

It was common knowledge that standard T-Craft were built smaller in size to make them affordable. Upscaling for atmosphere flight, even with the lift manifolds, was costly if you wanted a fast ship with good atmospheric flight capabilities. It didn't take long for DeCorp to streamline production on small to midsize fast T-Craft. The bigger the ship, the more expensive they became, from millions of dollars for slower, bulkier larger transports all the way up to the billions it cost to produce MMWs.

Ven continued the story as he remembered it. "What this kid's father was building was, as we all can see, at least three times bigger than your standard large T-Craft, like the SMTC."

"This thing is bigger than three times that size," said Taft.

"Yeah, like I said, that's just what I was told.

I think we had all seen the pictures and videos, but it's tough to sense scale unless you're standing next to it."

"Ven, do you really think this is as fast and as agile as any of our T's?" asked Kaytha. She knew her ships, almost as well—if not better—than Jebet, but the sheer size of the Anniversary made it tough to believe it could match the flight demands of even the most technologically advanced T-Craft. "This thing's sporting the biggest EnerCon Dual-Thruster package I've ever seen," she said, pointing to the robust gray engines on the sides to the rear of the vehicle.

The Anniversary was boasted as having a cargo bay big enough to house three full-sized T-Crafts and sleeping quarters for ten. Looking into the cargo bay, the friends were stunned at how much space was available.

"So, Ven, is it true that the dad died and his son took over? Again, I was told that the guy just made ships, not this ship," asked Taft.

"Yeah, as far as I know his son and several of his buddies spent another year finishing his work. See here, the carefully placed lift manifolds on the surface? Apparently it gives it flight advantages."

Oshly looked stunned and said, "I didn't even realize those panels were manifolds. Wait! You can do that?!"

Jebet bent down and looked under the rear of the ship. Pointing to the ship's undercarriage, she answered, "The thruster packages are tweaked. And, check this out, extra inputs for direct charging and fueling to the motors themselves. It's gotta be to allow for long-range flights without having to be worry about power consumption."

"Why is this thing armed?" Kaytha asked Ven, catching him admiring the mounted gun and missile racks.

"I don't know why it is *now*, but when I visited the guy's house, he had all kinds of weaponry, mostly for testing. I heard that his son liked to go blow stuff up at nearby abandoned airfields."

Kaytha said, "I remember reading somewhere that the son and some other kids took it on its first test flight on the *exact day* that his father died one year earlier. Local air enforcement picked up the Anniversary on their scanners almost immediately, but the kids —and the ship—up and disappeared before local officials could catch them. I'm guessing they knew that if they got caught, there was no way they'd be able to keep the ship."

Ven was nodding along as Kaytha spoke. "Yup, that's what I was always told. They never returned to the father's home again. Rumor was that they all kept a low profile living either on the Anniversary or at some secret location."

Oshly scratched his head absentmindedly, as he often did whenever he was hyper-analyzing a situation or data.

"Did you guys ever see a while back on one of those blogs that the son popped up at some underground T-Craft rally?"

"Yeah, but I always figured that was a bunch of bull," said Jebet, standing on a small ladder she'd grabbed, with her head inside the rear of the ship's biggest thruster. "Anyway, it's been a few years since I heard anyone even talk about the Anniversary, which is why I just figured it never existed and it was all faked. Obviously, I was wrong."

Everyone continued to explore and admire the ship's exterior. Finally, Kaytha said, "Ven, are you sure your scans showed a complete vacancy of the base?"

"Sure. Before we came in for an approach, I did a Moon-wide scan and grabbed the scanner repeater readings from the base itself. There is definitely no one here."

The Anniversary's rear bay door was open as they made their way up the loading ramp to examine the ship's interior.

Jebet walked over to the bay's data screen and began looking at the ship's systems log. "Looks like whoever brought it here left in a hurry and took what they could with them. The ship appears to be prepped for travel...fully fueled, provisions in the living area—even all the weapons arrays are loaded and charged."

While Jebet had been talking, Taft had been going through the crew storage lockers.

"Yeah, there's nothing personal around here either. No flight suits, no tools scattered about. Maybe we'll find more once we check out the flight deck system."

"Guys, are we going to talk about what's happening back home? What about those people that got killed? We have to go back..." Oshly's voice trailed off.

"Oshly's right. I say we use the STL to get home then destroy it and find our families," said Jebet as she sat down on a nearby stool, placing her head in her hands.

Kaytha was now examining the bay's data screen, pulling up Earth's network feeds. The voices from the reports got the attention of the other four.

"Hey, Kay, put that up on the monitor," said Taft, pointing to the massive HIREZ screen at the very back of the bay.

As the images came up, Earth's news reports gave them the clearest picture of the devastation: DeCorp and Enercon facilities were exploding one by one across the country, Yellowstone Park was still erupting as a giant ash cloud over the western half of the nation began to form, the Alaskan EnerCon plant was being evacuated as it was expected to blow at any moment, and that disaster meant that the deep sea pipeline to Europe was also compromised. Then came the reports of the global evacuations—thousands of ships leaving gave a clear sign of what would happen next.

DeCorp was said to be heading to Mars while EnerCon announced its first priority was to get as many people off-planet as possible before making any long term planetary travel plans.

Many departing ships were crashing in the ash cloud from Yellowstone Park building over the western United States; others got caught in the devastating blasts of exploding factories. A map of the US showed reach and impact of the destruction.

"Look! The ash cloud isn't expected to reach Arizona for at least a day or more. The jet stream is keeping it north and the DeCorp plant blast doesn't appear to have affected the field. We need to get home!" shouted Oshly.

"Osh, by the time we get there, even with the field on lockdown, there might not be anything left to go home to. We have to figure out our next move. Someone is looking for us, and while I want to go home too, I don't know if that's the best idea. With that being said, I don't have any good ideas either," Taft said, looking at Kaytha and hoping maybe she did.

Before she could answer, Ven spoke up, "Taft is right. Someone knows we have this thing, and I get the feeling they are not the ones who we should be giving the STL to. Plus, it's just too important. Right, Kaytha?"

"My dad wanted me to find this, but I don't believe it was so that I would destroy it. If it were, he could have done it himself. All I know is right now I don't trust DeCorp—especially with what happened at that O-Station. Ven, I defer to your military judgment on this—what do you think we should do?"

Ven didn't hesitate and was already forming a plan. "We need to get all the essential parts off my ship, along with the STL, load and attach them to this beast. We'll stow two T-Crafts in the bay, and have the other two follow in the stealth wake. We need intel into DeCorp and EnerCon—I am not going to get it out here. I'm sure the military back channels have already been closed off if they are following disaster protocols, which means I'd need to get to another O-Station in low orbit over Earth. Oshly, Jebet, how long will it take the two of you to get everything transferred?"

"Hold up a sec," Taft said. "Are we just going to *take* the Anniversary?"

"How about we just *borrow it*, right, Ven?" said Kaytha.

"Sure, Kaytha. If you all want to say we're *borrowing* the Anniversary, then we'll say we're *borrowing* the Anniversary."

"Works for me," said Kaytha.

"Ok, fine," Taft reluctantly gave his stamp of approval.

Sensing the group needed some reassurance, Ven said, "Look, everyone, when the Earth evacs get here, I can guarantee that whoever gets here first—whether it's DeCorp or EnerCon, my ex-girlfriend or the stinkin' Otto brothers, they're going to claim the Anniversary as their own. So, if we don't *borrow it*, someone else will."

"I see your point, Ven. Now what are Kaytha and I supposed to do?"

Taft was still looking at Ven, but Kaytha was the one to answer him. "You and I are going to go into the entertainment wing to look for some food, access a couple of rooms, and get some sleep."

Suddenly, the natural order of the group was retaking shape with Kaytha stepping back into an unspoken leadership position.

Turning to talk just with Taft, Kaytha said, "Next to Ven, you and I are the best pilots, so it makes sense that we stay in flight in case we come across trouble. Once we're outta here, the three of them can rotate sleep while we head back, so you and I need to get some rest." Leaning into Taft's shoulder, she whispered into his ear, "Don't worry, we'll share a room. But don't let my calm demeanor fool you, I can't be alone right now, apart from just wanting to be with you."

Ven had already headed up to the flight deck to get a look at the Anniversary's cockpit level.

"Ven?!" shouted Taft, as Ven opened the auto door to the flight levels off of the hangar bay. "How much time do you think we have?"

With a finger on the screen to keep the doors open, Ven quickly glanced at the monitors still streaming the news feed of the devastation on Earth. "None, but give yourself five hours. Let's plan on leaving in six." Then, looking back at Jebet and Oshly, who were already clearing docking space for their T-Crafts, he yelled, "Got that, guys?"

"Got it!" Oshly shouted back, as Ven walked through the doorway and the door closed behind him.

Walking off the loading ramp of the Anniversary and out of the base hangar, Taft saw rays of swirling neon lights coming off the entrance of the hotel club in the distance.

"You ready to go clubbing?" Taft asked.

"Heh. I don't think you're dressed for it," Kaytha replied.

Chapter 29

Moon Station

Taft and Kaytha made their way from the hangar bay where the Anniversary was stored. They passed their T-Crafts on the adjacent landing pad headed for the entertainment wing of MoonStation.

The multi-colored light display welcoming visitors washed over Kaytha. Taft couldn't hide his smile.

"I'm sorry, but how and why are you smiling?" asked Kaytha, a bit dismayed.

"I know the world's coming to an end and there're apparently some nasty dudes that I assume don't just want to use harsh language against us, but…"

"You're not helping your cause here, Taft." They continued to walk toward the two story spotlight-studded entryway to the entertainment complex. Its giant blue and purple holographic sign blazing overhead read, "Club Montepulciano."

"It's just this is the closest thing to a date we've ever been on."

"Ha, ha," was the only witty comeback Kaytha could drum up. She was feeling the same thing Taft was but had no practice in showing it.

As they walked beneath the swirling multi-colored lights, Kaytha reached down and took Taft's hand as the auto doors opened to the largest dance hall either of them had ever seen. The silence was deafening; the radiating dance of projections in the room was as if all the vibrancy of the entire galaxy was captured and put on display in one place. The design of the main space was like any typical dancehall one would walk into over the ages. The large dance floor in the center had a DJ stand and turntables that had been outfitted with lift manifolds to keep it aloft on one end of the room in front of the glass wall that looked out onto the Moonscape and the stars. On the other end was the largest bar either of them had ever seen. Every bottle of alcohol ever produced lined the shelves behind the space where bartenders would pour and mix drinks. Behind them was a wall made of one enormous HIREZ screen with famous clips from movies spanning the decades, the solar system, abstract arrangements of three-dimensional shapes in every color imaginable, and all designed to keep the patrons entertained. Every space in the room felt surreal. Holographic projections covered every table, stool, chair, and booth, giving the area a feeling like the visitors were transported into a simulation.

The silence in the absence of the music with nothing but a slight buzz from the power pumping through the room created a completely different vibe than what the designers had intended. It wasn't a simulation; this was no longer a place for hundreds to gather and forget about their interstellar worries. In this place, only Taft and Kaytha existed.

The room was laid out in such a way that they had to walk through the main area to reach the service desk. They both slowed, taking in the moment. Being a bit shorter than him, Taft hadn't noticed yet that Kaytha was standing in front of him as he stood in awe of the massive entertainment hall.

Kaytha let go of his hand, placed her palms on the side of his face, and tilted his head down toward her. His eyes grew wide as he found himself staring at that which was more beautiful than positively anything in the room they were in and, for Taft, anything he had ever seen. As she kissed him, Taft believed right then that everything would be all right.

As they pulled apart from their embrace, Kaytha was wearing a smile that Taft was sure he had never seen before. "Let's go get some sleep," she whispered.

Taft grinned, knowing she was deadly serious as she pointed her index finger to his heart and said decisively, "Yes, that's what we're doing…sleeping!" She then turned to make her way to the service desk.

"For a reason, boss, for a reason."

While Kaytha located the keycards needed for one of the larger suites, Taft made his way to the kitchen area. The production of large quantities of food was accomplished all by automation in a place like this. Storage of food, in a preserved state, could be thawed, cooked, and prepared in a reasonable amount of time. Utilizing the self-serve chef terminal, Taft ordered up a few personalized pizzas, cheeseburgers, chicken tenders, and sides, more than enough to feed all five of them and then some. Taft keyed his flight suit comm for "all." "Hey guys, Kay and I are about to eat and then get some sleep. I ordered food if you guys want to come grab it in the kitchen area. Pretty easy to spot behind the food service sign locator."

"Thanks. We got the Anniversary's food auto-machine up and running, but the options are limited. Time permitting, we'll run over and grab what you cooked up. You guys gotta rest, we're on the clock," said Ven.

"We're heading to our rooms now. Alarms are set for a few hours. Go to emergency calls if you need us sooner," replied Kaytha from her flight suit comm.

Back in the Anniversary hangar, Jebet chuckled to herself under her breath, "Ha, to *our* rooms."

"What was that, Jeb...?" asked a puzzled Oshly. "Wait, are they together?"

"What? No, no, I'm just joking...hey, do you have the angular hex wedge wrench in your toolkit?"

"No, but I've got one on my T-Craft. The space is already cleared on board for one of our ships. Tell you what, I'll run over to the food court and gather that food Taft said was ready and then on my way back, I'll just fly in the ship, so at least that part of the work is done." Oshly couldn't care less about anything but his stomach right now.

"Sounds like a plan, but hurry, I'm hungry too. And, like Ven said, we're short on time."

Back inside the club, Taft gathered up their dinner then placed it on a dining cart he found in the kitchen. As he rolled it out into the lobby area, a wall display caught his eye. "Hey, Kay, come over here really quick."

Kaytha had been waiting by the elevator lifts. "Oh, you're not really going to make me do that, are you?" Kaytha saw what had surely gotten Taft's attention: a sign on an adjacent wall that said "Holopic" in bold, neon letters.

A small two-person bench was positioned facing a shelf located on the wall where a small camera was mounted. The Holopic gave club-goers a chance to take a picture of themselves with the club itself as the background. The Holopic was one of the mini-attractions the club had to offer.

These included a Lunar Chapel where couples could get certified and married by an authorized AI, a standard gift shop, and a ride simulator where patrons could experience an old school automobile drive through various Earth locations.

"Come on, no one has to see it, just for us," Taft said with a smile.

"Fine. At least I wore the right shirt for the occasion." Kaytha unzipped her flight suit, pulling it off her shoulders to reveal a T-Shirt of one of her favorite retro-pop bands from the early 2000s called Chvrches. The shirt was black, adorned with a mostly hot pink photo featuring the female lead singer, with hints of blue and yellow for their album "Love is Dead." Kaytha sat down next to Taft on the bench.

"You *would* be wearing a Love is Dead shirt."

"Be thankful I wasn't wearing the necklace," Kaytha quipped back. "*And*, I don't really believe that. Now, can we take our picture, *please*." Kaytha threw her arm around Taft, moving her face next to his, smiling.

Taft had the biggest, most joyful grin on his face as he pressed the floor button with his foot to snap the picture. Immediately after the flash went off, a holographic version of the two of them appeared.

Staring at the picture, Taft noticed Kaytha's mood change. "What's wrong?"

"It's nothing. That's a great picture of us." Kaytha then rested her head on Taft's shoulder. The weight of what they were entangled in hung heavy between them as they sat together.

Taft made a few swipes at his flight suit's wrist data pad, then walked over and passed his hand through the holopic picture to his suit's OS storage. With Taft's back turned from her, Kaytha passed her wrist through the holopic too.

Soon after, Kaytha and Taft found the nearest room in the attached hotel. The standard suite had a full sized bed, sofa, and table. They sat on the floor around the coffee table and devoured the platter of food worthy of a 20th-century truck stop. Full from the meal, they climbed into bed. Taft had turned the AC down considerably in an attempt to match the temperature of his sleeping quarters at the airfield. They knew how important it was that they take advantage of the time and get some much needed rest. Kaytha felt secure with Taft lying next to her as she eventually fell into a deep sleep, exhausted from everything that they left behind and thinking about what awaited ahead. When Taft heard Kaytha's breathing become heavy with deep sleep, he, too, drifted off.

Chapter 30

Tober Rosel and his three T-Craft attackers were still several hours out from the Moon's orbit, but close enough to begin scanning the base. They were able to pick up the heat signatures coming from the Anniversary, due to Oshly's and Jebet's ships being docked in the belly of the custom freighter. The other's ships, which had not yet thoroughly cooled, were also showing on Rosel's scans. The bio life scans were indicating that people were present, but, because of the distance, the flight systems scanner couldn't determine how many.

Rosel relayed the data to the other three. "Everyone, continue to go over your flight systems. I want 100% readiness. The entertainment portion of the base is our target. I'll give out orders when we arrive."

****

Ven was sitting comfortably in the pilot's chair on the command deck of the Anniversary.

The ship was designed so it could be flown by one pilot, but co-pilots were necessary if you wanted to take full advantage of everything the ship was capable of. Ven decided that he would be the one to start at the controls on the flight back to Earth, giving Jebet and Oshly the opportunity to sleep. Then, hopefully, Jebet could take over in the pilot's seat while Oshly monitored Earth's activity and the STL.

Oshly had mounted the STL-5 in a compartment under the nose of the Anniversary and routed its power system into the larger ship, which was already connected to charging and fueling when they'd found her. With the STL-5 hard-connected, all Oshly had to do was find the shock-charger input on any of the Anniversary's data screens and route it to charge the device.

Oshly was working in the avionics area; the deck was situated one level below flight command and one above the hangar. While accessing the STL-5's central system, Oshly noticed that they'd used up more than he'd anticipated of the device's power. Oshly thought to himself, *This is going to be a problem.* He knew it wouldn't be long until they would run out of the energy required to maintain stealth, and without access to a source to recharge, the device could be rendered useless just when they needed it most.

Ven reached out to Oshly on the ship's internal communications to the mechanic's level, "Osh, are you up? You need to rest up, man."

"I'm trying to get the STL fully charged, and it's ticking me off. This is way harder than it should be."

Oshly then went into detail explaining what the issue was. Most MMWs would have the unique shock chargers on board, but very few machines used the type of power supply the STL-5 did, which was one of the reasons they came to the Moon in the first place.

"I was taking stock of what was available for power storage on the ship, when I noticed that there were two power blocks built into the ship in place of the standard fuel cells. I figured I could charge those blocks with the MoonStation shock chargers. Unfortunately, they were built into the electronics and could not be removed." Oshly sighed with frustration.

"You're tech-babbling, Osh. Get to it," said Ven.

"Ugh, sorry. So, anyway, I'm only going to get half of the usual charge into each power block, but that should be enough to keep the STL working, even if we need to make another planetary run after the return to Earth, and *that* really all depends on what crafts and how many we would be cloaking, draining more power. I'll offset the backup by maxing out the reserve power on the remaining four T-Crafts and the entire power supply module from your T-Craft, which we already gutted since we're leaving it behind anyhow. The power recharge and fuel bonding cables are already attached to our T-Crafts on board and Taft's and Kaytha's on the landing the pad.

I've taken the liberty of routing the power supplies to their respective locations."

"Osh, can you tell me just what I need to know and do it before we get back to Earth?"

"It's gonna take an hour or two for everything to charge and fuel. We should have enough juice in the cloaking device for the trip back and maybe, just maybe, we can stretch that. I can't take the recharging equipment with us. We're going to have to find the adapters I need to recharge the device someplace else."

"Keep me posted, but not before you get some sleep."

Oshly thought, *As if I could sleep with everything going on.* He wrapped up his work in the hangar bay, making the last fueling connections. Now that he was finished, he pulled a few mechanic's pads and a clean cloth tarp out of a supply closet, putting together a makeshift bed in the hangar bay for a nap. Jebet was already way ahead of him in the sleep department. She'd already gone to the crew's quarters where she found a bare mattress and plastic wrapped pillow. She stretched her arms, exhausted, and quickly passed out.

Ven continued to pour over data from the Anniversary memory bank. He first went looking for any crew logs only to discover that all the relevant info had been scrubbed.

The only information he could find was a file with clickable links that read:

A1: Operator Profile-N/A

A1: Flight Hours

A1: Power Plant Specifications

A1: In Flight Performance Data

A1: Travel History-N/A

A1: AI Assisted On Board OS

A1: Maintenance Records

Apart from where it had traveled, a complete picture of the Anniversary was all there. It was even more impressive than the rumors people told. Ven came to the conclusion that either someone was trying to sell it or needed to keep their identity secret but that didn't include ship capabilities.

A continuous series of three beeps came in rapid succession from the engineering terminal on the flight deck. Ven pulled up a duplicate screen from the pilot's monitor and realized that the sound was the fueling and charging indicator, showing that Oshly had finished up and they were now completely powered. Ven was keeping an eye on the time and estimated that a few more hours could be spared. It was just enough time for the others to keep resting.

Ven planned on using this rare moment of quiet to continue getting accustomed to the Anniversary.

Another alarm from the communications area rang out. The long-range scanners were picking up approaching ships. A quick look at the data display showed whoever was coming was still at least four hours out, even if traveling at max speed. Ven figured if he could see them, they were scanning too. Ven immediately pulled up the STL, which was now linked into the ship's systems, and switched it on. "What the hell?!" Ven cursed when nothing happened. Not wasting any time, he used the ship's internal BIO ID scan and located Oshly in the belly of the Anniversary. On emergency comms, he yelled, "Osh! Wake up! I need you on the flight deck!"

Ven also sent an alert to Taft and Kaytha that would override their "do not disturb" setting on their personal network devices. He knew they still had a few hours, but if the STL was offline, they no longer had time to spare without the ability to hide from whoever was coming.

****

Club Montepulciano Hotel, MoonStation

The hotel suite where Taft and Kaytha slept was pitch black and silent apart from the humming of the room's AC unit. Taft sat straight up in bed as the wailing clang of repeating tones that rang out through their room woke him from where his dreams had taken him.

Taft got up and stumbled barefoot across the floor toward the blue light flashing from the screen on his jacket's right sleeve. Not wanting to alarm Kaytha, he gently climbed back on the bed and nudged her shoulders softly.

"Kaytha, nap time's over. Something's up. We need to head back."

With her head still buried in the pillow, she mumbled groggily, "Didn't I tell you last night this was going to happen?"

"Yes, I know you did, you're always right. But can you blame me?"

"I was hoping for a few more hours, is it urgent?"

"Doesn't appear so. He's just wanting us to head back to the hangar."

"Alright, let me wake up, and we'll get out of here," replied Kaytha, yawning through the majority of her response. "I still need a shower too," she added.

While Kaytha and Taft made preparations to return to their friends, Oshly knew loud and clear the moment Ven comm'd him that this was an urgent matter.

Oshly, already on the flight deck looking over the STL-5 settings, said, "It's the same thing as before, Ven. I don't know what gives."

He stared at the HIREZ screen, clueless on what to do next.

"Should you climb under the ship and get a hands-on look at it?"

"There really isn't anything to look at. The device is functioning properly, just like it always has, but the stealth function simply won't turn on. It's like something just keeps switching its core functionality off. I don't know where the command to that is because it doesn't have one."

Ven knew that the more time that passed, the closer the cluster of ships was to arriving at their location. "Osh, if the STL isn't working then we gotta get out of here. We'll have to tell the others and leave right now!"

"Okay, okay, Ven," Oshly said in frustration. "I'll start preparations in the hangar. Can you keep an eye on the systems display? Every other time this happened it always turned back on when we needed it."

Ven knew there was no good reason to continue keeping his friends in the dark about the STL-5 issues, but he didn't want to lose their trust and a lot of time had gone by.

****

Kaytha and Taft were back downstairs in the central area of the entertainment ballroom. Kaytha felt the need to return the room access card from where she found it.

Watching Kaytha return the card, with a slight laugh Taft said, "What, are you hoping to get the security deposit back?"

"Ha, ha."

Taft found a sack near the kitchen area and started loading it up with processed packaged food bars and dehydrated packets of fruits and vegetables. Once he had all that he could carry, he walked over to the entryway and waited for Kaytha to catch up.

Before they walked out the doors, Kaytha grabbed Taft's free hand, stopping him before the automatic doors could be triggered. Taft spun around as she threw her arms around him and gave him a kiss.

"I don't know when we'll have the opportunity again. Now let's get going," said Kaytha, as she then walked past him out into the artificial air. Taft stalled in place for a moment, then hurried out the door to catch Kaytha, who was already jogging back to their friends.

****

Ven was seated at the flight operations console. For the Anniversary to be flown by a single pilot, the flight systems that would typically be operated by the co-pilot were either transferred to the pilot's flight controls or set to automation.

Automation for the co-pilot didn't offer the optimal flying options or ability to take full advantage of what the ship was capable of doing. However, with a skilled enough pilot at the controls, the ship could outrun and outperform most T-Crafts of smaller weight and size. Ven finished up the final automation implementations when he heard a familiar ping echo through the cockpit from his pilot's systems screen. The STL-5 had turned back on again. He looked over to view the monitor of the closed-circuit hangar cameras, confirming indeed that the Anniversary was cloaked once again by the STL-5.

****

On approach to MoonStation

Rosel had just switched off his comms when the large heat scan disappeared from his screen. Now only the faint signatures of the two ships on the landing pad and a few signs of life were visible. Rosel quickly did a rescan and checked for any craft leaving the surface, but there was nothing. He opened a direct comm to Uray Dow's ship. "One to Number Four, acknowledge."

"I read, Number One."

"I've patched my scan data to your craft. I'm going to replay the previous few minutes. Advise if possible."

Uray watched the same scan as Rosel, seeing the larger heat "sigs" disappear from the data screen.

"Four to Number One, this is the same anomaly I witnessed during my O-Station attack run. Given that the thermal signature diminished slowly, along with the remaining heat and bio scans, I can say with confidence that we have probably found what Commander Argum is looking for. The larger signature that dissipated could be where the device is located."

****

Kaytha and Taft arrived at the hangar bay. Taft had already stowed the food he'd gathered on one his T-Craft's outboard storage compartments before walking to where the Anniversary was parked. With the ship sitting idle, it was surrounded by the radiating wave distortions of light.

Jebet, Oshly, Taft, and Kaytha were gathered together again in the Anniversary's cargo bay.

"Are we getting outta here? Why is the STL cloaking the Anniversary?" asked a confused Kaytha.

"Ven will be here in a second to give all the details, but we have a handful of vehicles heading our way. He thinks it might be the party we left behind after the station attack."

Oshly, trying to avoid making eye contact with anyone, stared at the workbench, especially since he could feel Jebet glaring at him.

"We all better be happy the device is working because according to ol' Osh here, that hasn't always been the case, has it, Oshly?!" barked Jebet, who was clearly agitated with Oshly.

The door to the upper decks opened in the middle of Jebet's ranting.

"No, it hasn't, and I knew about it, too," Ven explained as he walked down the short flight of steps to the floor of the cargo bay. "We experienced the STL shutting down. Once, before we left. That was the first time. But in my and Oshly's defense, we figured we were in no danger at the time of using it to test and make this run. None of us could have expected what's happening on Earth."

Kaytha was growing angrier by the second. "What were the other times, Ven? Oshly?"

Ven continued to speak for Oshly. "It shut off for a brief period after the O-Station attack, but we assumed it was the blast that knocked it out. Then when I spotted the approaching craft, I tried to switch it on, and it didn't respond."

Oshly tried to lighten the mood. "But, like I told Ven, it's always worked when we needed it, like right now. Right, Ven?"

Ven simply stared straight faced back at Oshly.

"Any ideas what the issue is?" asked Taft.

"We've looked at all the data and it's running exactly as it should. Diagnostics don't show anything out of the ordinary. I feel like we're missing something, maybe a time delay or some sleep mode we're not aware of," said Oshly.

"Nevertheless, it's working now, and we have to get out of here before whoever is racing toward us gets here," Ven said.

"Whoever? Why don't we find out who these guys are?" asked Kaytha.

Jebet then asked, "What are you thinking, Kay?"

"Let's fly off the surface cloaked. We can watch them, and then, when they leave, we could even follow them back, while remaining in the stealth wake."

"Sounds good. We need to get to an O-Station and plug into the network, see if I can get any intel on EnerCon and DeCorp. Then we can look at heading home," said Ven.

"If home is still home," Jebet interjected.

With their next move in place, the friends worked to depart as soon as possible. Oshly and Jebet already had their ships prepared, and the STL-5 was as charged as it could be until the next time they came in contact with the right facilities or equipment to recharge it.

The question of power consumption by the device was on Ven's mind. When Kaytha and Taft initially found the device, it was technically turned on, so the only reference point Oshly had was based on the power usage since they had possession of it. Once they were back on Earth, the device might be useless in their own evacuation plans, which included, hopefully, joining up with someone trustworthy inside EnerCon. Ven would keep the others in the dark so as not to worry them and manage the STL-5 usage the best he could. If they needed to use the STL-5 beyond what he and Oshly anticipated, then they would have a discussion with the others.

The Anniversary was finally fully charged and fueled, as were its backup systems, which was more than enough to keep it flying with power to spare for the other T-Crafts for at least a few weeks. Jebet pulled the power charging and fuel lines to Kaytha's and Taft's T-Crafts once they reached their respective maximum levels. The friends and their technological gear were now all well rested, fed, fueled, and better prepared for the journey ahead than when they'd left Earth.

Kaytha and Taft, both strapped to their cockpit seats, began running over their ships' system gauges.

Taft was the first to direct comm with Kaytha as they waited for the Anniversary to begin its departure from the hangar. "You know, Kay, if it wasn't for the fact that we're apparently being chased by some bad dudes and the Earth's future's in jeopardy, we could all go wherever we wanted."

"You're not seriously joking again right now, are you?"

"No, of course not. It's just a better thought then whatever may lie ahead."

"It's for a reason, Taft. You know that."

"You're right," replied Taft, while he started the engine cycles on his T-Craft. "I want to know my family is safe—that your mom is safe. But apart from that, nothing is ever going to be the same."

Kaytha understood what he meant and felt the same. "We have each other right now—you, me, Ven, Jeb, and Osh. It's important we just take this one step at a time. We need to find out who's after us, then try and find someone who knows what's going on, either at NASA or EnerCon…"

Kaytha stopped talking as she heard the Anniversary rising up and out of the hangar, coming into view once it reached the hangar bay doors, close enough now to shroud their T-Crafts in its stealth coverage. The huge ship was a beautiful sight, impressive enough parked in the hangar and majestic as it flew completely out from the building it had been housed in.

Ven was at the controls while Oshly sat in the engineering comms stations and Jebet handled the flight systems and defenses, if needed. The Anniversary hovered above Kaytha and Taft, still parked on the landing pad as Ven swung the huge ship around to allow them to fly up behind them. Oshly had transferred all the custom STL-5 guidance systems he'd created to the Anniversary; that way they could keep in the stealth wake just as they had on the way out.

Ven comm'd to Kaytha and Taft. "Alright, guys, whoever it is we're waiting for is almost here. Go radio silent until you hear again from me."

"Ven, I trust your judgment, but we need to know who these people are, and if they are indeed after us," said Kaytha.

"I'll keep us at a distance so we can find out what we're potentially dealing with, but we're gone the moment I feel the situation is unsafe, copy?"

"Copy," Taft and Kaytha both responded, eyeing each other through the lifted visors of both their helmets as they rose side by side looking out their cockpit canopies.

With comms off, Ven, started his flight out to the perimeter of the Moon Station, throttling up the Anniversary, getting his first feel of its weight, power, and agility. *I'm never giving this thing back,* he thought, as a smile came across his face.

Chapter 31

Tober Rosel and his group of attackers now had the Moon in sight.

Rosel checked his scanned data. "Damn it!" He immediately realized he'd keyed all comms to the other fighters.

"Number Three to One, what is it?"

Trying to cover up his obvious mistake of allowing his pilots to hear his frustrations, Rosel replied, "Everyone, the contacts we were looking for have dropped from my screens. Number Four believes this is who we are looking for. However, we may have lost our opportunity. Stay in attack formation and weapons ready."

Tober switched over to comm with Sint. "Rosel, mission update for Argum, awaiting acknowledgment."

Sint, the Oberkorn, and its reduced fleet were making their way to rendezvous with Akens Ember's MMW. Ember, having barely escaped from Earth, was on his way with the supplies and crew to MarsCorp when Sint decided to regroup with him.

Sint was overly concerned while his best pilots were away on their mission. If anyone challenged him, he would be vulnerable. He was paranoid, which was what made him a threat to those under him. Sint rationalized all of his actions, his mind now hard-wired into believing that what he did was just and righteous. Because of the catastrophe playing out on Earth, no one would have time to worry about what he had done.

Sint keyed his comm to get the status update from Tober Rosel.

"Rosel, have you located our targets?"

"No, sir. We were reading life forms and vehicles signatures. Number Four..."

Sint cut off Rosel's train of thought. "Number Four?"

"Uray Dow."

"Oh, right. I forgot your cute way of numbering your pilots. Please continue."

Tober Rosel despised Sint Argum for speaking to him in such a condescending manner, but he also knew that if anyone would find the easiest of an excuse to end someone's life, it was Sint.

"We've lost all contact and your pilot, Dow, believes that they've gone dark again using the same method they used at the O-Station. We're on track and should arrive in less than thirty minutes."

Subdued anger could be heard in Sint's reply. "Do what you can to locate them. They cannot have gone far. When you have exhausted all options, execute Operation *Put a Bow On It*."

The communication went silent. Rosel knew what this meant and was stunned that Sint was going to take things this far.

Sint paced the floor while he waited for Rosel's confirmation and noticed that Director Vivsou had turned to look at him with a gaze that held a level of concern rarely shown. Sint stared back at Vivsou, then Sint keyed his comm. "Do you acknowledge the order, Rosel, or shall I comm one of your pilots to confirm my order instead? I'm sure any of them would be more than willing for a promotion."

Rosel fell in line. "Confirmed."

"Very well," replied Sint, a smirk appearing on his smug face, along with a raised eyebrow at Vivsou. "And do you, Vivsou, have a problem with my orders?"

Vivsou quickly convinced himself that Earth most likely had no future, regardless of what Sint Argum ordered.

However, he had a great desire to continue a future alive and in one piece, so Vivsou responded with, "No, sir. No problem at all."

Sint Argum had devised Operation: *Put a Bow On It* shortly before the disaster at the South Dakota West Quadrant DeCorp facility had spiraled out of control. He'd had the foresight to have a plan in place should things ever progress to the point of having to implement Operation: Hot Springs, and that mankind's future while away from Earth would be up for the taking. DeCorp already had a foothold on Mars plus other resources scattered across the planets of our solar system. Operation: *Put a Bow On It* was designed to finish the job of Earth's destruction—plain and simple.

Blowing up the power plant on MoonStation would lead to nothing short of the total destruction of Earth's Moon.

The infrastructure built on the Moon pushed deep beneath its surface. There were a few different outposts scattered across the lunar landscape. MoonStation was the central facility, the other locations were strictly for fueling/charging, some minor repair hangars, and a few larger housing units. All owned by various groups tied to either DeCorp, EnerCon, or UGEC. The power plant located in the center of MoonStation ran a pipeline through the entire Moon's core to all the other locations. Much like the chain reaction and destruction of Earth via the pipelines of EnerCon, Sint Argum planned to duplicate the destruction on the Moon.

****

Above Moon Station

The friends were back in formation. The computer program Oshly had installed to keep everyone in the stealth wake emanating from the Anniversary was again doing its job. Ven had the three ships flying in low orbit around MoonStation, taking the time to get familiar with the Anniversary as he took the ship through a series of banks and turns at various speeds. Ven had the sense to not simply waste time while they waited for the mysterious ships to arrive. The two following T-Crafts of Taft and Kaytha stayed right in line with the Anniversary as Ven proceeded with his impromptu practice flight. Ven was disappointed he had to leave his T-Craft behind; he was proud of that fighter (as he considered it). Ven was also aware that his friends were more important than any beloved ship. After flying the Anniversary in empty space above Earth's Moon, Ven all but forgot the now stripped out T-Craft he left behind on the surface.

Oshly and Jebet were keeping busy in their new positions as the Anniversary's flight crew. Jebet diligently did what she could to familiarize herself with the Anniversary's mechanics and how it functioned in flight. She was also searching for ways to maximize power output, depending on what systems were necessary, and what could be powered down to add to their advantage.

Jebet had been looking forward to getting acquainted with the Anniversary's weapons system—which was extensive. Most of the ship's weaponry was tucked out of view, hidden behind external compartment panels along the surface of the ship. But just under the huge front canopy window of the flight deck and the nose of the Anniversary was a menacing gun mount that housed a little of everything.

Pulling up the ship's defense capability manifest, Jebet took the liberty of sending it over to Ven's system:

A1: DEFENSE PACKAGE: Armament

Projectile Launch Racks: Port/Aft 20x Available Ports

 2x Compartment EnerCon Cannon (auto-reload)

Forward 100 Cal Machine Gun (auto-reload)

3x DeCorp IXZ Focus Plasma Blaster

14x EnerCon NUC-Propulsion Heat Seek Blast Tip Missile

The Anniversary wasn't created for war, but those that made it certainly liked to blow stuff up. For a ship that was built more for bragging rights and not combat, it was more than ready for combat, almost more than most military machines were.

Oshly was learning the Anniversary's digital language.

The ship wasn't all that different from most T-Crafts, apart from further redundancies being in place for a vehicle of its size. Once Oshly had a general idea of how the onboard operating system worked, he turned his attention to the inner workings of the STL-5. Oshly felt terrible for having deceived his friends about the random shutting off of the device and was now determined to figure out why it was happening. He created a duplicate of the STL-5 OS that was now running in tandem onboard the Anniversary. With the copy of the device operating system, he could delve further into its utilities, poke around, change settings, and monitor fluctuations without having it impact the device in its current operation.

Ven slowed up his flight practice. The incoming ships were now only several minutes out from reaching MoonStation. Ven's flight path took the Anniversary, with Kaytha and Taft in tow, into a circular pattern around the outskirts of the MoonStation. The tension, sense of unease and uncertainty was increasing within Ven; for Oshly it was curiosity.

Oshly's attention was hyper-focused on a particular set of graphic readouts from deep inside the STL-5 OS.

Oshly zeroed in on the output waves from the STL-5 and discovered that within the stealth stream was a secondary set of waves completely different from the ones creating the stealth wake. The secondary waves, fluctuating in tandem with the stealth waves, appeared to change the strength of the stealth wake itself.

Oshly was onto something, a theory was forming, but he wouldn't be ready to share it until he had more hard data to back it up.

Oshly was typing in notes to a text file; he was notorious for coming up with great ideas only to forget them later. His concentration was broken when he finally heard Jebet, who'd been attempting to get his attention for several minutes.

"Oshly! Dude, wake up! Jeeze, man, you're lost in your computer geek-dom."

"What? Sorry, I was onto something…" said Oshly, smiling knowing that redemption from his friends was in his grasp if he could crack the mystery of the STL-5.

Ven, while piloting the Anniversary, interrupted their exchange.

"They're almost here. Stay sharp. If anything goes south, I'm going to need you two to help get all of us outta here."

Jebet was quick in calling out Ven for talking like he was in charge. "Okay big guy, it's not like we haven't flown before. Don't go pulling rank on us."

****

Rosel and his team closed in on the Moon, unaware that those they were seeking were flying close by.

Rosel opened up all comms to the other DeCorp MTCs. "All craft begin scanning the surface. I want full coverage, so set your depth

200 feet, in case anyone is underground. Number Four, follow me to the E-section. Two and Three, stay together and give me complete over-flight coverage of the entire facility. Again, scan wide and deep and make multiple runs."

Rosel switched off his comms and keyed one-to-one with Uray Dow. "Number Four, everything is off my scopes. I assume whoever we're looking for is either a good distance away from here or, assuming your intel is true, they could still be cloaked in the area. Is there anything you can add?"

"For a brief moment at O-Station, I believe I entered into whatever field they were producing that was shielding them from view. If they are still in the area, we would need to figure out how to get inside their coverage zone, or…"

"Or what, Four?"

"Sir, after the destruction of the station, that's when I located them. The blast had apparently scattered them. It wasn't until they regrouped that I lost them," Dow replied.

"Understood. We're arriving over the area, so let's do a few passes."

"Should we land and search the area?"

"No need. I'm certain, based on our readings, that they already left the surface, but are still in the area."

"Why is that?"

"Because I would be," replied Rosel, assuming the targets were cloaked nearby, gaining intel.

Rosel direct comm'd to Sint Argum on the secure channel. "T. Rosel to Commander Argum."

Rosel hadn't used the symbolic commander title in a while, but seeing he was about to commit the Earth to total destruction, he was also investing his allegiance to Sint Argum and cementing his role within the ranks of Sint's military.

"Argum responding. Rosel, have you have found them?"

"No, commander. They disappeared from our scans before our arrival. We've detected no signs of life. I believe *Operation: Put a Bow on It* may assist in my efforts. Requesting permission to execute?"

Sint was beyond frustrated.

It was driving him mad not knowing who possessed the device he so desperately desired.

"Permission granted. Execute and destroy the Moon at your discretion." Sint didn't even bother with the official operation title. His arrogance and growing thirst for power made him proud of what was about to happen.

Chapter 32

Above Moon Station

From the moment the four T-Crafts came into view, Ven immediately knew who they were, where they were from, and that they were coming for him and his friends.

"The lead ship is Tober Rosel. He used to be military, now he's more mercenary. I heard he'd joined up with DeCorp. He's been flying that T of his for a year. He's not to be messed with," said Ven.

"Check it out. That's the scum that blew up the O-Station and spotted us. Appears he's working for DeCorp, too," said Jebet, gesturing toward her HIREZ monitor.

Oshly went back to his seat while Jebet and Ven watched as the four T-Crafts continued scanning the Moon base.

"Osh, can you send a message to Taft and Kaytha's monitors? One small enough that they won't pick up on the transmission?" asked Ven. "Let them know that these guys are DeCorp hired guns, definitely looking for us, and to follow my lead."

"Easy enough," Oshly replied, then added, "Done...and message received."

Ven wanted to watch the DeCorp fighters for a bit longer before they started heading home.

****

The four DeCorp T-Crafts made several passes over MoonStation but found nothing. Rosel decided he'd searched long enough.

"Two and Three, ready weapons and form up behind me. We're executing a new directive." Rosel swung his T-Craft up and away from the Moon's surface. Dow (Four) followed as Number Three, and Two changed their flight path, positioning behind Number One (Rosel). Once everyone was in place, Rosel changed his flight path, flying out away from the Moon.

****

Ven, with Kaytha and Taft still hidden in the stealth wake, continued following a circular pattern around the base's perimeter, keeping at roughly one thousand feet off the Moon's surface. Watching as the DeCorp ships seemingly began to fly away, Ven started breathing easy. He chose to maintain their current position since the DeCorp ships appeared to be heading home, and at that moment Ven got an idea.

The Anniversary, with Kaytha and Taft following behind, was about to pass over the massive power station that included the cylindrical power generation lines that ran from the structure to the rest of the Moon. Ven was about to relay his idea to Oshly, but then, a sudden turn of the DeCorp fighters caught him entirely off guard.

In an instant, Rosel put his T-Craft into a one hundred and eighty degree flip, and his three attackers followed. Speeding their way back toward where the invisible ships were still located, all four DeCorp T-Crafts angled down, heading straight for MoonStation.

****

On the flight deck of the Anniversary, Ven thought, *Surely they hadn't seen us. The device was still and they were all hidden in the stealth wake.*

Then he came to a shocking realization. Breaking radio silence, Ven comm'd Taft and Kaytha. "Escape and evade! They're about to attack the power plant!"

Ven went full throttle on the Anniversary's mighty engines, pushing the ship vertical. Taft and Kaytha desperately tried to stay in the stealth wake. Ven noticed on his HIREZ screen that the heat signatures were increasing from the mounted guns on the four T-Craft MTCs, indicating they were about to fire.

****

Rosel sent the attack plan to his pilots' data systems but decided to also give verbal instructions.

"All craft, fire on the power plant and supply lines, all weapons hot, launch at will!"

While Rosel was still speaking the command into his helmet microphone, he and the other three launched a pair of heat-seeking EnerCon thermal explosive tipped missiles. They followed the launch with multiple plasma cannon blasts and a barrage of high capacity rounds from their forward-facing guns. Everything they fired was on target to the Moon-base's power supply buildings. The plasma blasts struck the pipelines with punishing force, the ammo rounds shredded everything in their path. The four T-Crafts were flying at such a fast speed they sailed right past the missiles they launched, maneuvering up and over the colossal power generating structure, rocketing into space above the Moon as the building exploded behind them. It looked as if a nuclear bomb had been detonated. Huge chunks of debris went hurtling from the impact site. The four attacking ships were far enough away to be out of danger. The Anniversary, along Taft and Kaytha in their T-Crafts, weren't so lucky. The shock wave hit all three ships as they tried to escape the blast radius. Still protected from view, the first wave of energy struck the sides of the vessels, sending them spinning in different directions; it was a repeat of the O-Station attack.

****

Ven quickly went about utilizing all of the Anniversary's main and smaller directional thrusters to contain the spinning, while Taft and Kaytha struggled to keep their ships stable. Taft's thrusters were online as he searched for the Moon to find a direction out his canopy.

Kaytha was disorientated, flipping on the autopilot, figuring the onboard computer would do what she was currently unable. Kaytha's OS went to work adjusting the thruster speed to at least get the craft pointed straight. Seconds felt like minutes, and soon Ven, Taft, and Kaytha realized they were completely exposed. Taft and Kaytha's ships were too far away to hide behind the cloaking capabilities of the STL-5 on the Anniversary, as the situation was about to get much worse.

"The STL is offline again!" Oshly yelled out. However, Ven, Jebet, Taft, and Kaytha were already well aware of this fact, as they saw that the four DeCorp ships immediately changed direction and were splitting up to engage them.

Ven directed all available power to the thrusters, attempting to put distance between the Anniversary and two of the attackers, especially Tober Rosel.

Ven yelled out, "Jebet, put every weapons system we got online now. I'll handle all forward facing guns. Get into the secondary weapons chair and get on anything we can fire back at these clowns!"

Oshly, unsure exactly what help he could offer, thought, *Maybe I'll head to the hangar bay, jump in my ride and help Kaytha and Taft?* He quickly realized that wasn't the best move, opting to bring up the operating system for the STL-5.

If he was going to figure out what was shutting it down, he had to do it now. Oshly strapped into his chair as the Anniversary rocked violently back and forth thanks to Ven's evasive maneuvers. Oshly hammered in the data as he was receiving it from the STL-5. The stealth waves had gone dead, but the second set of waves were still active…

****

It soon became clear to Tober Rosel that the Anniversary was far faster than his DeCorp MTCs. Upon coming to this realization, Rosel barked out his next orders, "Number Two, break off your pursuit and reroute to the other evaders. The Anniversary will follow suit." Adding under his breath, "They're going to have to."

****

"Ven, they're going after Kaytha and Taft!" yelled out Jebet.

"Kaytha, Taft, we're coming around. The STL is offline, so we're going to have to fight this out if it doesn't come back." Ven didn't expect a response— they were too busy trying to outmaneuver the two other attackers.

As he pointed the Anniversary back toward his friends, Ven shouted at Oshly, "Can you hack into the lead the ship? We need the data from his on-board!"

Oshly hesitated as it looked like the STL-5 scanner was zeroing in on something. He feared this moment might be his only chance to solve this mystery.

"I'm on it, Ven!" Oshly yelled back, shutting off the STL's OS, bringing the Anniversary's small, rectangular dish online and directing it onto Tober Rosel's T-Craft.

Rosel was too busy navigating around the fragments of debris blowing off the Moon from its initial explosion. He didn't notice the external network attachment indication on his HIREZ on-board system screen.

Oshly murmured to himself while he broke into the OS system of the enemy, "I'm in now and invading your system…"

"Oshly, did you get in?" asked Ven.

"I'm in and running the system hack now…"

It took only seconds for Oshly to access Rosel's OS. Military T-Craft's systems were reasonably simple to crack, because even if someone did, it was easy to track the hacker to the source. All these things were irrelevant since Oshly didn't care if they found out it was him— he only cared about getting in.

"Ok, I'm pulling everything I can and transferring data back to our system."

Ven was catching up to Rosel and Uray Dow as they gained on Number Two and Three who were trying to take out Taft and Kaytha. The pilots were good but lacking in the experience Kaytha and Taft had.

The DeCorp T-Craft fighters were faster, but so far, incapable of getting a clean shot on either of their targets. The Anniversary was a fast ship, certainly much quicker than any other spacecraft its size.

As Ven began closing in on the dogfight taking place over the erupting Moon, Oshly yelled out, "The STL is coming back online. It keeps popping off and on, but I think we're going to get it back!"

Even if the STL-5 came back online, it did them no good unless they could get their friends safely into the stealth wake, and right now, they were too busy evading plasma blasts.

Ven direct comm'd with Kaytha and Taft. "Guys, as soon as you can, break, loop up and away, back toward my position!" It was a risk, but he assumed the DeCorp assassins were too busy to be dealing with monitoring their communications.

Ven was betting the other four T-Crafts would follow a direct path behind them, allowing Ven to arc the Anniversary up and toward them, hopefully giving Taft and Kaytha a chance to fall into the stealth wake. Suddenly, three plasma blasts flashed between Taft and Kaytha while all four DeCorp attackers were now fighting together in tandem, attempting to take them out.

Rosel was irate, his flying reckless, making him incapable of landing a shot on either of them.

Kaytha directed more power to her thrusters, throttling up as she quickly pulled back on her joystick, sending her T-craft upside down from where she'd been flying. Taft followed her lead as they made a full turn, spiraling their ships upright relative to the Moon, flying as fast as they could toward the Anniversary. The gamble paid off—the four attackers didn't react soon enough to adjust their course as they rocketed in the opposite direction. The moment Ven had Taft and Kaytha in his sight heading toward them, Oshly attempted to power on the STL-5 capabilities. To everyone's relief, it was operating again.

This was where all the lazy weekends of flying paid off. Ven knew his friends would keep to their course as the Anniversary disappeared in front of them. Ven swung the Anniversary around, putting Kaytha and Taft behind it and within seconds they slipped into the stealth wake, seeing the Anniversary reappear in front on their canopy windows. Taft and Kaytha pulled up the STL-5 program Oshly had created on their systems. They were in the green, safely hidden behind the stealth wake.

Ven made a sharp turn out and away from the four T-craft fighters, making sure they were out of their flight path. Oshly messaged Taft and Kaytha:

Oshly ID Taft, Kaytha: max speed to get out of destruction path. I've hacked one of their T-Craft, decoding the encryption now. Anniversary will maintain pace. Radio silence until Ven gives all clear.

Taft and Kaytha were flying aside each other behind the Anniversary and close enough to see into their cockpits, illuminated by their flight controls and internal helmet lights. In unison, they flipped up their visors to see each other. Taft didn't have to speak, and neither did Kaytha; their eyes said everything.

Onboard the Anniversary, after a few minutes of awkward silence, Jebet broke the mood. "Guys, that's twice now DeCorp jerks have shown up, blown stuff to hell, and basically knocked us on our asses. Next time, can we please just go the other way and not hang around?"

Ven acknowledged Jebet's frustration but was more concerned if Oshly got what they needed. "Did you complete the hack on the ship?"

"I got everything he had, but its security's encrypted. I'm going to run a hack to get the data."

As the Anniversary, now completely out of sight, powered away, Tober Rosel and his attackers also made haste away from the Moon. The destruction of MoonStation's power core began sending massive chunks of its surface flying toward Earth and deep space. Mini-nuclear explosions were occurring within moments of each other as the final remnants of the station's power supply lines exploded with intense fury. Over the next hour, the Moon would become nothing but millions of pieces of rock and debris that would spell further destruction to the Earth for centuries to come.

Many of the lunar fragments would be too small to bond back together via gravity and would quickly begin to spread. The more significant chunks of Moon debris would hurtle toward the Earth, eventually penetrating the planet's atmosphere. Fragments would turn into molten rocks of destruction. Whatever remained of the Moon would eventually enter the orbit of Earth's gravity, and, when it did, unlike rings of other planets, particles would break free and slam into the Earth's surface for years, continuing its bombardment without rhyme or reason. It was the stuff of extinction level event nightmares and a dream that only Sint Argum would have to help propel his plan to rule the galaxy through fear, might, and intimidation.

****

Far away from the destruction, en route to MarsCorp on the Oberkorn, Sint answered Tober Rosel's direct comm, "Rosel, I see by our long-range scanners you have proceeded with the operation as ordered?"

"Yes, commander. However, we lost sight of our target. We engaged two small T-Crafts, the pilots of which were well skilled. We also came across The Anniversary. Based on what we witnessed and with the intel Dow provided, I believe the device you seek does exist and is currently onboard the Anniversary."

Sint pounded his fist in agitation against the terminal in front of him on the flight deck. His best military man failed to gain possession or even destroy the device.

For now, the confirmation of its existence and the destruction of the Moon meant the mission wasn't a total loss. After regaining his composure, Sint replied tersely, "I'm disappointed, Rosel, in your inability to recover what I seek. Do you have any idea where the famed Anniversary might be heading?"

"The last supposed location was in southern Arizona, but it's been at least a year since the back channel networks reported its last sighting."

"Rosel, I want you and your pilots to plot a safe course back to Earth and the O-Station currently in orbit over the Southwest United States. Let no one stand in your way of refueling the crafts. Be prepared to depart in twenty-four hours. I'll order a bounty be placed on the Anniversary. These enemies of DeCorp will be discovered."

"We're currently en route to the O-Station now."

Chapter 33

Space, headed for Earth

Taft and Kaytha continued to follow the Anniversary, as they left the destruction of the Moon behind them. Ven, still manning the ship's controls, knew he needed to get some sleep but was keenly aware that he was responsible for putting everyone in danger since it seemed he'd been the one who'd persuaded the others to go on the Moon-run in the first place. He also believed that it was *for a reason*, but he still felt the burden of being the one with the most combat experience. Ven knew he could have handled things better and probably could have avoided the altercation altogether if he'd had them start back home before any threat arrived. He wasn't going to offer apologies. The team wasn't expecting it; he wasn't the type to provide sorries. *Team,* he thought to himself. He had been thinking of them as a team, ever since the O-Station. This team now had a job, a quest, a destiny, and Ven vowed to make better choices when it came to his friends' safety.

Ven slowed the Anniversary's average speed for the return trip. They all needed a little extra time.

Earth was in a state of disaster, and he knew it was more important for his friends to be mentally prepared for what would come next than to rush back to whatever was left. Setting the autopilot, he looked over the flight systems as he prepared to hand the flight chair over to Jebet, so he could attempt to get some sleep.

Now that they were clear of what used to be the Moon, Jebet began focusing again on the Anniversary's standards of operation. Learning the locations of the ship's essentials was of top concern. If anything needed fixing, she needed to find it. Jebet had already reprogramed the auto avoidance system and trained its relays from the front of the craft to the rear. The Moon's destruction created hundreds of thousands of tiny chunks of lunar surface flying like bullets toward them and Earth. The Anniversary was far enough from the blast that there wasn't a substantial threat, but Jebet was not one to take any risks—especially if there was an easier, safer option. By her calculations they still had plenty of time to make the journey back to Arizona before any larger chunks of the lunar surface started making their way through Earth's atmosphere.

Ven began to get up from the pilot's seat. "Hey, Jebet, have you switched over the guidance avoidance system yet? We have a lot of junk coming at us from behind."

"Already took care of it, but check your HIREZ screen display, just to make sure."

This was the final confirmation for Ven that he could sleep soundly, knowing Jebet was keeping an eye on things.

Jebet pressed off the brightly lit red and yellow transfer button to move the computer systems she'd been working with to the pilot control OS. With the flip of a blue toggle switch, the navigation screen switched off from where she sat. Jebet decided to stand up as Ven walked by. She was almost half his size, not petite by female standards but slight next to Ven's considerable build and tall stance.

He placed a hand on her shoulder and said, "Holler if you need me."

Jebet reached out to hug him. Ven, with the weight of putting his friends in harm's way, welcomed the comfort. It was the first time since they'd dated years ago that Jebet was physical. She wasn't known for being very being emotional. "Get some sleep. I'll wake you up when we're close."

Jebet watched as Ven made his way toward Oshly and the exit door. She hoped he would get the rest she knew he needed and deserved.

Oshly was so busy getting the decryption program up and running that he didn't even notice Jebet was now flying the ship. It was going to take an hour or more to decode the data hack from the DeCorp T-Craft Tober Rosel was flying.

"How's it looking, Osh? Can we read anything yet?" asked Ven.

"Not yet. My program will get us the information, but the military-grade crypto is going to put it through its paces. You want me to wake you once it's done?"

"I do, but use your judgment. I know it's not gonna be good, but I don't think much is going to change our current plan. If you think it does, then yeah, wake me."

"Will do."

Ven walked out the auto-door of the flight deck and made his way directly to the first crew quarters he could find.

Oshly went back to work combing over the data he was unlocking from deep into the operating system of the STL-5. Having the duplicate software of the device to run simulations on was proving more than helpful—it was getting him closer to discovering the reason it kept shutting off, which apparently wasn't an accident. The auto-shutdown was in the design, and he was convinced he partly knew why. Oshly knew he needed to confirm his suspicions in the time it was going to take to travel back to Earth.

After having exhausted all the available info, Oshly turned his attention over to Earth's network feeds.

They were close enough now to pick up the outgoing signals without the need to do any outbound scanning, avoiding detection by anyone who might be looking for that sort of thing. Jebet was already monitoring, as was Kaytha and Taft from inside their T-Crafts. The news from the planet was grim. A large group of various crafts were heading away from Earth in their direction. Everything from EnerCon MMW's, transports, T-Crafts, leisure vehicles—all trying to escape the calamity and hoping to find refuge on the Moon.

Jebet was currently in control of the Anniversary while Ven continued to sleep. She was going to reroute the path home when the departing ships from Earth slowly, one by one, began to change course after witnessing the destruction.

Jebet keyed in the Blaster news feeds, allowing the app to play audio from all the news outlets in short audio streams. During breaking news events, this was the easiest way to listen to all the angles being covered. The feed began in the middle of a broadcast from a female reporter.

"...reporting live from just outside the Yellowstone blast radius as I'm just now receiving word that more factories are exploding. The chain reaction of the underground connections across the planet's pipelines...Wait, producer, that can't be right. This is planet-wide?..."

The first live streaming report cut off and immediately another one started. Jebet, Taft, and Kaytha were listening to the same scan feed as Oshly.

"...two companies that supply the world with the energy and fuel for our flying machines may also be partly responsible for our destruction. More reports are coming in as I speak. People by the thousands are fleeing the destruction and heading to the farthest reaches on the globe that are not caught in the blasts and shock waves that followed...."

"...experts are stating that Yellowstone will continue to erupt and as it does there will be nowhere to hide from the ash cloud and endless toxic winter to follow. The fate of the planet is sealed as... now I am receiving word that...our moon has...I'm sorry, my producer is telling me the information in my ear...The Moon has been destroyed?..."

"...Yes, to repeat, we can report that something has happened to our moon. Witnesses report a blinding light outside, and now officials inside DeCorp on their way to the MarsCorp facility are confirming that something—or someone—destroyed MoonStation..."

"…speaking on condition of anonymity, some inside DeCorp are saying a group of ships from Earth may be responsible for destroying the Moon, and that currently one of the leaders inside the company, namely Sint Argum may be launching a search for these people. We'll keep you informed…"

"…saying it's most likely EnerCon employees that did this to the Moon. Some are even speculating, Phil, that they may have sabotaged DeCorp here on Earth. We've attempted to reach officials in EnerCon, but they have not answered our…"

As Taft listened, he tried to figure out what the rationale was—why blow up the Moon? He came to the same conclusion that those inside EnerCon did. They figured DeCorp must have done it as an opening assault to try and lay claim to what would remain of the human race among the stars.

****

The Oberkron was still moving away from Earth, heading for Mars, as Sint sat on the flight deck. His twisted plan of making Earth completely uninhabitable was playing out better than he could have imagined, and with it, he was creating a much-needed division between what remained of Earth's biggest corporations. He alone had set DeCorp on a path to becoming the solar system's most significant superpower. Sint Argum would soon learn that he now had the power of propaganda to convince everyone under DeCorp that for the moment it was EnerCon who took away Earth's ability to survive past the planet's catastrophe. The only thing that could possibly stand in his way were heading back to Earth, custodians of a device that could shift the balance of power to whoever had it. They were also witnesses who could expose his part in the murder of his own people at the O-Station and ultimately the real destroyer of the world.

****

Inside her cockpit, Kaytha opened her comm channel to talk with Taft.

She could hear the slight buzz of an open frequency behind the music Taft was playing through his helmet speakers. "You awake in there?"

"I wasn't sure who was going to break the silence first." Taft knew as well as Kaytha did that they were close enough to Earth that they were safe from anyone scanning ship-to-ship communications.

"Have you looked at the net feeds? It's unbelievable."

"I was, but I've been trying to give my brain a rest until we know what's going on. I want that data Oshly said he hacked from that T-Craft fighter."

They continued to chat for several minutes. It was a circular conversation not amounting to anything of substance, but it provided them both the opportunity to distract one another with their speculations as they waited for an update from Oshly. They could then decide their next course of action.

While Oshly continued to monitor the network feeds, he also kept an eye on the area around the flying field, which seemed undamaged so far by the disaster.

Most of the reports confirmed that it would be a few days before the first chunks from the remains of the Moon would hammer through the Earth's atmosphere. Additional reporting stated that the worst was yet to come from Yellowstone. The first eruption was just the precursor to a potentially larger one. The clock was no longer ticking; time had run out.

Oshly's mind was so overwhelmed by the info streaming in that it took a minute for him to realize that his decryption of the hack data was finished. His computer made a consistent, distinctive *ping* as he moved his chair to get into a position behind the data monitor. A quick look at the hacked material gave Oshly an idea of what he had—and it was dense. Flight path instructions, operation code names, MarsCorp schematics, and more importantly, Sint Argum's name was attached to almost everything. Anyone who paid attention to geopolitical news knew who DeCorp's Sint Argum was. Oshly knew of Sint through Ven and his military background, but Ven did not speak highly of him. Oshly really didn't want to wake Ven up just yet, that was until he read some of the operation details and the order to attack the O-station. The particulars of Operation: Hot Springs—DeCorp's evacuation plan—was pretty standard. What wasn't standard was the addendum his hack revealed that was only available to those on a need-to-know basis, like Tober Rosel. The additions to the evacuation plans included the Operation: Put a Bow on It to destroy the Moon, along with the Argum's home base facility.

Hot Springs also included orders in place that gave authority to Sint's "military" to take out MMWs from EnerCon and even DeCorp were anyone to become a threat to his plans. It all painted a clear picture that DeCorp, under the command of Sint Argum, was making a major move to control as much as they could. And to get

266

that control, Sint was murdering millions on Earth by ensuring its destruction. Now Oshly knew he had to wake Ven up.

****

Tober Rosel, Uray Dow, and the two other fighters were quickly catching up to the Anniversary's location heading back to Earth, but they wouldn't know it. Jebet performed a long range scan and picked up on the DeCorp attackers signal. The enemy was flying in an almost parallel track of their cloaked ships.

"Is that the group we left behind?" asked a still groggy Ven as he looked over Jebet's shoulder. Oshly woke him up after he saw the information in the hacked data. Before Ven reviewed the material, he wanted to be sure everything was running as smoothly as possible as they neared the end of their journey home.

"Yep. Looks like they flew out and away from some of the debris. They've been flying like two- hundred miles off our left and catching up, given our range of speed," answered Jebet, as she started transferring some of the controls back to the station she had been manning.

Ven leaned in toward the HIREZ tracking screen, tapping away and inputting commands. "If they stay on their current track, they'll intercept DeCorp's O-Station over the western part of the US. My guess is they'll rest, recharge, and fuel up." Ven was unsettled by the fact that they'd appeared to be heading for that location, but he didn't want to say it out loud and concern the others. As long as the STL-5 remained working, they were safe.

Jebet went back to her maintenance station while Ven took back over in the pilot's seat. "Has anyone checked on Kaytha and Taft?"

"Not yet. We were waiting on you."

Ven keyed in all comms so everyone could hear. "We're about an hour to the atmosphere at our current speed. How are you two?"

In unison, Taft and Kaytha answered, "Pretty tired."

"I think it's safe to say we all are. We have some new intel. Oshly, what do we know?" Ven was in military mode.

With that, Oshly began to go over the data he was able to decrypt. Having spent a lot of time watching and dissecting movies, he was definitely the biggest nerd of the group. It was a skill set that paid off in this instance.

Oshly carefully told a story that he was able to piece together, not just from the hacked data, but also from what he already knew about Sint Argum and DeCorp and all the events that had led to this moment. It took about fifteen minutes for Oshly to lay out how the initial fire damage at West Quadrant in South Dakota had led to the chain reaction and the failures of the fail-safe systems. How Yellowstone likely erupted because of destruction in the adjacent state at DeCorp. How Sint Argum destroyed his own airfield before departing and then ordered the attack on the O-station, killing everyone onboard, including most of the influential individuals central to DeCorp's leadership. Oshly was convinced that Sint had made a significant play to control DeCorp and it was probably working. EnerCon was in disarray, and while DeCorp was heading to Mars, EnerCon would be slowly heading into space to allow the evacuating ships to catch up with them. The data showed that

DeCorp was monitoring their travels, and it looked like a small number of EnerCon ships may have been heading toward Europa, while Sint and DeCorp were all making their way to Mars.

Oshly also discovered other potential operations including and most importantly, a planned attack on EnerCon's lead command ships, once they were identified and circumstances justified it. The EnerCon convoy—basically everyone not headed to MarsCorp—could be seen as a potential threat. At this point, Sint Argum would have all the justification he would need, blaming the Moon destruction on a small group loyal to EnerCon. The media was already helping Argum in his propaganda campaign.

Ships evacuating Earth were choosing sides, either following DeCorp to Mars or joining what remained of EnerCon, as they started pushing into space.

Chapter 34

Space, just outside Earth's orbit

Kaytha glanced over at Taft flying beside her and sighed. The turn of events made her thankful she got to spend time alone with him. She only wished she hadn't waited so long to make her feelings known. Kaytha was always goal oriented and now those goals were changing. Where once she focused on achievement and success, now it was survival. Not just for herself but for her friends and the one she cared deeply about.

Kaytha opened up the communications screen on her HIREZ monitor. It wouldn't be too much longer until they got to Arizona, and she needed to make sure they were all on the same page before they arrived. "Hey, guys, once we reach the airfield, we need to talk about getting the STL-5 to EnerCon. I don't see any other choice."

"I say we fly out to that O-Station and take out those DeCorp-ers who keep blowing stuff up!" said a frustrated Jebet.

Oshly was quick to agree.

"I'm okay with that. If we can get our ships out of the hangar bay with all five of us invisible, we could easily take them on before they knew what hit them."

Ven swiveled around to look at Oshly and Jebet. "Then what? We start our own little war? What happens if the device shuts off? What if we have to split up and one of us gets exposed? Kaytha's right. We need to regroup at the field and pray no one knows who we are. Then we head out to find the EnerCon evacuees and hope we aren't too late."

Taft asked, "Oshly, that operation you mentioned, the one to attack the lead EnerCon ships, was there any kind of timetable included?"

"Yeah. It was an order that said pending Sint Argum's approval and circumstances."

Ven picked up on Taft's line of thinking He suddenly regretted questioning out loud starting "our own little war."

"My guess is they'll wait until most of the departing ships join the convoy. Sint is as lethal as he is smart. If he's talking about taking out command ships, he's going to expect everyone to fall in line, join with DeCorp or face the consequences," said Ven.

Kaytha summed things up. "Getting to that convoy is our first priority after we regroup at the airfield."

She was starting to realize that this may no longer be just about the device and their own safety.

She opened a direct comm to Taft. "I'm afraid we may have to take matters into our own hands, Taft. We've been attacked twice now, and we're the only ones who know what's happening. If we can't get to EnerCon, we need to start thinking about taking action once we get to the field."

Taft was taken back by what he was hearing, but didn't necessarily disagree with her. "Let's talk it over with the others. I'm with you, Kay, but I don't know what we do right now."

The Anniversary, with Taft and Kaytha following, was now minutes away from entering into Earth's atmosphere. Ven open comm'd to Taft and Kaytha. "Hey, you two. Back off from our rear as far as the stealth wake will allow. Jebet and Oshly are going to depart the ship and join you guys. I'll keep the Anniversary cloaked behind you all the way home. Once we get into the departing Earth traffic, you four will be safe with all the chaos."

The lights of the hangar made it look like a hole of bright light just opened in the middle of space. Jebet's T-Craft slowly floated out the back, her thrusters a glowing yellow as she powered up to drop into position behind the Anniversary. Oshly already had his ship pointed nose first out the bay entrance. He manipulated his lift manifolds while they kept magnetic contact with the floor of the hangar bay.

Releasing his ship for the bay flow, he drifted out and gently throttled up his power systems, swinging his T-Craft around as the bay door closed in front of him.

"Okay, guys, we're coming up on heavy traffic. Those DeCorp attackers are well past us now. Everyone back out of the stealth stream. Kaytha, you're lead. Everyone follows Kay, and I'll keep up from the rear," said Ven.

One by one, they flew out away from the Anniversary and watched it disappear before their eyes.

"Ven, with the rest of us out in front and out of the stealth stream, let me know if you run into any issues with the STL shutting off? You'll notice there is a system power indicator widget on your HUD. Green you're good, red you're exposed," Oshly tried to explain without sounding too nervous.

"Sounds good, Osh." Ven flew into position behind the others. It would be tricky for the Anniversary to remain cloaked since other ships wouldn't know to avoid him. He was counting on the other four clearing a path and do the avoiding for him, like following a person through a crowd.

On all comms from the lead ship, he said, "Everyone keep an eye on the outbound traffic. After we're into the atmosphere, we'll maintain a high altitude to avoid the chaos below until we're over the airfield, then we'll drop steep into the valley."

And, like it was any other day, they went through their roll call.

"T on the ready."

"J on the ready."

"O on the ready."

"V on the ready, Kaytha."

"For a reason...K, on the ready."

Kaytha led them on the descent, for what may be the last time, into the atmosphere of Earth.

****

Space, destination MarsCorp

The Oberkorn, along with support craft in Sint's entourage, met up with Akens Ember in open space, far from Earth, but still a day or more at their current pace to Mars. Many of DeCorp's MMWs that had made it off planet were now en route to MarsCorp and the planetary settlement there. MarsCorp had two large swaths of the planet, several hundreds of miles covered in breathable air from its advanced atmospheric processing towers.

A dome-shaped bubble of H2O could cover almost the entirety of installations and reached up to the planet's own loss of atmosphere. One section was dubbed "engineering" with miles of block concrete buildings that housed the mechanics needed to keep the other section known as the "colony" running. Both the colony and engineering took decades to build and hundreds of supply missions to get the needed equipment to make it happen. The colony only had a hundred people who flew in on some of the supply runs, but it could and would house hundreds of thousands. Oversight of the Engineering District was handled by Sint, and just like everything else, he did what was required by DeCorp. But he also did what he felt was necessary to preserve his own self-interests. Engineering also housed a massive military arsenal that Sint kept relatively secret, using his own men and packing the buildable vehicle parts and sections in with the power planet component shipments. Sint commanded a sizable crew of loyal men who oversaw the buildup of everything flown to the red planet. His military firepower sat quietly in over a dozen hangars built to look like the rest of the power plant. Even if the moment never came to use it, Sint had no fear of being found out. None of this mattered now; Sint would not have to face any questioning over his quest internally to make DeCorp into his own military superpower—he was now the defacto leader of that superpower.

****

Skies above the United States

Aboard Oshly's T-Craft, a program that monitored the Anniversary's power usage, including the drain from the STL-5, had updated its projections. The monitor displayed that the STL-5 power supply was falling faster than his earlier projections. He examined the data while doing what he could to keep in formation with his friends as they passed through the thick clouds over the Midwest.

Oshly ran a quick calculation, then opened up the comm channel to update Ven. "We're losing power faster than anticipated on the STL. There's plenty of charge, but if this keeps up and we don't find a place to power the device back up…"

Ven cut Oshly off, "I hear you, Osh." Then he keyed all comms. "Does everyone read me?"

One by one the friends copied back.

"Oshly says we're losing power on the STL. I'm going to shut it down. Having the Anniversary out in the open is a risk I'm willing to take. I don't want to *not* have the power to hide when we need it most."

No one was going to disagree with Ven, but they all knew that the sudden appearance of the Anniversary would draw attention.

Kaytha glanced at her rear camera HIREZ monitor as she sliced through the clouds. She watched as the Anniversary materialized at the rear of their convoy. *If we ever get out of this, I hope I can fly that thing,* Kaytha thought.

Ven considered taking over in the lead of the group but decided against it. Kaytha would take them in on final approach. The air traffic wasn't what any of them were used to or expected. A majority of the larger transports, those with evacuation protocols in place well in advance, had already left the surface. Smaller vehicles, no longer traveling across the country, were taking a direct route to space.

Kaytha opened up the all comms channel while they continued to fly in and above the cloud layer, which was turning gray the further west they flew. "We're almost over home. Everyone, get ready to begin our descent."

Kaytha knew she didn't need to call out specifics; they had flown together hundreds of times, including the route they were about to take back to the field. But because of the seriousness of the situation, her gut told her to be overly cautious and specific.

The five vehicles started their steep descent coming out of the cloud and smoke layer just south of the flying field and over what remained of Camelback.

"Oh my gawd!" They all heard Jebet gasp into her mic as they got their first look at what remained of the largest city near their homes.

"There's nothing left!" croaked Oshly.

The city which was home to over five million people had been completely destroyed. The location of DeCorp's facility was nothing but a smoldering crater with flame licked smoke plumes billowing up from its deep, steep concave pit. Like a rock dropped into a motionless body of water, the blast wave that had radiated from the destroyed facilities extended in a circular pattern for miles. Neighborhoods were leveled, reduced to rubble, as were parks, businesses, and life that used to occupy the now charred burning and smoking remnants. The downtown skyline looked more like a burnt forest of massive blackened trees than anything close to what was a skyline filled with dense high rises. No vehicles could be seen in the air or on the ground, clearly a sign that when DeCorp was destroyed, everything in the air also went with it.

Kaytha closed the channel to her friends. Flipping up her tinted visor to clear her watery eyes, her gaze moved to her left as Taft pulled up alongside her in the sky.

"You all right in there?" Taft, while devastated by the sight of what was left of the city, was still focused on Kaytha's well being.

"I can't believe it's all gone, T. I mean, I knew what had happened, but this bad. Worse than I could have imagined."

"You want me to take the lead?"

She flipped her visor back down into place. "No, I'm getting it together. Let's get back to the field. I'm just praying it's still there."

Once they were clear of what remained of the city, Kaytha picked up the caravan's pace; time suddenly now seemed of great urgency. They were only a few minutes out from the flying field. Based on the untouched barren desert landscape beneath them, it was a positive sign that their collective "home away from home" would still be there.

Scanner pings started sounding, indicting aircraft were coming up from behind their group.

"I'm getting multiple signals popping up on my scanners. Are you guys seeing this?" Taft asked on the open comm channel.

"I'm seeing it too, Taft. It's like we woke everyone up," said Oshly.

"Are we under threat, T?" asked Kaytha.

"I can't tell. Ven, what do you think?" asked Taft.

"Given the scattered nature of the ships, I really don't know what to think.

I say we stay in the skies until we can get a better gauge."

"What in the..." Kaytha stopped talking as the flying field came into view.

Dozens of T-Crafts were parked all around the secured buildings and hangar, and the concrete runway was dotted with people milling about. Suddenly, hundreds of heads all turned their attention toward the South at the approaching group.

Kaytha slowed their approach as she continued talking on the open comms channel. "Who *are* all these people?"

Taft said, "I recognize a lot of those Ts. It looks like the landing lot on the first day of high school."

"Lots of them are from the Raider and Ultra Clubs," added Jebet, noticing that many of the T-Crafts carried the symbols of the flying clubs that most of the locals belonged to.

"What the heck are they all doing here?" said Oshly, as they all continued to cautiously fly toward the field's main hangar bay.

The incoming T-Crafts they'd been monitoring came roaring past them, flying over and under their five ships, making their way to any empty space they could find around the scattered buildings.

The arriving T-Crafts were joining the group of almost one hundred pilots, mostly recent high school graduates, some even younger, who were already located at the field waiting for them. There was a large open spot left open for the friends to land right by the hangar door that still remained locked shut.

Kay's Field and the five pilots that used it were well known in the area. They were also well respected, being slightly over the average age of the pilots in the clubs.

The flying club members—like Taft, Kaytha, Jebet, Oshly, and Ven —also strived to be better pilots, and masters in their crafts. These kids had been waiting for them for the past 24 hours, gathering at Kay's field hoping that its occupants would return. They waited, speculating whether what they had heard was true, that they were in fact in possession of the Anniversary.

Ven maneuvered the Anniversary past his four friends' T-Crafts, setting down just in front of the hangar bay doors. The size of the huge ship was accentuated by the fact that the air field's hangar bay was definitely too small to house a ship of its size. The four others landed around the Anniversary, and from a bird's eye view, they looked like they were leaders of an army—or the main attraction at a sizeable T-Craft rally.

The bay door opened on the rear of the Anniversary as Ven appeared, albeit a little worse for wear based on all that they had been through.

As he made his way down the platform, he recognized some of the younger pilots who were making their way over to greet Ven and the others. Two of the most popular young locals were leading the growing crowd, whose chatter got louder the closer everyone got to the Anniversary in front of them.

Kaytha threw her arms open wide as she gave a huge hug to Marrett Toppest. Marrett was widely regarded as one of the best female pilots in the region, but you wouldn't know it from looking at her. She was shorter than average and had a stocky build which was misleading considering how fierce she was in the air. Her straight blonde hair was always pulled back into a ponytail, because it was practical and comfortable, seeing how she spent the majority of her day in a flight helmet. She was kind and unthreatening in every way, looking more like a bookworm than a pilot ace. When Marrett got behind the control stick of her T-Craft, like Kaytha in the skies, she was not to be messed with. Of all the locals, she could rarely be outmatched in her skills. Because of this, she had a fan base in the form of many young admirers.

"It's great seeing you, Marrett, but what are all of you doing here?" asked Kaytha.

Marrett was the head of the Ultra Fliers, one of two of the largest groups of young pilots in the Southwest. The other was the Raiders, and at its lead was Anorant Dashel, having just turned eighteen days before.

Anorant was piloting T-Crafts almost before he could walk; at least that's what he told anyone who'd listen. He didn't look eighteen, which helped gain him respect beyond his skills in the skies. Anorant stood almost six feet tall with dark skin, wavy jet black hair, and muscular build. He too, like Marrett, had his share of older and younger admirers, not just because of his looks, but also his quiet confidence. One-by-one, Anorant gave handshakes and half-hugs to the five friends whom he hadn't seen in many weeks.

Taft interrupted the warm reception. "I'm with Kaytha. We're relieved to see you all, but, yeah, why are you here?"

Marrett and Anorant gave each other confused glances. Marrett said, "So, clearly you haven't seen the network feeds? There's a bounty out for your whereabouts and rewards for any information leading to where you guys are."

"But the reports don't show your identities yet," Anorant quickly clarified.

"What do you mean *yet*?" asked Kaytha.

Marrett pulled out her personal data device and held it up to show the group a photo. "Apparently you guys haven't seen the picture?"

Taft immediately dropped his head in embarrassment at the sight of the holopic he had taken with Kaytha on the Moon.

Jebet let out a burst of laughter, while Ven and Oshly just looked around confused. All Kaytha could do was grimace at Taft while shaking her head.

Anorant said, "So far, they're only seeking information leading to the Anniversary and your ships. They've been repeating footage of you guys taken from the MoonStation before it exploded. Anyway, they're after you guys because they say you blew up the Moon."

Marritt added, "We instantly recognized Kaytha's T-craft. None of us could believe you guys would do that."

"We didn't!" Taft assured them. "It's a long story, and we'll give you all the details, but just know that we're not a part of any of this. It was a group of mercenaries out of DeCorp that destroyed our Moon, and they're responsible for that and a lot more."

"So that kinda explains why *you* guys were here waiting for us, but why are any of you here at all? Why haven't you evacuated?" asked Jebet.

Marrett and Anorant went into great detail explaining that the evacuation happened so quickly that it ended up causing too much confusion for the efforts to escape to go as planned.

"We made plans to join up with EnerCon's MMWs leaving out of Camelback. A lot of the transports were supposed to be routed to come out here," said Marrett.

"The ships were being filled with our parents and employees of both DeCorp and the EnerCon power plant."

Anorant continued, "But before they all could leave, DeCorp was caught in the apparent chain reaction. Outbound MMWs were either destroyed in the air or left sitting on the ground. The few that did escape the blast continued off planet."

"Why haven't you all tried to join up with those that got out?" asked Jebet.

Marrett said, "We were preparing for that, but then we lost all communication with the ships that got out. It's either interference from orbiting communications relays, or, as some have speculated, intentional jamming."

"And we didn't want to risk heading out blind. Then, we saw the network feeds. Kaytha and the Anniversary—we all assumed you guys would be together. So, those of us left decided to come out here, hoping you would show up," said Anorant.

"Ven, why don't you get these two up to speed on what's going on. Taft, let's get inside and see if we can round up food for everyone," said Kaytha.

Before walking away, she called Taft to her side. "Let's not talk about the device just yet," suggested Kaytha.

"I totally agree," whispered back Taft.

Ven, Oshly, and Jebet watched the exchange, deciding to wander over and join in the conversation.

"You guys talking about the device?" said Jebet.

"Yeah, we're gonna hold off on letting anyone else know about it. It's safer for everyone," said Taft.

Jebet was still concerned. "What about the Anniversary? It's just sitting out in plain sight. Is it worth the risk not to hide it? We could flip on the STL now and…"

Ven cut her off. "If Oshly's right, we have the power drain issue to contend with. We all know we can't stay here long. If someone spotted us already, it doesn't matter. They'll be on their way. No, let's stick with what we're doing. We'll get organized and get out of here."

"Besides, we have the firepower if we need to defend ourselves. The kids must have raided moms' and dads' ammo closets. Most of those Ts are armed to the teeth," added Taft.

"It's settled then, let's get some food going, figure out our next move, and like Ven said, get out of here," said Kaytha.

As Kaytha and Taft started to make their way to the main door of the facility, Oshly caught Ven's attention. "I'll be right back."

Ven and Jebet stood at the base of the Anniversary's bay door and told the large crowd of young, scared pilots what they had been through and that they were going to get some food together and then decide what to do.

Oshly jogged over to Kaytha. "Yo, Kay! Before you guys head in, can I talk to you for a minute? Just the two of us?" he said while looking at Taft.

Taft complied, a little confused and curious as he watched an animated Oshly talking to Kaytha off by themselves. Kaytha was clearly intrigued by what Oshly was saying. Taft kept his eye on their discussion that he desperately wished he could hear. Punching in the needed codes, the sound of generators powering up began to echo as Taft was about to walk inside, but not before he looked back to see Kaytha giving Oshly a hug. Taft noticed that Oshly definitely seemed relieved as he made his way back to Ven and Jebet. Kaytha quickly made her way to where Taft was standing, just outside the door to the living space.

"What was that all about?"

"Oshly needed to share some info with me, but I can't talk about it now."

Taft tried not to sound annoyed. "Oh-kaaay…"

Kaytha gently nudged Taft in the chest, causing him to take a step backward and trigger the sensor on the auto door.

She pushed him into the adjacent room as she stepped forward, waiting for the door to close behind them, putting them out of sight of anyone else.

"I'll tell when I can, but you trust me right?" Kaytha leaned in close, sending Taft's heart rate higher than where it was when they were in space under attack.

"Of course I do," he managed to get out.

"Good." Kaytha smiled. Putting her hands on his shoulders, she rose up on her toes to match Taft's height, and kissed him. Taft managed to refrain from letting out an audible sigh, though not without minor difficulty.

"Now, since the world is apparently ending, that's all we have time for, so let's find some food," said Kaytha.

"Right...food." Taft, lost in the moment, came back to reality when she reminded him about the dire situation they were currently in.

Over the years, Taft and the others had stockpiled tons of non-perishable food items. They always grabbed extra protein bars, freeze-dried fruit, cans of soup, and pasta in bulk when shopping at the nearby essential living warehouse store. The extensive food storage locker had been converted from the standard living quarters used to house the pilots that had trained there when the flying field was still active.

 It was still over a quarter full of boxes filled with single meal packages that could last a decade. Once taken from the packaging and in bulk placed inside the vast meal radia-cooker oven in the mess hall, the SMPs could be warmed and ready to eat within a few minutes. The food tasted as good as any freshly cooked meal.

The friends took up their usual spaces inside the hangar. Jebet was in the maintenance area assisting a few of the pilots with an issue they were having on their vehicle. Oshly sat at his computer terminal inside the hangar and was running over system data from the Anniversary and connecting all the T-Crafts currently at the field on a single private network. After that, he switched on the field's facility scanners. It was the easiest way to get a head count of how many people they needed to feed. In all, there were 98 mouths who'd joined them, having flown in on roughly 70 different vehicles. Oshly picked up a handful of signals just outside the valley, assuming it was more locals coming to join them. Several of the Raiders had informed him that there were others who hadn't made it their location yet.

Ven was still onboard the Anniversary, along with over a dozen of the teenagers, getting more familiar with the ship. While this was occurring, Taft and Kaytha directed a handful of Anorant's and Marrett's club members to cook up the meals. The clock was ticking and the five friends all knew it.

Several of the young pilots informed Taft and Kaytha that Sint Argum had been flooding the network feeds with a new narrative to the propaganda story of the Anniversary and the occupying craft being responsible for the destruction of the Moon.

The plan now was to gather everyone into the hangar, eat, and then discuss their next move. One thing was clear, they couldn't stay there. Not just at Kay's Field, but Earth itself. Once they were ready, it was time for them all to evacuate as well.

Chapter 35

Earth's orbit

Tober Rosel, Uray Dow, and Rosel's other pilots, Numbers Two and Three, were docked at the West US Orbital Station. Now on rest rotation, Two would eat and sleep while the others monitored the Earth's departures and incoming responses to the posted bounty searching for the Anniversary. Rosel was already growing impatient with the process. They had not been at the O-Station long and the lack of a substantial lead was frustrating him. The only good intel submitted was scan data received from a departing EnerCon MMW. Someone on board went back and looked at the avoidance system feeds on board almost all vehicles, and from that, he was able to retrieve what appeared to be the heat signature and outline of the Anniversary. The intel wasn't enough to warrant the bounty that was placed on whoever found the infamous ship, but that was irrelevant—Sint Argum had no intention of ever paying it if the Anniversary was found. This did, however, give Rosel confirmation that not only did the Anniversary return to the planet, but it was apparently heading east to west.

Sint was right to route the search party to this O-Station, but Rosel still had no clue where to start looking.

Rosel leaned into the thick bubble viewport of the O-Station. From this height, the Earth usually looked peaceful and beautiful despite what was happening on its surface, but not now. The planet looked like it had been ravaged by an interplanetary war. The white clouds that would ordinarily drape over the globe, pushing up against the atmosphere, were now replaced by dense, thick clouds of toxic smoke. The western portion of the US they floated above was hardly recognizable. Pieces of departing ship debris hung in the sky just outside the gravity field. The fragments were from ships that made it past exploding DeCorp and EnerCon facilities, only to have suffered too much damage in the blasts. The evacuees in their escape vehicles either broke apart or they exploded from the pressures of space and came raining back down into the atmosphere, streaking the skyline with falling fireballs and smoke trails. In a few days, it was going to get even worse. What remained of the Moon would start its assault on the populated planet—that part was Rosel's doing, but he didn't care. Tober Rosel was only worried about his mission and only cared because it secured his future with what he believed would be the winning side.

"Number One?!" shouted Uray Dow.

"Yes, Four, what it is?"

"We just received a report out of Arizona. Someone claims to know where the Anniversary is. They apparently have a visual on the ship."

It was the break Rosel was waiting for and a chance to redeem himself from letting them slip away.

****

Kay's Field, Arizona

A few of the younger pilots asked Oshly if he could run a check on the flight manifests from the MMWs that did make it out from Camelback. Oshly obliged, tapping into both DeCorp's and EnerCon's network systems and running a search program. All the pilots were gathered inside the hangar, eating and having conversations in small groups while Taft, Kaytha, and Ven discussed what their next move would be.

There was a growing desire by some of the pilots to leave and join up with the MMWs that survived the evacuation. Especially by those who'd discovered that their parents had indeed made it off-planet based on the info Oshly was able to pull from his manifest search. Before anyone left, Taft, Ven, and Kaytha decided to lay out what they were up against so that they could all make the best decision. Oshly relayed one more vital piece of information to his four friends. After a brief discussion, they were ready to address the group.

Standing on a workbench, Taft told the group about what they had been through. He omitted the STL-5 from his explanation, sticking with the idea that they chose to only make a Moon run for fun and that DeCorp sent the four attack craft to destroy it. Taft went on to say they were now being hunted because they were witnesses to the event. It was the truth, just not the whole truth. Taft also let everyone know that they would understand if anyone wished to leave to find their family.

Jebet leaned over to Kaytha and whispered, "You gonna take over and give the boy a break?"

"Nah, I think he's doing a good job, and it looks like he's enjoying himself."

Jebet could tell Kaytha was a bit starry-eyed and for a good reason. Taft looked every part a leader as he continued speaking.

Taft laid out how there was still danger ahead. They believed Sint Argum now had complete control of DeCorp and its military arsenal, adding that they had reason to believe DeCorp planned to launch an attack on Enercon's evacuated convoy of ships or anyone that Sint might feel stood in his way.

The information Oshly gave at the last minute was vital as it would point them in the direction of what would happen next.

Taft would only share some of the truth that Oshly discovered: a small group of EnerCon's more advanced ships, including one MMW, was heading toward Europa. EnerCon placed an atmosphere processor there over a decade ago on Jupiter's moon. The speculation was that EnerCon may attempt to set up an interplanetary staging area while its convoy of ships pushed out further into space in search of a new home. Proxima B was everyone's guess. Next to Mars, Proxima B was widely regarded as the most viable planet to sustain human life, but it would take a few months to get there.

What Taft didn't tell the crowd was that part of the payload EnerCon stored on that MMW on Europa included the needed equipment to recharge the STL-5, the parts they used on MoonStation but couldn't take with them.

Oshly only found it while conducting his manifest search for everyone's parents. The parts they needed were slated to be transferred to an existing maintenance facility on Europa's surface.

Much to Kaytha's surprise, Taft turned over speaking duties to her. "You guys all know Kaytha. She's going to wrap this up with our plans from here on out."

Taft walked down from the table he'd been standing on. He gave Kaytha a slight wink and a head nod as she stepped up to begin speaking.

"As Taft already explained, now that many of you know where your parents are, we realize that you may not wish to stay. For those that choose to leave, we completely support you. For any of you that stick around, we hope you join us in finding a way to not only keep the evacuees not heading to MarsCorp safe were DeCorp to attack, but also find a way to prevent an attack from ever happening."

Kaytha wasn't exactly sure what else to say, so she stepped down.

The crowd immediately started having side discussions. After twenty minutes, about half of the young pilots decided to leave. Most of them would be going to go find their families, while others just decided to go it alone. All of them vowed to keep the location of the Anniversary hidden, while those that planned to find the EnerCon evacuees said they would relay what they heard today to anyone who would listen.

And with that, forty-five young pilots in about 30 T-Crafts departed Kay's Field for the convoy of EnerCon ships and those not loyal to

DeCorp.

After watching the T-Crafts venture into the skies above the valley, the remaining pilots went back to eating and talking. A plan still needed to be formulated. Ven asked the other four if they would gather in Taft's converted field office. Just like they used to on long weekends, the five friends gathered around Taft's massive HIREZ television screen.

The TV was tuned to a national news outlet giving minute by minute updates on the disaster taking place. The world was finding out what they all knew: it would be coming to an end.

Sitting around Taft's coffee table on the sofa and love seat, Ven laid out his idea. "Taft and Kaytha, with Oshly's hack data in hand, I think you should fly out to Europa."

"Why don't we all go? We need the STL fueling and recharge adapters anyway?" asked Jebet.

Kaytha answered, "Because we've got, what, forty or fifty kids out there we need to watch out for. Anorant and Marrett are great leaders, but they're just as young as the rest of them. Taft and I can get to Europa in half the time and maybe see if we can't find someone inside EnerCon to trust with the device."

"That's assuming they believe the data I hacked about DeCorp's plan in the first place," Oshly said.

"If no one believes us, they won't know about the device because we obviously won't tell them," said Taft.

Kaytha continued, "Either way, we secure the parts we need to adapt the charging system and meet up with you once you arrive."

"It's also a good idea to split up for now. We double our chances at success were anything to happen to one group," said Taft.

"So, I guess you guys don't need me at all, I'll just show my way out." Ven was half joking, but slightly annoyed. "I'm going to go consult with Anorant and Marrett. We'll get a game plan for when we meet up in the Jupiter system."

Jebet, having a better understanding of Kaytha and Taft's current status than the others, got up to leave the room. "Okay you two, let's get moving and let them rest. We've got a lot of planning to do."

Jebet, Ven, and Oshly made their way back to the others in the hangar bay.

Taft and Kaytha were happy to be alone again. They had a long flight ahead of them, and while the massive show of force was surrounding them, it was relatively safe for the time being.

Taft gathered up what valuables he wanted to take with him, just enough to fit into the some of the storage space on his T-Craft. Before they would leave the Earth behind, Kaytha needed to go to her home. She was confident the blast had reached her city, but she needed to be sure. Before they departed, they both decided to sleep for as long as they could. Taft blacked out the windows and set the security measures.

Still in their flight gear, Taft and Kaytha climbed into his bed.

Neither of them realized how exhausted they were until they laid down in each other's arms and fell fast asleep.

****

Marrett, Anorant, and Ven stood together on the same table as earlier, looking out toward the remaining pilots who'd decided to stay behind at the airfield. Marrett was first to address them. "We don't know what the future will bring. DeCorp and Sint Argum have already murdered hundreds and will be responsible for the deaths of potentially millions more, so we need to get out of here as soon as we can. Rest now while you can, eat more if you need to. Myself and Anorant, along with Ven, Oshly, and Jebet, will let you know what our plans are after we talk. Kaytha and Taft will be departing soon for Europa."

"Oh, and one last thing," said Anorant. "For a reason, you're all Ultra Raiders now. Welcome to the revolt!"

Ven, Oshly, Jebet, Marrett, and Anorant worked out new plans while Taft and Kaytha continued to rest. While Ven and his military expertise guided the discussion, the newly labeled Ultra Raiders continued to eat and load up what provisions they could fit for the long, unknown journey ahead.

Many of Ultra Raiders took advantage of the large gathering of T-Crafts, with well over forty ships sitting on the tarmac of Kay's Field and a hangar bay of tools at their disposal.

They repaired their own ships and upgraded them by trading with each other thruster packages, gun and plasma blaster arrays, missile mounts, and various communications mods.

They were all young but experienced as fliers. Some had already gone through some form of military training.

The leaders of this newly formed alliance quickly put together a plan. So far, it would involve the STL-5, while hopefully stopping DeCorp and Sint Argum from being successful in his efforts to wrestle control in the wake of the disaster. In doing so, they would keep the traveling EnerCon and non-DeCorp convoys safe while they made their way away from Earth. The first action of the plan, stopping DeCorp, took some convincing for Marrett and Anorant to get on board. It would amount to what could only be described as a preemptive strike on a private facility.

Despite the concerns, the basis of their plan was set. The Ultra Raiders would be given the necessary details and then provided the option to join in or leave. No one was forcing anyone to partake in anything they didn't want to. At this point, everyone was putting their faith and trust in what Ven, Oshly, Jebet, and ultimately Kaytha and Taft had told them. It was already a burden on them that their world was literally coming to an end.

It seemed way too much to ask these kids to take part in a mission that was going to risk their lives.

Those who decided to volunteer would be split up into two groups. The most skilled pilots who volunteered would stick with Ven, Jebet, and Oshly, first to meet up with Kaytha and Taft, provided they were successful on Europa in finding help within EnerCon. Everyone was praying that they would be able to recruit more fighters to join in their cause, but they were prepared to go at it alone. The remaining pilots would be sent on a separate mission that only they would be made aware of to secure its success.

Anorant was the most hesitant and wanted to do more to recruit others to join their cause. Oshly shared with him the data files, the destruction of Sint Argum's headquarters along with the O-Station, and the murder of innocent lives, not to mention the destruction of the Moon. Anorant wanted to join up with the convoy and try to convince them to fight, but time wasn't on their side. There was no telling how soon Sint might attack, or predicting how many people would be skeptical, believing that data was forged.

The club pilots, when waiting for the Anniversary to arrive, had kept an eye on the network feeds. It was being widely reported that even many of the evacuees not a part of the DeCorp convoy already bought into Sint's propaganda. Anorant agreed to go along with the plan only because he knew Taft and Kaytha would be meeting with most likely the highest ranking EnerCon officials on Europa.

If they didn't believe them, it didn't matter who else did.

Chapter 36

Earth's orbit, south-western United States

"Otto, sir, local brothers. I haven't done the background search yet, but they have eyes on a flying field north of Camelback," said Number Four.

The Otto Brothers had no family, no allegiances to anyone, and both chose to stick it out on Earth for now. The Ottos were the first to spot the Anniversary officially. They were after the bounty placed on its whereabouts.

"So, is the Anniversary there? Do you have confirmation, Four?" asked Rosel.

"Yes. They are sending data of the field. I've been monitoring the location since they initially contacted us."

Tober Rosel looked at the streaming footage displayed on Number Four's HIREZ screen, seeing the Anniversary and numerous T-Crafts surrounding the hangar bay.

"A large group of ships departed about an hour ago based on the footage, sir. I tracked their signals, and the majority of them are heading to the growing group of ships moving out into deep space."

"Does it appear that any of the DeCorp evacuees of Operation: Hot Springs are in that smaller escaping group of ships?"

"No, sir. This smaller convoy looks almost entirely made up of EnerCon and random evacuees. The DeCorp caravan is quite large and also growing. That group is on track to MarsCorp. I noticed that Sint Argum's fleet is within a few hours of that group. It looks like a handful of EnerCon MMWs and over a dozen smaller ships have broken off from their original convoy. They're also making their way toward the DeCorp group."

"Hostile intentions, you presume, Number Four?"

"No, sir, quite the opposite. When the commander sent out the bounty on the Anniversary, transmissions were sent from these ships to the lead DeCorp ships requesting to join them," replied Uray Dow.

Tober was puzzled by this. "How are you aware of this?"

"Before I was a pilot, I was in communications and, more specifically, collection of data.

With the current chaos, systems are no longer being monitored and are easy to access."

"So, you hacked in?"

"Yes, sir."

"What about those ships that left this field?"

"Don't know, sir. I did try to zero in, not only on any private networks but also the field's feeds. They're heavily locked down. It just appears they left to join the convoy."

They continued to look at the incoming feed from the Otto brothers. "There's a lot of activity on the tarmac. Those T-Crafts look like they're ready for a fight," Dow observed.

"Did these Ottos give you a clue as to who these people are?"

"Apparently the field is occupied by a Taft Gaurdia. He's a local boy, mid-twenties. Parents both worked for DeCorp and EnerCon throughout the years. Also, a Kaytha Morrow. The picture we secured from the Moon, I crossed referenced it and it's absolutely these two. The girl's background is interesting— lots of flight training, father worked for..."

"NASA. Wilicio is his name, correct?"

"That's him," said Dow, growing curious.

"I met that man a few times. Brilliant mind, apparently an engineering legend, died not too long ago." Tober Rosel was putting the pieces together now. Wilicio, his daughter, the others they were pursuing, and, most importantly, it was beginning to make sense why they had a cloaking device. "Anyone else I should be made aware of?"

"Yes, sir. The others we've been tracking appear to be an Oshly and Jebet? The Ottos didn't say their last names, but, after some cross-referencing, they seem to be locals also. Oshly Flocca and Jebet Ponets. The girl's a fairly successful T-Craft mechanic. I don't have anything on Oshly. Lastly, this guy." Dow pointed to one of his data screens showing a military background file and photo from Ven's time in service. His retro flattop haircut and tense slightly battle-scarred face made Dow, a skilled pilot-mercenary, cringe. "This dude looks like bad news."

Tober Rosel's eyes narrowed as he glared down at Uray's face. "Do I look like one of your *buddies...FOUR*?" Rosel hissed. "Do you think it becomes you to show me that this man, whom you have never met, apparently has a resume, of all things, that intimidates you?"

"No, sir, I do not. I apologize."

Rosel straightened back up. The truth was he knew Ven Rivel well. They never served together, but his time in service was well documented.

Not just because of his accomplishments, but because when his duty was up, despite all the military could do to convince him to stay, he left.

Everything was making sense now. Suddenly, this was no longer a mission to retrieve a vital piece of technology—this group was now looking like a threat. Rosel composed himself and mentally calculated his next move.

Uray Dow was getting a better idea on how to track and ultimately lead to retrieving the device. "Sir, I've run a variance and anomaly scan on all the data from ships during the encounter with this group and picked up on an unknown energy signal coming from the Anniversary. This same energy pulse was picked up during my first contact during the O-Station Mission.

In both circumstances, the pulse disappeared when the ship went stealth. This signal has to be the device we're looking for. I've now coded into the scanning the specific signal, assuming they're not using the device to cloak their whereabouts. We will, at least maybe, know which ship is carrying it."

"And, where is it located now?"

"Current reading shows the energy pulse emanating from the Anniversary."

Rosel was pleased, but also finding himself further on edge. He didn't want to be bested by these "kids", as he thought of them. Even if they did have the help of Ven Rival, Rosel's arrogance was getting the best of him, having not secured the device before they destroyed the Moon. He started to value revenge more than his mission.

"Number Four, compile this data and send it to my personal systems file. Commander Argum will want this information," said Rosel.

"Yes, sir. Should we prepare for departure?" Uray assumed that they were launching an assault on the field.

"No. I don't wish to stir up the hornet's nest with that many armed T-Crafts to contend with. I am sure we could take them, but it's not worth the risk. No, we'll wait until they make their next move and then make ours."

"Understood, sir."

Tober Rosel was walking away when Dow noticed something new on the streaming video of the field. "Excuse me, sir."

Rosel, on the edge of annoyance, turned back around. "What is it?"

"The scan program just ID'd the ships belonging to the five people we have identified." Dow pointed to the HIREZ stream with several screen grabs. "These two here appear to be Flocca and Ponets. I haven't identified any vehicle belonging to Ven.

Although there are several attachments to the Anniversary registered to Rival."

"Yes, I imagine it would make sense, Four, that Ven is flying the Anniversary, not just because our device is on board, but I should have known it was someone with military training when we last encountered them. Anything else?"

"These other two." Dow singled out another image showing Taft's and Kaytha's T-Crafts. "Prophet 6-0091 and SH1-0151—they belong to Guardia and Morrow, and they look to be preparing for departure."

"Continue with my orders. Wake up Two and Three. Rest now but be ready to leave at a moment's notice."

"Yes, sir."

The O-Station floated in a stationary orbit over the western United States, utilizing small thrusters placed throughout the structure that kept it in place. The control deck itself consisted of a circular room with bubble viewport windows wrapped around the dome-shaped top of the platform. Under the control deck housed the sleeping quarters and vehicle docking station, both twice the size yet same shape as the control deck space. EnerCon built a majority of the O-Stations orbiting Earth and designed them with particular attention to art and aesthetics.

Once Uray Dow left his control desk, entering the elevator to travel to the lower level, Tober Rosel took the seat at his terminal. Using his priority access, Rosel logged back into Number Four's system. Finding the initial contact from the Otto Brothers, he wrote back a private reply.

Attention Otto: This is T. Rosel, security liaison for DeCorp and Commander Sint Argum. I've been authorized to reward you with the discovery of the Anniversary. Before you accept the bounty, a new offer is now available. Upon destruction of Prophet 6-0091, SH1-0151, and their pilots, you will be given full access to living space and full accommodations on DeCorp Mars station and double the bounty payment. All communication will remain confidential. Full denial if leaked and forfeit of the offer. Proof of achievement required.

After sending the transmission, Rosel brought up live Earth feeds, leaning back in his chair to gather his thoughts and take in the latest in ongoing catastrophic events unfolding and evacuation efforts. Rosel knew that he should have consulted with Sint Argum before making the offer to the Otto Brothers, but he wanted to do things as much his way as possible. The choice to put a hit out on Taft and Kaytha was one done solely out of the need for progress. Rosel had a clear idea who created the device—Wilicio Morrow. His daughter now represented an obstacle that would be best dealt with by not being in his way. If the Ottos were successful, it would be easily explainable that they died while in pursuit.

As for the Otto brothers, Rosel had no intention of making good on his offer. If they were successful, he would order them eliminated as well. Rosel was feeling more at ease now that he had some control over what would happen next. He would still have to wait until Ven, the Anniversary, and the young pilots made their next move before he could plan his. But the murderous goal created with the Otto brothers was enough to equal progress in his mind.

The elevator lift door opened with Number Two and Three on board, arriving to take over for Uray Dow while he went to rest. Rosel was about to get up from Dow's terminal when the message indication ping sounded from Number Four's computer.

Attention T. Rosel: Offer accepted. Will notify upon completion with confirmation. Otto

Chapter 37

Kay's Field, Taft's living quarters

A few hours had passed, and the room was still darkened with the ambiance setting set to evening. It was approaching noon as Taft started to wake up from his nap. Lying under the sheets, he rolled over, barely awake, and expected to find Kaytha next to him, but she was already out of bed. Taft had slept hard for those few hours, and his body had absolutely needed it. Wiping the sleep from his eyes, he heard soft sobbing coming from his system's workstation on the other side of the room. Looking through the darkness of the room, he saw Kaytha, wrapped in a blanket from his bed, the light of the HIREZ screen illuminating her face. Taft liked to keep his living space cool and kept a few layers of sheets and comforters on the bed. Grabbing a blanket, he wrapped it around his body and up over his head as he walked across the cold floor to Kaytha. She was staring at the transport MMWs' flight manifests from both DeCorp and Enercon. Taft pulled up a chair to sit beside her. With concern in his voice, Taft asked, "Bad news, Kay?"

"I found my mom." She pointed to the manifest of a DeCorp transport on the screen. "She must have gotten priority boarding because of my dad. The MMW she's on was heading to MarsCorp, but now it seems like it's staying with the EnerCon ships. Look here, this shows two convoys—one heading toward Mars, and the other's destination is unknown, but maybe it's pushing out beyond the other group. Unfortunately, there's no way to get a message to her. They took all the in and outbound transmissions offline. I found your parents, too."

Kaytha slid her finger across the HIREZ screen, bringing up another flight list. "Looks like your family flew out on one of the housing transports. If the information's correct, they've already reached the convoy of EnerCon transports heading into deep space."

"But that's the same group of ships that Oshly said Argum had plans to target, isn't it?"

"It is, but that's part of what's bugging me. Both our families are at risk, and I don't know what to do about either."

"I think all we can do is stay on track with what we've planned so far. We need allies on our side. Argum has to be stopped," said Taft.

Kaytha turned her attention toward another monitor showing recently recorded footage.

Taft recognized some of the landmarks, half destroyed buildings, and the remainder of a skyline that used to exist now just barely resembled the former outline of the city that once was. Taft then realized why Kaytha was so upset. "Kay, I'm so sorry."

Kaytha's home was less than a mile from where the footage showed the downtown devastation of smoldering buildings and at ground level, nothing but scorched earth. Kaytha for the moment assumed her home was gone.

"Thanks, T." She rested her head on Taft's shoulder. He felt horrible for his friend and worse because of his love for her.

He took comfort in knowing that at a minimum he could be there for her. Kaytha was accepting of his love and friendship. It showed in her vulnerability. Taft would cherish it and never betray that trust.

"I've got plenty of supplies for the journey. Plus, you have clothes over in the housing unit right?"

Her head was still resting against him, tears slowly rolling down her face. "No, I brought my stuff over. Well, the stuff I cared about and didn't want Jebet borrowing before we left."

Taft had to force himself not to crack a smile at Kaytha's admission. He knew now how much she cared for him but still carried a certain sense of insecurity and fear and that it would go away.

 Kaytha's minor revelation chipped away a little at the uncertainty, but only a little.

Kaytha continued, "And, anyway, it's not about the stuff. I'd be more upset if I'd left this T-Craft there." Kaytha motioned in the direction of the hangar where her ship was parked as she continued, "I flew my favorite today. It's just a shame my other ships are gone. It was just my home. We've all lost our *home.*"

Taft felt the same way. "I know, Kay, but we've got each other, and, *for a reason*, once we get through all this, we'll make a new home somewhere."

"I wish we could stay. I want to stay, now more than ever, here... with you."

Taft knew what he wanted to say, he'd wanted to say it for longer than he could remember, but this again just wasn't the time—they had to leave. There would be another time, a better time. "You *are* with me. We're going to see this through."

Kaytha sat up, wiping her face clean. "Let's see it through then."

****

Oshly had been running an operating system upgrade on Taft's and Kaytha's T-Crafts while they were resting. This was standard procedure on all his friends' ships.

They trusted his expertise. During the process, Oshly not only was running Taft's and Kaytha's T-Crafts' power plants through a series of reset cycles and calibration in preparation for the extended interstellar travel, but he also synced Taft's ship to his central computer mainframe.

While Kaytha was in Taft's bathroom space of his converted living area, Taft was sitting at his computer workstation when he noticed the T-Craft sync notification on his main HIREZ screen. The situation was becoming all too real again. The sync between his ship and his computer system was one of the last things he would need to do before they left. Taft transferred everything on the Kay's Field operations system. Anything personal he needed not at the flying field was available via a Cloud Over Air network. Taft downloaded the terabytes of data, then deleted the network account. He had no intention of physically returning to his actual home. Kaytha was right. They had no home now. For now, Kaytha was his home. Taft punched in the necessary commands to start the data transfer.

Then, he created a backup file with essential information that he could keep on a condensed data chip and attached it to his flight suite's limited microcomputer.

During the system upgrade, Oshly uploaded an additional program to Kaytha's operating system. She would be expecting it to be there when they departed. Oshly also placed a duplicate version deep inside Taft's T-Craft OS that could only be accessed if he knew where to look.

It would take about an hour for the transfer and duplicate to finish filling up the data banks. After which, Taft would also erase his entire Kay's Field OS. Oshly made a small notation on the transfer notification for Taft to include all the entertainment, movies, music, and games. This was something Taft would not have forgotten, but Oshly would have been remiss had he not reminded him. Besides, all of them had a good amount of personal items on the field's system. All logins were accessed for the data transfer, and he routed Kaytha's to her T-Craft OS, even though he had it as well. Kaytha had lost almost everything and hoped to be able to at least access some of her personal data that would provide some level of comfort while piloting her T-Craft.

The clock was ticking on their departure time. Once the transfer was complete and Taft and Kaytha were fully packed, they would make their way off the planet and head for Europa.

Plans were now in place, everyone knew what their roles would be and what the intended goals were. Taft and Kaytha would be attempting to gain support from those who would listen and weren't loyal to DeCorp. Ven, Jebet, Oshly, and the newly formed Ultra Raiders would make their way off the planet and await word from Taft and Kaytha. If everything went as planned, a serious attempt would be designed to stop DeCorp and Sint Argum's ability to launch an attack. One that would most certainly put lives at risk and ultimately the future control of humanity among the stars.

Fifteen young pilots in ten standard T-Crafts were already suited up and heading for their ships. They had their own mission, one that may prove vital when the time comes. Ven, Anorant, and Marrett stood together just outside the bay doors as they watched those ten ships depart on an almost vertical trajectory toward space, praying they would see them again.

Anorant's eyes glistened as the departing ships disappeared into the graying cloud cover. Marrett placed a hand on his shoulder and said, "For a reason, guys, so let's get back to work." Oshly had never stopped working. Applying system upgrades to all remaining T-Crafts wasn't all he was up to. Oshly had Jebet pulling out stacks of thruster filters, retrofitting each one to meet the various shapes and sizes on all the remaining T-Crafts. Kay's Field had more than enough supplies in its warehouse. Hundreds of T-Crafts used to be flown out of there before the airfield was eventually abandoned. Stacks of vehicle parts were left behind when its last occupiers left.

Oshly, Ven, and Jebet knew that they could not run the STL-5, not just because of the decision to withhold its existence from the others, but also because they were going to need the ability to go stealth when the time came; they couldn't risk draining its power should Taft and Kaytha not be successful in getting the recharge components off Europa. Oshly had his own reason for not wanting to attempt turning the STL-5 on as well.

Because of this, and the decision to stick together, there was a fear of drawing too much attention with such a large contingency of T-Crafts. The Anniversary stuck out like no other craft did. They collectively decided to attempt avoiding detection leaving Earth by flying north, into the growing ash cloud of the Yellowstone eruption, before exiting the atmosphere. The filters being outfitted on all the ships were generally reserved for desert conditions and would keep the thrusters from getting clogged by dirt and sand—a common nuisance, especially in this part of Arizona. Unfortunately, this was still risky since no one really knew what effect the ash smoke would ultimately have. Given that sand and dirt was denser than ash, Oshly was confident that the filters would hold up long enough until they were safely in open space and the filters could be jettisoned from the T-Crafts. It was starting to look like everyone's departure times at Kay's Field were lining up, with everyone leaving for the last time together.

Chapter 38

Kay's Field, Arizona

Everyone was so preoccupied at Kay's Field that no one was keeping an eye on the short or long range scanners. Just over the ridge, the Otto brothers sat parked in their dilapidated, barely-worthy-of-space-travel-yet-heavily-armed T-Crafts. Neither brother was a skilled pilot. However, what they lacked in piloting ability, they managed to overcompensate with DeCorp THX Thruster packages several grades beyond the stress levels that their T-Crafts were supposed to sustain. Each of their ships carried just two of the massively boosted power cores, enough to keep up with most any custom advanced ship they came in contact with. They also loaded up their T-Crafts' arsenal with a stacked array of EnerCon short and long-range target tracking explosive tipped missiles. The Thruster package mounted to the sides of the ships served not only the function of speed but also power enough to carry the explosive payload. It, too, was well beyond either Otto's T-Craft's safety rating. The two vehicles were almost as deadly for the pilots as they were for whomever they came in contact with.

The brothers themselves looked better suited to be found in a back ally living in a box in a downtown cityscape, making signs begging for money. Their flight suites looked like they'd been lifted off of pilots found in the wreckage of some long forgotten war. Their clothes, made up of a patchwork of tans, greens, and grays, were tattered and torn. Their flight helmets were beaten up to the point that it was a miracle they didn't just crack apart when being strapped on their heads. These two high school dropouts somehow wore it all with a sense of delusional pride and arrogance.

After having exited their ships, both brothers were now lying down on the ridge mount looking out on the airfield, passing back and forth a bottle of cheaply made clear alcohol strong enough to be used for paint thinner in a pinch. The Otto brothers watched and waited for their opportunity to make good on the bounty request. This was their ticket to freedom and riches off world.

Sint Argum's fleet of support ships, including the SMTC-Oberkorn, was closing in on Akens Ember's MMW and other DeCorp vehicles making their way to MarsCorp. Sint had only just returned to his commander's chair on the command bridge after getting several hours of sleep. He immediately received the communication data from the West O-Station and Tober Rosel. Swiping his finger to open the file, Sint studied the information Uray Dow had compiled regarding the details on the evaders who continued to elude his grasp and the device he now knew they were in possession of.

Seeing their faces, learning their names, the background that Uray had culled from his scouring of what data was available, he already hated them. Before, they were just random people who might get in the way of his grand plan; now they were Taft, Ven, Oshly, Jebet, and, worst of all, Kaytha Morrow. If Kaytha's father weren't dead already, he would be hunting Wilicio Morrow down too.

Morrow was the man who most likely created the device Sint so desperately wanted. His daughter carried the genes of the man who may have given these children, as he viewed them, the capability to evade capture by his best men. They also carried hope.

Hope he absolutely did not want anyone to have as he sped toward his goal of having ultimate power over the future of mankind away from Earth. His anger and drive to stop them and obtain the device, to wield its power, to cause fear in others, was now renewed.

"Director Vivsou, make speed to dock with Ember's O-MMW as soon as possible. We must double our efforts and advance our plans. The situation is now more urgent than ever," said Sint.

The handful of DeCorp ships that were in tow of the Oberkorn broke off from their flight path with the DeCorp armada making its way to Mars.

With Akens Ember's O-MMW in view, Director Vivsou took control of the Oberkorn. Approaching from behind Ember's ship, the Oberkorn moved in over the top of the massive vessel, matching its speed as it reached position just behind the O-MMW's command deck. Akens watched Sint Argum's lethal war machine on the outboard monitors begin its landing cycles.

Gregor Digby, being the only one on board who had served on its design team, knew the Oberkorn better than anyone. Sitting in the chair usually occupied by the MMW Vehicle's specialist, Digby at the moment was in charge of preparing for docking of Sint's ship to the MMW. Toggling the switches required to open up the connector ports on the roof of the massive vehicle, Digby watched through the huge upper viewport windows as Sint's SMTC arrived. Wendal Hindley sat in the designated fueling specialist seat and turned the analog dial to begin pressurization of the dual fuel and recharging cables that would connect to the rear of the SMTC.

Director Vivsou on board the Oberkorn switched the OS of the ship to the command controls of the MMW flight computers while the remainder of the landing procedure was executed with mathematical precision. The Oberkorn was now firmly docked into place.

A smile crossed Sint Argum's thin-lipped mouth as he looked out the massive canopy window of his SMTC, now perched above the O-MMW command center.

In his mind this was his O-MMW now; he was the commander and it was his personal warcraft.

Akens Ember waited for Sint to make his way off of the Oberkorn. Looking up out of the viewport window gave him a direct line of sight to the Oberkorn attached to his ship. Akens feared Sint Argum and, like so many others, had little respect for the man. Seeing the Oberkorn sitting piggybacked on his ship was a visual reminder of where he stood in the grand scheme of things. He had no love for EnerCon, so he also wanted DeCorp to be the dominant power; however he felt remorse for the innocents caught up in the building conflict that Sint Argum was creating. Akens quickly pushed that thought out of his mind, justifying the loss of life by simply assuming people would be dead regardless. Akens Ember believed everything that was happening was for a reason, and the future would be better served under the rule of DeCorp, even if that meant Sint Argum was in power.

The power door to the O-MMW slid open as Sint Argum arrived on the command deck.

"Good to see you again, commander," said Ember, standing near the command deck flight chair.

Sint wasted no time asserting his position of power in a not so subtle fashion. "I'm glad to see you survived your little mishap during the evacuation, Ember. I trust you've put everything in the storage bay back in its proper place and things are as they should be?"

Aken was immediately reminded of why he had so little respect for the tall, gangly *commander*. Sint's arrogance and condescension oozed from his mouth, needlessly reminding Akens of the difficulty they had escaping the devastation back on Earth that was completely not his fault.

Akens knew it was unwise to push back. "Yes, commander. It's as if nothing happened and the flight crew handled themselves admirably."

"The flight crew should have had you away from the blast wave, but never mind that. Are we still on schedule at Mars Station?"

"Yes, Engineering has preparations well in hand and ahead of schedule. Residency is already prepared for when we arrive," said Akens. Engineering maintained the needed infrastructure at MarsCorp to keep the huge DeCorp facility functioning. However, Sint was actually referring to DeCorp's military component, which was preparing for the possibility of battle. "We are about half a day out from MarsCorp, unless you wish to speed up the fleet?"

"That won't be necessary at the moment. I am awaiting word from Rosel and his pilots. We are tracking a handful of ships that could potentially cause problems in our current plans. Tell me, Ember, are you keeping watch on those departing Earth? Especially EnerCon's evacuees?"

"We are, sir. A large convoy is making its way out toward Jupiter and, based on their rate of travel, they are planning on pushing out further. The network feed reporting indicates they are heading for Proxima B. There is a smaller group of EnerCon MMWs— personal, supply, and support ships—heading back our way. After word got out that MoonStation had been destroyed, and the details of those responsible, we received and accepted the requests from those in charge of the vessels. This new group of ships is planning to join us on MarsCorp.

"And what about the remaining convoy? Have they responded in any way?" asked Sint.

"No, they seem to be loyal to EnerCon and have not replied to our requests to join us. Several hours ago, one MMW along with a few medium sized EnerCon ships and T-Crafts flew to Europa. We believe they're on its surface. The EnerCon facility is located on the atmosphere processed portion of Europa."

Making his way to the captain's chair, Sint Argum took this moment to remind Akens that he was in charge by sitting down in the pilot's seat. "Ember, we have a sizable number of Drone Ts onboard, do we not?"

"Over two dozen in the bay, fully fueled, armed and cells charged," replied Ember.

"Inform those in the hangar bay to finish prep and prepare to dispatch them. I want them in open space between Europa and us."

Akens Ember was beyond annoyed at having been relegated to Argum's assistant. In his mind, it wasn't Argum's O-MMW to command, but there was nothing Akens could do about it now. "Very well, commander," Ember replied, as he made his way to the flight director's chair on the command deck. Once seated, he sent out the needed protocols to initiate departure procedures of the pilotless T-Craft drone squadron.

Chapter 39

Kay's Field, Arizona

Taft and Kaytha gathered the last of what would be going with them, looking around the room at everything that would be left behind. "Do you want to say goodbye in some way to this place?" asked Kaytha as she and Taft started making their way out of his living space, toward the hangar bay and their ships.

"Nah, the file transfer is complete. Everything I need is safely in my flight suit's memory bank and on board on my T. This, well, it's just a place."

While it had been just a place, it was primarily his home. Taft spent his days during the week in his apartment while working. But Kay's Field was indeed home, and it was mostly because of Kaytha. She only came over to his apartment a few times and always with the others. Kay's Field was special only because after meeting Kaytha, he had even more reason to spend his time there. It was always where he wanted to be most, and that was with her.

He didn't think it was necessary to make a scene in his final moments there. He preferred to remember that the things which mattered most were going with him.

They stepped through the doorway that led to the hangar bay together. Taft took one quick look back at the room space before using the voice command on the room's system pad, "Taft's living quarters: authorize. Complete system shut down."

The room went dark and eerily quiet. The usual humming of the appliances had stopped. Taft had already erased the computer system's drives after the data download was complete. With a smile on his face, at peace with never seeing this place again, Taft followed Kaytha as they made their way toward their friends and their T-Crafts out on the flight line.

Just outside the hangar bay, Ven packed up more gear to stow away on the Anniversary. Jebet was tinkering with an ammo rack mount for one of the Ultra Raiders. Meanwhile, Oshly hammered away at his keyboard, wrapping up the coding that was needed, which would allow for the filters installed on all the T-Crafts to be jettisoned with the flip of a designated switch once they served their purpose.

One of the young pilots, a 15 year old boy named Gander, walked over to Ven, who was standing just outside the Anniversary's rear hangar bay door.

"Excuse me, Ven. Would you mind if we used some of that paint over there on the wall?" asked Gander, pointing to a dozen cans of spray paint in an array of colors.

"Nah, go for it. We're leaving that behind anyhow."

"Thanks, Ven! Come on guys!" Gander said, motioning to his pilots buddies to join him in raiding the shelf of paint.

It didn't take long for them to grab every can of spray paint off the shelf. They thanked Ven as they went running back out to their T-Crafts. One by one, each pilot painted a large U in one color, then an R, using the right portion of the U, in another color.

UR for Ultra Raiders was their logo now. The U and R painted on every ship was done in a number of color combinations—red and gold, blue and yellow, green and purple.

Kaytha and Taft walked through the hangar bay, heading for their ships on the tarmac. They watched the impromptu paint party. Taft thought of asking one of the young pilots to paint the letters on his T-Craft, but then decided not to. This was their moment. They needed this opportunity to bond, and he didn't want to take anything away from it.

"You guys ready to get outta here?" Ven asked Kaytha and Taft, walking toward the runway.

"Yeah, we're all set," Taft said, slowing his pace but not stopping. "How long until you guys get moving?"

Jebet looked up from her project when she heard Taft's voice. "I can't speak for these two, but I should have my work done in the next half hour, and I'm already packed."

"I was just about to log off," said Oshly, without looking up from his screen. "I'm ready when everyone else is."

The mood turned somewhat somber. The time had come when these five friends would be apart for the first time since Kaytha and Taft returned with the STL-5. No one knew what to expect or what would come next, and no one wanted to say goodbye.

"Anorant and Marrett have the young guns ready to fly. I imagine we'll be out of here in an hour, give or take," said Ven, as he zipped up a large forest green duffle bag.

Ven looked confusedly at Kaytha, as she let out a slight chuckle. "*Young guns*? Huh. Rant and Mar are younger than half of these young guns. Too young to have to be faced with what's happening."

They all looked around at the group of Ultra Raiders when Taft said what they were all thinking, "For a reason."

Focusing their attention back on the mission, Kaytha said, "Once we get within scanning distance of Europa, we'll try and contact you." Jebet walked over to join them as Kaytha continued, "Take care, you guys. If all goes as planned, we'll see you just outside Jupiter."

"Should be a beautiful sight..." said Jebet, poorly hiding her emotions, as tears began to fill her eyes.

"Talk to you guys soon. Be safe," Taft said, catching Ven giving him a subtle head nod.

Taft and Kaytha approached their T-Crafts with a sense of fear and excitement. The rumble of their custom vehicles was a welcoming sound, it had to be. These were, for better or worse, their homes for the foreseeable future. Kaytha ran her hand over the clear canopy of her T. Some of the Ultra Raiders must have done a quick cleaning of both their ships because they seemed newly washed.

They stowed their baggage into the empty rear compartments. Standing between both of their ships, there was nothing left to do but get on board. Before they did, Taft walked over to stand in front of Kaytha.

"You ready to get outta here?"

"No, not really," Kaytha said, smiling.

Taft stared at her and noticed she was different, that her guard was down. Taft felt a sense of comfort he never knew existed. He thought to himself, *For a reason, indeed.*

Opting to not make much of a scene in front of everyone, he threw his arms around Kaytha. When he did, he heard her whisper, "Okay, now I'm ready, Sandy."

Kaytha's demeanor changed back to the familiar confidence Taft was used to as she turned her attention to the task at hand. She pressed the illuminated yellow button outside the cockpit to open her T's canopy. Her helmet—in all its custom-painted gray, black, and candy apple red artistic glory—was waiting for her. She reached down and set it on the small ledge above the cockpit dash as she climbed in. Taft was already sitting inside his T-Craft, strapping his helmet with the visor up, as the onboard system cycled through its departure procedures. With both their canopies still open, Taft looked over in time to catch one last glimpse of her. She gave him a slight wink before her gray smoked out windshield started to close and she flipped down her visor. With their canopy windows magnetically sealed airtight, it was all business now as they pulled their seat belt straps tight. Their collective thrusters began to squeal as they spun up. Reaching back to the left sides of their flight controls, each of them pushed their levers forward, applying power to the lift manifolds.

Kaytha comm'd Taft as their T-Crafts slowly lifted from the concrete. "I say we fly south and keep below the cloud cover before we head out of the atmosphere. Let's try to avoid flying through that ash cloud. The smoke from Camelback will be bad but avoidable."

Their Ts slowly gained altitude and, following Kaytha's lead, Taft turned his ship to face south.

"Looking at the weather data, there seems to be a patch of blue sky just past downtown and nothing but evacuating traffic. We can go off-world at that point, mix in with the others leaving," said Taft.

"Sounds like a plan." Kaytha powered up her thrusters as Taft did the same, keeping just behind and to the right of Kaytha as they gained speed and altitude up and over the valley ridgeline and out of sight. Their three friends left behind went quickly back to work; they had their own departure to deal with. None of them liked seeing their friends leave, but all prayed that they would see them again soon and hopefully with help.

The older Otto brother looked through his sensor enhanced viewer at Taft and Kaytha embracing before they left the valley. With an audibly disdainful grunt, he said to his brother, "Ugh, I thought the reward would be worth it, but now I want to take these two out just because they're so obnoxious."

Still looking through the lenses, he hadn't noticed that his younger brother had fallen asleep next to him. "Let's get moving. We'll take a high, wide path to the east. Keep them on our scanners. Once their out in the open we'll drop in on top of them. They'll never know what hit them." The elder Otto's eyes were still locked on the flying field. "You got that?" Finally, looking to his left, he realized his brother had passed out from drinking.

"WAKE YOU UP YOU IDIOT!" He smacked him upside his already severely damaged flight helmet.

"Hey, yeah, what the?!"

"Just get moving! It's time we go collect our reward, you moron."

The two brothers got up and boarded their poor excuses for T-Crafts. The older brother knew he was going to have to move on their two targets before they left the planet. He was less than confident that either of their ships would survive in space.

As they were departing, the older brother keyed his comms, "Send a message to that Rosel guy, tell him we're going after them and we'll let him know when we're finished. Oh, and find out if there're any DeCorp transports we can hitch a ride with? Otherwise, we'll need to steal some space worthy rides."

As they took to the air, both of their ships left behind thin contrails of escaping oxygen, dripping oil, and smoke from the residue burning off of their latest alterations. The younger brother followed the older Otto as they somehow managed to stay close enough behind Taft and Kaytha, keeping them visible on the long-range scanner. The two nitwits kept just beneath the cloud and ash cover as they flew south toward Camelback.

EMBARK

****

The large group at the airfield was in their final stages of stocking, charging, and fueling their vehicles. Ven was already finished loading as much equipment and tools onto the Anniversary in the hangar bay as he could. He and Jebet had worked hard to make sure they could still fit at least three T-Crafts, and maybe even a fourth if they had to, on board the ship. Jebet was making a third pass through her flight checklist on her T-Craft, while Oshly was busy wrapping up the final file transfer.

As Oshly was about to execute a hard erase of the remaining memory left in the airfield's operating system, one of the Ultra Raiders walked over to talk to him. She'd met Oshly earlier, and, after talking briefly earlier, she'd taken a liking to Oshly.

"Hey, Oshly. Um, can I ask you a question?" asked Torian, who was a fellow computer geek herself.

Oshly, like usual, was focused on the screen in front of him. Barely looking up, he said, "What's up, Torian?"

"I was just wondering, um, do you really think we're going to be able to pull this off?" Nervously she tried to exude a little more confidence than her initial query. "I mean, don't get me wrong, I'm ready to fight, too, if...I mean *when* we have to. But I was just curious if you were worried at all."

Oshly never had much skill in being tactful or cautious with his words, and it certainly didn't make an appearance at this moment. Being an only child, he had very little experience with people younger than himself. Oshly was also the least mentally mature of his friends. He pressed enter to start the file erasing program and continued staring at his HIREZ screen, when he said, "Well, Torian, provided we make it from here to Wyoming without drawing too much attention, there's going to be what, forty maybe fifty ships? Oh, and that's including the Anniversary which isn't exactly the most inconspicuous ship. After that, if my smoke filters do their job and our ships hopefully don't choke, crashing to the lava below, then we just need to make it out to Jupiter. Which should take at least a day or more, maybe a little less as long as our T-Crafts hold up. This will, after all, be the longest any of you will have traveled in the interstellar lanes."

"Oh, okay...Uh, thanks?" said Torian, confused. She was looking for some reassurance and received the total opposite.

Oshly was completely clueless that he was scaring Torian; the fact that he was still staring at his screen didn't help. Unfortunately for Torian he wasn't finished. "Because we have to rendezvous back with Kaytha and Taft and pray—for a reason, of course—that they got help. Now, if they did, then great, our lives got easier. But if they didn't, we have to successfully launch an attack, on our own, mind you, at DeCorp's military assets on Mars. If that is successful, then we have to get far enough away, as fast as we can, from whatever DeCorp has left that can fly.

Hopefully we can reunite with those who aren't loyal to DeCorp on their way to God knows where. Then we need to convince them that we were completely justified in taking the preemptive strike, since we'll have blown to crap a whole bunch of stuff and probably killed quite a few of DeCorp's worst in the process."

All Torian could do was stand there, frozen in place, with wide eyes and her mouth agape.

Thankfully, Jebet had walked over to hear the last part of Oshly's rant. She shook her head, and put her arm around Torian's shoulder. "Don't you listen to him, Torian. He sniffs thruster grease when no one's watching. We'll be fine. Just follow Ven's instructions. He'll take care of us. Great t-shirt by the way."

Torian was wearing a blue Sad Milkshake Weekend shirt that featured a plain yellow frown face emoji on the front and concert dates from their last tour on the back.

Torian was excited Jebet noticed. "They're my favorite!"

"Mine too. Although I think I prefer their last album over the new one," said Jebet.

"Me too."

Jebet walked with Torian to her T-Craft. Oshly shrugged, confused as to what he'd done wrong.

Jebet looked back at him and gave a clueless Oshly the hardest side eye she could.

Chapter 40

Earth Orbit, O-Station over the south-western United States

Tober Rosel leaned into the giant bubble viewport window, looking down on Earth. But it was an Earth he no longer recognized. The usual swirl of the white cloud cover was replaced by vast swaths of gray. The initial blast from Yellowstone had created an ash cover over half the continental United States. Patches of smaller smoke clouds from the destroyed factories covered every part of the globe that wasn't water. Thousands of ships could be seen flying off-world. While in the upper atmosphere, hundreds of thousands of metal debris pieces littered the skies. It was all that remained of the ships that were caught in the blast waves and tried to escape the clutches of Earth's gravity or were not ready for space flight. The rush to escape led to a lack of safety preparedness, leading to many larger transport ships exploding on takeoff. Rosel watched as more and more ships suffered the same fate, like some twisted deadly fireworks display.

Number Two was currently monitoring the flying field. "Sir, the Ottos. We've received a new message. They're currently tracking the two targets, heading south toward Camelback."

Rosel stood up straight and, without speaking a word, turned back toward the operations consuls in the center of the room. Number Two continued, "Also, there appears to be a lot of movement at that airfield. If I were to guess, they're getting ready to evacuate."

"Wake up Number Four and inform Three to prepare for departure to the surface," ordered Rosel.

Number Two went immediately to work. "Should I also add reports indicating Yellowstone Park is beginning to erupt again? Experts on the private feeds believe this may be bigger than the last eruption."

"Package the info, Two, and send via my private channel to Commander Argum. We leave in less than a half hour. Time to go hunting."

****

In the skies south of Kay's Field, Arizona

Not wanting to draw attention to themselves, Taft and Kaytha took it slow to Camelback. Kaytha knew her home was gone but intended to make a quick flyby to put her mind at ease. Taft understood why Kaytha wanted the confirmation.

Taft also agreed with Kaytha's logic for departing the planet surface in the only nearby blue sky available. He knew that they could have easily made quick work of the dense cloud layer, even where they currently flew, but he didn't question it.

"Kay, check your rear scans. I see two ships at high altitude in the east. They just made an abrupt turn in our direction. Signatures look strange," said Taft.

Kaytha pressed the small black button to bring her radar dish online.

A small door opened just above the T-Craft's power plant on its top rear, and out popped a plate-sized dull green dish that aimed in the direction of the new contacts. "Scan data coming in now. Ah, crap. Looks like the Otto brothers. And based off the heat signatures, they're overloaded on power and heavily armed."

"What do you think, do we try and evade now? There's not much between us and the downtown area ahead. If they're coming after us, they might engage before we have cover."

"Let's not act like they see us. We'll see what they do. If we reach what remains of the city, then we have options," said Kaytha.

The Ottos were indeed making their turn for their targets. The younger Otto always followed his brother's lead.

Keying his helmet comm with his older sibling, he asked, "What's the plan?"

"Keep our present altitude, increase speed. Once we're just about on top of them, we'll dive down and take 'em out before they reach the city."

The younger brother's T-Craft was already red-lining. The thrusters output was too much for his abused T-Craft. The alarms warning him went ignored. Sirens always seemed to go off on both brothers' vehicle systems. The Ottos took the wailing alert sounds as more suggestions than anything else.

Taft didn't much care for this game of chicken they were playing. It was clear the Otto brothers were on an intercept path to their location. "Kay, we're about two minutes out from downtown. I say we boost now and close the gap to the buildings in front of us."

"I know. I thought that too, but I think they have some long-range seekers attached. And if we gun it, they'll know we spotted them. Those seekers might be tough to evade."

"Scratch that! Prepare for evasive maneuvers, T!" Kaytha called out.

The older Otto called out on his comm, "Dive! Get after them!"

And with that, they both started full speed at Kaytha. Spiraling their T-Crafts down through the clouds, they sent out a massive smoke trail behind both their howling ships.

Taft and Kaytha closed up their formation. Using the collective strength of their thrusters, they made haste to the destruction of what remained of downtown Camelback. Seven of the tallest high rises still stood, but they were smoldering, hollowed out shells of what they once were. The top floors, roofs, and vehicle landing pads were torn away, exposing giant gaping holes and ripped apart chunks from the barely standing structures. The destruction served for the only cover Kaytha and Taft had to run from their reckless pursuers.

The Ottos were quickly gaining on the two evading T-Crafts. The older Otto was shouting out quasi-military jargon. None of it served any real purpose apart from pretending that they were on some military mission and not a murder-for-hire bounty. The younger Otto couldn't hear anything over the squealing thrusters and cautionary alarms ringing out.

More warnings sounded by the second as the younger brother's ship began to shake violently. "I need to back off, I can't take the abuse!" comm'd the reckless youngster.

"Just hang on to it! We'll slow down when we get closer. Now arm your seekers. Point them at the gray one. I'm taking out that hot rod myself!"

"But…" he replied, as his ship violently shook.

"No buts! It's not gonna break apart!" The older brother was relentless in his pursuit.

Flames suddenly started fanning out from the upper right thruster of his brother's ship. He had four other engines to work with, but the first one failing was only the beginning of his problems. One of the heavy cannons attached to the gun rack on the nose of the younger brother's T-Craft snapped clean off, smacking the canopy before being flung past the rear of the ship.

"I'm losing it! I gotta back down!" the younger Otto cried out.

The oldest brother kept advancing and now was more focused on his future than his brother's. "I'm gonna line up with hot rod! You get that gray one! Lock on, fire off that seeker, then back down!" The older Otto continued ignoring his brother's pleas.

Taft's target alarms sounded. "Kay! They're trying to lock on!"

"Keep with me, we're almost there! Split up when we get into the buildings. If they launch we should be able to dodge—" Kaytha cut herself off mid-sentence.

The oldest Otto brother pressed down on his thumb trigger as hard as he could.

The blast from the seeker missile fired from between the lift manifolds created a massive smoke cloud as the explosive tipped projectile rocketed toward Kaytha's T-Craft.

The younger Otto's ship was breaking apart as panels were flying off. A huge, black smoke trail filled the sky behind them. Barely audible in the echoing warning alarms blaring, a loud set of *dings* rang out as Taft's T-Craft was now locked on. Pressing his launch button, the seekers jet started to launch, and in an instant the leaking oil and fuel that coated the entire undercarriage of the T-Craft caught fire. Before the missile could leave its launch tube, the younger Otto brother's ship exploded. The thrusters, fuel, recharge cells, thousands of rounds of ammo, and a dozen explosive missiles all detonated in one massive fireball then crashed down to the ground the below.

"No!" the older brother shouted, watching the carnage from behind him on his rearview screens. Slamming the thrusters to max power, he continued after Taft and Kaytha.

Kaytha was approaching her maximum safe speed for atmospheric flight as the heat seeker was closing. She flew as straight as she could, hoping to reach the smoking damaged buildings in front of her. The contact *pings* were sounding off closer together, letting Kaytha know how quickly the destructive force trailing her was. She was about to reach a high rise as she prepared to start banking at precariously dangerous speeds to dodge the incoming ordinance.

She angled her T-Craft sideways, preparing for the g-forces of a turn at that speed.

The warning alarms immediately stopped. All Kaytha could hear was the quick wail of thrusters buzzing across the rear of the T-Craft. She then eased slightly up on her thruster speed and flew between several of the buildings.

Taft successfully crossed between the missile and Kaytha. His ship was putting off enough heat that at the moment he got in front of the missile, it tracked onto him and off of Kaytha's T-Craft. With the missile now tracking him down and Kaytha safe for the moment in the cover of the buildings, Taft pulled back on his control stick, making a sharp turn skyward, moving his T-Craft back in the direction of the remaining Otto brother.

The missile was running out of fuel as Taft dove for the desert terrain. Otto saw Taft and the missile heading back his direction but he was flying too fast to fire any of his weapons, and he didn't want to use another seeker, not after what had happened to his brother. He let Taft and the missile pass several hundred feet below him as he continued on after Kaytha.

The pings in Taft's T-Craft were now ringing out like they had in Kaytha's. The fuel continued depleting on the seeker, yet it still had more than enough to meet its mark before it ran out.

Taft had other ideas as he sped toward a smoke cloud rising up from the ground half a mile ahead. He aimed his T-Craft right for it as the seeker closed in. Plowing through the cloud of black smoke, he slammed his throttle forward. The surging thrusters thundered to deafening levels as Taft yanked the control stick back, rocking his T-Craft vertical into the air. The seeker missed the rear of Taft's ship by mere feet when it struck the ground, causing a mini mushroom cloud explosion and hurtling debris and dirt hundreds of feet in the air.

Taft gambled that the heat from the fiery wreckage of the younger brother's T-Craft that had crashed to the ground would be enough to take the seeker off his ship's track. He was right—the missile landed in the center of the burning wreckage. Still flying vertically, Taft barrel rolled his T-Craft back into the direction of downtown to engage with the attacker before he could get to Kaytha.

The smoke was thick and heavy in the air surrounding what remained of the Camelback skyline. Kaytha cut a path in the sky as she flew her T-Craft in between the buildings. The older Otto was having difficulty reading her heat signature amid the fires raging on the ground below. She had wound her way in and out of the crumbling high rises and flown straight out past the downtown area. She'd had it with being followed and attacked; it was time to go on the offense. Kaytha flipped the switches on all her sensors, scanning the entire area for the person trying to kill them.

Taft tried to zero in on their pursuer's location by spotting his smoking T-Craft. He was now flying his way through the downtown maze, catching quick glimpses of the evading T-Craft, then losing sight of him.

"Kaytha, you read? I don't see you or the other T? Acknowledge."

But Kaytha didn't respond—and for a good reason. She feared that the Otto might be frequency scanning and didn't want to give up her location. Taft flew between two high rises and out into the open air, flying out south from downtown in an attempt to regroup.

Just as he reached the edge of the city, the Otto brother came screaming down from above the skyline, firing a barrage of large high capacity sabot rounds from the mini-cannon he'd mounted on the nose.

Taft put his T-Craft into a cylindrical spin, powering up the throttle control and aiming for the heavens. The whooshing sounds of ammo flew past him and, for a brief moment, he thought that this was it. This desperate Otto brother was about to take him out. Taft twisted and turned as fast and hard as he could, dodging and weaving from every blast the smoking T-Craft could fire at him. The brother locked on with his one remaining seeker. Taft knew the guy was too close not to land his shot. As he was about to key his comm directly to Kaytha and say goodbye, he was blinded by the sight of gray, black, and red streaking past him.

The wailing of Kaytha's T-Craft as she blasted right past Taft's cockpit canopy was a welcome sound as he yelled out loud, "Yes!"

Kaytha unleashed two huge destructive bursts from her forward facing thruster cannons while flying directly at the Otto brother. After releasing the fatal shots, she pitched her T-Craft down under the incoming T-Craft right as the blasts connected with the Otto brother's cockpit, instantly destroying his ship. The explosion reduced the T-Craft to explosive dust, creating a rain of tiny bits which fell from the sky like burning confetti.

Taft slowed his T-Craft, catching his breath as Kaytha flew back around and pulled alongside him. Flipping up her visor and taking her cockpit canopy off its smokey tint view setting so Taft could see her, she keyed the comm to him. "You all right in there?"

"Yeah, a little shook up. I thought I was done for. I owe you for that one," Taft said, still breathing heavy.

"You don't owe me anything. You totally saved me from that seeker."

"You do make a good point."

"With the Otto brothers coming after us like that…there must be a new bounty out there? Which just confirms whoever is tracking us knows who we are now," said Kaytha.

"It doesn't matter. I mean, sure, it matters if now we have people out there trying to kill us. But it doesn't change our plans," Taft replied.

Kaytha turned her T-Craft to the east. She hadn't forgotten her personal reasons why she wanted to fly south. They weren't far from where her home was. "We just have to get more aggressive, T. We're at war now, whether we want to be or not."

"Should we warn the others?" Taft asked.

"They already have enough to worry about. Ven knows what he's doing. They'll be cautious enough."

The destructive path from the nearby DeCorp power plant and factory reached farther than either of them imagined and traveled miles past where Kaytha's home had been.

The two passed over the area of her neighborhood as Taft pondered saying something, but he opted to stay quiet. Kaytha slowed up her T-Craft as they flew past where her home would have been. There was nothing left, no evidence that a community ever existed in the charred remains of the blast radius.

With Taft still following her lead, they headed toward their atmospheric departure point. Kaytha pointed her T-Craft at a large open area of blue sky, so far untouched by the clouds of smoke and ash.

The space was roughly twenty miles wide in the vast empty desert between Arizona and California. Kaytha changed the view setting on her canopy, smoking the glass once again. They were heading into the sun, so Taft did the same.

"No easy way to say goodbye to this place, is there?" said Taft on the ship to ship comms.

"Everything has gone too far to go back. Makes it easier, I guess."

A large group of various T-Crafts and transport ships had the same idea as they did.

Taft kept an eye on his radar as they approached their departure point thinking, *If Ven and the Ultra Raiders decide to go the same route, then someone will absolutely spot the Anniversary.*

"We have an escort of medium-range EnerCon transports converging from the north. Let's mix in with them," said Kaytha over comms, turning in the direction of the evacuating ships.

The transports Kaytha had spotted were close relatives in design to the commercial jumbo jets of the past. The bodies were about the same shape as a typical airliner, but with a circumference twice the size. Underneath carried two rows of lift manifolds. Like most other modern crafts, they had no wings.

The rear of the ship housed two large EnerCon long range thrusters on each side and one short duration thruster to the rear at the top of the ship. The third engine helped in escaping Earth's atmosphere and gaining needed speed in space.

Flying into formation around the various vehicles, they all began to make their ascent into the blue sky above. Taft and Kaytha took one last look at the landscape and horizon. The sun was shining, lighting up the barren mountains in a brilliant display of orange, red, and yellow. It was the perfect view to remember planet Earth as the sky grew darker in front of them, with no sign of devastation yet.

As they reached the beginnings of space, the view was drastically different. The planet from this height no longer looked like Earth found in history books. It was covered with devastation and neither of them could stomach to stare at it. They were now flying with a group of over a hundred ships all heading in the same direction. Most would either join up with the EnerCon convoy or head to MarsCorp.

Now heading into the darkness of space, Taft and Kaytha removed the smoke tint again from their canopies.

Taft opened up his comms to Kaytha, saying, "When we break off, let's attach and get clear of the crowds quickly. People will be watching, but the sooner we're out of sight, the better."

"I'm ready when you are," Kaytha replied.

T-Crafts had the ability, similar to swapping parts, to be combined into essentially one ship. This was only possible in space. The T-Crafts connected via the lift manifolds under each ship. The power that radiated from the manifolds that provided the needed lift would now serve as magna-connections. By reversing the power flow, the connection could be achieved and was nearly unbreakable. Once they were sealed, with the press of a few buttons from the cockpit, two panels would open on each craft— one would sync the power distribution so thrusters would work in unison, while the other would sync the ships' operating systems.

"You don't mind if I lead this dance, do you, Kay?" asked Taft.

"Go for it."

They both spun up their long-range thrusters' energy cells. The extra power to the main boosters would send them hurtling through space at close to light speed. This "speed jump" was yet another reason Taft and Kaytha flew out ahead to Europa before their friends. Two ships in tandem could drastically cut the travel time.

Having now distanced themselves out away from the gathering of ships, they both flipped their visors down again to prepare for the jump.

Taft looked down at the floor of his cockpit. It was silly to do. But in his mind, he was looking straight through both ships and picturing Kaytha. "You ready?"

Kaytha, unbeknownst to Taft, was looking down at him through the floor too. "Yup, I'm just along for the ride. Now take us outta here."

"On my mark... three, two, one... Now!"

Taft went to work flipping the switches to direct all power to the engines, while he also pushed his throttle control forward to maximum output to all their thrusters. The two T-Crafts, now joined as one, shot off into the dark star field ahead like a bullet from a gun. Moving as fast as their combined T-Crafts would carry them, they were on their way headed straight for Europa.

Chapter 41

O-Station, Earth's Orbit

Tober Rosel, Uray Dow, and Number Three were strapping up their flight suits in preparation for departure to intercept the Anniversary once they left the flying field. They planned to take out as many accompanying craft before they reached space. Once the Anniversary was vulnerable, they would cripple the ship and secure the device for Sint Argum.

Number Two was already suited up as he continued to monitor the situation. "Number One, sir?"

"What is it, Two?" answered Rosel.

"Activity on the surface. I'd been monitoring the departing ships from the field. The two we placed the bounty on have left their location. They came in contact with two other T-Crafts in Camelback. One of the T-Craft went down quickly. I lost its signal. Then another T-Craft went down shortly afterward. From what I can gather of the data, the two that were destroyed were those Otto brothers. I assume it was them, sir," said Dow.

Rosel was annoyed. He had wanted those two, Taft and Kaytha. His priority was the device, but he was still upset that the others had slipped through his grasp when he had the chance. "Have you been tracking the other two T-Crafts?"

"Yes, sir. I was, but they joined up with a large group of outbound departing ships, west of the city. I lost them with the other ships. I'm continuing to monitor in case the scanner is able to isolate their signal again," replied Dow.

Rosel was trying to maintain his composure. The hit he had ordered was not authorized, and he feared this whole episode would turn on him, causing more problems than it was now worth. Rosel was about to tell Number Two to get ready to leave when Dow received an alert notification.

"Wait, sir. The scanner just picked up SH1-1051 and Prophet 6-0091. They just left a large gathering of ships right outside the atmosphere and jumped at speed out of the area."

"Can you plot a course to wherever they're heading?"

"Based on their trajectory, they appear to be heading straight for Jupiter. Doesn't EnerCon have an atmos and assets on…" but Dow was cut short.

"Europa, Number Two, they are heading for Europa. Put the data together, transfer to my onboard flight OS, then meet us in the launch bay."

"Sir, I don't mean to question, but would you like me to erase any of the data or shut the system down?"

"No need, Number Two. We'll destroy this floating office before we make our way to the surface," Rosel said.

Once they were locked into their attack ships, the tight quarters of the hangar bay decompressed, the O-Station equalization machine sucked all the air from the space. The T-Crafts were magnetically attached to the floor as the bay door slid open. One by one they flipped the power for the magna-connections into the off position. There was no need for the lift manifolds, as the absence of artificial gravity allowed the vehicles to float. Following Tober Rosel's lead, they each throttled up slowly and flew out from the O-Station in order by number.

"Number One to Two, Three, and Four, begin your descent to the planet at cruising speed. Watch for outbound ships and I will catch up with you," commanded Rosel.

Two, Three, and Four did as ordered, pitching down to begin the journey into Earth's atmosphere. Rosel kept them on his scanners as he powered forward with a quick boost out and away from the O-Station. Picking up speed, he traveled a few miles before throwing his control stick back, making a U-turn. Now speeding toward the O-Station, he slid the hand-sized red lever forward.

Rosel moved forward the small lever on the weapons control panel, charging the pulse blaster located at the front of his two largest DeCorp multidirectional cannon and thruster packages. The O-Station was getting big out his window as he closed in on his target. Using his trigger finger which was now assigned to unleash the power of the pulse blaster, he fired. Two huge, green energy blasts cut through the open space between Rosel and the O-Station. The moment the bursts almost simultaneously connected with their target, the O-Station completely erupted in a circular fireball, vaporizing the entire floating structure. Rosel continued his path directly into the chaos. His T-Craft cut through the carnage, emerging out the other side with his ship trailing fire and smoke. He kept up his speed and made for the three attackers just entering the gravity and air of the world on the brink of total collapse.

****

Mars' Orbit

The O-MMW, with the Oberkorn still attached, along with the dozens upon dozens of support ships in tow, were dropping down to the surface of the red planet. Sint Arugum was no longer sitting in the command seat. He was now standing in front of the bridge's biggest window looking out at the atmodome as they approached and the miles of geometric patterns created by all the DeCorp structures and MMWs that covered the region.

Leaving space, entering into Mars' gravity, and then through the dome took a bit of skill. Even with the power of the lift manifolds keeping everything afloat, the differences in air density required quick calculations to ensure a smooth flight. Akens Ember usually did not care how bumpy the trip to the surface was, but with Argum on board, it was best not to give him a reason to complain.

Sint didn't care about the dazzling dreamlike display flying through an atmodome created. Nor did he much like the outward displays of awe the crew would show when witnessing the colored vapor dance that occurred as each ship flew inside.

As the O-MMW breached the manufactured breathable air, the lift manifolds, outboard thrusters, and dozens of micro-jets kept the huge ship stable.

With the colliding atmospheres swirling all around them, Sint turned from his window toward the crew. "Pilot! Set the ship down and make your connection to Engineering Hangar Bay One. Ember, inform the rest of the following vehicles that, unless they are carrying equipment, to proceed to the habit portion of the compound. Ember, what is the status on the T-Drones you released?"

"Sir, the twenty-four attack drones have arrived just outside the Jupiter sector. They're in standby mode and awaiting orders," said Ember.

The twenty-four T-Drones flew in a programmed formation to an area of space in equal proximity to Jupiter and Europa. Once they arrived and left the regular travel lanes, the twenty-four pilotless ships magnetically connected together in a tightly formed group and powered down. They would stay dormant in order to avoid detection until given their commands. Unless someone was processing an active scan in the region, they would go unnoticed.

The O-MMW landed adjacent to the largest hangar bay on the planet. Behind the two enormous sliding doors, almost four stories tall, sat hundreds of DeCorp vehicles. Housed inside the huge building were T-Drones, attack craft, supply ships, Mars landscape traversing T-Crawlers, and dozens of sport vehicles of all manner of size and shape. The O-MMW slowly floated via the power of the lift manifolds until it rested flush with the wall of the complex. Once in position, the needed flight mechanisms started to fold back into the interior with the flight deck along with the outboard thrusters disappearing behind doors and panels. The O-MMW, now attached to the main building, was lined up with the entrances covering several floors. Once the sealed connections were locked in place, the crew of the vessel began to depart into the compound to continue working.

Sint Argum gathered up what few things he had on the Oberkorn and started making his way to the personal living space he had prepared in the heart of the engineering sector of the DeCorp operations. Before departing, Akens Ember had one more item to share with him.

"Commander, it appears Rosel and his team are preparing to engage the hostiles in hopes of securing the device. Also, we retrieved a transmission. It appears Rosel put a bounty on the two young people identified as a part of the conspiracy. From our data analysis, the bounty failed to yield results. Two potential profiteers tried to claim the bounty, but lost their lives after they engaged with the two who were the intended target," explained Ember.

"Where are they now?" Sint barely managed to contain his anger.

"They left the planet shortly after the fight with the bounty hunters. We did track two T-Crafts that bonded their ships before jumping to speed. Based on their trajectory, they too are headed to Europa."

"Have your drone captains be prepared to deploy and give me an estimated arrival time for our wayward friends headed to that floating frozen block," said Sint.

"I'll report what information I can as soon as I have it."

"And Ember, one more thing. If failure continues, someone is going to be held fully accountable."

Chapter 42

Kay's field, Arizona

Everything they could take with them was now loaded on the fifty-five interstellar ships of the newly formed Ultra Raiders and the Anniversary. Most of the T-Crafts were single seat vehicles apart from the handful of support T-Crafts, with some that seated two and a few that seated four. Anorant and Marrett decided to pilot one of the dual seated support craft, allowing for two of the Raiders to have their own ships to pilot. It was best that everyone get as much experience now and not later when they're under stress. None of the support ships were all that much larger than your standard Ts. They had extra storage areas attached to the rears of the ships plus larger, lower mounted thrusters. And, with larger fuel cells and charging loads, they could handle the energy drain from the extra weight in atmospheric conditions. Just like all the other ships, they were armed with whatever weaponry they could handle.

The Anniversary was already outside the hangar, with Ven, Oshly, and Jebet all sitting in their respective places on the bridge of the famed vessel.

Oshly was still patched into Kay's Field's hangar operating system.

With a few keystrokes, he shut and locked down the facility for the last time. Everyone assumed whatever they left behind would be plundered, but it just didn't feel right to leave the place they'd all grown to call home completely vulnerable.

"You two ready to get outta here?" Ven asked Oshly and Jebet.

"I'm ready," said Oshly.

"I'll never be fully ready, but we gotta leave at some point. So, sure, let's go," Jebet said with a hint of sarcasm to mask her nerves.

Ven went live on the comms to all the Ultra Raiders who sat idle on the tarmac. "Okay, pilots, the Anniversary's gonna take the lead. Everyone stay tight together. There's a lot of evacuating traffic being flown by scared and desperate people, but they're not our problem. Remember that the filters Oshly installed are gonna rob you of some power but they're necessary. We're gonna make our way north into the Yellowstone ash cloud. Because we're such a big group, we're gonna draw a lot of attention until we find the cloud cover. When we do and we're out of sight, we'll head out of the atmosphere. Once we're all off planet, we'll jettison our smoke filters and make the speed jump to Jupiter. Anorant and Marrett will fly to the rear of our group, call sign Supply One.

Me, along with Marrett and Anorant, will do everything we can to keep everyone informed of what lies ahead.

When we know, you'll know. Anorant, Marrett, are you guys ready?"

"Ready, Ven. The Ultra Raiders, they'll do a good job," said Marrett.

"I know they will. Keep comms to a minimum. Direct open communications only if completely necessary. I know you're scared, we're all scared. But let's remember, it's for a reason. Happy flying everyone," Ven said then switched off his mic.

Wasting no time, Ven powered up the energy cells feeding the lift manifolds to raise the Anniversary off the ground.

Throttling up the thrusters to 15% was enough to get the ship moving forward. As the Anniversary rose up from the valley floor, one by one the Raiders' T-Crafts followed suit. They gathered together flying behind the Anniversary, creating a three and four wide, two and three T-Crafts tall convoy. Supply One, the support T-Craft of Anorant and Marrett, followed as the last ship in line. Moving to a low altitude and into the increasingly gray cloud cover, the parade of assault ships disappeared from sight, heading north into the cover of an exploding volcano.

As the last T-Craft flew into the clouds, four DeCorp MTC fighters entered the airspace to the west of the air field.

They made a quick pass while monitoring the path of the newly departed caravan, but kept a safe distance. Rosel wanted to wait until they were clear of Earth before he and his fighters launched their attack and, more importantly, retrieved the device.

Rosel comm'd to the others, "Let's begin our tail of the targets. Do not engage until I give the go ahead. Remember, we need the Anniversary intact."

"Why are they heading north?" asked Number Three.

"I don't know, but stay sharp."

Uray Dow (Number Four) said, "Sir, did you happen to see that pile of smoke filters on the flight line?"

Rosel then figured out what their plan was. "Good observation, Four. They won't be staying this close for long. They're heading for the ash cloud, probably going to attempt to get off-world under the cover of Yellowstone. Let's pick up the pace. This expedites our mission."

Rosel knew he could go into the upper stratosphere and catch them in open space. But he also knew that they would probably pick up their signal, and he would lose the element of surprise. An attack in the ash cloud could provide an advantage, dispatching as many of the smaller T-Crafts before chasing the Anniversary into space.

As the DeCorp ship started their turn north, Number Two opened up comms to the other three MTCs. The four DeCorp MTCs quickly left the field behind and entered the growing cloud mass as they chased down their target.

****

The Ultra Raider convoy was approaching Yellowstone as the sky grew darker. The Anniversary shook violently as they maneuvered it through the chaotic weather, made all the worse by the rising ash plume. All the ships in the caravan struggled to stay straight.

Ven opened all comms to every ship behind them. "Listen up. If you're not already, go active on your lift manifolds for stability while we ride this out. We need to get further north until we have the open air space above to start our run."

"Ven, I'm getting a massive heat signature about twenty miles out. Oh my—" Oshly's voice broke off, and the color drained out of his face. Out the flight deck windows, the gray clouds of wind, rain, and ash were suddenly entirely washed out in a flash of bright light.

Within seconds, every ship traveling north in the convoy, including the four DeCorp attackers who were now less than a mile away from the last of the group, was stopped in midair and thrown backward from the shock wave. Yellowstone's biggest eruption had begun.

Every vehicle flying within a fifty-mile radius was tossed through the air. Two of the Ultra Raiders flying in the middle of the pack were thrown into each other and exploded instantly upon impact.

****

Uray Dow was the first to go on all comms to the other three DeCorp pilots. "The park is erupting again! Waiting for your instructions, Number One!"

Tober Rosel was dazed from the blast. As his T-Craft went into emergency mode, he attempted to manually gain stability.

Hearing Dow's communication, Rosel replied, "Begin engagement of the smaller T-Crafts. Take out as many as you can before they try and leave the planet. DO NOT ENGAGE THE ANNIVERSARY!"

****

"All Raiders, break formation, split up and head for open space!" Ven shouted on all comms. The ash cloud they were flying through was now thousands of feet thick above them as the Anniversary and young pilots started their climb, their ships rocking back and forth as they fought the dense smoke and wind. The center of the park, now a volcano, was shooting ribbons of lava into the air. Red-hot molten rocks were rocketing upwards and falling like bombs! The DeCorp attackers now had the tail of the convoy in their sights as burning smoldering chunks of earth flew past their ships.

Anorant and Marrett were the first to pick up the signal of the four ships chasing them down. "Ven, it's Anorant! We've got company! It looks like four heavily armed DeCorp crafts are closing in on us!"

Ven watched on his screen as Number Three launched two heat seekers from the belly of his fighter. Within seconds, the missiles connected with an Ultra Raider and blew the entire rear of the ship completely away, then it burst into flame and went nose first back down to Earth.

Seconds later, a huge chunk of burning rock struck dead center on the lift manifolds of another Ultra Raider.

"I've been hit!" comm'd the teen as his ship went tumbling forward and smashed into the Raider he had been following.

Both pilots struggled to regain control. The first ship, burning from the impact, erupted into a massive fireball. One of the main thrusters, still being fed power, broke free from the exploding T-Craft and, like a rocket, launched forward to connect with another ascending lava rock. The rock flew directly into the side of yet another Ultra Raider, splitting the T-Craft in two as it plummeted to the surface. With two missiles, Number Three had inadvertently disabled one T-Craft while taking out his intended target.

Six Raiders were already down as Anorant and Marrett struggled to fly their own ship.

They were desperate to find a way to help the others, but not without risking the supplies they carried.

Doing everything she could to sound rational, Marrett said, "There's nothing we can do. The ship is loaded too heavy for combat. Unless we break free of the atmosphere, we have to protect the supplies, or we're all in trouble."

"There!" said Anorant as he pointed toward a ray of light that had broken through the chaos around them. "We can make for that patch of blue sky!"

Marrett immediately direct comm'd to Ven. "Ven! It's Supply One. We've found a clear exit point and we're making a run off planet. Once we're clear, we'll wait as long as it's safe to. If not, we'll see you at the rendezvous."

Ven didn't reply, and Marrett didn't have time to think about why.

"I'm transferring controls to you. You're better at this than I am," said Anorant.

Without saying a word, Marrett took over. Throttling up the bulky supply T-Craft, she mashed the thrusters to the point of redline and shot directly toward a sliver of blue sky. Number Two was chasing behind and fired a plasma blast at the ship, but Anorant and Marrett had already disappeared into the haze above.

Uray Dow and Tober Rosel were in pursuit of at least twenty Ultra Raiders as they all pitched their T-Crafts toward the heavens. Rosel fired off round after round from his auto-cannons, showering the metal explosive tipped shells into the ash cloud. Sounding like popcorn cooking, the sound of the deadly ammunition struck the back of two Raiders' T-Crafts as they flew in close formation. Within an instant, they exploded in a shower of burning hot metal pinging against Dow's and Rosel's cockpit canopies.

The attack by the DeCorp pilots temporarily stopped. Everyone was too occupied with dodging the molten debris falling from the sky. Number Three joined up with Dow and Rosel flying along behind them. Rosel was about to give his next command to begin tracking down the Anniversary when a giant block of rock and lava came bursting down at them from the clouds above. The boulder had been blown from the heart of the exploding volcano. Rosel jerked his control stick back as hard as he could, almost stopping in midair as his T-Craft dropped from the sky to avoid hitting the burning chunk of earth. Number Three had fallen in line flying behind Rosel. Looking forward, Number Three had no time to react as his T-Craft flew directly into the massive rock. The giant mass of soil was so hot that the nose of Number Three's T-Craft punched into the white-hot molten core of lava rock instantly setting his ship on fire as it continued its fall to the ground. The rock and ship had melted into one, as the energy cells and fuel ignited. The combination of scorched earth and disintegrating T-Craft sent pieces of debris flying in all directions from the exploding center of blinding light.

Uray Dow continued to follow the convoy, wondering if he would ever make it out of the endless ash cloud. He continued to see T-Crafts in front of him but failed to fire.

Number Two was now following a group of twelve T-Crafts, fighting between flying and taking aim at the ships whenever he had the chance.

****

Torian, the young Ultra Raider, watched helplessly as rounds of ammo and energy blasts flashed by her and her friends from the attacking DeCorp ships. She worried that the air was starting to darken ahead with the ash cloud reaching all the way to the edge of the atmosphere.

Still being fired upon, Torian had had enough. She went on comms directly to a handful of friends flying closely with her. "Keep going, guys. I'll be right back."

Shutting the power off and putting her T-Craft into a stall, Torian nosed her ship back toward Earth. It didn't take long until she could see the DeCorp attacker screaming toward her. Pressing the missile arming buttons on her ship's weapons panel, she squared the T-Craft in her sights. Torian squeezed the trigger on the control stick assigned to launch dual heat seekers. A double blast of light was all she needed to know that her delivery was on its way. Before it would reach her pursuer, she slammed down the power lever; her thrusters let out a loud growl with the increase in power. Torian looped her T-Craft back toward freedom.

Number Two never knew what hit him as both missiles directly impacted his T-Craft, instantly destroying him and everything around where he sat.

The fireballs being thrown from the Yellowstone blast were fading into the gray skies below. The Anniversary and remaining Ultra Raiders continued their rapid ascent into space. Anorant and Marrett in their supply ship were already clear of the atmosphere. They watched and prayed as they waited for their friends to emerge below them from the ash cloud as they floated in space.

Ven had been right. There was no evacuating traffic from where they entered space. They were the only crafts within hundreds of miles.

"Oshly, do you see the remaining DeCorp ships on your scopes?" called out Ven, knowing they would be in open space soon and most likely have to fight the attackers one-on-one.

"No. I've got most of the Raiders accounted for, but I can't zero in on those a-holes," Oshly said.

"Hey, Osh, I know we're fighting for our lives and all, but can you keep it clean?" said Jebet.

"For a reason, Jebet, for a reason!" Oshly quipped back. "Ven, our raiders are struggling to keep up."

Oshly glared back at Jebet and continued saying, "If those *bad guys* are still out there and catch up, they're in big trouble."

Ven did a quick scan of the remaining ships trailing behind. A handful of the Raiders were flying separate from the others. One by one, those few left behind dropped off his radar. Ven tragically assumed the eruption must have taken them out, and he was right.

The Anniversary was about to enter open space while the remaining Raiders were going to be vulnerable once they breached the ash cloud. "Oshly, you have any ideas?"

"Well, I could—"

"DON'T QUESTION IT, OSH! Whatever you're going to do, just do it!" Ven yelled as the Anniversary rocketed clear of the planet's gravity and into open space.

Just then, the two remaining DeCorp MTCs appeared behind the leading group of escaping Raiders, firing on the ships with wild abandon.

Oshly pulled up the operating system screen where he had granted himself control of the individual systems on all the Ultra Raiders' ships. With a single swipe across his screen, he implemented the command to jettison all the smoke filters he had installed on the Raiders' thrusters.

Once the filters dropped off, the Raiders' thrusters were able to open up, allowing their T-Crafts to immediately gain power and increase speed. Coming as a shock and relief to the remaining pilots, each ship pulled away from their attackers.

All Rosel and Dow could do was watch as the ships they had been pursuing disappeared into the gray ash around them. Adding insult to injury, they were bombarded by the air filters flying off from the evading ships.

Once Anorant spotted the Anniversary, he powered up the guns of his ship and primed the missile launchers, expecting a fight. Ven spun around the Anniversary as they all waited for what remained of the Ultra Raiders. Then, one at a time, the young T-Craft pilots shot out from the grey smoke clouds below them. Anorant, Marrett, Ven, Oshly, and Jebet watched and counted as each craft broke into open space. Oshly kept an eye on the scanner and at a count of forty-two saw what he knew was the last of the Ultra Raiders.

****

Tober Rosel and Uray Dow continued their climb when Rosel comm'd, "Slow up your speed and turn east. We're leaving."

Dow didn't question it. They didn't take out nearly enough ships, and, with Numbers Two and Three dead, they would be sitting ducks if they were to engage again.

"I'm setting a course for MarsCorp. Compose a message and inform Commander Argum of the situation and the loss of Two and Three.

We'll regroup with the fleet and reconfigure our plan," Rosel said in defeat.

"Yes, sir," Dow replied, as the two DeCorp ships flew east into the ash cloud still within the stratosphere. They soon arrived to clear skies where they joined in with a group of evacuating ships heading into space.

362

EMBARK

****

The crew of Anniversary and the Ultra Raiders all sat in the silence of space while the violent destruction occurred below them underneath the stratosphere.

"That's all of them that are left," Oshly said somberly. "And it looks like the remaining DeCorp ships left the area."

"They knew they were outgunned," replied Ven. Then, going all comms to the survivors, he asked, "Any of you injured?"

The communications stayed silent.

"Everyone, drop in behind the Anniversary. We'll have time for sorrows later. Right now we need to speed jump out of here in case any more unwelcome visitors arrive."

Ven then looked over at Oshly and said, "Send out the flight parameters for a speed jump to take us just outside Jupiter's orbit."

As per protocol for a group speed jump, Oshly punched in the needed information to all the ships' flight computers so each ship would match the lead ship's speed.

"Done, Ven. We're good for the jump."

With all the ships now behind the Anniversary and pointed the same direction at the open space ahead, Ven gave the command. "All pilots, for a reason. Jump in three, two, one."

The remaining ships shot away from Earth to join their friends heading for Europa just beyond Jupiter.

Chapter 43

In the engineering wing of MarsCorp, a single tall circular coning tower sat in the center of the sprawling complex. At its top sat the facility's main command center. Inside the room showcased a center stage where a large bank of HIREZ screens and computer consoles were located along with an auto chair for easy access to the equipment. The chair's position enabled whoever was utilizing the space to effortlessly move around to any portion of the technology available. The entire structure at the top of the spire was made of shatter-proof poly alloys and was completely transparent except for the titanium support bars that ran between the geometrically shaped panels. Looking out around the room, there was nothing but crystal clear views in every direction. From the outside, in the light of day, the panels gave off a bright, yet still transparent, emerald green glow. From a distance, the complex looked more like a wizard's staff, adorned with an obnoxiously large green gem on top of the hi-tech control center.

Until Sint Argum arrived with his fleet and the first of Earth's evacuees, the space had sat empty. Argum commissioned it to be built when the construction on Mars began.

No one was ever authorized to utilize the area in the years since its completion—until now.

Upon arrival, Sint ordered all his operating system's files transferred to what would now be his personal command and control center. This was always his intent. At the base of the spire, the tower fanned out to provide space for a medium sized hangar bay and living quarters that could efficiently and comfortably fit a small crew, but would only house Sint Argum. His personal belongings were moved to this location, unpacked, and prepared according to Argum's exact preferences. And of course, this included his decadent luxury T-Craft.

Sint Argum traveled alone up the high-speed elevator to his new C&C center. As the doors slid open, he could already hear the transmission exchanges echoing from the workspaces in the raised center of the room. All computer systems were online, with supplies laid out in the utility area near the elevator entrance. In this moment, Sint felt satisfied at his accomplishments so far. He knew his efforts were proving successful, and even though it had come with a horrible price of the massive loss of life, in his mind, it happened for a reason. As he looked out over DeCorp's creation, a notification ping sounded from the room's main computer terminal.

"OS, play the latest message received," Sint said.

"*For Command Argum's ears and eyes only. Private message from Uray Dow. Authorized by T. Rosel,*" replied the female voice of the OS system.

On the terminal's main HIREZ screen, a command flashed. There was a request in small, white letters against a black screen which read simply *Acknowledge*. Sint requested that all available logins to every system in the command control center set to his signature, his fingerprint serving as the only necessary ID for the OS System. Touching the screen, the system confirmed that the user was indeed Sint Argum.

Next, the display opened a video stream of Uray Dow from inside his T-Craft, recorded after he and Tober Rosel had broken off from their attack on Earth. Speaking through his flight helmet, Dow explained the events that had unfolded. Sint could see the look of strain and frustration on Dow's face. He was clearly in rough shape.

"Commander Argum, our target consisting of roughly fifty light heavily armored Traverse craft, along with a modified support ship and the Anniversary, left the flying field north of Camelback and made their way for Yellowstone. Rosel believed that because of the large contingent of ships, the targets were attempting to utilize the volcanic ash cloud to depart the planet with as little attention drawn to them as possible. We spotted T-Craft smoke filters scattered on the tarmac before our pursuit of the target. As we were about to engage, Yellowstone erupted.

We attacked the convoy and took out a handful of light craft before losing Number Two and Three during the engagement of the enemy and the volcanic activity." Dow was attempting to explain why they had failed, again.

Sint Argum dug deep to control his emotions. While he had acquired success getting to Mars and was ever closer to his goal of complete control of DeCorp, he was inevitably failing. He needed to get his hands on the one thing that could either give or potentially strip him of power. Without the device in his own hands, everything Sint had worked so hard to achieve was threatened. He believed he was still destined to attain the device and that this setback was minor.

Taking a deep breath, he continued to watch the stream. "Rosel believes, and I concur, that the targets are heading toward Jupiter and its moons. We also believe they're attempting to meet up with SH1-0151 and Prophet 6-0091. At no point did the Anniversary, which we think still holds the device we're searching for, engage its stealth capabilities. We are now making plans to begin heading to Mars station. We await response or further orders, sir."

Sint knew Rosel was a stellar military strategist and why he broke from the mission parameters. This didn't change the fact that Sint believed they should have gone after the device sooner. But there was nothing that could be done about that now. With the garrison of T-Drones as backup, he had another opportunity to retrieve the device and take out this alleged resistance.

Sint considered for a moment to connect directly with Rosel. His patience was wearing thin however, and he instead decided to record a video stream with new orders, rather than waste his time with unnecessary conversation.

"Rosel and Dow, set a course for Jupiter immediately. There is a moderate fleet of attack drones in a stationary position between your destination and Europa. They await your arrival to engage. I am also ordering a strike on the Enercon facilities. Whatever Prophet 6 and SH 1 are looking for, I will make sure they don't find it. I'm contacting Akens Ember immediately to dispatch the closest manned T's to assist you in retrieving the device and the

Anniversary before they can escape the Jupiter system. Contact me when you have reached the outer edge of the system. And do *not* fail me again," Sint concluded.

Chapter 44

Jupiter was now in sight out of both Kaytha's and Taft's T-Craft windows. For the time being, Kaytha was the only one awake to see it. The navigational system operated solely from Taft's T-Craft while they were connected in tandem mode. The guidance computer would know when to begin to slow up their approach. A prolonged burst from their thrusters when they departed Earth allowed them to reach the speed needed for the jump. Once the increase was achieved, the engines would shut down as their ships maintained their momentum. To slow the T-Crafts, the computer started firing tiny boosters located on the nose of the ship pointed forward.

A few hours into the flight, they both had an onboard meal. Some prepackage processed fruits, grains, meat with water, and milk, but nothing too filling as their flight suits were only designed for urination relief into the waste compartment. Anything beyond that and they would need a proper rest stop. After they ate, the onboard AI took over so they could rest.

The small boosters slowing their speed as the ships started their final leg of the journey to the icy blue moon was enough to wake Kaytha up. Europa was the smallest of the four moons orbiting Jupiter. Its size and surface made it perfect for the EnerCon

Atmosphere Processor to cover the majority of the surface infrastructure they'd built.

Looking at Taft's vital signs, she could tell he was still in a deep sleep. *He probably didn't notice the change in power output, since his music is still playing*, Kaytha thought to herself. Curious what he was listening to, she directed his audio output into her helmet headset. The music was vaguely familiar, symphonic. *Not a band, most likely a soundtrack*, she thought. She didn't much care for movie soundtracks and wasn't nearly as big a fan of films as Taft was, but she always appreciated his passion for movies. She thought about waking him up, but based on the current calculations, she decided to go over both their ships' diagnostics. Plus, she was actually enjoying the music. A few tracks into Taft's playlist, Kaytha finally guessed that it had to be one of the Star Wars films. They were his favorite and most likely it was from one of the older ones. Taft told her many times of how he appreciated the movies that were made while the creator (some guy named Lucas, she recalled) was still alive and especially the ones he was involved in. Whatever movie this particular track was from was apparently a love theme of some kind.

"Hey, you awake up there?" Kaytha's voice roused Taft from his deep slumber.

For a moment, he had forgotten exactly where he was, but the stale taste of recycled air was an instant reminder that the space he was currently occupying was the cockpit of his T-Craft.

Taft broke through the music in Kaytha's speakers, still groggy. "I'm up, sort of. I didn't realize I was that tired, wow," he said, wiping the grime from his eyes.

"Yeah, I was just going over our systems. Everything is running smoothly. We aren't using up nearly as much power as I expected. Can you see Jupiter out the window?"

Taft stretched and, behind a stifled yawn, said, "Wow, that's quite the sight. How much longer you think? Hey, you listening to my tunes?" Taft noticed the system share indicator on the playlist patched in from his flight suit to his console.

"I figured the music was keeping you asleep. What is this anyhow? I assume it's Star Wars?"

Taft chuckled. Anytime she would acknowledge his fondness for old-school nerd culture, it made him happy. "You, my dear, are currently experiencing none other than John Williams. One of the, if not *the*, greatest film composers to ever have lived." Taft imagined she was probably rolling her eyes at this.

Kaytha decided to indulge him. "Huh, it's not so bad. This one's a little overly dramatic, but okay."

"It's from *Attack of the Clones*. I made you watch it last year. Pretty sure you fell asleep. This particular track is called *Across the Stars*."

"Of course it is." Taft knew this was Kaytha's way of saying the moment was probably over.

"I'll make sure I put together a playlist and include it for next time we aren't running for our lives." Taft tapped the pause button on his player.

Kaytha let out a slight laugh, but his words instantly broke the mood. They were running for their lives and, while it was nice to have forgotten the situation, it was time to get focused again.

"Kay, looks like we're close enough. I'm transferring flight controls back to you now," said Taft as he made ready the separation of their T-Crafts. Kaytha's controls lit up like tiny Christmas lights as she prepared to regain control of her ship.

"Detaching in three, two, one." With a press of an illuminated purple button, while still flying toward their destination, the T-Crafts separated. Kaytha loosened up her arms by pitching her ship through a few cork screw turns out away from Taft.

While she continued course correcting, Kaytha flew up next to Taft. Her helmet visor up, she looked over at him for the first time in almost a day. "Hey, handsome."

Taft still wasn't quite used to Kaytha's outwardly vocal signs of affection, but he wasn't complaining. Besides, it wasn't like anyone was around for her to be embarrassed in front of. "Good to see you too, K."

Kaytha had no intention of always being so direct but enjoyed this deviation from her typical personality. It reminded her of what it was like trying out a new hair color or style of clothes.

As Europa came into view, her mood quickly changed. There was an abundance of debris floating just outside the man-made atmosphere. Heat signatures off the surface location they were heading for showed clusters of random readings. Nothing that looked like a typical moon or planetoid civilization. Something terrible had happened. Someone got here before they did.

Making their approach, all visuals of Europa's surface were clouded behind a smoke cover that pushed up against the atmodomes' processed air.

Usually, any surface particulates would escape out into space when vehicles would breach the engineered atmosphere arriving and departing a planet or moon's surface.

It looked as if nothing had breached the dome as smoke and gasses from whatever occurred on the ground filled the breathable airspace. The moment their ships passed through the thin differential that kept the atmosphere from pushing out into space, a whirlwind of dense gray smoke swirled out into the weightlessness of space behind them. As they flew closer to their intended destination of what they hoped would be evacuees of EnerCon, the devastation came into view. The handful of structures and buildings were utterly destroyed—burning and crumbled. There was nothing left of the company's assets. Then the horror came into view as dozens of ships lay in ruin, scattered across the entire region.

"Did DeCorp know we were coming? EnerCon is no threat. Why murder so many innocent people?" asked Taft over the comms to Kaytha.

"They were easy targets. EnerCon had built a sizable presence here, and DeCorp's staking their claim. I don't think they knew we were heading here or they would have waited. Clearly, they were caught off guard." Kaytha tried to keep it together. Any doubt of the growing danger Sint Argum and DeCorp posed was gone. "It looks like some of the ships might have been in flight. Maybe they tried escaping at the last minute? My scans show no sign of life."

"I'm in the process of a deep surface scan. It looks like there's a series of power lines feeding from a power generator burning in the north sector. The generator is destroyed.

It's looking like the backup power cells are buried deep beneath the surface ice. They feed to a location on the other side of the Moon. Maybe DeCorp missed something?" Before Taft finished, Kaytha was already turning her T-Craft toward the direction of the power line feeds.

The smoke-filled Atmodome was starting to dissipate as Taft and Kaytha flew toward the underground power lines. The power needed to keep the processors working was almost drained, which meant that the protective layer of breathable air would soon evaporate under the pressure of Europa's natural atmosphere. The backside of the moon didn't have any air processing.

"I think the attack was a hit and run, probably not carried out by any manned craft. I assume drones would be focused on the highest concentrations of activity and human life. Without an atmodome drawing attention to it, it's easy to understand why they didn't pick up on the power line feeds," said Taft as they quickly approached the area the lines were feeding.

"Yup, just as I suspected, looks like a supply depot and power replay substation," Kaytha said, pointing to a group of buildings in view.

"How are the lights still on?"

"Most of EnerCon's facilities store a certain amount of power in the cells just in case the plant goes down.

I'm hacking into their OS system now to see if I can retrieve the current level of power generation left. Here we go, got it. The facility is on backup power now, and it looks like at least three, maybe four, days before the place goes dark."

Kaytha and Taft flew over the row of silos along with rectangular, box-shaped buildings, all stacked on top of each other, each only a few stories high. The structures were covered in piping with brightly lit neon tubing running from one building to another and antennas poking into the sky.

"EnerCon always did make their infrastructures look fancier than they should be," said Taft.

"Look, there's a hangar off to the south. I think I can open up the flight entrance door."

They slowed over the flight hangar located outside on the harsh, deadly Europa surface. The hangar itself was designed to get the ships into the bay and allow the pilots to exit into the building's airtight safety of breathable air. The landing procedure was reminiscent of entering buildings in the cold weather climates of Earth. Two sets of doors would keep the heat inside and the freezing temps outside. In this case, the Enercon hangar's first entry was a massive, hinged door that opened from the top half up, like pulling up a lid on a beverage cooler.

Taft and Kaytha, utilizing their lift manifolds, flew into the top portion of the building and hovered while the door closed above them. A loud, mechanical whir followed by a magnetic slam informed them the doors were sealed properly. Huge fans on each corner of the room filled the space with oxygen. After only a few seconds, another door slid open in front of them. The bright white lights inside the hangar caused them both to flip down their visors to avoid the glare. The hangar was big enough for a dozen or more T-Craft sized vehicles. The room was vacant of any ships but filled with supplies. Whoever was last to leave left a lot of gear behind. Taft and Kaytha slowly pushed forward into the room. Once clear of the door, it closed and sealed behind them.

Kaytha keyed the comm one last time as they landed their ships and prepared to examine the hangar bay's contents.

"I didn't pick up any signs of life, but let's be on guard anyway. EnerCon's security drones are a bit sketchy—if there are any left wandering around."

Taft said, "I just hope we find the parts we need to fuel up the STL-5. If not, this was a wasted trip."

Even though it wasn't visible from the exterior of the building, there appeared to be a crew headquarters built into the structure.

"Looks like living quarters over there, next to the computer systems." Taft pointed to the back of the room.

A series of stairs headed beneath the surface with dormitory and kitchen signage.

"I'll log into the OS system. Maybe I can find a supply manifest. Plus, the antenna arrays and dish outside should be capable of long-range transmissions."

Taft made his way to the other side of the hangar.

Large black metal fences with stacks of equipment behind them were providing the best visual hope he had in finding the parts that they needed. Specifically what they were searching for was required to retrofit the standard fuel loaders and energy chargers unique to the Anniversary.

Looking back over his shoulder, Taft yelled out, "Looks like we lucked out! The gates were left open so I'm going to go poke around."

Annoyed, Kaytha said under her breath, "So much for keeping quiet."

"What was that?" Taft yelled back

"Nothing. I'll yell if I find anything." She figured there really was no point anymore maintaining a low profile. If there'd been security drones around, no doubt they would have attacked by now.

Taft sensed Kaytha's annoyance and then realized why.

He considered yelling back once more to apologize but decided to leave well enough alone. It didn't take him long to wander past three rows of parts and boxed up nonperishable food supplies to come across exactly what he was looking for. "Hey, Kaytha!" Taft yelled at the top of his lungs. "Looks like we struck gold!"

Kaytha didn't hesitate to get up from the terminal and jog over to Taft. "What are we looking at?"

"These EnerCon guys were stocked up all right. Check it out, this entire rack is dedicated to different fueling and charging systems. Over here we have DeCorp craft stuff—fuel cell adapters, quasi-nuke transfer pods, thruster recharge flux boxes. And here, these are what Oshly was talking about. Refuel Snap Charger Adapters with multi-size energy links. With these, Oshly can retrofit the STL to virtually any charging station." Taft was feeling some relief until Kaytha noticed another problem.

"T, I don't think we have enough storage space with the gear we're carrying to cart what we need outta here. Besides, there's a lot more here we could use," said Kaytha.

"What if we get a message out to the group? Tell Ven to send everyone here. If they take an indirect route to this side of the moon, they stand a better chance of not being detected. Chances are DeCorp—or whoever attacked—aren't coming back. If they missed this place, there's no reason to.

If they come in from the far side, even if those responsible are still in the neighborhood, they probably aren't looking for incoming traffic coming from that direction," said Taft with confidence about his plan.

Kaytha walked outside the supply area to get a better look around. "There isn't enough room to get all the ships in here, but the rest can attach outside. Their flight suits will safely get them into the building. We can use the facility as a staging area, no wasting time. Who knows how long until DeCorp goes after the evacuees."

"Then let's make time. Unload what we don't need now and get the parts for the STL. Our ships are already fueled, and the auto charging started the moment we locked to the floor. With the attachments—if the STL still needs a boost—Oshly can connect inside the Anniversary's hangar." He was growing even more optimistic and could tell that Kaytha was too.

"You start making room and loading what we need. I'll see if I can't get the communications towers up and running."

"Why not just message Ven from your Craft?"

"We're better off using EnerCon's logic crypto messaging. Ven will know how to retrieve it. We get the info to him, then he can relay the relevant data to Anorant, Marrett, and the Raiders."

"I'm not sure it's a good idea for the two of us to just wait. We'll be safer once we're with the others. It may take them a while to get here."

"We're not sticking around, T. Once I message Ven, we're charged, and everything's loaded, we'll make a straight flight out to the Anniversary while the others take the long way, like you suggested. Plus, when we reach the Anniversary and charge the STL, we won't have to worry about being spotted. Then we can return back here and plot our next move," said Kaytha.

"Almost sounds easy?" Taft's light tone contradicted the reality. It was anything but easy, but it was a plan. And right now, it was better than nothing.

"For a reason, right?" Kaytha then surprised Taft by grasping his jawline in her hands and kissing him. "There! Motivation! Now, I'm going to go see if I can reach our friends." She turned to walk away but called back to add, "You, sir, need to get to work."

Taft could only smirk and cock his head as he watched Kaytha jog back to the other side of the bay. Taft decided that Kaytha for sure had faith in him and, more importantly, in them.

"Stop smiling and get to work I said!" Kaytha shouted on her way to the computer terminal.

"Yes, ma'am!" Chuckling to himself, with two fingers to his brow, he playfully mock-saluted in Kaytha's direction. Turning back into the gated supply area, Taft was very much motivated.

Chapter 45

Space, destination Jupiter

Ven sat in the flight chair, nodding off and on while the Anniversary autopilot kept the ship flying true to its destination. The remaining ships' pilots of the weary band were resting as best they could while their operations systems executed their flight orders. Even Anorant and Marrett were sleeping as the remaining few hours until they were due to meet with Kaytha and Taft ticked down.

Ven's message alert chime woke him up from the longest stretch of sleep he'd had since they left Earth. Groggy and not quite alert, Ven lazily swiped his finger across the screen to open the message. It was a video stream from Kaytha. The moment her voice began to echo through the flight deck, Jebet and Oshly, also napping at their respective posts, jumped up and hurried over to Ven's HIREZ view screen. Kaytha was quick to point out that the message was for Ven's eyes only. That only meant that everyone other than the three of them shouldn't be viewing. Ven, Jebet, and Oshly watched and listened while Kaytha updated them.

Behind Kaytha, they could see Taft pulling out the parts, supplies, and adaptors that Oshly had requested. Unbeknownst to Kaytha and Taft, there were now far fewer young pilots than when they'd departed.

Kaytha quickly laid out the plan for the Ultra Raiders, including the supply T-Craft with Marrett and Anorant, to change course by plotting a longer indirect route to the far side of Europa. Once they arrived at the EnerCom facility, they could utilize it as a makeshift base of operations. Next, Kaytha detailed how she and Taft would fly directly out to meet the Anniversary in space above the moon.

Oshly left for the hangar bay to start prepping his and Jebet's T-Crafts. They would need the space for Taft and Kaytha to dock inside the ship to unload supplies and begin the process of converting the Anniversary's fuel and charging systems. Before Kaytha's message concluded, Jebet too rushed to get straight back to work. She and Oshly would both be off the ship in their T-Crafts, and Ven would have to handle all the systems of the Anniversary alone. The mighty freighter was built to be piloted by a single person if need be, but it would take an hour for Jebet to route all her navigation and fire controls to Ven's captain's system. Kaytha ended her video with Taft saying over her shoulder, "See you guys soon." Then he added, in the sincerest way he could, "For a reason."

"Jebet, plot a course away from the current path we're on to the far side of Europa.

Keep the group clear of the nearest system but not so much that it's going to take them forever to get there. Just far enough to be safe and close enough to still be efficient," Ven said, going through a mental checklist. "Once you do, go ahead and log into Oshly's system and load it up on all the Raiders' nav networks. Make sure Rant and Marrett get it too."

"Why don't they just wait for us where they are?" asked Jebet, as she ran the needed calculations for the caravan's course change.

Ven said, "I know that facility and it's not the biggest. The Anniversary would take up too much space. Besides, if those DeCorpers are still hunting for us, even Taft and Kaytha know it's better not to drag everyone into battle with those guys. With the device, assuming Oshly gets it working, we should be able to avoid detection on our own without putting everyone else in danger. The less they know, at least for now, the better."

Jebet transmitted the details to the remaining ships, with each of them pinging back after receiving the latest instructions. Everyone was still flying at incredible speed through open space. Ven, now awake and alert, sat reviewing the flight systems Jebet had transferred.

Anorant and Marrett would now lead pilots in their forty-three ships to Europa.

Marrett was in direct communication with the other pilots, giving instructions and checking on their well-being. She turned off the transmissions to the Anniversary. They were now on two separate missions for the time being, and everyone need only worry about their task at hand.

Ven watched as Supply One, on the tail end of their interstellar wagon train, picked up speed and changed course. Supply One passed the others to assume the lead of the caravan. Guided by the onboard navigation systems behind the Anniversary, Anorant and Marrett were now on the new path Jebet formulated for them. One by one, the Ultra Raiders peeled off and followed one another, trailing behind Supply One, in the same direction. It took only a handful of minutes for the entire convoy to gather and head for the long way around to Europa.

Once the Ultra Raiders were out of scanner range, Ven opened up the communications channel to the Anniversary hangar bay's audio system. Ven's booming voice echoed loudly off the metal walls of the bay. "Oshly, how much power is left in the STL?"

Oshly was sitting in the pilot's seat of his own T-Craft with the canopy open. He brought up the flight deck on his console's computer to reply, "Well, it's got a charge, but I'm hesitant to bring it online until I have my hands on the parts we need for refueling and recharging."

This was a version of the truth. but Oshly wasn't ready to share everything he knew. Not even with Ven and Jebet and definitely not until Kaytha and Taft arrived. He sat nervously in his seat waiting for Ven to respond, worried Ven would press him on the issue. And he definitely didn't want to lie to his friend.

"Okay, Osh. We're not that far out now. Just make sure you guys are ready to head out when Kay and Taft get here." Ven knew Oshly's tone well enough to suspect that something wasn't right. But he also trusted his friend and now was not the time to get into a discussion based on emotions and assumptions.

Jebet closed out her terminal and made her way down the ship's central hallway to Oshly and her T-Craft. As she walked, she could barely make out the low hum that reverberated throughout the interior of the Anniversary. Jebet found the various processing whirs, bright alert chimes, and beeps surprisingly comforting.

Ven was diligently bringing the main systems back online while the Anniversary winded down from its speed jump. Several sets of small, embedded thrusters fired from the nose of the ship. Very soon, the Anniversary would be flying at cruising speed as it reached Jupiter.

Ven was slightly unnerved at the changes in tone on the Anniversary as it reduced its speed.

Being that he was unfamiliar with the ship's normal acoustics, they served as a reminder of what was at stake and the uncertainty of their future.

Chapter 46

Sint Argum listened as the elevator arrived to his top floor MarsCorp tower command center. Akens Ember stepped into the room while Sint, standing at one of the windows, continued to look out over the Martian landscape. Sint watched a flurry of T-Crafts flying about, surface T-Crawlers transporting personnel and supplies to the civilization sector a few miles to the east of E-District.

"Look, Ember, more MMWs are arriving, a new home for so many. So many that will be kept safe under the warm blanket of security only we can provide them," Sint Argum said confidently.

Akens eyed a quarter full brandy glass sitting on a small table next to a chair in the center of the room, then swept his gaze to the nearly empty bottle of alcohol left on top of a cart with a variety of barely touched refreshments on the other side of the room. He didn't know how much was in that bottle to begin with, but, given Sint's current demeanor, the answer seemed clear.

"Yes, commander, quite the sight," said Akens, still not entirely sure why Sint had called for him.

"Ember, I'd like you to assist me here, for now, while we engage in

386

the final phases of transition." Sint turned around and slowly made his way back to the command center's main terminal. "Please, have a seat there. I've transferred the communications systems to that terminal."

Akens Ember did not like where this was going. Sint was making him his personal assistant, and there was nothing he could do about it. He sat down as Sint had politely demanded.

"Gregor Digby will be joining us shortly. I will be using him to help execute our plans." The alcohol combined with his deadly arrogance and ego were doing all the talking. Pointing at Akens, he continued, "You, Ember, will be my right hand man. I assume you wish to help all these people, don't you?" Sint's towering posture leant more of a threat than a question to his words.

"Yes, absolutely. Everyone's safety is of utmost importance."

A forced grin cracked across Sint's flushed face. "You are so right, Ember, the utmost importance indeed!"

Sint's dramatic positivity and fake compassion faded as quickly as it had appeared.

Sitting down in his command chair and leaning back, Sint Argum's true nature began to reemerge. He didn't care about anyone but his own ambition and desperation for power.

"And, in order to keep these people safe, we must be sure those who would oppose us are no longer a threat. Therefore, Director Vivsou is already hard at work down there with the many loyal, trained DeCorp personnel." After a brief pause, he continued, his voice now dripped with disdain, "The fleet of EnerCon evacuees had already been invited but ignored our charity, so now preparations are well underway to deal with them. They will either join us, or we will be sure they have no worries at all."

Ember couldn't help but interpret Sint's last statement to be like that of a parent telling a child to eat their vegetables or get no dessert.

"I am certain, sir, that with the proper persuasion, the evacuees will make the right choice." It was all Akens Ember could think to say, now that he was at the mercy of his commander.

"We just have one other problem." Sint's mood changed again, this time to controlled frustration. "That small band of pesky evacuees. This Taft Guardia, Kaytha Morrow, and their friends. They continue to evade me. I have laid waste to any chance they may have at reprieve on Europa. Yet I still have not heard from any of the assets you placed in the system whether they arrived there."

Fear gripped Ember. The reason Sint had received no information about ships in the system was because the T-Drones had been placed in standby mode. Ember never turned on the regional alert scanners. He had figured that any ships entering the system would pick up the signal and destroy the attackers before DeCorp could be alerted and power them up in defense. It was the right call, but Akens did not dare challenge Sint's logic, which was clearly clouded at this point. All he could do was lie.

Turning to face his HIREZ communications terminal but making sure to block Sint's view of the screen, Akens Ember brought up the drones' control settings. "I'm going over diagnostics now, commander. If anyone is in range of the scanner around Jupiter and Europa, your terminal system will be alerted." While he spoke, Akens powered up the long-range scanning system on just one of the currently idle attack drones that sat still in a joined cluster. The machines were hidden from any passers-by in the darkness of space.

Sint said, "Fine. Send the control data to Tober Rosel. He and Dow are currently on a path to the area. Inform him that if the drones pick up any signals, they are only to engage with the smaller T-Crafts. Rosel and Dow will personally deal with the freighter we're after."

"Commander, there are eight manned and armed DeCorp T-Crafts within short range of the Jupiter system, part of an MMW group that evacuated late. Would you like me to send them in case they could be of assistance?"

Sint rose from his chair and strolled over to the refreshments area. "Give Rosel control of them. They will follow his orders."

Akens crafted the message and sent it off to Rosel's ship. Shortly after, a message received notification pinged from the communications terminal. "It's Rosel, sir. Message was received, and, by the looks of it, they're close to arriving at the destination."

"Very well. Feel free to help yourself to anything here, Ember. You've done well. Oh, but before you do, can you comm Digby? Have him send a fresh case of beverages, I'm running low."

****

Tober Rosel and Uray Dow were closing in on Jupiter. Both DeCorp MTCs were starting their arrival procedures. Their ships were starting to slow in speed when an alert sounded to their on board flight OS systems from the nearby scanning T-Drones.

Dow comm'd Rosel out of habit, even though Rosel could see the same data. "Two T-Crafts matching the signatures of SH1 and Prophet 6 recently left the surface of Europa."

Rosel responded, "Yes. Power up all the T-Drones, give them the signatures and kill order, command to engage."

Just as Rosel finished his instructions, another signal popped up from the drones scan data.

"Ha! Looks like we found the Anniversary! Quickly, Dow, send the freighter's signature to the attackers with the program code for NO ENGAGEMENT! We need that ship intact. We'll deal with the freighter ourselves as soon as we arrive."

****

The Anniversary slowed to its cruising speed. Jebet and Oshly were already suited, strapped in, and waiting for the hangar bay door to open. Kaytha and Taft, loaded with the parts and supplies they needed, flew out from the EnerCon power facility. The building would sit empty until Ultra Raiders arrived in a few hours.

"It's good to see the Anniversary on the scopes," said Kaytha on a direct comm to Taft. The Anniversary was passing Jupiter, heading for Kaytha and Taft, but still several minutes out from reaching them.

Ven pressed the command to open the bay doors when alarms for both the short and long-range scanners began blaring from flight deck speakers. Jebet and Oshly immediately disconnected from the hangar bay and drifted out the rear of the Anniversary. They cleared the ship and throttled up to match the freighter's cruising speed while the alarms continued whining.

"What the hell is this?" comm'd Oshly.

Looking over the scanners, they all spotted the signals of the DeCorp T-Drones powering up. The fast attack, pilotless ships were positioned close to Kaytha and Taft. It would take several minutes for any of them to arrive to assist. Ven immediately opened the operations screen for the STL and started the power-up sequence, but nothing happened.

"Oshly, the STL—it's offline again?!" Ven called out on a direct comm.

There was nothing Oshly could do, not yet. Wasting no time, Jebet and Oshly hammered down their throttle controls to reach their friends. As they did, Ven saw two DeCorp attackers coming into the region. They were the same ships from Yellowstone. All Ven could do was turn toward Jupiter and hope the gases would provide him cover.

When the scanner alarms started sounding, it took only seconds for Taft and Kaytha to see the T-Drones heading for them from their cockpit windows.

"Kaytha, evasive action now! Break off!" yelled Taft over the comms. Their instinctive reactions sprung into action, as they swiftly spiraled away from one another. Plasma blasts from the drone attackers flew past them as they twisted and turned their ships to avoid getting hit.

Kaytha made quick work of the DeCorp drone attack ships. Their avoidance sensors were the best ever made but still proved no match to the training Kaytha had put herself through and her natural skills as a pilot. She was chasing down the drones one by one, using her T-Craft's dual nose weapons arrays. The ship didn't have an infinite supply of fuel and ammo, but she was far from empty. Taft continued tracking her, assisting where he could and keeping up as best as possible.

"Why are you using smaller weapons? You know the Thruster Blasters are a one-shot kill," asked Taft.

"Waste not, want not," Kaytha replied, as she fired off a series of rapid bursts, disabling two T-Drones in a barrage of blasts. As they went spinning out of control and out of sight, she spotted the two T-Crafts heading straight for them. "Taft! We got two piloted T's heading our way! We have to split up!"

Kaytha grabbed the throttle stick and thrust it forward, surging her T-Craft as she began a quick spin, down and away from the incoming T-Crafts, which were heading straight for Kaytha and Taft.

Jebet and Oshly finally reached their friends fighting off the ineffective T-Drones, while Ven kept the Anniversary shrouded behind the gases of Jupiter. The scanners would undoubtedly pick it up, but he knew that the device was the end game of those attacking them and needed the Anniversary hidden as best he could to keep them at a visual disadvantage.

Ven struggled with the need to help his friends. He knew DeCorp wouldn't destroy the ship, but if the Anniversary's power plant were disabled, he would be helpless. With his eyes on the battle being waged outside, Ven didn't even think to look to see if the STL-5 was operational again.

"Oshly! Jebet! Incoming Ts and these got butts in the pilot seats!" Ven called out on the comms.

Jebet and Oshley ramped up their attack pace. Jebet comm'd, "Oshly, pick up your firing rotation! We gotta take care of the rest of these twits before we help engage with the live ones!"

Oshly succeeded in firing off multiple blasts from his M-Cannons and took out two T-Drones that were heading straight for Jebet. The destruction debris created a maze of metal bits right in Jebet's flight path. She opened fire on all her blasters and cannons, maneuvering her ship as fast as she could. Blasting big broken pieces into little broken pieces, she quickly made it out of the destruction path of the metal scraps in her wake.

"Yes! Good shooting, Osh!" Jebet cheered.

Another group of signals popped up on their scanners. More piloted DeCorp fighters were joining in.

The moment the drones engaged SH1 and Prophet6, Rosel commanded the eight manned T-Crafts from an MMW on its way to Mars to assist them in the attack.

They were about to arrive just when he needed them.

Taft said over the comms to the entire group, "I don't think we can make a stand here. We're going to have to try and fight them off in the planet gases."

Ven immediately responded, "It's really rough in here, Taft. We'll be as blind as they are!"

Taft already had his ship pointed toward the Anniversary while Kaytha still had a few seconds before the two manned DeCorp fighters were on top of them. She turned to follow Taft and the others toward the planet's outer gases.

Kaytha switched on the comms to talk directly with Taft. "Taft! What's the move? We don't have much time!"

"Our best bet is to get Ven to depressurize the vehicle bay, open the rear, and we fly in at speed."

"WHAT?! *That's* your plan?!"

"I don't see any other option. Once on board, we go stealth and get out of here—KAYTHA, YOUR SCOPES!" Taft cried out.

They had taken too long, and Uray Dow was right on the rear of Kaytha's ship.

"Go tell the others! NOW! I'll catch up," she said.

Taft immediately relayed the plan to Ven, Oshly, and Jebet as

Kaytha made an aggressive vertical flip to evade her attacker. The ship moved right with her and began blasting his directional cannons. Spinning, turning, and varying her throttling speed, Kaytha kept her enemy at bay.

****

Tober Rosel broke off to chase Taft. "Number Four, you take out SH1. Prophet6 is heading toward the planet gases and the Anniversary. Once you've destroyed her, come assist me. Backup should be arriving any moment."

****

Kaytha watched and prayed Taft was far enough away that he could reach Ven and the others before he could catch up, all while she was having more trouble than she expected.

Dow's ship was surprisingly faster than Kaytha's, and she was getting worn out. Fighting for her life, she did everything she could to get behind her nemesis. Watching his moves, she realized the pilot was decent at flying but not so good at aiming. She made a quick decision to slow up while she continued her chaotic evading space dance. It was hard to ignore the laser blasts zipping past. One blast created a heat streak above her cockpit canopy.

It was at that moment that Kaytha was half throttle with the DeCorp fighter directly behind her. Anticipating his next move, she slammed the throttle control, and, like a bullet from a gun, her T-Craft launched forward, the thruster wake knocking him off his course.

Uray Dow skillfully regained control of his ship. Kaytha had covered enough distance that there was no way he would catch up before she reached Jupiter's gases. Determined to finish the job he was paid to do, he pursued her anyway.

In the distance, Kaytha could see the other attacker ahead of her. She took a moment to breathe a sigh of relief that he hadn't already caught up to Taft when her ship rocked violently forward. Uray Dow had concentrated his long-range master cannon and connected enough with Kaytha's ship to knock it out of control, sending it spinning through space end over end. She scrambled to get the thrusters back online, but the heat from the blast caused the charging reactor to trip. She knew it would be at least 30 seconds before they came back online, but it was 30 seconds she didn't have as the fighter screamed closer toward her.

"The weapons systems are still online," Kaytha said the words out loud while she looked out the canopy at the spinning star-scape. Every completion of her off-axis rotation she got a glimpse of her attacker closing the distance between them. "He's waiting for the right shot," Kaytha continued talking to herself.

Every half a second her ship, for a brief moment, would be pointing straight at the DeCorp fighter. Her T-Craft tumbled helplessly as Kaytha switched active all the available weaponry. With only seconds to practice, she quickly worked out the timing of her only shot.

"Now...now...now...NOW!" Kaytha fired her four directional thruster blasters, launched the two guidance missiles, and went full active on her dual nose gun mounts at the exact moment she saw the fighter out her window.

Uray Dow waited too long before squeezing the trigger of his weapon. Before the system could register the digital instruction to fire his guns, his ship exploded in a blinding blast of light and metal debris.

Even with her auto shade visor activated and the ship still spinning out of control, Kaytha still had to look away from the blast. Like chunks of ice in a hailstorm, bits of Dow's ship pinged against the hull of her T-Craft, chipping away her custom paint job, punching tiny holes in the metal side panels. As the overheated systems buzzed and beeped back to life, Kaytha's thoughts immediately returned to Taft. She regained control of the ship and headed straight toward Jupiter.

She caught a quick glimpse of Taft before disappearing into the planet's gases. Tober Rosel was far enough behind Taft that she was confident he wouldn't catch up. The question now was how was she going to get on board with the others while eight manned DeCorp fighters were entering the fight against them.

Ven wasted no time securing the interior bay doors before opening up the lower rear hatch of the Anniversary.

As the massive door opened, the vacuum created by the change in pressure sucked a bunch of hangar bay tools out into space.

Jebet and Oshley were already heading for the ship. "Look out, guys, there's a lot of crap trailing behind me from the hangar bay!" Ven alerted everyone over the comms.

Oshly said, "Nothing important, I hope."

"Stay focused. You've got a ladder in your path," said Jebet, as Oshly spun his ship quickly to avoid it.

Once the cargo debris was clear, they pulled in behind the Anniversary. "Jebet, line up your run and fly as deep into the bay as possible," Oshly suggested.

"See you inside, Osh."

Oshly then comm'd directly to Ven, "Can you see the STL screen? Is power-up available?"

"Hang on. I'm going to fly deeper into the gases and give Taft some cover. The D-Creep is closing in fast. Nope, still nothing!"

Oshy did a quick scan of Taft's and Kaytha's positions. Then, Oshly comm'd to Jebet, "Match Ven's speed and get as close as you can. You then gun it into the bay. I'll follow behind and provide you and Taft cover."

Both T-Crafts were in the wake of swirling gases behind the freighter. Jebet on all comms said, "Oshly, I'm heading in."

Jebet gave a sharp burst to her thrusters and was instantly covered in the light of the hangar bay. She pushed forward the power to her forward facing reverse thrusters while simultaneously switching on the magnetic fields of the lift manifold to secure in zero-G. The ship slammed to the deck of the hangar bay in a shower of sparks and screeching metal. "I'm locked in, everyone. Far left corner of the bay. Osh, your turn. Oshly, come in?"

Taft now had a visual on Oshly, after watching Jebet load into the rear of the Anniversary. He direct comm'd Oshly, "Oshly, fly on board, power up the device, and make your way clear of the planet."

"But where's Kaytha?!"

"Osh, there's no time. My ship's taken heavy damage. I have to draw this guy away from the Anniversary, and I have to get back to Kaytha. Get on board and get clear!"

Parallel to the fight, the eight manned T-Crafts in tight formation were closing in and heading to cut off Kaytha before she could reach Taft or the Anniversary. Oshly suddenly realized what he had to do.

Breaking off from his current flight path, Oshly pointed his T-Craft at the eight incoming DeCorp fighters.

Switching all power to the thrusters, he made an attempt to close the gap between them and Kaytha before they could engage.

Going one-on-one comms to Jebet, he said, "J, my OS on the ship—search it. Kaytha...without her none of this matters. Goodbye." Oshly turned off his comm.

"Oshly...OSH?!" cried Jebet.

He could hear Jebet over the comms, but was ignoring her, focusing on what he needed to do. "What are you doing, man? Get *your ass* on the ship!" Jebet patched in her on board HIREZ screen to the Anniversary's outboard monitors, watching her friend fly away from her.

Ven watched as Oshly made his run toward the deadly ships. Quickly pulling up the available weapons packages equipped on the Anniversary, he found three long-range programable rockets. Using his scan data, Ven targeted three of the eight incoming T-Crafts and launched them. A panel on the upper rear of the Anniversary opened and almost instantaneously the blast of the three projectiles erupted toward their target.

The three launched missiles from the Anniversary flew past Oshly as he continued to close in on the incoming ships, seconds away from confrontation.

Kaytha was desperately trying to catch up to Taft, who continued using evasive maneuvers to keep Rosel from taking him out. All were weary and exhausted, fighting for every ounce of energy to stay alive. Both the bad guys and the good were fatigued. Someone was going to win, but it would be a sloppy victory.

Oshly looked at his scanners. Examining the positions of his friends relative to the Anniversary, he direct comm'd to Ven, "Ven! Ven! Look again, the device. Is it available?!"

Ven looked at the device's operating screen and once again, when everyone needed it most, the cloaking ability of the STL-5 was operational. Ven wasted no time powering it up as the Anniversary disappeared from view with only the swirling planet gases to show for it. Taft was already close enough to slip into the stealth wake.

Jebet was still seated in her T-Craft, helpless to leave her cockpit until Kaytha and Taft were on board and the bay door was closed. Kaytha watched as the Anniversary and Taft disappeared from view. A devious grin crossed her face. She was in range of Tober

Rosel and, with Taft out of sight, she could line up the clean shot. Just as Kaytha was about to launch a heat seeker, Rosel violently pulled back on his control stick and throttled away from Kaytha, making speed to join the other fighters who were about to engage with Oshly. Kaytha was planning to turn after the evading DeCorp fighter, but it was too late.

Three DeCorp T-Crafts exploded as the Anniversary's missiles met their mark, throwing the remaining attack ships of course briefly. Oshly took advantage, flying straight at the remaining five manned T-Craft fighters and firing everything he had on board all at once. He immediately destroyed two ships as the other three opened fire and then attempted to evade him.

Taft followed in the stealth wake of the Anniversary, his ship battered. He waited for Kaytha to catch up. Her ship was bleeding power from the fight. Kaytha, as everyone else did, knew there was nothing they could do to help their friend as he fought for their survival. Ven turned the Anniversary toward Oshly and flew the ship close enough to Kaytha so that she could slip into hiding under the power of the STL-5.

The Anniversary appeared from out of nowhere, flying right past Kaytha's cockpit window, startling her as she flew in behind the stealth wake. Kaytha throttled up to fly in alongside Taft.

Oshly was taking multiple hits as he continued to fly right at three DeCorp ships and now Tober Rosel was closing in behind him. With the remaining fighters focused on him, Oshly knew this was the only chance the rest of them had. Tober Rosel was now engaged behind Oshly and knew he needed a victory, of any kind, after so many DeCorp losses.

With Rosel firing bolts of plasma energy frantically, Oshly still managed to take out another attacker while the remaining two regrouped.

"Get out of here, you guys! For a reason!" was the last thing his friends heard Oshly say.

"NOOOOO!" Jebet screamed, sitting inside her ship in the freighter's hangar bay.

Firing what ammo he had left, Oshly hoped he could at least keep the enemy busy long enough for his friends to escape. Racing as fast as he could to head off the DeCorp MTCs, he now had the attackers in range. Oshly threw his T-Craft into a violent spiral then shot off round after round from his nose cannons at the incoming enemy ships. With his friends flying to safety, Oshly's time had all but run out. Tober Rosel was closing in.

The remaining two attackers, dodging his chaotic assault, opened fire in front of Oshly. A few blasts connected with his ship; smoke and fire billowed from one of his booster. He was damaged but still fighting. Meanwhile, Rosel had flown into position and had locked Oshly in his ship's inescapable sights. But before Rosel could attack, Oshly overloaded his fuel and charging systems, at the same time that he fired the one remaining on board missile left without launching it. All the explosive energy combined together as Oshly detonated his own T-Craft.

Watching through the viewport windows, Ven saw the blinding rays of light shooting out from the center of where the ships had been fighting each other. It was tragically beautiful as he realized what his friend had just done. Sacrificing himself to keep them all safe.

Tober Rosel was far enough away. Not being destroyed by the blast, his ship was sent spinning from the carnage. Able to regain control before debris from the explosion could dissipate, Rosel scrambled to put in the coordinates for a speed jump.

With tears in his eyes, Ven saw the one remaining DeCorp T-Craft. He reached over to switch the weapons selection to the fire position on the control stick, but it was too late. Before Ven could fire, Rosel speed jumped and escaped.

Jebet sat in her cockpit quietly sobbing, watching what was visible on her ship's screen. Now that the area was clear of all hostiles, Taft and Kaytha lined up to join Jebet in the hangar bay. There was no telling if more attackers would arrive, and they needed to get the parts and supplies on board.

"You first, Kaytha," Taft said.

Still stunned, Jebet keyed all comms, "I'm deep in the hangar far left side, so throttle in slow. It doesn't take much to clear of the bay door. Reverse thrust and magnetize the lower landers."

Kaytha did exactly what Jebet suggested. With the reverse thrusters spinning her ship around so she could see out the hangar, she locked to the bay floors as if she had done it a thousand times.

"Taft, let me know when you're in and we'll make for..." but before Ven finished his comm, Taft was already inside the hangar bay. He throttled in too fast and was struggling to gain control. He switched on the lander mags, sliding hard and fast on the metal surface, sparks flying as his T-Craft came to a stop right next to Kaytha's ship.

"Ven, we're all in. Close the bay doors. Let's get outta here," said Taft.

Kaytha and Taft removed their helmets and at the same time placed their hands on their cockpit windows as if reaching out to each other while the sound of the hangar bay's pressurization could be heard in the background.

Chapter 47

MarsCorp

Sint Argum sat in his commander's chair, anger building inside of him as Akens Ember informed him that Rosel was en route to MarsCorp. Gregor Digby gathered the final signals sent from the manned and unmanned attack crafts involved in the skirmish around Jupiter. Sint desperately desired to fly into a rage.

Tensely still, he stared at the data indicating the number of men and hardware destroyed, all amounting to a growing list of continued defeats. "We've had our best pilots, bounty hunters, and drones created solely to take out *anyone* who has the misfortune of getting in our way. Dozens loyal to our cause are now all dead all because of a handful of untrained desert rats! And all we have to show for it is one pilot running back to us after getting his ass kicked—again!" Sint was about to lose control, and neither Ember nor Digby was confident they would survive whatever action he took to unleash his emotions. Their concerns were only heightened by the fact Sint was currently being fueled by his current alcohol consumption.

Akens Ember cleared his throat. "What would you like me to do, sir?" was the only thing he could muster the courage to say, trying to appeal to Sint's desire to control everything around him.

The words were enough for Sint Argum to realize he did have an option. Turning his head slowly with an uncomfortable level of seriousness to his tone, he said,

"I will tell you what we are going to do. We are going to send these traitors—these murderers who think they deserve a power that does not belong to them—a message. There are consequences for those that would push back against the generosity and power of DeCorp." Sint pulled up his communications screen as he continued to speak. "I am going to contact Director Vivsou. The Enercon evacuees, those who have chosen to not join us, who ignored our protection, will soon find out what a mistake they've made. Earth is no more, gentlemen. We are on our own and the galaxy needs us. People need to feel safe and secure, and that cannot happen when people fight against us," Sint concluded.

****

The Anniversary hovered stationary in open space between Jupiter and Europa. The STL-5 shut down while they mourned the loss of their friend, who had not only given them the ability to effectively use the device, but also sacrificed himself to keep them and it out of harm's way.

They sat around the leaking and still slightly smoking T-Crafts in the hangar bay. Neither Jebet, Taft, nor Kaytha had left to the other parts of the ship, all of them battered, physically and emotionally. Taft and Kaytha felt responsible, thinking it was a mistake to not just wait in Europa, letting the Anniversary arrive with the rest of the group still in route from their departure off course to the facility on the surface of the moon.

"Even if you decided to stay until we arrived, those DeCorp'rs or the T-Drones would have picked up our presence and attacked us on the ground. We all could have lost our lives, not just Osh," Ven said, trying to reassure them. "Besides, now they think we've gone."

"You're right," said Taft, pointing at Ven then turning to face Kaytha. "And, Kaytha, they assume we flew in, saw the destruction, and flew out. That's when they realized we were here. Those other two were probably told to track the Anniversary. It's all for a reason."

"And what reason is that, T? So, Oshly could die? What's the reason for any of this?!" Kaytha's head dropped as she started to cry, sitting on a work bench stool.

"We don't always know the reason," Taft immediately replied. "I don't. Oshly didn't. But Oshly didn't die for nothing. We didn't just make a mistake. If it even was a mistake, for nothing. They still don't know of that other facility, and they assume we've left.

In no way does it make up for losing Oshly, but his sacrifice has secured us a safe location for now. I can't tell you why any of this is happening. All I know, all any of us knows, is that it has happened. People are counting on us. Our friends heading to Europa, our family, and the thousands of lives in the darkness right now that have no idea the danger we are in." Taft gestured with his hand toward his and Kaytha's battered, still slightly smoking T-Crafts. His genuine emotion and encouragement was exactly what everyone needed to hear.

Sitting on the floor of the hangar bay, resting her head on her bent knees, Jebet listened to Taft finish giving his impromptu speech. With tears rolling down her face, she looked directly at Kaytha and said, "Oshly comm'd me right before... He told me to go into his files. He was asking me to help you the way he would have helped you. This isn't over, and for his sake, we need to see this through."

Kaytha nodded. "We brought along the fuel and charging adapters. They're stowed away in storage on Taft's ship. Do you think you can figure out how to convert the power connections to get the STL charged?"

"I think I can manage. I've seen Oshly make the changes before." Jebet's words had an air of confidence everyone needed to hear.

Taft said, "Our rides are pretty beat up. Kaytha and I will start getting to work."

"Before I came down from the flight deck, I checked the ETA on the others. If they maintain their speed, it's gonna be a few hours before they get here," Ven said, checking the clock on his flight suit wrist OS screen. "I'll move the Anniversary into that outcropping of gases coming off Jupiter and have us hold there. It's enough cover to keep us hidden, more or less. I'll keep the active scanner on. When they're in range, we'll head back down and work on our next move. Until then, you all need to eat and get any sleep you can. For a reason, right, Taft?" No one disagreed.

Jebet noticed the makeshift nap area Oshly had created in the far corner of the workspace in the hangar bay, complete with a thin pad to rest on, along with some blankets and pillows he'd pulled from storage. Standing up, she reached into the cockpit of her T-Craft and pulled out a nutrition bar and her water canister, then walked over to the area of comfort Oshly had made.

Ven was solemn in a way none of them had seen before. "I'll go get the ship in place and set up the proximity alert sensors before I rest. We'll get woken up if anyone comes around or when the rest of us arrive." Ven then turned and made his way up the small flight of stairs to the passageway into the heart of the ship.

Kaytha stood up straight, trying to keep her emotions in check. "Let's grab some food and head to a room. We both need the rest."

Taft knew Kaytha was barely holding it together as he walked over to give her the embrace she needed. They wrapped their arms around each other. "Think we can sleep for a few hours, try to forget about all this, again, while we can?" said Kaytha.

Taft kept quiet, holding her tightly just enough to acknowledge. Kaytha pulled back, eyes red and puffy. Taft's were in no better shape. A slight smile of contentment crossed her face as she kissed his cheek and took his hand. "Come on, T. Let's get going. For a reason, right?"

"I'm already regretting that speech," said Taft.

They walked together to leave the flight deck together. "You should," was Kaytha's sarcastic reply.

****

MarsCorp

Sint Argum, after sleeping off his frustrations at yet another loss, and the copious amounts of alcohol consumed, made his way down from his perch in the command tower, driving a T-Crawler to the largest building in the entire engineering wing of Mars station.

T-Crawlers were one of the few surface bound vehicles still in use. Travel around the red planet wasn't always conducive to flying and much of the time moving from building to building was still better achieved with land-based vehicles.

The lift manifolds didn't react well to the dirt, and DeCorp also deemed it a waste of time to put in place paved roads. T-Crawlers were a hybrid vehicle with the strength of T-Craft power plants and highly efficient fast spinning alloy and rubber composite tank-like treads. T-Crawlers were built in all manner of sizes, not unlike the cars of old.

Sint's single seat T-Crawler was decked out with plasma blasters and conventional firing auto-cannons loaded with metal piercing rounds. He drove his overly armored land tank straight into the massive building, more than five times the size of a typical MMW. Inside sat the bulk of the DeCorp fleet of deadly ships. Sint's 4 MTCs, rows of T-Crafts, the Oberkorn, and even a few MMDs located just outside, all being prepped for battle at Sint's request. Hundreds of employees, soldiers as far as Sint was concerned, mercenaries in reality, were scattered about doing their business. Sint exited his T-Crawler and walked over to a waiting Director Vivsou standing next to his personal T-Craft.

"Welcome, commander. Everything is moving forward as planned," said Vivsou.

"Is this your personal T-Craft?" asked Sint.

"Why, yes, it is. It also is being prepped for the operation." Vivsou was curious at Sint's inquiry.

"Would you mind if I took a look inside the cockpit?"

"Not at all," replied Vivsou.

A small footstool of only a few steps was needed if one wanted easier access to most T-Crafts. Argum's arrival elicited the attention of most everyone working in the area. His climbing into the seat of Vivsou's personal ship was enough to pique everyone's curiosity.

As Sint sat inside the craft looking over the gauges, Vivsou was beginning to think his commander intended to go for a flight. "Its cells are fully fueled, and the charges are at one hundred percent if you want to take her out. Although I would like to mention that Rosel should be arriving at any moment. I did send word that you personally requested his presence at this location."

Sint had yet to close the canopy or start up the ship's power plant. With a computerized whir, Sint did turn on the main OS system, the first step in the preflight procedure. All the onboard avionics were now running along with the location scanners, guidance, and targeting operations all at his disposal.

Sitting up from the seat for a moment, Sint looked out across the nose of the ship.

Addressing half a dozen workers in his line of sight, he called out, "You there, would you be so kind as to step away from the front of your director's ship, please."

He motioned with his hands for them to move off to the side. Sint's words, while polite, were contrary to the tone which dripped of condescension.

Everyone's attention turned to the familiar roar of an approaching T-Craft. Tober Rosel was a legend among those willing to fight for what DeCorp stood for. The eyes of the men and women widened as Rosel slowed his ship just outside the hangar bay. The combination of the lift manifolds and the force created from easing off of the thrusters kicking up dirt pushed the dust of Martian soil inside of the hangar where they all stood.

"Enough of this nonsense," said Sint to himself as he pulled the main weapons trigger on the ship's control stick. Everyone jumped at the sound and sight of a single powerful silver plasma blast erupting from the forward cannon under the nose of Vivsou's ship. In a blinding flash the focused energy connected with Rosel's T-Craft just outside the entrance of the building. The explosion knocked back a handful of DeCorp employees who stood closest. Staff and crew looked on in horror as they shielded their eyes from the explosion. Tiny shards of metal, debris, and dirt flew everywhere. Even Director Vivsou stood stunned in disbelief at witnessing Sint Argum murder Tober Rosel.

Sint powered down the OS systems and stepped out to the top of the footstool. He stood for a moment and sternly glanced over the faces of everyone around him.

"Now that *that's* settled, allow me the opportunity to briefly explain why Tober Rosel, one of DeCorp's best, had to die. Everything is for a reason, is it not?

There are a group of renegades, terrorists really, who have taken it upon themselves to threaten everything we have to offer. While there are those who have simply turned their back on us, this group, this rebellion, seeks to harm our attempts at a new life. Not only for you but for everyone who has wisely chosen to join us. Tober Rosel failed to stop them on too many occasions. They were the ones who destroyed our Moon. They were the ones who sealed our fate. And, while we continue to hunt them down, you will seed a message to those who have chosen against us. The evacuees who have decided to side with the rebels will pay the price. You will succeed where Tober Rosel failed. You are the future of humanity in the stars, and together we will provide security and safety to all those who chose to join us."

The speech was inspiring enough to motivate the DeCorp men and women who not only feared Sint Argum but believed in his justification for killing Rosel. They would now fight for the cause of preserving their way of life. Director Vivsou knew the truth but was also keenly aware that his future, and that of those he loved, now rested in his allegiance to Sint.

As the workers dispersed, Sint made his way back to the T-Crawler as Vivsou followed in his wake. "Fantastic speech, commander, but it's a shame Rosel had to die."

"Strength and, more importantly, resolve needed to be shown, Director. Besides, five manned T-Crafts will make up for one Rosel. Now, I'm going back to my quarters. Continue preparations and send out a scouting party to monitor the traitors' convoy. I'm going to give them one last opportunity to hand over what I seek. And if they don't, they will see what real resolve looks like. Once our forces are ready to deploy, notify Akens Ember and await my orders."

"Yes, sir," replied Vivsou.

Sint reached the T-Crawler and pressed the illuminated green button to open the top opening side driver hatch. He turned back toward Vivsou and said, "I do hope they choose to give us what we seek. It would be a shame to waste all that firepower just to punish them."

Sint drove away, leaving a trail of red dust behind. Director Vivsou stared at the still burning mound of metal debris outside the compound. It was all that remained of Tober Rosel. Vivsou was about to order a crew to clean it up but decided it best to leave it as a reminder. Not so much as to what their leader was capable of, but just how dangerous Sint Argum actually could be.

Chapter 48

Peacefully quiet, the ship's ambient noise and random, faint electronic sounds were all that could be heard as the Anniversary floated relatively still while Jupiter's gases swirled around it. Small stabilizing thrusters, half foot in diameter tubes embedded all around the freighter, did their job keeping the ship in one spot. The little motion there was felt reminiscent of a boat floating on calm waters.

Ven was asleep in the large captain's chair. When reclined, the seat provided enough horizontal padded area comfort for even someone as large as Ven. The electronic repeating whoop of the long-range scanner roused Ven from a deep sleep. Looking at the digital clock readout, still on Earth time, he was surprised that over five hours had passed. The long-range tracking was picking up on several incoming ships to the far side of Europa. Ven assumed it was the Ultra Raiders, but just to be sure, he entered in the tracking number for Anorant and Marrett's supply ship.

He hastily composed a message to send to Marrett directly to make them aware of their location and give a brief summary of the events that had unfolded.

The text ended with: <u>message me once everyone is safely inside the facility, glad you all made it. Ven.</u>

The door to the rear of the flight deck slid open and in walked Jebet. "Did I hear the scanner alarm?" she asked, followed by a yawn.

"Yeah, they're all just now arriving. I messaged Marr the situation," Ven replied.

"And *what exactly* is our situation?" Jebet walked over to the terminal Oshly had been using.

"I figure we give them enough time on Europa to get settled in before we go and join them. In the meantime, once the other two are up, we can formulate a plan to present to the group."

Jebet logged into the computer using Oshly's ID on the Anniversary's OS. She needed to get familiar with the STL-5, especially since she'd been tasked with fueling and charging the device. Most importantly though were Oshy's words during the battle, "…OS system on the ship…Kaytha…without her none of this matters." Jebet thought about asking the others, but Oshly didn't tell everyone on all comms; he specifically only told her.

She needed to figure out what it meant. She wouldn't be able to focus until she did.

"Looks like Kay and T are up." Ven pointed at a screen. "Activity in the kitchen wing."

But Jebet had tuned out, already searching through the files on

Oshly's OS. She found a group of folders within the STL-5 program and quickly noticed it had a set of subfolders. Each one was labeled under the T-Crafts' signatures of all their ships. It was the signature on Kaytha's that caught her attention. Not only was her file the most recently updated, but Kaytha's signature was wrong, reading STL-0151 and not the SH1-0151. It could have been a typo, but that's not something Oshly was likely to do.

As Jebet opened the folder, Taft and Kaytha entered the flight deck. Taft was carrying a tray of food: processed scrambled eggs, toasted bread, bacon—all cooked by the Anniversary's kitchen automation.

Kaytha carried two carafes, one with water and another with coffee. Jebet barely noticed them enter as she continued looking over the details in the subfolder she'd discovered.

Taft and Kaytha set down their breakfast near the communications terminal. While the two of them ate, both Ven and Jebet were so busy they appeared to be completely oblivious to the fact that the others were in the room.

Noticing this, Kaytha made her way to see what Jebet was working on.

Jebet continued to look over the information. Oshly had filled the folder with lines of data and notes on the STL-5. There were dozens of readings he had collected during the times the device was in operation. It looked as if he had compiled the data to see if there was something specific that was causing the STL-5 to shut down in a seemingly random way. Jebet, quickly scrolling through the notes as Kaytha walked over, sensed that Kaytha was now standing behind her but was too focused to acknowledge it.

417

She read the words on the screen out loud to herself, "STL-5 Shut Down Data Calculations: Conclusion."

Kaytha was now reading along with Jebet over her shoulder. Both remained silent as Jebet discovered the truth that, up until then, only Oshly and Kaytha knew. Jebet's eyes widened as she finished reading the report. She turned her head slowly to look at Kaytha, stunned at the revelation. Kaytha simply nodded to confirm what Jebet now knew. Jebet mouthed the words, "And the others?" Kaytha raised her left index finger to her mouth and slowly shook her head. Kaytha had her reasons why Taft, Ven, and the others could not know what Jebet now did.

****

MarsCorp

Hundreds DeCorp MMWs from every corner of Earth were arriving at MarsCorp. Thousands of other ships followed, carrying millions of souls fleeing Earth. Many of the arrivals were former EnerCon employees or supporters. They had abandoned their convoy, believing in Sint Argum's propaganda that a group from EnerCon was responsible for destroying the Moon and so they chose safety over any allegiance they may have had.

A part of Sint Argum's Operation: Hot Springs was expediting the travel from Earth to Mars. All ships under DeCorp's control were to travel as fast as allowable, while anyone joining DeCorp would also be requested to keep up. It was said this was for their own security. That wayward ships would leave themselves vulnerable were they to fall too far behind the massive space "wagon train" that had stretched for hundreds of miles. The truth was that Sint Argum wanted the might of DeCorp established as quickly as possible. This meant the new citizens of Mars needed to feel secure under his rule while he worked toward his intended goal.

Millions would be left behind on Earth, eventually succumbing to a grim fate, while hundreds of thousands would choose to look to the stars alone.

Sint and his underlings at MarsCorp referred to the remaining evacuees, those aligned with EnerCon who had decided not to join DeCorp, as the EnerConvoy.

The EnerConvoy carried far fewer souls than those under DeCorp's umbrella and traveled more slowly as they pushed their way deep into the solar system and beyond, praying to find a new home. These were the people that posed a threat to Sint Argum in his mind. These were the people that the friends knew Sint planned to attack. The EnerConvoy included their families and the friends needed to protect them.

The EnerConvoy's pace as it moved away from Earth was slow, traveling on a path that would avoid Mars. However, in the next twenty-four hours, the convoy would be at its closest point to the Red Planet. This provided the opportunity Sint Argum was counting on to eliminate the threat. His plan included a search party of T-Crafts he instructed Director Vivsou to deploy.

Back in the command control tower, Akens Ember briefed Sint on the scouting party's report. "Sir, the EnerConvoy is smaller than anticipated, although the team did see a large contingent of armed support ships. Also, a few of our own MMWs have joined them."

"Traitors, Akens, traitors to our cause! It's just more reason to wipe them out. Have you heard from Director Vivsou? Are our forces ready to deploy?"

"No, sir. I mean yes, sir. What I mean to say is, yes, Director Vivsou relayed the report for the scouting party, but our military is not yet ready. He stated he still needs at least a day."

"And what about our targets? The farther they travel, the more likely others will join them," Sint said.

"Commander, the director assured me our forces will be ready to deploy when the EnerConvoy is closest to our system."

"Very well, Ember. We'll send our annoying little band of freedom fighters a message. Once the EnerConvoy is reduced to floating trash, I will personally see to it that, where Rosel failed, we will succeed." *And Kaytha Morrow will no longer be a concern to me,* Sint thought to himself. He continued, "We will not give them the satisfaction of *hoping* they can save *anyone.* Besides, with the convoy wiped out, they'll run aground eventually. Continue keeping me posted."

Sint walked out of the room in frustration at not having already retrieved the device. In the wrong hands it could prove devastating to his plans. For now, he would focus on the anticipation that his attack on the EnerConvoy would draw Kaytha and the others out into the open.

EMBARK

****

Inside the Anniversary, Jupiter

The Ultra Raiders had settled in on Europa. Anorant messaged Ven directly that most of them were resting after the journey, but still eager for a fight after losing so many during the volcano eruption as they departed Earth and were attacked.

Oshly's death weighed heavily as they worked out a strategy and course of action for their next move. Taft and Kaytha were even more motivated after hearing about how so many of their brave new friends had lost their lives on Earth.

It had been enough justification already to save their parents and the evacuees headed out into space, but their choice to take on DeCorp directly was now crystal clear.

Jebet was done going over the data Oshly had obtained from his hack on the DeCorp attack ships just a few days ago. She transferred the files containing all the relevant information, including the detailed schematics of MarsCorp, down to the surface of Europa. Marrett and Anorant could now begin identifying vulnerabilities and weaknesses—an attack on DeCorp would need to be swift and precise.

Taft, Kaytha, and Jebet were on the flight deck with Ven as he readied the Anniversary to travel down to Europa and join the Ultra Raiders.

Before leaving, Kaytha felt like she needed to make sure they were making the right move. She asked Ven, "Look, before we head down there, are we sure we looked at all the options? Are we missing something? Anything?"

"What if we flew out to the convoy and convinced them? Showed them the evidence?" Jebet offered.

"We've got a bigger problem now," said Taft. "I've been on Earth's networks, listening to the evacuees posting audio on Blaster. Sint's propaganda campaign's clearly working, from what I'm hearing."

"How are you still on the net?" Kaytha asked, confused.

Jebet hadn't had time to tell the others what she'd discovered on their trip to Europa, until now. "DeCorp's communications MMW took control of the OverAir network. For now, everyone still has network access."

"They're all calling the group not heading to Mars the EnerConvoy," Taft said. "People now believe it was a small group of terrorists, with support from EnerCon, who destroyed the Moon. We're officially the bad guys now, us and EnerCon. Sint has been posting audio Blasts from his personal account. He's vowing to hunt us down. And from the Blaster responses I've heard, people are believing it. Sint Argum is setting them up and made us the enemy."

"I think Jebet's right. We have enough evidence with all our combined data to prove it was Sint Argum and not us. But, do we have time?" Kaytha asked Ven.

Ven said, "We can speed jump to Mars from here in a few hours. Looking at the calculations of the convoy's current location, it'll take a lot longer to get to them. By the time we reach them, we'd have little time to mount a successful defense when DeCorp does attack." Ven looked at Jebet and asked, "Do you think the STL-5, if it was leading the convoy, is powerful enough to cloak the whole fleet?"

She sighed, "Oshly would know. All I can do is theorize and, *in theory*, it's possible. But getting that many ships in the right formation to ensure they're all in the stealth wake without months of planning is virtually impossible. Even with the computer guidance program, if one of the larger ships were to slip out, it's game over."

The room got quiet for a moment until Taft spoke up, "Well, it's up to us to stop the attack before it happens. It's the best chance they have against Argum."

Jebet said, "And the biggest risk for all of us, but I don't see a better option."

"I don't either. We have to launch a preemptive strike," Kaytha agreed.

Ven stood up from his seat and said, "So, with the Anniversary in the lead, we can relatively, safely, and effectively put the forty or so of our ships into the stealth wake and attack virtually unseen. If we conduct multiple attack runs, they won't have the ability to target us. We get in, take out their capabilities to attack the convoy, and get out. As long as they have time to put as much distance between them and DeCorp, they have a chance. Once they reach a habitable planet, they can set up their defenses. We need to target their core defenses. It would take months, years, if at all, for DeCorp to build up their forces once we're finished with them. At a minimum, they won't be able to launch an attack on the same scale they can now. This, what we're planning, it's the best shot we all have." Ven pointed out the flight deck window.

"For a reason, everyone?" Kaytha, looking around the room, asked her friends.

"For Oshly," Jebet answered while Taft and Ven nodded in agreement.

Chapter 49

Ven sat down in the pilot's seat and powered up the Anniversary's thruster drives. As the engines roared to life, Taft, Kaytha, and Jebet were already in the hangar bay looking over their T-Crafts, now in desperate need of repairs. It was a visible sign the fight was far from over.

The gases swirling around the Anniversary surged as Ven pushed the ship forward, out and away from Jupiter, heading back to the surface of Europa and their friends.

****

Most of the Ultra Raiders were fast asleep inside the maintenance crew facility. More than enough housing space was available for the forty-eight teens to each have their own room, although several decided to bunk with one another. Marrett and Anorant worked together to keep the scared pilots positive and motivated, like captains of a sports team.

Most of the Ultra Raiders' T-Crafts actually fit inside the hangar.

Those that didn't attached to the outside of the building. The structure had built-in entryways for ships that needed to dock on the exterior. Plenty of provisions were left behind by the last occupants. Based on the station's previous computer entries, there was a skeleton crew working to keep the lights on, and most likely they were on the other side of the Moon when DeCorp struck. The majority of the operations were automated. This particular hangar and quarters area was initially designed to house the construction crew for EnerCon.

While everyone tried to rest, Anorant and Marrett spent time looking over the holographic schematics of DeCorp's Mars station. Placed at the center of a table, a small rectangular box projected from its tiny shimmering dome on top a green transparent three-dimensional image. The hologram was complete with text identifiers of all the buildings and structures of the sprawling facility. It was obvious DeCorp went out of its way to keep the population centers entirely separate from the power and engineering portions. What the hologram didn't show was where the armories were placed. It was clear to Anorant, based on the size, location, and what power lines were feeding certain buildings, where DeCorp's vast array of vehicles and weapons could be stored.

Marrett said, "We need to be able to reduce their ability for attack while also keeping the civilian population safe and able to maintain their power generation. We can't just sacrifice the people on the planet, or it makes us no better than them."

"Our target selection needs to be focused and strategic," Anorant agreed. "Like here—this large building with the MMD attached to it—it's essentially their mechanics' garage. If we destroy the power lines running to it, we can take out their ability to make repairs. And here, this is manufacturing. We could level that building."

"Rant, isn't there any way we don't..." Before Marrett could finish, Anorant cut her off.

"Mar, there is just no way around the collateral damage."

Marrett solemnly lowered her head in agreement.

Anorant went back to identifying potential targets, making a list to give to Ven once they arrived. The goal was to minimize casualties and take out their military capabilities. Marrett would play a key role in figuring out the priority targets that would diminish DeCorp's ability to have tactical and firepower strength. The ultimate goal would be peace, but with how aggressive DeCorp had been against even their small group, they knew that defense and a preemptive strike were the only options for now.

****

Ven reduced speed and powered up the lift manifolds on the belly of the Anniversary as he approached the streaked frozen blue, white, and gray ice surface of Europa.

He engaged the levers that lowered the Anniversary's five sets of gray landing gear. Ice and steam rose up from the ground as Ven gently landed the large ship just outside the moon's hangar. Because this portion of the Europian moon had no atmosphere processing, the four of them suited up with the appropriate gear to venture outside of the Anniversary and into the harsh environment. Exiting the Anniversary from the rear hangar bay door, it was a short walk to the entrance where the Ultra Raiders waited for them. The four entered into the maintenance facility decompression anti-chamber before being able to step into the breathable air-conditioned life-sustaining air inside.

As they walked into the main hangar, Kaytha and Taft gave each other a side glance with raised eyebrows as if to say, "Weren't we just here?" Hugs were shared and greetings exchanged but little time was wasted before everyone directed their attention to the hologram that was still up.

Anorant showed Ven the completed list of potential targets, then inputted the list into the holographic program which then displayed the targets in red next to each location. Ven was skilled in military strategy and agreed with the others in trying to reduce the casualty count while taking out DeCorp's armed forces.

Taft and Kaytha took the time to study the map while Ven formulated a plan. "It's all about their ability to launch an assault, right? We can't take out the entire fleet of manned and unmanned T's.

But we can take out their main fueling depot and their recharge silos. This building here, I agree, has to be the main hangar. If we surgically strike the opening of the hangar bay, we would at least trap the bulk of their fighters inside," said Ven, as his plan was starting to come together.

"Wait, it looks like they have two power generators, one for each district. In theory, couldn't we destroy the engineering generator and the adjacent construction depot? It could take at least a year to rebuild," said Anorant.

Marrett asked, "But what about the power for the populated district, the fueling and recharging for them?"

"Almost all the housing consists of transportation MMWs. Look here, very minimal actual infrastructure was built," Anorant explained, pointing to an empty area on the hologram.

"The remaining power generator is more than enough, and most of the long-range housing transports run on quasi-nuke drives." Anorant's confidence was all the convincing Marrett needed.

Ven said, "Plus, see this shorter tower next to this command control spire? That's the flight operations for their drone fleet. If we take this building here out, it should disable the drones. I assume this building with the hangar doors is probably where the drones are located. We could level it.

We can't leave DeCorp anything they can attack us with. All that being said, I think everything so far is feasible and I agree with Rant. At least a year if we are successful for them to get everything back online."

"Even longer if we took out the engineering atmodome," said Kaytha, as they all started to get on board with what needed to be done.

"Without breathable air, power, and the equipment to rebuild, it should not only set them back long enough for the evacuees to be safe for now, but also send a message of just what we and the device are capable of." Kaytha reflexively covered her mouth, hoping no one had actually noticed what she'd said.

Ven, Taft, and Jebet's eyes got wide as their stunned faces focused right on Kaytha. The young pilots heard what Kaytha said and all of them looked as confused as Anorant and Marrett did.

Torian was the first to ask, "What device?"

"It's time, guys," Kaytha said. "We have to tell them."

Taft, Jebet, and Ven looked at each other, and then again at Kaytha, as if trying to pass off the responsibility of explaining what the STL-5 was. Each of them had a part to play in the story.

Taft started with the short version of how Kaytha received a message from her father and found the device at the crash site of a T-Drone in California. All the Ultra Raiders were now gathered around the main control room, riveted by the tale. From there, Taft told a little more of the story until Jebet, with a certain sadness in her eyes, picked up the technical details where Oshly would have. They took turns explaining how it was because of the device that they'd been attacked at the Moon, witnessing the O-Station destruction before that, and why they'd decided to wait to tell everyone until now. Ven finally filled them in on why they all needed to be told about it now: the device would prove crucial in the effectiveness and success of their attack.

Anorant and Marrett were understandably both angry that none of them had revealed being in possession of such a power. "You mean we did all that, and you were holding on to information that could have proved useful in the planning?" said a frustrated Anorant.

Ven wasn't in a mood to be questioned or lectured, especially considering the age difference. "And exactly how would the knowledge of a cloaking device change your list of targets? Nothing would have changed, except now you know that we have the advantage to add to our already thorough planning."

Anorant kept a straight face and his mouth shut, just nodding along.

Ven said, "Jebet will familiarize you all with the stealth wake program that Oshly created. We'll install software on all your OS flight on board systems."

"Actually, Oshly already loaded the program in everyone's systems before we left. I'll tell everyone where to look," said Jebet.

She kept talking, laying out in detail everything the Ultra Raiders would need to know about their onboard STL-5 guidance system. While the education continued, Kaytha and Taft decided they needed to get back on board the Anniversary to resume the last of the minor repairs on their T-Crafts.

"Ven will now finish the lesson, letting you all know what to expect when traveling in the stealth wake," said Jebet. She smiled at Ven, who was less than pleased about playing the role of teacher. She walked over to Ven and leaned in so the others couldn't hear. "Just give them the basics. They'll figure it out, big guy."

"Anorant, you get caught up. You're flying anyhow. I need to check on a few things in communications," said Marrett.

Kaytha and Taft were already suited up and heading out the depressurized door into the harsh, dark, frozen wasteland of Europa. "You know, I bet the atmodome sector of the planet was pretty interesting.

Before the attack, that is," Taft spoke through his flight helmet mic as they made their way up the rear loading ramp and into the hangar bay.

"Yeah, it's a little too cold for my taste. But I could see a visit being all right," Kaytha said, as she pressed the round, red button from inside the Anniversary, closing the bay door and pressurizing the room. Once the chamber was sealed, it took only a few seconds for the fans embedded in the wall to blow fresh, cool, breathable air. With a buzz and electronic ping, the red alert lights that lined the walls turned green. Taft watched as Kaytha unclasped her helmet and pulled it off her head, messing up her tangled, brunette hair which fell onto her shoulders. Taft couldn't help but fall into a goofy daze, like he often did.

"What are you staring at?" Kaytha asked in mock annoyance. Taft just shook his head quickly, acting as if he was being snapped out of a trance.

"I'm not sure if I should be impressed that, on the edge of oblivion, you still gawk at me, or whether I should be concerned that something must be seriously wrong with you," she joked while Taft removed his flight helmet. "Well, either way, there's no doubt ya like me, but I've known that for a long time."

"All right, all right, don't get too arrogant."

"But you make it so easy." Kaytha nudged him with her elbow. "Let's grab a quick bite and get back to it. My girl needs work."

Back inside the crew operations building, Ven and Anorant continued going over the holographic map, making slight changes to their plans. Ven also admitted that the order of attack should change based on the fact they planned to remain hidden under cover of the STL-5.

The Ultra Raiders spent the time working on their ships and getting familiar with the STL-5 onboard operations screen. Jebet helped out when she could. Going from ship to ship, computer to computer, talking to the teens, she tried to give them every ounce of confidence and encouragement she could.

An hour and a half had passed when Marrett finally got up from her terminal and made her way to Ven and Anorant who were still going over the attack plan.

Marrett interrupted the discussion. "I received inside word from the other group. They say the attack will commence within the next ten hours. We have to get going or we'll never make it."

"Did they say anything else?" asked Anorant. He was glad to receive word but desperate for anything that showed potential for success.

"They didn't. The message was short and encrypted. Most likely it's all we'll hear from them, and I obviously can't message back," Marrett said.

"Alright, everyone, listen up! The time is now," said Ven looking at all the nervous pilots. "If you're eating, take your last bite. If you need to use the restroom, go now. Otherwise, suit up and head for your ships. We'll open communications once everyone's on board, before we take off. Marr and Anorant will provide rear support. Everything that happens is for a reason! Now, let's go!" said Ven.

Chapter 50

MarsCorp

Sint Argum left his command control tower. He wanted to be at the center of operations near the surface to witness Vivsou direct his armada off to their mission. Still hours from launching the attack, Sint left Akens Ember and Gregory Digby at command control atop the tower. They were to keep him posted of anything out of the ordinary. Several plans were now in motion, which Sint believed would assure him success in not only taking out the EnerConvoy, but also any contingency plans should any attempts be made to disrupt his efforts.

At the bottom of the command control tower was a small hangar with room for a few standard T-Crafts. Sint was planning on flying his personal luxury T-Craft he had transported from Earth. Upon entering the hangar, he changed his mind after spotting one of the newer DeCorp T-Craft. This particular model had two oversized fusion drive thrusters attached to the side of the streamlined version of a typical ship.

The reinforced titanium barred shatterproof canopy set at the nose of the T-Craft wrapped underneath, giving the pilot an almost limitless view from where he sat in the cockpit. The operator would have a clear line of sight from any direction. Many civilian pilots disliked the feeling of sitting out in the open and vulnerable. However, it was the complete opposite for combat pilots. For Sint, he fed off the uneasy feeling, thinking himself as being brave.

It was a relatively short flight from the base of his command control tower to the operations center. The ten-story building resembled a standard control tower from airports long ago. Various control operations were placed on every level leading to the top. The globe shape flight control center gave a 360 degree view of the engineering district. Jutting out the side at the top base of the tower rested a landing pad capable of parking three T-Crafts. As Sint reached the tower, he took his T-Craft and flew it at the same height as the top of the structure, sweeping all the way around as if to announce his arrival and landing next to Director Vivsou's slightly larger personal vehicle. The cockpit canopy swung forward for Sint to exit the craft. His signature purple accented cape attached to his gray designer, custom made flight suit billowed behind him, blown by the Mars breeze as he walked to the entryway with his helmet tucked under his arm. As the automatic door slid open, all eyes turned toward him.

Director Vivsou stood observing the hangar below that housed the fleet still in preparation for departure, his hands clasped behind his back.

When he heard Sint Argum's footsteps behind him, he turned around and said, "Welcome, sir. Glad to have you with us."

Sint raised an eyebrow in response to Vivsou's greeting. "I assume we are going to get our forces heading to their destination soon and on time."

"Yes, sir, we will. Digby is keeping me posted on the convoy's location relative to us," Vivsou replied.

"The EnerConvoy. Let's not give anyone any reason to believe these traitors and murderers are anything other than what they are."

Sint wanted the label to stick. EnerCon was the enemy.

"Yes, sir. Help yourself to sit in the flight operations chair if you wish while we continue our preparations. It's going to be some time before the operation is underway."

"I will." Sint Argum then spread his arms wide, raising his voice to address the hundred or so employees and staff. "Everyone, give me your attention! Thank you all so much for your efforts. What we do, what you *all* do…" Sint pointed at the faces of the individuals closest to him. "Yes, you and you… What we do today will set us all on a path of security as we look to our future. Thank you again, thank you ALL! Now, be vigilant, for this is all for a reason!"

****

Europa

Jebet and Ven were now onboard the Anniversary. Kaytha and Taft, having made the needed repairs to their ship, waited onboard their T-Crafts inside the hangar of the ship. Once they were all clear of Europa and flying in open space, Taft and Kaytha would both depart out the rear and lead the Ultra Raiders while they followed behind the Anniversary. Anorant and Marrett would fall in behind everyone else. The plan was to speed jump to Mars without the STL-5 powered up. They would save the power of the device until it was time to attack.

Jebet had retrofitted the Anniversary's charging connections and begun the power-up process, carrying more than enough energy cells to completely recharge the device. They would finish the process halfway through their journey. Everyone would stay in formation during the jump, like a dry run as if the STL was on. Before arriving, they would turn on the device to (what the Ultra Raiders referred to as "ghosting") remain in the cover of the stealth wake for the duration of the attack. Anorant and Marrett would stay behind, just outside the red planet's orbit. Once the attack commenced, DeCorp would be distracted enough to, hopefully, not be paying attention to a random ship in the system.

Once everyone was strapped in and powered up, the hinged door of the hangar opened to the bitter cold of Europa's atmosphere as the Ultra Raiders inside started switching on their lift manifolds. The pilots parked outside followed suit, while Ven spun up power to the Anniversary's massive thrusters. Taft and Kaytha kept their onboard OS and avionics up and running while waiting to fire up their own T-Crafts' power plants.

Taft said on his direct comm, "We're gonna get through this, Kaytha."

"I know we are. At least by tomorrow, it'll all be over, right? It's just another day," replied Kaytha, staring at Taft out her cockpit canopy with her visor up.

Jebet sat at the terminal designated for communications which now would also be handling flight operations and weapons control after some clever remapping of the Anniversary's computer systems. Once all of her HIREZ screens were positioned in place, she gave Ven the thumbs up that she was ready.

Ven went all comms to the entire group. "V-five, on the ready."

"J-two, on the ready."

"K-three, on the ready."

"T-four, on the ready."

Ven invited everyone in on the ritual, "Ultra Raiders, Supply One are you ready?"

A chorus of nervous and excited voices spoke over the open comms, "Ready!"

"Supply One, ready."

Ven, deciding to change his normal close to the roll call, said, "For a Reason, everyone."

The entire region surrounding the facility shook as more than forty-five ships rose from all around and inside the building. The Anniversary slowly roared into the sky. Shards of ice crystals flew off the ships that were parked outside. As the Anniversary ascended with its nose pointed to the stars, the other T-Crafts quickly fell in line behind. The glowing of the yellow thrusters combined with the ice falling off the ships that moments before were sitting on the frozen surface created a dazzling display.

Supply One was the last to lift off as the newly formed strike force entered into space with Jupiter in front of them and Europa now behind them. Ven completed the depressurization process for the hangar bay. Taft and Kaytha pressed the square illuminated blue button they each had in order to turn on the power to their engines. Their T-Crafts came to life. Positioned facing out the hangar bay door, they watched as the blackness of space appeared in front of them.

Once opened, Taft and Kaytha saw the Ultra Raiders' ships glowing like Christmas lights with reds and greens from the plasma blasters and cannons, flickering blues from the cockpits, and the faint yellows of the thrusters—all being dangled against the stark backdrop of space as the ships drifted to maintain their positions.

"You first, Kay," Taft said.

Kaytha hastily did a once-over of the space between them and realized the rear of the ship didn't offer enough clearance. "Actually, we'll leave together," she said decidedly, as she flipped down her visor.

Taft did the same then called out the countdown, "And in three… two…one."

In unison, they floated off the hangar bay floor, releasing the magnetic docking like they were one ship. They matched the slight throttle up of their thrusters as their T-Crafts drifted slowly out the rear of the Anniversary and headed straight for the caravan of young pilots.

Kaytha said, "You go right, I'm going left, T." They each made a 180 turn to fall in line behind the Anniversary as the hangar bay door closed.

"All right, everyone, access your STL flight program. Once you're locked in the cruise position when everyone is in the green, we'll be ready for our jump," Kaytha said on all comms. Since most of them were already in position, it only took a few seconds before Kaytha comm'd the Anniversary's flight deck. "Ven, we're ready."

"Ready indeed. Heads up, everyone. We're in position, so begin throttle up procedures," Ven said on all comms.

Jebet would now have control of the entire group. Oshly had included the ability to "group fly" under one controller, but this would be the first time it was being utilized. Once the collection of thrusters trailing behind them were powered up, Jebet would engage everyone together for the jump.

Jebet said on all comms, "Okay, people, get ready for a kick! And here…we…go!"

A split second later, they blasted off away from Jupiter. Apart from Ven, all everyone had to do was sit back and enjoy the ride.

Chapter 51

Open space, destination Mars

An hour had passed, and the remote piloted speed jump was unnerving everyone. Unlike autopilot, here you had over forty ships in close proximity to one another, the flight computers always adjusting the ships, jockeying to stay in position at just under sub-light speeds. For Taft and Kaytha, they needed to fight the urge to correct their flight paths if they felt they were drifting too close to each other.

Kaytha reached out on a direct comm to Taft. "This really sucks. I don't mind the ship flying for me, but I do mind all the other ships around us flying for them."

"I just keep telling myself that if the auto-flight program wasn't working, we'd have known by now," Taft replied, fidgeting with some of his cockpit comfort settings.

Jebet's voice broke through the conversation on all comms. "Wake up, everyone. The STL-5 is fifteen minutes from a full charge.

Once it's finished, Ven will enable the device. Ultra Raiders and Supply One, listen up. Your STL flight program *ghosting* indication lights will soon be up and running. You'll have control of your ships again when we arrive. Oh, and remember, if you slip out of the stealth wake, you *will* be visible."

Ven chimed in, "What Jebet's saying is mind your STL program monitor and stay in the wake. If not, you'll be on your own."

Jebet picked back up the comms. "We're about halfway into our trip, so if you want to nap, now's the time."

Jebet, monitoring one of her HIREZ screens, noticed various signals being picked up on the scanners and then dropping off as quickly as they showed up. The group was traveling at exponentially faster speeds than what was being picked up on their scanners.

"Ven, there are so many ships out here, and most of them don't appear to be functioning at all," Jebet said.

"People weren't prepared for what happened. Unless they were already attached to EnerCon or DeCorp, chances are they're going to die out here before they even have a chance to reach a destination."

****

MarsCorp

Sint Argum watched the DeCorp T-Crafts flying in and out of the hangar bay from the comfort of the flight director's chair. The ships buzzed around the engineering district as they continued to prepare for travel to intercept the EnerConvoy.

From the communication terminal of the operations center, a young woman received a message, turning in her chair towards Sint. "Commander, sir, Akens Ember needs to speak with you."

"Send him to this terminal," Sint replied.

Sint reached down to bring up the incoming video feed. "Yes, Ember, what is it?"

"Sir, we just received the footage from one of the last remaining transmitting orbital stations. Debris from the Moon's destruction has begun striking the planet." Akens Ember was having difficulty hiding the sadness in his voice.

Sint Argum's treacherous plan to secure Earth's fate was coming to fruition. The first of the destroyed Moon fragments that reached the Earth's atmosphere burned up on entry. Shortly after, larger pieces fell from the sky and were set ablaze on their way to the ground.

Chunks of the Moon, half the size of most single occupant T-Crafts, carried enough velocity to leave a crater five times its size and a blast radius almost a mile wide. Many fragments would land in the oceans, others in remote, uninhabitable areas. However, the real devastation was occurring in the most populated areas around the globe. Hundreds of thousands of people, who were still scrambling to either get off the planet's surface or trying to find shelter, had to outrun the fury of what remained of Earth's destroyed Moon. Not long after, larger pieces of rubble began arriving. Each one, the size of a city or larger, brought with it a potential for an extinction level impact. Scores of escaping vehicles filled with evacuees were being wiped out. Ships fleeing the planet were now being brought crashing back down after getting caught in the repetitive blast waves of each rock's impact.

"Oh, no, that is truly horrible, horrible news. So unfortunate for those left behind." Sint did his best to show some semblance of remorse, though those close enough to watch his reaction were not convinced. "Do you have the footage available, Ember?"

"I do, sir. Shall I send it to you?"

Sint thought for a moment. He indeed wanted to see the destruction, but then had another idea. "Yes, patch me into the feed. Also, have Digby prepare a planet-wide emergency broadcast."

"Plant-wide, sir. You mean everyone, commander?"

"Yes, Ember, everyone. Every functioning screen on every ship should receive this message. Tell Digby to patch me into this video you are watching. I will address the population directly, and I want this footage to be shown while I speak," said Sint.

"When would you like this to take place, sir?" Ember didn't like where this was going.

"Right now, Ember. I prefer there be no delay."

"Yes, sir," Akens walked off camera to find Gregory Digby and deliver Sint's request. It took only a few moments for Digby to route the necessary feeds for Sint Argum's address. Digby gave him the needed information to inform their leader and a thumb's up that he was ready to broadcast. Akens stepped back in front of the camera.

Seeing him, Sint asked, "Are we ready?"

"Yes, as soon as you see the green light appear in the upper left corner of your screen, you will be live. Starting with you, and then the feed from the O-Station."

Straightening his posture and lifting his head high, Sint waited for the light to appear. He took a few deep breaths and began speaking the moment it came on. "Hello, this is Commander Sint Argum. As you know, upon evacuation of Earth, we received word that an attack on its Moon—our Moon—was carried out by a group who now travel in the EnerConvoy.

The convoy consists of EnerCon assets and many people who have chosen to ignore our offers of security here with us. Those responsible for destroying the Moon have doomed any hope of returning to our home planet."

He continued to narrate, lying to justify his attack, his war, before it began. "As you can see on your screens, the effect of their murderous act has begun. Witness city size boulders of our Moon as they impact the planet. Tidal waves created from debris falling into our oceans are already crashing on the shores of the continents. Each destructive piece that impacts land is like a nuclear bomb being dropped. More will die than needed to. Many still trying to escape will no longer have that opportunity."

The footage was short but effective as the hundreds of thousands of evacuees on Mars, plus those still arriving, watched the further destruction of Earth.

The camera focused back on Sint. "Those responsible, traveling in the EnerConvoy, will suffer for what they have done. As will those who choose to side with them, believing the lies that they have told. In a matter of hours, we will strike at the heart of them, enacting swift justice. This has all happened for a reason.

And it's for that reason the hundreds of our bravest souls will have their revenge for what they have done," concluded Sint, leaning down to turn off the feed.

The screens and monitors of everyone in the tower returned to their previous modes. Suddenly, yelling of support and applause broke out. Sint simply nodded his head. The last piece of his plan worked better than he could have possibly imagined.

Aware of the truth, Director Vivsou stood stoically as he watched Sint's military gather for their upcoming attack. Out on the Martian surface, rows of armed T-Crafts and support ships were being placed outside the hangar as they were prepped for launch.

****

The Anniversary

Ven started the deceleration procedure as they neared Mars. He was directly tied into the program keeping the other ships in sync together during the jump. The STL-5 was now up and running, cloaking everyone behind the ship.

"Ven, you seeing this on the scanner? We're coming up a line of ships still headed for MarsCorp. At least a few hundred extending out to space from the planet's surface. Looks like they're all landing in the population district," Jebet said, looking over the long-range scanner at her now multipurpose terminal on the Anniversary flight deck with Ven.

"I noticed, all right. They're cutting a line right across the path I plotted for our attack," said Ven, already reviewing other options. "Looks like Anorant's idea of coming in low on the horizon is going to be plan B."

"There're a lot of ships stranded by the looks of it. Probably not enough power to land in the atmosphere. You know what, Ven?"

"I was thinking the same thing!"

Ven direct comm'd to Supply One. "Marr, Rant, it's Ven. You guys awake back there?"

"Yeah, Ven, just going over the latest deceleration readings. I assume we're close?" Marrett replied.

"We are. Rant, we're going with plan B. Jebet will alert everyone in a minute. There's a line of ships from off planet blocking our run. I'm going to swing us around. Come in from the east, low to the terrain."

"I guess you've finally come around," Anorant said.

"No choice. The good news is, however, we have a bunch of derelict ships in orbit around the planet, and you two can hide among them. They'll provide great cover during the operation."

"Will do, Ven. I'll wait until we slow up some more and find a spot. Going crypto comms from here on out."

Marrett said, "Ven, take care of the Raiders. Come back to us safely, for a reason."

"For a reason, you be safe too. Ven, out."

As soon as Ven closed his communications with Supply One, Jebet opened the channel wide all comms to the ships that followed.

"Everyone, we are currently ghost status and slowing for final approach. Mind your STL program, stay in the green during our run, and follow Taft and Kaytha's track. Ven's leader." Jebet then handed the comms to Ven.

"No motivational speeches needed. You know why we are doing this. We are going with option B from the mission plan. A line of ships blocked our access to the surface. We are about to reach cruising speed, and Jebet will count you down to manual control take over. Jebet, we're all yours."

"Taft, Kaytha, Raiders, if anyone isn't ready, sound off now." Jebet waited a few seconds.

Giving Jebet a familiar voice, Kaytha replied, "Hey J, we're ready."

"You will have manual control of your ships in three...two...one," called out Jebet as the pilots regained control of their ships.

Supply One, carrying Marrett and Anorant, already left the group and were in the process of reaching the tail end of ships arriving on Mars.

As soon as Jebet switched off the remote speed jump program, several Raiders' T-Crafts started slipping out of the stealth wake.

"Ven, we have some loose T's in the middle of the group!"

"Just give them a minute, J. You remember when we tested back at the field, it takes a second to adjust," Ven replied.

Ven was right. Following the computer guidance of the STL-5 stealth wake program, the Ultra Raider pilots quickly flew back into formation.

Ven opened the all comms channel. "Raiders, we are going crypto comms in a minute. Maintain radio silence and follow my lead. I'll be calling out orders. Only break radio silence if you must. We'll be working our way wide around the line of ships off the planet and making our approach low, from the east. For a reason, and good hunting."

Taft direct comm'd to Kaytha, "Kay, if the group gets split up..."

Kaytha cut Taft off, "I've got your back, T. We're seeing this through together."

"Together for a reason," Taft spoke the words as a declaration.

"For a Reason, together, T," was Kaytha's reply.

Chapter 52

The forty-six ships and Supply One, now floating in orbit above
Mars in between a half dozen ships stuck in space, made up the
strike team. As they began their run, they were all well hidden
from view in the stealth wake of the STL-5. Starting their attack
run, they stretched out their distance, ship to ship from each other,
forming a double wide line with the Anniversary in the lead as they
approached Mars' surface.

While they had stayed in tight formation during the speed jump
from Europa, they now had plenty of space to maneuver. The
Anniversary picked up speed entering the native atmosphere of
Mars. Each ship maintained just enough distance so as not to slip
out of the stealth wake and risk being exposed.

Kaytha and Taft had arguably the most challenging task. Following
behind the Anniversary blocked their forward view of the targets,
more so than any of the other T-Crafts that followed. If they came
under any fire, Kaytha and Taft were to break free and draw away
any potential defense from DeCorp.

With the entire strike team now inside the atmosphere, Ven took
the Anniversary and everyone following into a low position over
the red and orange covered Mars terrain. Flying at a lower altitude

than the mountains on either side, they twisted and turned through rocky Martian canyons. They were invisible to the eye; however, they cut an unmistakable massive dust trail plume behind them while heading toward the engineering district of DeCorp.

With less than fifty miles to go, they were closing in fast on the atmodome at MarsCorp. Ven opened up the crypto channel to address the Raiders. "We're keeping at this speed for now. Targets coming up. Wait for my signal." Inside the flight deck, Ven was both nervous and excited now that he finally was getting to put the Anniversary through its paces.

"Jebet, ready the seeker missile packages! We can make multiple runs, but I really don't want to!" Ven shouted out, having to yell over the sound of rushing wind blowing past the ship and the roar of the engines. Ven had one hand on the flight stick and the other gripping the throttle.

****

MarsCorp Communication and Control Tower

The atmodome towers that surrounded the miles of the sprawling complex began to shake, setting off the ground sensors and alerting the flight tower. Earthquakes on Mars weren't uncommon, but specific sensors being tripped was.

"Director Vivsou, east atmo ground sensors are showing minor fluctuations!" a DeCorp staffer shouted from across the room.

"Stagnant or growing?" Vivsou asked her.

"They're growing, sir. It doesn't appear to be a quake, but if it is, it's one of the smallest we've registered. I'm not sure what to make of it."

"Do you have visuals on the perimeter monitors in the east?" Vivsou knew there was most likely one thing that would cause this type of low seismic disturbance—invasion.

"No, director. Wait…It looks like a dust storm, but it's close to the ground and growing, however. I can't tell what's causing it."

Realizing what would cause that, Sint Argum sprang from his chair and moved in close to Vivsou. "If that's the Anniversary, who knows how big a group is creating it! We're blind!"

Director Vivisou thought for a moment then called out his orders. "Operations, tell all flight crews and pilots to prepare for departure and await my signal to launch. Ground defenses, go full alert. Activate all weapons and focus them east. Prepare for incoming targets!"

Across the vast array of buildings, doors slid open on their roofs.

Spiraling out from their hiding spots were dozens of gun turrets, each equipped with short-range plasma cannons and missile launcher racks. In unison, the turrets turned into the direction of the east and dust cloud.

****

The Anniversary, above MarsCorp

"Raiders, we're scanning defensive artillery ahead. I'm going to take a higher flight line over the area. Keep in formation. Break off and evade only if you have to," Ven said over the crypto comms.

They were about to pass in between two atmosphere processors and into the atmodome as Ven drifted the Anniversary a few extra hundred feet to stop the dust the trail they'd created. As the Anniversary flew through the thin differential layer of atmosphere, swirling, colliding, particles passed all around the ship and everyone that followed. They rapidly made their way toward their first target, a large warehouse building, home to all of the E-District's construction equipment and the fueling power recharge station located next to it.

****

Back at the communication and control tower, one of the MarsCorp spotters zeroed in on the hole created in the atmodome as the last of the Raiders' T-Crafts flew past it. "Director! There! Something is creating a disturbance in the atmosphere layer!" shouted one of the tower spotters.

Vivsou called out, "Weapons control, plasma fire now to the east, sweep wide right, into the sky."

"Director, what are we firing at?!" a weapons controller shouted back.

Vivsou grabbed the moveable desk microphone. Pressing the talk button, he spoke to the entire tower, "Weapons, follow orders now! Fire to the eastern skies, plasma only. Our attackers are using a cloaking device. Everyone, call out anything that might give us their location!"

****

The Anniversary, with T-Crafts in tow, were far enough away from the incoming energy blasts to worry about being stuck. Ven had been keeping the crypto comms open for the duration of the attack. "I'm angling in to line up our target. Watch your fire, use your weapons' guidance, and follow my lead."

The Anniversary then dove down toward the building.

"Jebet, now!" Ven yelled out, fighting the G-forces caused by the aggressive maneuver.

Not wasting what ammunition they had, Jebet fired only two missiles from the forward launchers under the nose of the ship. One was for the construction warehouse, the other was aimed at the fuel-recharge power station. Once the missiles blasted away from the ship, Ven pulled back the control stick, lifting the Anniversary up toward the sky.

With the Anniversary clear from blocking their view, Taft and Kaytha each fired off a round of plasma blasts. The glowing silver destructive energy mass followed right behind the missiles as they made direct contact with their intended target. Like a roller coaster on a track, swooping low before going high, each pair of Ultra Raiders' T-Crafts followed the same path with the same number of blasts, connecting with the multi-story warehouse, every explosive hit doing more and more damage.

****

"Oh my God, director! LOOK!" called out one of the tower spotters as she pointed to the series of massive explosions in the direction they had all been told to fire upon.

"Director, launch the ships! Launch them all— NOW!" Sint shouted, knowing if they didn't get the fleet off the ground, they were going to be taken out in the attack. Sint Argum had no patience to wait for Vivsou to weigh all the options. "WHAT ARE YOU WAITING FOR?!" he screamed at Vivsou.

Director Vivsou snapped out of his moment of hesitation to make his next move. "Operations, mission Convoy is a go, launch immediately!" he shouted.

Sint Argum rushed back to the flight director's chair. Pulling forward the movable HIREZ screen, he quickly called on direct comms to Akens Ember in the command control tower.

Akens was waiting by his terminal. With panic in his voice, he choked out, "Commander, we're under attack!"

"Ember, engage Recondite Protocol. Execute as soon as possible," Sint told Akens.

"Yes, sir." Ember then called out to Gregors Digby, "Digby, execute Recondite! Go on their authority, fast readiness. It's been approved."

****

On the Anniversary, Ven felt confident that their first attack was a success. They were already turning to take out DeCorp's drone armada. Ven snaked the trail of T-Crafts up toward the sky and over into a loop for another drop down attack. The Anniversary completed a tight turn, the angle forcing Ven and Jebet into their seats. Ven had the ship flying upside down for a brief moment, before heading back toward Mars, having to send the Anniversary through a barrel-roll to get her right side up.

The Ultra Raiders followed suit, pulling through the same maneuver, one that the friends had done many times over Kay's Field.

"Raiders, we'll handle the housing, you take out the base of the tower," Ven called out.

Jebet then fired off a series of four plasma blasts in succession from two rooftop cannons. The bolts connected with the top of the building directly above the massive exit door. Chunks of concrete flew in all directions amid the fire and billowing smoke, as the entire front of the building collapsed. As it did, the Anniversary made a hard right turn, again clearing the way for Kaytha and Taft to start the attack on the small control tower.

Kaytha switched her weapons selection to the forward facing energy blasters of her sturdy thrusters. Before Taft could even fire a shot, two blasts of red-hot thermal energy exploded from Kaytha's thruster cannons. With tremendous force and speed, the energy pulses landed at the base of the drone control tower. The entire structure was instantly reduced to rubble as Kaytha whipped her T-Craft around to follow the Anniversary toward the next target.

Ven dropped the Anniversary low, skimming the tops the buildings. The flying train of forty-five T-Crafts still in tow wound in between the larger towers, buildings, and silos.

The MarsCorp defensive gun turrets fired away indiscriminately, making it safe to fly below their line of fire. The heads-up display showed in real time the holographic image of the E-District, giving Ven the needed layout as they continued their attack. They were only seconds away from approaching the vehicle hangar and engineering spaceport.

Knowing he had a few moments until they started the next attack on the hangar and power generator, Taft broke radio silence to comm one-on-one with Kaytha. "How you holding up in there?"

With her right hand firmly gripping the control stick, Kaytha twisted and turned her T-Craft over the industrial landscape. "You mean, did I like doing your job for you?"

"It was impressive but don't take away all my fun," Taft replied, jerking back on the controls to bring his T-Craft up and over the top of one of the taller buildings.

Marrett's voice broke through Taft and Kaytha's direct comm. "Ven?! Ven, do you copy? This is Supply One. We're picking up a mass of heat signatures." Before Marrett could finish her warning, the Anniversary was already flying above the massive vehicle hangar. Ven saw exactly what Marrett was alerting them about.

Taft watched the Anniversary make an aggressive 90 degree spin off to the right, away from the flight path he and Kaytha were currently on.

Taft didn't have time to work out why Ven would be so reckless. With his comms to Kaytha still open, he screamed, "LOOK OUT!"

The DeCorp fleet of over a hundred T-Crafts was lifting off the flight line and directly in front of them.

"Raiders, break off! Evade! Evade!" Ven called out as he struggled to keep the Anniversary aloft in the manufactured Mars air.

Ven's efforts to warn the others were too late. Kaytha, Taft, and the Ultra Raiders flew directly into the path of the DeCorp fleet lifting off the surface.

Chaos immediately broke out as the Ultra Raiders attempted to wind their way at high speed through the rows of rising attack ships. Two Raiders' ships plowed directly into the sides with a pair of rising DeCorp MTCs, exploding in the sky before they could think about getting out of the way. Everyone was now exposed, no longer hidden by the STL-5.

The Anniversary had turned away in time to avoid any collision. Jebet, already prepared to deliver the strike package, recalibrated the onboard targeting computer to account for their new flight path as she executed their next targeted attack. Within seconds, two small doors on either side of the Anniversary flipped open. Spinning out away from the ship was a set of long-range remote driven fusion drive cluster bombs.

With her small weapons joystick, Jebet piloted the highly explosive projectiles back in the direction of the DeCorp vehicle hangar. The Anniversary flew farther away as the bombs locked on and struck the building directly. The explosion caused the hangar to collapse, demolishing the bulk of DeCorp's military might.

Taft continued flying at full speed, focusing only on avoiding the ships in his path. Every DeCorp attacker that was passed by a Raider T-Craft engaged and gave chase. Taft was almost through the crowded airspace, having broken past the last of the enemy ships in his way, when he caught a glimpse of Kaytha still struggling to get clear. Knowing better than to break her concentration, he shut off the comms between their ships and spun his T-Craft around to go help her. From out the right of his canopy window, Taft watched another fireball erupt as a DeCorp fighter took out one of the Raiders, sending them crashing to the red Martian dirt below.

With the last of the DeCorp ships blocking any clear pathway to airspace above, Kaytha pulled back on the joystick, throttling up her thrusters, to head vertically into the sky. An Ultra Raider who'd been following her hadn't anticipated her maneuver and attempted to dive beneath her. Flying too closely, the roof of his T-Craft clipped one of Kaytha's thrusters and sent her upward, flipping violently end over end. The top of the Raider's ship was torn to shreds. Flying out of control, the Raider couldn't avoid crashing nose first into a DeCorp ship rising from below. The collision took them both out in an instant, as they fell tumbling to the ground.

Kaytha's T-Craft's momentum carried her vertically for a few seconds before it stalled in midair. Then, spinning like an arrow, it dove toward the ground. Kaytha instinctively scrambled to ignite her thrusters.

Switching from the main power to auxiliary, she rhythmically slammed the throttle stick back and forth trying to jumpstart her ship. Taft raced through the sky to reach her location, taking out several DeCorp T-Crafts with his ship's nose cannons, watching helplessly as Kaytha dropped from the sky.

Seconds from impact, Kaytha's ship roared back to life. The powerful burst of power from her thrusters kept the ship, for the moment, from crashing, but now it fishtailed back and forth, sputtering through the air.

Taft had nearly caught up to Kaytha when a DeCorp fighter positioned itself behind her. She had no control as the MTC opened fire. Taft quickly locked on, aimed, and fired a short-range guided missile. It took just a second after pulling the trigger for the DeCorp ship to explode in a shower of burning debris. Taft flew his T-Craft directly into the smoke, metal bits, and flame of the destroyed ship and pushed through the carnage only to see that his shot had come too late. The DeCorp attacker had riddled Kaytha's T-Craft's power plant with bullet rounds as she started falling again toward the surface.

Taft tried to reach her on his comms. "Kaytha, your flight suit! Pressurize and seal your flight suit!"

Taft realized that Ven and the Raiders might soon destroy the Main Power Generator, shutting off the atmosphere processors. If Kaytha survived the crash but the hull was breached, she would be dead in seconds. Taft stared as her ship spun closer and closer toward the ground below. Stunned by fear, he was incapable of looking away.

At the very last moment before impact, a sudden yellow flash burst from one of her thrusters straightened out her ship as the purple glow of her lift manifolds appeared. The surge in power was all she needed to keep her T-Craft from total destruction, but not enough to stop her from violently slamming into the hard surface. Upon impact, her ship shifted onto its side. Watching from above, it felt like an eternity seeing Kaytha's smoking T-Craft come to an abrupt halt against a mound of rocks jutting up from the ground

Taft, still connected to Kaytha's systems, was receiving data from her flight suit, indicating her vitals were fine, but he wasn't picking up any movement. *She's gotta be knocked out,* he thought as his T-Craft took a hit from a plasma blast. A trio of DeCorp fighters hadn't given up on trying to take him down. Thankfully, the blast was from such a long range that, by the time it hit the rear of Taft's ship, it had lost so much energy that it hardly caused any denting to the metal panels. He knew he'd gotten lucky and still needed to concentrate. He'd be no good to Kaytha if he wasn't alive to help.

"Ven! Ven?! Call off the attack on the generator! Kaytha is down, and I don't know if the ship is depressurized! Copy?!" Taft yelled desperately on the comms.

Ven and a handful of Raiders, who'd been able to avoid the carnage over the hangar bay, were heading for the main power generator, which sat completely vulnerable in the distance. Ven hesitated to call off the attack. He thought, *Lives are at stake, not just Kaytha's.* But as quickly as the thought to go forward with the attack came, so did hesitation. Ven turned to see Jebet staring at him, her face filled with panic not knowing what choice he would make.

"We're *not* losing Kaytha too, J," Ven said, as he opened the comm to all channels. "Raiders, disengage from the target and follow me." With absolute resolve, Ven believed this was happening for a reason.

Ven comm'd Taft, "We copy. We'll wait for your word. Go get her out of there."

"Copy, Ven. Thanks."

Taft then turned sharply to evade the fighters still on his tail. Spotting a huge smoke cloud billowing up from the damaged facility, he got an idea. Slamming forward the handle to provide full power to his engines, Taft was able to put some distance between himself and the DeCorp MTCs that chased him.

Pitching down to skim the tops of the engineering buildings, he flew into the massive cloud of gray smoke hanging heavy in the artificial air of the Mars atmosphere. As soon as he was out of sight from his pursuers, Taft switched on his lift manifolds and immediately opened up his T-Craft's speed flaps and drag fins. Slamming his control stick sideways, his ship did a full 180 in the sky, and came to a stop. Floating, Taft positioned his ship to face in the direction of the incoming enemy. A second later, both MTCs burst through the smoke cloud where Taft waited. He targeted both ships and unleashed the fury of his forward facing plasma cannons. The energy blasts were spot on, connecting with the DeCorp fighters, shredding directly through their hulls, which sent them exploding to the ground beneath Taft's T-Craft.

Finally clear of the immediate threat, Taft powered his engines to speed back to where Kaytha had gone down. Again staying low to avoid attracting attention, Taft pressed a bright blue illuminated button to bring up the scanner overview of the battle that was still raging. Based on the identity markers, twenty or so Raiders were still in the fight, outlasting the fragmented DeCorp military. Locating Kaytha's distinct craft signature, Taft could see three surface vehicles heading her direction. Taft knew that if she were captured, DeCorp would not risk injuring her. They would have the only bargaining chip that they could exchange for the device.

Taking a deep breath, Taft forced himself to focus on what needed to be done.

Swinging his ship around, he shot off in the general direction of the other side of the complex, back to where Kaytha had crashed. Keeping low, dodging in and out of some of the taller buildings, Taft maneuvered his way at breakneck speed through the explosions, ash, smoke, and debris coming up from the surface. Like a knife piercing him in the heart, he genuinely understood what devoted love meant. Taft had never been so certain of anything in his life as he was now. Irrational and, perhaps, selfish as it might be, nothing mattered more to Taft than getting Kaytha back—or die trying to save her life.

****

Inside the communications tower, total chaos had broken out. Tower spotters called out targets while damage assessments were being made on a second by second basis.

"Commander, there's a T-Craft down near the airfield. Looks like it's intact," Director Vivsou said.

Sint Argum brought up the surveillance imaging to his HIREZ monitor, enhancing the location of the wrecked ship.

"I've already dispatched a ground crew to retrieve the pilot, assuming they're still alive," continued Vivsou.

Sint ran the verification scan and confirmed his suspicions. "SH1-0151, Kaytha Morrow, I hope you're still breathing," he said under his breath.

Sint then responded to Vivsou, "When the crews gather her up, immediately fly her here."

"Her, commander?" asked Vivsou.

"Yes, director. That's Kaytha Morrow, and, if her terrorist friends want her alive, they'll give me what I want. So, getting that girl in a ship and on that landing pad," Sint said, pointing out the side of the operations tower, "is our priority."

****

Slowing his speed, Taft closed in on Kaytha's T-Craft. He could already see that the canopy was open and she was gone. He did a quick flyby, keeping an eye out for any threats that would take advantage of his vulnerability. The three surface vehicles were already on the move, and they had Kaytha, making their way into an open smaller vehicle hangar. Taft could see dust from the red surface still hanging above the tracks left behind the trends of the small T-Crawlers. He knew landing and trying to find Kaytha was no longer an option as two DeCorp fighters seemed to have spotted him and were heading his way. *Dammit!* Feeling frustrated and hopeless, he made for the clear space above. He would have to regroup with the Anniversary and figure out a way to get her back.

Ven continued to fly the Anniversary upward, well above the battle below but just below the planet's orbit.

"Hey, Ven, the STL is offline," said Jebet, not entirely surprised by the revelation. The truth was the device had gone down prior to when they'd left the atmosphere. But, since there wasn't any immediate danger, she'd kept the news to herself. Jebet figured it was more imperative that Ven focused on getting them all out of harm's way.

"Ugh, of course it is," replied an exasperated Ven.

Ven took the Anniversary and the Raiders that followed into open space, keeping the ships low enough to engage back to the surface in a moment's notice. Having picked up a few more Raiders, many were still missing or fighting it out with the DeCorp T-Craft MTCs that made it airborne. Ven wanted to get back into the fight, but he knew these battle worn, inexperienced pilots needed to catch their breath. Once the generator was destroyed, they'd be done with the mission. But now, with Kaytha missing, the danger for all of them was rising with every second.

Just as Ven was about to comm all the Raiders that they'd soon be getting back in the fight, the Anniversary's surface scanners picked up a new bunch of signals. Directing the imaging onto the flight deck heads-up display, Ven counted roughly 25 large signatures rising off the ground in the population district.

Marrett and Anorant, who were still monitoring activity from their position outside Mars' orbit, hidden among the ships that had evacuated Earth, direct comm'd the Anniversary. "Are you guys reading this?!" Marrett's voice was calm.

Ven opened up the comm channel. "Yeah! What the—they're MMDs! Those bastards hid them among the evacs. Oh, hell, they're coming up off the surface fast!"

Even with the all Raiders launching everything they had at the colossal flying blocks of military might, it wouldn't be nearly enough to take down even half of the fully armed and operational MMDs. Worst of all, if they formed into the Massive Mobile Station-Adaptation (MMSA), they could still launch an effective attack on the EnerConvoy.

"We have to abort the mission, J! We can't take out those ships. And, if we try, none of us will make it out of here alive!" Ven was angry that he hadn't seen this coming. And worse, it looked like their mission was about to fail and he didn't know what he should do about it.

Jebet's head dropped as tears welled up in her eyes. Her mind raced with images of worst-case scenarios. She thought about how Kaytha was captured or maybe dead, how so many Ultra Raiders were still dog fighting on the surface, and it'd be all for nothing. Jebet smacked her hand against her thigh in an effort to regain her composure. She opened up the crypto comms to all the ships. "Raiders, break off! Get outta there and regroup with the Anniversary. We'll cover you as best we can."

Ven looked at her and said, "Once we get these kids clear, you know we're gonna have to figure out a way to get Kaytha."

Jebet nodded. "I just picked up Taft's signal. He's heading our way. Still a few minutes out. The others can't be too far behind. But, Ven, how soon till those MMDs are on us?"

"Not long. We'll deal with that when we have to."

Chapter 53

MarsCorp Communication Control Tower

A DeCorp transport craft pulled up alongside the landing platform but didn't land. A walk ramp slid out from beneath the ship as the large passenger side door swung up. The vehicle was about twice the size of standard T-Craft. Used for transport, it stood taller than most ships to accommodate passengers. Its two main thrusters were positioned almost perfectly center to the side of the ship on top of the fuselage. It was a T-Craft equivalent of a helicopter.

Two armed DeCorp security personnel, dressed in red, orange, yellow, and gray colored digital camouflage fatigues to match the Mars landscape, stood on either side of Kaytha. Their faces were protected by full-faced military grade helmets, and they carried— of all things—EnerCon pulse blaster rifles. The guards escorted Kaytha, still in her flight helmet and her hands cuffed, out on to the landing pad.

"Your guest has arrived, commander. Shall I alert the men to bring her in?" asked Director Vivsou.

Sint was already up from his seat, throwing on his cape over his shoulders. "That won't be necessary. She can remain outside.

467

Hopefully, this won't take long." Sint knew precisely what he planned to do. There was also no need to parade her in front of his people. If the situation with Kaytha had to get ugly, it was best that it happened with fewer eyes around.

The doors to the landing pad opened and let in a burst of the thick, smokey air that lingered over most of the burning E-District below. Sint strolled confidently through the smokey stench and onto the landing pad. The doors automatically slid closed behind him, and he walked directly up to Kaytha with her helmet on and her tinted visor lowered. Burning particles and dense smoke swirled all around where they stood.

Pointing to one of the armed men, Sint said, "You, there. Take this poor woman's helmet off. Let's have a look."

The security guard strapped his rifle to his belt and proceeded to lift the helmet from her head.

"The lovely Miss Kaytha Morrow. You look more like your father than I expected." Sint's tone was sardonically polite.

Kaytha's brow furrowed. Fighting the instinctive urge to lunge at him, she simply stared at her captor. Her forehead was slightly bloodied from a small gash and a bruise bloomed on the right side of her jaw from the crash.

Her dark brown hair, matted with Martian dirt, blew in the hot, acrid wind that blew around them.

Sint read the curiosity on Kaytha's face. "Yes, I knew your father. Brilliant man, shame what happened to him." Sint stalked around where she stood and stopped to stare briefly at the transport ship still floating above the landing pad.

Furious, Kaytha could hardly believe that the man in front of her could possibly hold the key to how this all began. She made the decision then and there that she would hold firm and never give him what she assumed he wanted.

Sint returned to stand in front of Kaytha. While being anywhere near Sint was enough to make her stomach churn, he was now close enough for her to catch a hint of body odor. Condescendingly, Sint said, "Look, *dear*. I'm not going to waste yours or my—" Kaytha tensed her clasped hands and, in one swift motion, lifted her arms, handcuffed together. The metal bindings hit Sint Argum right under his chin, knocking him backward.

A guard smashed the blunt end of his gun against the backside of Kaytha's legs, bringing her to her knees.

Sint dabbed at his mouth with his sleeve. A single drop of blood trickled from his mouth as he laughed while regaining his composure. "While I am sure you believe I deserved that, it doesn't change the fact that I am going to get what I want!" He drew himself up to his full height.

His face turned from amused to furious anger as he locked eyes with her.

Picking up Kaytha's helmet from the landing pad surface, Sint dusted off a smudge. "Let's get this over with, shall we?" Sint motioned for the guards to pull Kaytha to her feet.

"You, my dear, are going to comm whoever it is I need to speak with to get the device your father created. Once I have the device in possession, they can have you back *alive*. If they refuse," Sint paused for dramatic effect, "Well, let's just say they can have you back *after* I toss you from this ledge."

Kaytha finally broke her silence. "You can go ahead and ask whatever you want of my friends, but you're never going to get what you're after. All of this…it didn't have to be this way. The people on Earth still had a chance. But it was you—you who destroyed our Moon. You who ordered the murder of countless evacuees. We're here to defend them *because of you!* For a reason, this is happening. And, for a reason, you'll get whatever you deserve."

Enraged, Sint bellowed. "IT IS FOR A REASON THAT YOU'RE STILL ALIVE AND FOR A REASON THAT I WILL GET WHAT I WANT!" Taking a deep breath, he continued, "Now, girl, patch… me…through!" He thrust Kaytha's flight helmet at her face.

Kaytha lifted her cuffs and motioned for the guard to remove them.

With the cuffs off, she could comm Taft on her flight suit's operations pad on her wrist which was connected to her helmet mic. Opening up the comms, she carefully punched in two sets of ID numbers, Taft's and Jebet's.

Taft was just leaving the atmosphere of the planet when he heard the buzz and crackle of his helmet comms. Without looking down at his data screen, he knew it was her. "Kaytha?! Kaytha, you there?"

Taft's voice echoed from inside the open visor on Kaytha's helmet.

Speaking loudly toward the mic inside the helmet, Sint said, "Taft, is it? This is Sint Argum, Commander of DeCorp. I don't wish to waste your—or, I mean, Kaytha's time. Basically, you have something I want, and, when I get it, you can have your girl back."

Taft needed the proof of life first. "I'm not making any deals or talking with you any further until—"

"Yes, yes. You need to know she's alive. Of course she is. Otherwise, what would I have to barter with? But, fine, let's do this just to make you feel confident." Sint continued to play up the sarcasm. "Kaytha, dear, why don't you go ahead and tell your friend Taft that he *shouldn't* give me what I want."

She couldn't believe Sint's arrogance, regardless of how right he was. Sint shoved the helmet into her face. Kaytha gritted her teeth, nearly refusing to speak. She squeezed her eyes closed and thought of Taft and the danger he would be put in. Burning with hatred, Kaytha opened her eyes and stared straight at Sint. "Taft..." She clenched her fists to keep from begging him for help. Instead, she yelled loud and clear, "TAFT! DO NOT GIVE IT TO HIM! You and the others, do what you need—"

"That will be quite enough of your predictable comments," said Sint. Sint yanked the helmet away from Kaytha and turned his back on her as he went back to speaking into the helmet mic. "Now, you bring me the device, and, in exchange, I'll give you back the girl."

Taft's mind raced. He already knew he was going to give Sint what he wanted but didn't know if the others would see things his way.

Sint grew impatient waiting on Taft to reply. "I hope for her sake that you're still there."

"I'm still here, *Sint*," Taft replied.

"I'll tell you what, *Taft*. Let me sweeten the deal." Sint flipped over his wrist. Attached was a tiny square OS device no bigger than an antique watch. He punched in the code for Director Vivsou, "Director, do you read me?" Sint spoke closely enough near Kaytha's helmet for Taft to hear.

"Yes, commander, I read you."

"Director, I want you to halt all operations. Call back our remaining MTCs to the nearest landing location possible and tell the MMDs to hold their position," commanded Sint.

"Very well, sir." Vivsou could be heard barking out orders just before Sint closed the comm to him.

"As you no doubt just heard, I have called off my military operations. So, Taft, I will not only give you back Kaytha, but I'm giving you the opportunity to save your friends and all the others. See, I'm even more generous than I need to be."

As he continued flying toward the Anniversary, Taft looked over the scanners to confirm that DeCorp's forces were indeed returning to the surface.

****

On board the Anniversary, Ven could hear Jebet listening into the communications. He was too busy to focus on who or what she was listening to, assuming it was operations from below. Ven looked over the heads-up display to see that the MMDs were sitting in stationary positions in the Martian sky. The remaining Raiders were now heading to them without anyone following.

"Jebet, are you seeing this?" Ven asked.

****

Sint Argum gave his last request to Taft. "I am sure you are conflicted, but I don't see that you have any other choice. I'm certain you couldn't have gone far. And neither could your friends nor the device, for that matter. So, I will give you forty-five minutes to bring the device to me at this location, which you can track off our comms. You come to me, drop off the device, and I give you Kaytha. We get what we all mostly want. Do you read me, Taft?"

"I read you," Taft replied through gritted teeth.

"Good. I'll see you soon." Sint glanced back at the guards. "Thank you for the help. Hand me one of your weapons there and return to your post." Sint needed the available space on the landing pad for Taft to land for the exchange.

"So, Kaytha, I hope your friend returns promptly. Can I have someone bring you anything?" Sint asked, returning to his polite self.

Kaytha glared. Keeping her mouth tightly closed, she refused to give Sint Argum the satisfaction of making small talk.

"Fine then. We will just watch the fire and the clock." Sint looked at his wrist OS and tapped the screen.

****

Meanwhile, just above Mars' orbit, on the Anniversary's flight deck, Jebet switched seats, moving to a new terminal adjacent to the one she was using. Ven was busily monitoring the incoming Raiders, trying to figure out who, and how many, they had lost. Jebet logged into the ship's operation system. She worked furiously, searching for the right operating commands she needed, knowing she didn't have a lot of time.

Taft pushed his T-Craft to its limits to reach the Anniversary. He assumed his only shot at getting the STL-5 was through Jebet. He knew to trade the device into the wrong hands was putting so many lives in danger, but Taft had made a commitment to Kaytha, so, right or wrong, he believed deep down that he was saving her for a reason.

Taft now had the Anniversary in sight as he opened up one-on-one comms with Jebet. He made an effort not to yell, in case Ven was listening. "Jebet, it's Taft."

"No time, Taft. Transfer power to magnetize your center lift manifolds. It's the only way you're going to be able to grab it," Jebet said in a hushed voice, as she opened the doors to the belly of the Anniversary, just behind the weapons mount on the nose of the ship. She then swiped *unlock* from the STL-5 program on her

HIREZ screen.

Taft was confused by Jebet's cryptic directions, but then, in an instant, knew what to do as he watched the STL-5 float down out of the ship and away from the Anniversary.

"JEBET! What the hell are you doing?!" Ven boomed, as he looked out the Anniversary to see the device floating away from the ship.

"Ven, I can't explain now. But trust me, this isn't over."

"Wait! Is that fool planning on trading the device for her?! Jebet, there has to be another way of getting Kaytha back!"

Jebet stood up from her chair and yelled out at Ven, "Kaytha is the key! Alive or dead—we have to get her back! There isn't time for me to explain."

In one fluid motion, Taft angled his T-Craft sideways, relative to Mars beneath him, and pulled up alongside the device. He got just close enough for the magnetized lift manifolds to connect with the metal panel at the top of the device. The sound of metal slamming against metal was all Taft needed to hear to confirm he had the STL-5. Pushing the power lever forward, Taft's T-Craft thrusters burst to life, as he went rocketing back toward the surface.

"Taft? Taft, it's Jebet. Whatever happens—if you give them the device—you have to get Kaytha, no matter what!" Taft heard her but didn't respond. He was too focused on getting back to Kaytha before time ran out.

****

Sint Argum and Kaytha stood silently as they waited. Kaytha knew Taft wasn't going to listen to her, but she counted on it.

Director Vivsou's voice buzzed from Sint's wrist. "Commander, we have one lone fighter approaching from space, north-west at a high rate of speed."

"Keep me posted. Do not fire upon him," Sint said.

Glancing over at Kaytha, Sint grinned. "Looks like I am getting what I want." He turned around to watch the skies from the direction Taft would be approaching. As Taft flew through the atmodome, Sint could just barely make out his glowing, yellow thrusters in the failing light of day.

"See, here comes your rescuer," Sint said, almost gleefully. He motioned his head toward the growing speck in the sky that was Taft's T-Craft.

Kaytha easily homed in on Taft speeding toward them. That was until the STL-5 came to life once more. Because the device was on, but no longer attached to a program, it automatically cloaked Taft from their view.

A smile crossed Kaytha's face. She knew exactly what had happened. "Well, Sint, my rescuer *was* there," she said with a shrug of her shoulder.

Sint looked and saw nothing of the ship, apart from the swirls of rising black smoke Taft was flying through.

When the device turned on, the stealth wake caused a brief, but noticeable, visual disturbance. Like being inside a bubble, Taft knew he was cloaked. He briefly thought he could target Sint on the landing pad without hurting Kaytha.

Sint wasn't stupid and knew he was suddenly at risk. Walking over to Kaytha, he grabbed her arm and shoved her to the edge of the landing pad, leaving her only a foot from the ledge. Sint lifted the rifle to her head. Taft was close enough now that he could see what Sint had done. Sint was standing too close to her for Taft to line up an accurate shot, and he couldn't bear to see Kaytha in such danger. Flipping the switch for the remaining lift manifolds, Taft slowed his T-Craft as he approached the operations control tower's landing pad. Everyone inside, including Vivsou, watched, not exactly sure what was happening outside.

Taft's T-Craft roared as the air around the landing pad became chaotic. Lifting up his visor to clear his view, Taft moved his T-Craft right over the top of Sint and Kaytha. Even though they were unable to see him, they knew he was there. Taft started his descent onto the landing pad, close enough now that the stealth wake washed over the structure below him, along with Sint and Kaytha. Once Taft's T-Craft materialized before her eyes, Kaytha's face lit up. An audible gasp could be heard inside the tower as everything they were watching outside vanished.

As he reached the landing platform of the command and control tower, Taft flipped the four toggle switches, lowering his landing gear. Taft struggled briefly to land his T-Craft. With the STL-5 magnetized to the bottom of his ship, he didn't have full use of all his lift manifolds to help him keep stabilized while aloft.

Sint watched Taft's arrival, and immediately noticed the device attached to its undercarriage, now just a foot away from the surface beneath the ship. Sint then motioned for Kaytha to walk away from the ledge and toward the parked ship.

The cockpit canopy swung open forward, exposing Taft, who was still strapped in as he removed his helmet. "We had a deal! Let her go, and I'll release the device."

Sint knew if the boy had come this far, he intended to go all the way. If Taft tried to re-magnetize before he lifted off, Sint was certain the pulse rifle he borrowed from the guard would be enough to take out the ship's power plant with just a few blasts.

Sint moved in closer behind her. "Go ahead, Kaytha." Then, positioning his head over Kaytha's left shoulder, he said calmly into her ear, "I told you I would get want I wanted." Sint, undeterred by a lack of reaction from Kaytha, reached his lanky arms around her body to unlock her wrist bindings. Now that Kaytha's hands were free, he gave her a slight shove with his rifle to get her walking.

As she began to move away from him and toward Taft, Sint sneered, "It is too bad I didn't have more time to tell you about your father." He watched as Kaytha turned her head briefly and saw only sheer loathing.

Taft felt like it was taking an eternity for her reach him. Once Kaytha reached the side of Taft's ship, she placed her hands on the outer ridge, where the cockpit would seal closed. Just as she was about to climb on board, Sint fired a blast from his rifle across the nose of the ship.

"Not so quick! Release the device," Sint pointed the rifle back at Kaytha's head.

Taft already had the lift manifold operations screen up. Reallocating the center panels' power, thus turning off the magnet mechanism, the device dropped from beneath the T-Craft with a loud clunk.

Sint pulled back his weapon and pointed it away from Taft and Kaytha. Taft tossed his helmet behind the seat as he leaned out to help the wounded Kaytha into his cockpit. She would have to curl up on his lap since the ship was without a co-pilot seat. Taft's height made it possible for him to give Kaytha just enough space to curl up and position herself against him, but not take away from his ability to pilot his ship.

"This is new," said Kaytha, sore and beaten from her crash.

"Let's just get outta here," he replied.

Taft lifted off the platform even before the cockpit canopy could close. The wind violently rushed through the cabin as Taft piloted away from the tower. Then there was silence as the canopy sealed airtight and pressurized for the journey back into space.

The landing pad was still invisible when Sint walked over to examine the device. Everyone in the tower looked on in awe of seeing absolutely nothing. Sint used his wrist OS to contact Vivsou. "Director, send out our remaining fighters and order them to re-engage with the hostiles in the area. Also, inform the MMDs to continue their operation. They are to depart for the EnerConvoy immediately."

"Right away, sir."

Kaytha and Taft remained silent until they were clear of the atmodome. While Taft concentrated on getting them to the safety of the Anniversary, Kaytha shifted slightly to open the comms on her own. Before bringing up the Anniversary on the screen, she told Taft, "I gotta warn them."

"Warn them about what, Kay?" Taft asked.

Kaytha didn't have a chance to answer. Now connected with the open comms on the Anniversary, she said, "Ven, Jebet, tell the Ultra Raiders to get ready!"

Ven turned to look at Jebet, and, when he did, the holographic surface projections showed at least fifty of the remaining DeCorp T-Craft fighters departing from various locations.

Along with them, the MMDs started to rise, lumbering their way from a stationary position still inside the atmodome.

Taft and Kaytha now had the Anniversary in sight, along with the trailing Ultra Raiders.

Chapter 54

Sint Argum, using what limited strength his gangly body could muster, moved the device over to his DeCorp T-Craft sitting on the landing pad. The noise from the T-Craft fighters taking off across E-District had drowned out Director Vivsou's attempts to communicate with him. The door to the operations control center slid open as Vivosu rushed out, but Sint was too distracted with trying to determine how he would transport the device.

"Commander, are you okay?" Vivsou halted in front of Sint, catching his breath.

"Yes, of course, director. Everything is fine. We have the device, and, soon enough, the enemy will be—"

"But, sir, you were gone! The platform—most of it wasn't visible," said Vivsou.

Still caught up in his own triumph, Sint pointed at the device and continued, "Director, this is the cloaking machine. We are unstoppable now.

As soon as we get it to the DeCorp techs to determine its potential power and function, nothing will stand in our way."

"Yes, but how did you turn it off?"

"Turn it off? All I did was move it. Wait, how did you get out here?"

Sint then looked back at the windows of the tower and the dozens of faces staring back at him.

"Commander, you disappeared. Then, just a moment ago, you reappeared standing next to your ship. So did the landing platform."

Sint turned around, staring into the direction that Kaytha and Taft had flown away, fearing now he'd just been played a chump in the exchange. "Get this device into a secured location, director. Now!" Sint ordered.

Pressing the orange button on the side of his T-Craft to open the cockpit, Sint climbed inside.

"Commander, you don't have a flight suit on. You won't have your helmet!" Vivsou hastily stepped back away from the ship.

"Just get clear and lock up that device, director!" Sint yelled over the sound of his already wailing engines.

Sint Argum didn't bother strapping in as his T-Craft rose from the platform. Director Vivsou was nearly knocked off his feet as Sint cleared the landing pad and headed toward the MMDs to the west.

****

Just outside of Mars' orbit, Ven sat in the pilot's seat, mentally running military scenarios. He couldn't come up with one in which they made it out of the situation in one piece. He rubbed his hand over his bald head.

Taft and Kaytha were now on final approach after handing over the STL-5 to Sint Argum. He and the Ultra Raiders had failed to take out all their targets. And, to keep them on their toes, a lethal fleet of MMDs was making its way off the surface.

Jebet opened up the crypto channels to all the remaining Raiders still following the Anniversary. "Raiders, Taft and Kaytha are closing in for docking on our ship. Those following closest behind, we need you to make room for them to board inside the rear hangar."

Ven took over the comm. "Raiders, we have incoming attackers! Be prepared to engage and follow my orders."

Just then, Marrett's voice broke through the channel. "Negative on those last orders! Ven, as soon as Taft and Kaytha are on board, take the Anniversary and jump out of the system! Ultra Raiders, look for our signal low on the horizon to the east of E-District. Lock in on our signal and follow Supply One! We're going to finish this!" Marrett, piloting Supply One, was already skimming the surface, making their way for the E-District.

Anorant was busy readying what weapons they had on board. The first target had to be the atmosphere processing towers. Anorant identified two of the towering, monolithic wonders of technology.

Without hesitation, he locked them into the targeting computer and fired two fusion-fueled missiles from the undercarriage of the ship. Supply One, nearly matching the missiles' speed, was about to enter the false atmosphere of the MarsCorp facility as the base of the towers exploded and both life-giving air processors came crashing to the ground.

"Raiders, go help Supply One!" Ven called out on the comms. The Ultra Raiders, one by one, peeled off, flying down and away from the Anniversary.

Jebet already had the hangar bay open when Taft and Kaytha arrived at the rear of the ship. He slowly drifted his T-Craft into the Anniversary's hangar bay, and the familiar sound of the landing gear securing to the metal floor echoed as the door shut behind them. Taft tilted his head back and breathed a sigh of relief.

Wishing he could make time stand still, Taft waited for the hanger bay to pressurize. Kaytha then lifted her head off his shoulder and stared into his eyes. Not wanting to miss this opportunity, Taft kissed her and Kaytha passionately welcomed it. The loud buzzer, indicating the pressurization was complete, interrupted their embrace and put an end to the moment—a sad reminder that their work wasn't done.

Taft whispered, "Let's get you up to the med bay."

"No. Get me up to the flight deck."

Ven saw through the ship's deck monitors Kaytha and Taft exiting Taft's T-Craft in the hangar. Jebet called over to him, "Hey, Ven. I've got the jump calculations in place. It's not going to be exactly where the EnerConvoy is, but it'll be close enough."

Ven busied himself with getting the Anniversary pointed in the needed direction, but, inside, he struggled with the idea of leaving the Ultra Raiders behind. He knew the remaining Raiders weren't enough to take out the MMDs. If Supply One and the Raiders engaged them alone, it would be a suicide run.

****

Marrett was starting their run toward the main power generator. "Anniversary, why are you still here?!"

"Don't engage the MMDs! Hit your target and retreat!" Ven shouted back at her.

"We're all set, Ven. Whenever you're ready." Jebet glanced over her shoulder as the flight deck door slid open. In walked Taft, doing his best to assist Kaytha as she struggled from her injuries. "Buckle up, you two. We're about to jump outta here."

Marrett opened comms on all channels. "This is Supply One. Raiders, continue to engage with hostiles. Keep them busy. We're seconds away from taking out the generator."

The Ultra Raiders were fighting the DeCorp MTCs and taking them out one by one. DeCorp ships fell from the sky as the motivated young pilots continued to keep the enemy busy while Anorant and Marrett closed in on the main power generator.

Ven finished up the last settings needed before the jump then turned his attention to keeping an eye on the battle on his heads-up display. He watched as the MMDs were about to reach the edge of the Mars gravity. Once the MMDs were in space, with the powerful thrusters they carried—eight on each vessel—they could easily take out the Anniversary.

"Ven, we have to get outta here! Like five minutes ago!" said Jebet.

Supply One finally reached its target. Anorant took aim and fired off four consecutive plasma blasts from the dual purpose thrusters of the EnerCon-built ship. Marrett already had Supply One turned and heading away when the MarsCorp main power generator for the Engineering District erupted in a massive explosion of fire and fury. Connected power lines erupted all over the region as burning concrete, machinery, and metal debris scattered for miles in every direction.

Watching the destruction from out his cockpit window, Sint Argum was now hell-bent on revenge, flying as fast as he could to reach the MMDs. He planned to board one of the massive ships. He now wanted to carry out the attack on the EnerConvoy first hand. Closing in on the last MMD in the group, he comm'd to the flight director to open the rear hangar.

Back on the Anniversary, Ven knew he could jump to safety at any moment, but waited. He knew there was still time to escape as long as the DeCorp armada were still tethered to Mars' gravity.

The Ultra Raiders had all but taken out a handful of the DeCorp T-Craft attackers. The few that remained were also heading to the MMDs, under orders from Vivsou. The Director was still in the communications control tower.

"Raiders, lock on to our signal, our work is done. Anniversary, I told you guys to get outta here, don't worry about those MMDs!" said Marrett.

Ven didn't understand but trusted Marrett and just as he was about to jump out of the system, he understood.

Sint Argum was moments away from reaching the MMD he planned to dock with. As he slowed his approach, the gigantic weapon of war lost power and began to slowly drop from the sky. One by one the MMD's engines fell silent. The vessels began to tumble slowly in the air, falling from the sky and heading for the ground below. All of them but one was destined for disaster.

The lone MMD still under power was still picking up speed from its enormous thrusters, breaching the Mars atmosphere and into the weightlessness of space.

Sint, without his helmet or flight suit, didn't dare attempt to follow the MMD and could only watch as dozens of huge Massive Mobile Defense ships came crashing to the ground, each one erupting into a massive mushroom cloud from the exploding fusion reactors on board.

High above the Martian atmosphere, Marrett went all comms once more, "Raiders, drop in behind us and head for that MMD!" On a separate frequency, they all heard Marrett's voice again, "Fliers? Do you copy?"

Ven looked back from the Anniversary's pilot's seat at Jebet, Taft, and Kaytha, confused. Then it hit him—they were never alone.

"Ultra Raiders, good to see you. You're safe to board us. Swing around the rear of the ship and land in docking bay 94. Once you're secure, we'll jump out of here. Anniversary, we look forward to seeing you guys soon," said the voice on the other end.

"Goodbye, you guys. Get to the EnerConvoy. We'll see you there. If they don't believe your story, don't worry, we're right behind you. And I think we've got a big piece of convincing evidence," Marrett said before closing out her comms. Supply One reached the open hangar bay door leading into the rear of the huge MMD.

Ven looked around the room. "Everyone ready?"

"J, on the ready."

Kaytha just nodded and smiled.

"Take us home, Ven," Taft said.

Using both hands, Ven pushed forward the cold, steel handles that powered up the engines for the jump. The thrusters roared to life as the Anniversary shot away from the planet.

****

Sint Argum flew in his T-Craft back to the command control tower and was already reaching the top of the spire as the Anniversary jumped into deep space. The door slid open as Sint entered the room, seeing Akens Ember and Gregor Digby facing out the wide sweeping windows. Sint walked slowly to his commander's chair and sat down. He leaned back in the seat and slumped his head forward. "Ember, quit staring at the fire and bring me that bottle of

Nubian Brandy," Sint said. Akens Ember did as requested, after which both he and Digby returned to their designated terminals in the tower.

The viewing glass of the command control tower swept all the way to the top of the dome, out of which was now the beautiful night sky on Mars. Lifting his head, Sint Argum trained his eyes on the stars above. Just then, he witnessed a flash and streak, like the most brilliant shooting star. It was the stolen ship, the last of his remaining precious MMDs, the final insult added to his complete failure.

Chapter 55

Everyone sat quietly, still strapped in, for several minutes as the Anniversary reached maximum speed for its jump.

Jebet asked, "So, what the hell just happened? I assume the pilots were the ones that left Earth early? They hijacked an MMD?"

"Not just that, they must have sabotaged all those other MMDs too," said Kaytha.

"Why didn't anyone let us know they were there?" asked Taft.

"For the same reason we didn't tell them about the STL? They wanted to keep the Fliers safe, I assume?" Ven said. "When the Fliers left, I asked Anorant where they were going and he wouldn't tell me. He was insistent that no one know the specifics of what they were up to. His involvement in our plan was contingent on us being in the dark."

Jebet said, "I can't wait to hear *that* story."

An awkward silence fell over the room. Ven then stood up from his pilot's chair and walked over to where Kaytha and Taft were sitting. "First off, are you okay, Kay?"

490

"I'm fine, just a little beat up." The fatigue and pain showed as Kaytha sat slightly slumped in her chair, looking exhausted.

Ven said, "I know I speak for everyone when I say we're all glad Kaytha is back. But now DeCorp has the device. Look, even if they can't wage war now, when they do, they—"

Jebet interrupted Ven's rant before it got started. "Ven, stop. You don't understand."

Ven threw his arms in the air. "Well, will someone explain it to me?"

"They can't use the STL-5, and they'll never be able to. Well, at least if I'm not around, they won't," Kaytha said.

Taft and Ven exchanged confused glances.

"The device—it's attached to Kaytha. It only works when she's within a certain range!" said Jebet, shaking her hands in the air trying to get the explanation out as quickly as she could.

Kaytha continued, "It's coded to my DNA. Oshly figured it out before we left Earth. I told him not to tell anyone."

"I don't get it." Ven displayed a look of shock none of them had ever seen. "Why didn't you tell us?"

"Because!" Kaytha said, then took a deep breath to calm down. "Because I knew that it could change the decisions being made, and I didn't want that."

Taft was visibly shaken. "Then why the hell did you tell me NOT to come get you!?"

Kaytha got up from her chair and limped over to where Taft sat. She knelt down in front of him and took his hand. "Because I knew you would come anyway." Kaytha smiled. "And Sint needed to believe that he could use it."

Taft knew she was right, and she knew he wouldn't get mad with her looking at him like she did.

"While these two share their, uh, *moment,*" said Jebet with a roll of her eyes, "allow me to explain further."

Kaytha, knowing she was back in Taft's good graces again, turned to help Jebet ease any of Ven's still confusion and concern.

"My father, Wilicio, must have known a device like the STL-5 couldn't be allowed to fall into the wrong hands and that it could be a valuable means of protection. I assume that's why he built in a safeguard. Jebet can probably explain it better."

"Thanks, Kay. We gotta give Osh credit. So, basically, the STL actively scans its surroundings. It only comes on—or stays on—when the right DNA—Kaytha's DNA—is identified. Oshly figured out its mechanics, but the program and coding that's crucial for its operation are protected and impenetrable without it verifying the DNA."

Kaytha chuckled. "Exactly. Sint Argum has in his possession a useless hunk of technology."

"Okay, okay. I can buy all that. But, Jebet, when did *you* find out?"

asked Ven.

"Before we lost Oshly. He told me where I had to look. He buried a file that had the data he'd collected in the STL's operating system."

"I was there when she found out. I told her to keep it secret. Again, guys, I'm sorry. This was my burden. I did it for my reasons. *For a reason*, right?" said Kaytha. She was confident she did the right thing, but still felt a small sense of remorse for not telling her friends, especially Taft.

Ven recounted all the circumstances when the device had turned off. It finally all made sense.

"So, now what? Do you think DeCorp could reverse engineer it?" asked Taft.

"Not without me. You can't even access the system unless the active scanner picks up my DNA or I assume that of my family."

"What about EnerCon? Or us, for that matter. Can *we* create another one?" Jebet said.

"Oshly collected all he could. But he said he would need the coding, and he didn't have time to retrieve it. Maybe if we had access to my father's files.

But who knows if that ever made it off Earth."

Kaytha yawned. Taft could see the exhaustion in her eyes. "So, Ven, how long is this jump?"

"At least twelve hours at our current speed. Everyone, go on, get

493

some sleep. I'll stay up here and mind things. Try to get some rest myself." Ven turned around to head back to the pilot's chair, but Jebet had other ideas. She threw her arms around him. Taft and Kaytha followed her lead and they shared a group hug before going their separate ways.

Jebet made her way back down to the spot Oshly'd created in the hangar while Kaytha and Taft found their way to the main captain's cabin.

Taking off his flight boots and jacket, Taft watched as Kaytha did the same. "You gonna get cleaned up, Kay?"

"Nah, we're just going to go to bed. I wanna wake up and start our new life."

"I love you, Kaytha. I always have."

"I know you have, Sandy, and I know you always will. I've always loved you, too. Since I saw you standing there looking ridiculous with that crowbar in hand. But it wasn't until you helped me find what my father left for me that I started to learn *how* to love you. It was all *for a reason,* Taft. It all always happens *for a reason.*"

Kaytha kissed Taft, and he kissed her back as they fell onto the bed. They pulled up the sheets as the Anniversary's room monitor scanned their bios and heart rhythms and automatically turned down the lights.

Chapter 56

One month later…

Space, edge of the known solar system

The EnerConvoy was growing larger every day. Thousands of ships continued to join, many having fled DeCorp and MarsCorp after learning the truth of what Sint Argum had done. The story of Taft, Kaytha, Ven, Jebet, Oshly, the Ultra Raiders, and Fliers gave everyone hope.

Most of the world leaders never made it off Earth. Those who did were killed by Sint Argum's mercenaries who destroyed the O-Stations. In place of the UEGC, a council was formed to help guide the people in the EnerConvoy. With a majority vote of all the evacuees, the new council made the decision to head for Proxima B, a planet far beyond DeCorp's reach.

Shortly after they arrived, Taft, Kaytha, Ven, and Jebet located their families.

Ven's and Jebet's loved ones had made it onto the same EnerCon MMW during the Earth evacuation, while Taft's parents were a few weeks behind the rest of the convoy. They'd departed Earth on one of the last MMWs leaving Arizona before the lunar debris began to strike the planet.

After spending some time reuniting with their families, Ven and Jebet quickly found new roles for themselves helping assist with repairs on the many ships and flight training for the youth population. All was done in preparation for when they reached their new home.

Kaytha found her mother, Tellsea, within days of regrouping with the EnerConvoy. Being the widow of Wilicio Morrow, Tellsea was given a seat on one of NASA's evacuating shuttles. Her mother, unfortunately, couldn't offer any answers to the mystery of why her father allegedly crashed the drone carrying the STL-5. Nor did she have any clue as to who may have sent the message. According to Tellsea, she hadn't seen Wilicio for almost a month before she was contacted by NASA officials that he had died due to heart-related complications. After spending some much needed time together, they both decided it was best that Tellsea go back to using her maiden name of Gannon. Kaytha wanted to keep her mom safe. If DeCorp or Sint Argum came looking for her, her mom could also be at risk. It would be left unknown to the public that Tellsea and Kaytha were mother and daughter. The secret would only be known to the friends and a handful of trustworthy newly formed leaders.

Taft became one of the founding members of the space force entrusted with the responsibility of protecting the newly formed union that was renamed the Envoy, until a more suitable name was decided upon.

His squadron consisted of five other pilots made up of former Ultra

Raiders, including Torian, who'd insisted on joining. Their primary job was maintaining the forward scouting party to Proxima B, or what everyone now called Xima.

Kaytha took on a position as one of the heads of flight direction for all of Envoy. Kaytha originally wanted to only be a part of the space force with Taft. She was convinced by the council to become one of the flight operation leaders under the condition that she had the option of assisting the Envoy Space Force, (ESF) if she desired.

****

Kaytha stood on the flight deck ahead of all the Envoy ships. The stolen MMD was now the lead craft, and she was its commander. Looking out the massive flight deck window, she stared at the glowing yellow thrusters of the six T-Crafts.

Taft went one-on-one comms directly to her terminal. "Kaytha, we're about to make the jump. I'll keep you posted during the regular comm cycles."

"Sounds good, Taft. Be safe…I love you."

"I know you do, Kay. Love you too."

The comm connection went silent as the ships launched away from the ship, disappearing into the star field ahead. She smiled but only for a moment as reality set in. She didn't like watching Taft go off without her.

She watched the display screens closest to her as they made their ever-changing calculations, keeping the ship on course to its destination. Normally, Kaytha would take even the smallest portion of automation offline so she could be engaged in the MMD's operations. But if the adventure she had just played an active role in taught her anything, it was to take not only comfort, but enjoyment, in letting go.

$$****$$

Standing just outside the MMD flight deck door was Sabast Ooker. He was wearing his flight suit, which was too tight for his current weight. Sabast had docked his ship and made his way directly to the command deck. Sabast, like so many now, found himself personally alone in the wake of the Earth disaster and the battles that came after. He had but one thing left to do that was attached to his former life before he could find a new one out in the stars. He hesitated to open the door. He was nervous about meeting Kaytha and delivering the message he'd rehearsed so many times earlier.

Kaytha glanced at the door monitor screen and saw a man standing there. He looked to be in his late 40s and stocky. He was slightly disheveled but also a little sad. Kaytha keyed the outer door comm. "Is there something I can help you with?"

Sabast peered up at what he assumed was the camera. "Hello. If this is Kaytha, I'm here to see you. I, uh, have something for you actually." He nervously glanced around. "Kaytha, my name is Sabast Ooker. I knew your father. We used to work together."

Kaytha figured since he had reached this door he had proper security clearance and was not a threat. Kaytha slid the options bar on her touchscreen controls to allow him to enter. Sabast walked through the threshold, and the door immediately slammed shut, startling him slightly.

Kaytha remained sitting forward in her chair, her back to Sabast, triple checking the auto controls.

"Sorry about that. All these doors are pressurized. I still haven't gotten used to them shutting either." Kaytha swiveled around to face her visitor.

"I'm sorry to bother you, but, like I said, I knew your father very well. I worked for him. He trained me, taught me everything I know." Sabast's attention darted around the room, looking anywhere but directly at Kaytha. "It was such a shock when he died. Especially the way he did. He took great care of himself. His heart attack inspired me to take better care of myself. I do my best anyway."

Tears welled up in Kaytha's eyes.

"I am genuinely sorry about your father's passing. Because of the security protocols surrounding our work, your father wasn't able to send out any messages to you and was only allowed to make monitored calls to your mother. He recorded messages for you, a few times a week, but he could never send them... He desperately wanted to. As you know, he wasn't a very emotional guy."

"That's very kind of you to say. I really miss him."

"I do too." Sabast fidgeted, obviously uncomfortable and nervous.

"Not to be rude, but why are you here?"

"Those messages…I wasn't supposed to, you know, but after your dad died… Well, I wasn't supposed to go into his computer system, but your father gave me special access to help speed up our work. No one at NASA knew."

Sabast held up a small data card.

Kaytha recognized what it was Sabast was holding. Based on this poor man's skittish demeanor, Kaytha wouldn't be surprised if he ran out of the room at any moment. "Is that for…"

"Yes, yes it is. Before they could erase the data, I retrieved all his messages to you. I also erased the files—everything—this is the only evidence left. The only record of his work and his messages to you."

Sabast reluctantly extended his arm to give Kaytha the data card. It wasn't that he didn't want Kaytha to have it but that he was trusting to her to keep him anonymous. No one could know he took the information. Sabast, having listened to the recordings, knew there was more than just sentimental words from a father to his daughter.

Kaytha's eyes widened. In the wake of everything that had happened, Kaytha now recognized the importance of how it had all started and how this odd man held some answers. "It was you who sent me that message telling me where to go."

"I did. Whenever he talked about you, it was always about your camping trip, when you were a child. I knew that message needed to get to you. I decided I had to risk sending that transmission. In the wake of the evacuation, well, thankfully no one investigated or noticed, as far as I know."

"But why, then…why wait?"

"It wasn't at all intentional." Sabast blushed at hearing Kaytha's frustration. "There was a lot that needed to be sorted out with his work. We were on the verge of finishing a big project, and, unfortunately, before your father passed, the project suffered a huge setback. I was tasked with trying to duplicate his work. I was paranoid about letting anyone know I had your father's recordings. It took some time for me to get that one message to you, and even after I did, I was sure someone would have intercepted it. I barely made it onto one of NASA's evac-crafts.

I would have been here much sooner but my ship was held up at the tail end of the convoy. I only found out where you were a week ago."

Kaytha processed Sabast's explanation. He had no idea its significance—how could he. Only she and her friends understood the importance of that single message. Kaytha realized that Sabast would have probably been the only other person to know what Kaytha assumed her father had done, crashing the drone carrying the STL-5, but apparently even he didn't know that.

"Your father was a great man, and I know how much he loved and missed you," Sabast said.

"I know he did. And I can't thank you enough for bringing this part of him back to me."

"You're welcome. But, please don't tell anyone. Not that there's really anyone left who would care, but I prefer to keep to my old rules." Sabast was happy for the first time since his friend died. Now that he'd accomplished what he'd set out to do, he could finally pay his respects to the man that was so impactful on his life.

"Well, it seems I've accomplished what I set out to do. I think I can..." Sabast started making his way to the door.

"Wait! You said the project my father was working on suffered a setback?"

"Yes. Your father had spent over a decade on it, and, well..." Sabast stopped himself, even after all this time, he still kept it sworn to secrecy.

"It's okay, Sabast. Listen, the device—the STL-5—I found it." Kaytha got up and walked over to him. "The message you sent me —my father's message—led me right to it. That's how we won."

Two people, who had never before met, discovered that they not only shared family but also events that would forever shape their lives. Kaytha threw her arms around Sabast.

Kaytha pulled over one of the secondary crew chairs and proceeded to explain how everything had unfolded. She knew the story of their journey was safe with Sabast. Kaytha also knew that if there was anyone who would be able to fully understand the device and, more importantly, her connection to it, it was Sabast.

He declined Kaytha's offer to stay on in a permanent position on the ship, at least for now.

"I need to find my home first. But, after I do, I'll be in touch about that job. I've kept you from your father long enough." They gave each other one more hug.

Sabast then stood up. "Well, I must be on my way. Say hello to your dad for me."

"Good-bye for now then, Sabast." Kaytha watched as he walked out the door of the command bridge. The door slammed as it always did, but this time, it gave Kaytha a smile.

Kaytha returned to her pilot's chair. With her mind racing and a sudden burst of adrenaline rushing through her body, she hurriedly looked over the ship's latest course correction data and calculations. Once she was satisfied that the ship was set and heading in the right direction, Kaytha engaged the MMD back to full auto pilot.

Bringing up the communications screen, Kaytha tapped in the code to the next person on flight deck watch in the crew quarters.

"This is Kaytha Morrow on the flight deck. Please inform my relief pilot that I am leaving my post early. The ship is on full-auto."

"The pilot is standing right here. We'll handle it," the crewman comm'd back.

"One more thing. Take me off flight deck duties for the foreseeable future. I'll send more detailed information soon."

"Understood, Kaytha."

After closing the comms, Kaytha inputted the code for Jebet, who was currently stationed in the MMD hanger bay.

With the comm channel open, Jebet broke in before Kaytha had a chance to speak. "Well, it's about damn time you comm'd."

"J, I'm heading down to the hangar. What's the Anniversary's flight —"

"She's fully charged, fueled, and waiting for you. Just get your butt down here."

Kaytha didn't even say good-bye as she turned off the comm between the two of them. She logged out of the OS and sprinted for the flight deck door. She followed the short hall down to the elevator which would take her to the hangar, and her friends.

Jebet and Ven were inside the Anniversary's hangar locking down some equipment and magnet-securing Jebet's T-Crafts to the interior floor of the ship. They both chuckled as the elevator door opened and they saw Kaytha standing there.

Kaytha immediately noticed her T-Craft parked next to the Anniversary with the cockpit open. She ran over and up the Anniversary hangar ramp. "What are you two doing?"

Ven went back to tightening some straps on two metal containers as he said, "I cleared Sabast to come see you. I'm guessing you two talked already?"

"Yeah, but that doesn't explain why you guys apparently assumed I'd be coming down here?"

Jebet stopped putting away some tools, walked over to Kaytha, and put her hands on her friend's shoulders. "We knew there was no way you weren't going to follow after Taft. The only question was how long until you realized it." Jebet laughed as she stepped away from Kaytha and over to a control panel where she pressed the large illuminated red button to close the hangar door.

Ven said, "Yeah, I talked for a few minutes with Sabast. He said he needed to talk to you about your father. So, we've just been getting the Anniversary ready, waiting for you. We knew it was just a matter of time."

"You didn't really think we were going to let you go without us, did you?" said Jebet standing next to her T-Craft.

"That's a lot of assumptions you guys made. You weren't wrong, but still. By the way, did someone clean my ship? It looks brand new."

"Taft cleaned it up before he left. I think it was his way of saying he wanted you to follow him. We would have boarded her in here, but we need the extra space. Besides we knew—"

"You knew I'd want to fly my own ship." It was a comfort to Kaytha that her friends knew her so well. "Did you happen to grab—"

Jebet said, "We've got everything already loaded: your flight suit and helmet are waiting for you in the cockpit.

We've packed up plenty of food and equipment. Honestly, your ship's been ready for days now. I only opened the cockpit after you comm'd down to us."

"So, get in your flight suit and let's get out of here before someone starts to question it, including me!" said Ven.

It didn't take long for Kaytha to change into her flight suit. While she did, Ven and Jebet finished preparing the Anniversary and were already on its flight deck waiting for Kaytha.

Jebet watched from out the windows of the Anniversary as Kaytha strapped into her cockpit and sealed the canopy shut.

"You ready to go after your boy?" said Jebet over the comms to Kaytha.

"Let's disappear," replied Kaytha

Ven smiled at Jebet as he powered up the Anniversary's engines. Jebet then remotely depressurized the MMD hangar.

"Kay, you can open the main bay door. Ven and I are already strapped in. We'll follow your lead for the jump. Have fun, Kay!"

Kaytha opened the hangar bay door. The moment she did, radio communication chatter could be heard from the communications console. Kaytha turned them off.

Her gray and candy apple red T-Craft and the Anniversary both faced out the rear of the MMD.

The huge metal sliding doors opened and Kaytha could see thousands of ships trailing behind the massive vessel. Powering up her thrusters, she floated the ship slowly out of the hangar. Pitching the T-Craft vertical, Kaytha spun her ship like a corkscrew up and over the top of the MMD. Ven followed in the Anniversary right behind her. Slowly pushing the main engine power lever forward, she flew directly out in front of the MMD. She was now in the same position that Taft was before he took off for Xima. Punching in the same coordinates as Taft's, with the Anniversary following beside her, they were ready to start their next journey.

Kaytha heard a slight crackle on her comms. "Hey, Kay, we're ready for our jump. Are you good to go?"

"Yeah, Ven. You and Jebet get started. I just need a second. But I'm right behind you."

"Copy that. See you soon."

The comm channel closed.

Kaytha watched as the Anniversary's engines started to glow a brilliant neon orange and the ship rocketed away from the Envoy.

As she kept an eye on the countdown to her speed jump, Kaytha inserted her data disc into the flight deck system.

On the audio options screen, countless dated entries appeared for her to choose from. Kaytha thought about starting at the beginning of the list but then decided to randomly pick from one of the final entries, labeled KLM122423. Her father's voice, a voice she hadn't heard since the message that started the chain of events that changed everyone's future, played over the sound of the ship's thrusters coming to life in the background. Kaytha pulled her seat belts tight one last time as her T-Craft launched at top speed towards Taft and the future.

"Hey, Kaytha. It's Dad again. First off, I love you. And, with that out of the way, do I have a story to tell you."

The End

EMBARK

ABOUT THE AUTHOR

Jon "Justice" LoGiudice lives with his wife, Melinda, and their two sons, Logan and Kyle, in Blaine, Minnesota. Jon is a full-time talk radio personality and host of a weekly Star Wars Podcast: My Nerd World. His work is inspired by God, family, Star Wars, music (especially Depeche Mode), NASCAR and the films he loves.

Twitter: @TheMyNerdWorld @JonJustice

Instagram: TheJonJustice

Facebook: Jon Justice

Made in the USA
Middletown, DE
10 November 2018